THE AVON ROMANCE

Four years old and better than ever!

We're celebrating our fourth anniversary...and thanks to you, our loyal readers, "The Avon Romance" is stronger and more exciting than ever! You've been telling us what you're looking for in top-quality historical romance—and we've been delivering it, month after wonderful month.

Since 1982, Avon has been launching new writers of exceptional promise—writers to follow in the matchless tradition of such Avon superstars as Kathleen E. Woodiwiss, Johanna Lindsey, Shirlee Busbee and Laurie McBain. Distinguished by a ribbon motif on the front cover, these books were quickly discovered by romance readers everywhere and dubbed "the ribbon books."

Every month "The Avon Romance" has continued to deliver the best in historical romance. Sensual, fast-paced stories by new writers (and some favorite repeats like Linda Ladd!) guarantee reading *without* the predictable characters and plots of formula romances.

"The Avon Romance"—our promise of superior, unforgettable historical romance. Thanks for making us such a dazzling success!

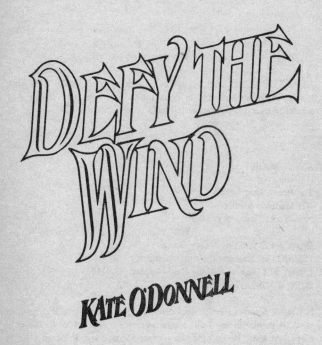

DEFY THE WIND

KATE O'DONNELL

◆ AVON
PUBLISHERS OF BARD, CAMELOT, DISCUS AND FLARE BOOKS

AVON BOOKS
A division of
The Hearst Corporation
105 Madison Avenue
New York, New York 10016

To My Sons, Gregory and Gary—
Because of You

Part I

Chapter 1

Huddled on a large rock, Meghan stared down the trail by which her father and Llewelyn ab Gruffydd, Prince of Wales, must return. Her arms were wrapped around her legs for warmth. Her small, square chin rested on her knees. She was swaddled in a cloak borrowed from a warrior, but it was sodden. As was all their clothing, as was the whole world, it seemed. A drop of water plopped on her head from a tree above and Meghan stood, silently cursing Edward I of England, accusing him of every crime she could think of. Then her fury relaxed, driven from her by misery.

She was not being just. She had heard much of Edward's justice and mercy, his lack of pettiness. Nor was he to blame for this foreboding that had grief cradled within her like an egg, its cause not yet hatched. Her sad presentiment might mean nothing. She had felt it before and it had come to nothing. Nor was there anything left for her to lose—except for her father and he had gone down to the English under Edward's safeguard. Little harm could come to him there.

Edward was not to blame for all male creatures and their will to quarrel—Welshmen no less willing than others, perhaps more so. They thought it such sport to raid in the Marches, into England itself! What made stolen beef and other men's women seem so much sweeter than their own she wondered.

That battle lust had, in truth, brought them here; that, and the Welsh passion for their old laws and ways, their

3

own land, their freedom. At first, as they won battle after battle, it had seemed that Llewelyn would bring his warriors victory. But Edward had not proved as unfit a commander as his father had. Then, even nature had seemed to cast her lot with the Norman king. Famine had followed the unseasonal rains and Llewelyn had seen the clans dissolve around him as his allies made their excuses. Those not brave enough to face him had slipped quietly away in the night. Soon there had been no food. Soon their horses, the famous milk-white horses of Wales, had fallen to their knees and could give no more. Then Llewelyn had sent away the remaining clans, keeping only the most loyal chieftains and a few men. With those, he had ridden down to meet with Edward. Perhaps a voluntary surrender would bring easier terms and leave Wales strong enough to rise again one day.

"'Twas at cock's crow three days ago that they left," Meghan whispered. "If we had a cock to crow. And if he did crow, he would sign his death warrant into the cooking pot afore noon."

Meghan's stomach cramped at the thought of food and she peered down the trail once more. The trees were stripped of leaves and half shrouded by mist. Beyond, hidden by clouds, were the towering crags of Snowdonia.

In the gathering dusk she caught a glimpse of movement and waited, poised to shout an alarm. Then she recognized white horses, their hides dulled to pewter by the damp, and the dragon pennant of Llewelyn of Wales, and she relaxed with a sob of relief.

When her father reached her, Meghan turned to walk beside him, her hand resting on his horse's stirrup. He did not speak, did not comment on her damp cloak or her determination to join him. He refused to meet her eyes until he had dismounted. Then he turned to her, his features harsh and unyielding.

There was no comfort he could give her for the despair his news would bring and to acknowledge his own sorrow would surely break him. They had had enough grief, he and this girl before him. Like two cripples, they supported each other in a too-precarious balance. Now there was to be yet another loss to bear.

"Edward asked that we relinquish all claim to South Wales," Gavin ab Owen told his daughter. "We are to pay a fine of fifty thousand pounds. We are to give hostages to guarantee the peace of the clans. You are all I have left. You go to Edward and on to England three days hence."

Meghan stood, stunned by his words and by his unspoken grief. He left her there, her face buried in the mane of his weary horse. She felt little, only the rain pelting her uncovered head.

Life had been good once, she thought. Even after her gentle mother had died. For there was still her father and the forever brawling, wenching, laughing brothers of the clan Owen—and a bard to sing of their history, of the saga of their heroic deeds, their bold, defiant sins. But word had come last winter that the ancient bard ap Anyon had died, and his son before him, in battle. And a clan with no bard was without history, without song.

The song had died a little more with the death of each tall, lusty brother. It had left forever the day Kay, her oldest, her favorite brother, had come home tossed over the back of his horse like a sack of English meal, the grimace of battle still twisting his features.

Bran, too, her gentle foster brother, was gone. On the day Gavin ab Owen had received Llewelyn's summons to war, Meghan had requested her father's permission to marry Bran. She smiled into the horse's mane, remembering his reaction.

"You'll not!" he had yelled. "Not with my permission or blessing, you'll not!"

"I don't need your permission or blessing," she had calmly reminded him. "I haven't since I was thirteen."

"Bran is too gentle, too scholarly for you," ab Owen argued. "He is better suited to the priesthood than marriage."

"Those are the qualities I love," Meghan stated.

Her father shook his head. "And how long, girl, do you think such a man would hold you? Besides, this is not a good time to marry any man. Do you want a whelp in your belly," he taunted, "with your husband off to war? Or do you already carry his?"

Meghan's jaw tightened. "I do not! He's not touched me! He's not like you and those"—her chin jerked toward the sound of her brothers' swords' clanging in the ward—"ever ready to wallow with every available wench, agreeable or no! And be damned to your insinuations! I would be agreeable!"

Ab Owen snorted and rocked back on his heels. "In truth, I thought you not yet a woman, at least not by that one's hand. He reeks too much of the clergy to lift a skirt—the English clergy! Methinks his nether sword is as much a mystery to him as that hanging so limply from his baldric. Methinks, too, such a tumble would do you good. Mayhap 'tis its lack that makes your temper so vile and your tongue so sharp."

Meghan refused to be drawn into a shouting match. Her face grew calm and hard; ab Owen, knowing well the will behind that obstinate expression, began to bluster. He continued to reason and plead, but her features only set more firmly. At last it had been agreed: let Bran prove himself a warrior worthy of the daughter of the Clan Owen. Then, when the war was over, or if he should come home in the meantime, they could wed, if not with her father's pleasure then with his blessing. Ab Owen, Meghan had known, did not think Bran would live so long. Nor had he.

Why was it, Meghan wondered now, her hair slicked to her head by rain, her face buried against the horse, that she could not even recall Bran's features?

Now, but for her bastard brother Caradoc, there was no one left. And no one knew Caradoc's whereabouts, which was for the best. He brought only trouble and contention with him wherever he went, as though he verily carried them in his baldric. And for her, he brought a sense of fear, of disgust and foreboding.

She straightened at last and drew the horse on up the trail. She dared not give in to the despair she felt. After all, she might not be in England for long. Surely Edward would not be so cruel, for her father needed her. She would come home to him after only a short time and he would live to be an ancient, to die, at last, in his own bed. It was a fate he would hate but the one she wished for him.

It was the time until then that she grieved over. When Kay had died, her father had at least had her. He had had, too, his vast pride, his duty. Llewelyn had needed him and ab Owen's loyalty to the Prince of Wales, to the son of his foster brother, had gone beyond personal grief. But that, too, was past, gone with Wales' defeat, as now Meghan herself would be gone. Her shoulders slumped again.

Three days later, November 9, 1277, Llewelyn ab Gruffydd led his chieftains and the promised hostages down from the mountains. Only the Welsh prince's squire and bard attended him. The squire was necessary for the prince's dignity and rank; the bard was for his clan and honor—and because the song the bard would compose of this event might one day lift up the hearts of other, younger men against the foreigner. They carried no arms but for the lance borne by the squire and the swords at the baldrics of the nobles. From the lance flew Llewelyn's pennant, symbol of the Pendragon of Wales, which had once belonged to the legendary Arthur.

Meghan rode beside her father, her head high on her long, slim neck. Her features were carefully composed against her grief, for to give way to it would forever disgrace her father.

The English, it was said, were a cold people and her coming exile was only just becoming a reality. She was to live among strangers with foreign ways who scorned her people and their ancient customs.

Shock protected Meghan, but her hate waited within. She had enough hate, she thought, to entirely destroy Edward's army—if she could but direct it, if she was one of those witches the English believed abounded among the Welsh. Without the hate, she would be empty.

Her father's features were also blank, yet she knew he, too, was a caldron of rage and despair. He had come to her the day before and they had talked. She had longed to cling to him, to ask him to keep her by him somehow.

But she could not add her fear and desolation to the burdens he already carried.

"We can go into the hills, girl," he had whispered as he held her, reading her mind.

But they could not, not against Llewelyn's word. He had lost too much already. So many men were dead, the clans sundered. The beautiful Eleanor de Montfort, Llewelyn's betrothed, had been captured by Edward and was perhaps gone from his life forever. The defection of ab Owen, his most loyal chieftain, would be too hard a blow. Nor was the life of a fugitive easy or the mountains kind to a woman. Her father was growing old. His warrior years, his sons' deaths, the defeat of Wales had all taken their toll.

Ab Owen had given her the belt he had worn for as long as she could remember, as it had been worn back more generations than even the bards could cite. It should have gone to a son, even to Caradoc, perhaps; he had always coveted it. But it was ab Owen's to bestow and he had clasped its heavy length around her waist twice, the second loop spanning her hips like a girdle.

They had said their farewells then, away from alien eyes. This last parting was but a formality they had to endure without giving the English the satisfaction of seeing their grief.

Our appearance, Meghan thought, will give them gratification enough. If there is one whole garment amongst us, I know not where. My father has but one gauntlet and I no hose and, all said, we go like jesters to a fair, wrapped in nothing but rags and dignity. Our horses are no better, poor, ill-used brutes, belly to backbone, the famous milk-white horses of Wales. All but Llewelyn's, and where his came from, no one tells. Mayhap from Edward. 'Tis the sort of gesture he would make; the Normans do love chivalry. Ah, but no matter. Llewelyn ordered us to go at a walk, that 'tis more fitting. But methinks 'tis more that the horses would fail us if we pushed them harder. The sun shines for the first time in months, but 'tis now too late.

Tilting her chin skyward, Meghan allowed the music in her soul to rise in a keening lament.

Where were you when we needed you? She silently asked the sun. Even you deserted us! Where were you when our grain rotted in the valleys, when the pride of the Welsh huddled in caves or hovels that a villein would have been shamed by, half of us and more shaken with ague, and the English snug in silken pavilions and castles? Now you shine on their victory and on our shame, but where were you when Welsh cloth shredded on Welsh bodies and Welsh bellies whimpered with hunger?

Suddenly aware that she was weeping, Meghan drew her horse from the column. Her father followed her. Leaning over, he laid a finger on Meghan's cheek to wipe a tear away.

"Why weep now," he asked, "when all is done? You haven't wept since your brothers refused your company on the raidings, and you with your first long skirt and gawky legs. You could not understand why they did not want your company."

"Aye, but I could shoot as well as they and ride, too," she stated indignantly. "'Twas at thirteen the boys went, if only to hold the horses." Then she broke, as he knew she would, her sobs ripping from her.

"Ah, let it go, girl," ab Owen whispered, his throat thick. "Cry as I cannot."

Covering her with his cloak, he clasped her to him, shielding her. He gazed at the mountains, his mountains, as he held her, feeling her agony as his own. He held her for a long moment after her weeping was done, then lifted her face to his. He wiped the tears away with his cloak and offered a corner of it for her to blow her nose on, as he had done when she was a child.

"Don't be shamed, girl," he ordered when she caught her lower lip between her teeth. "You've never given me cause for humiliation; your tears cannot do so now."

Ab Owen held her head between his hands and wiped the last tears away with broad thumbs. He gazed into eyes so like her mother's that they caused him pain—Irish eyes, leaf-green rimmed with jade. "Are you finished, wench?" he teased. "You keep the most important man in the kingdom waiting!"

"It cannot be Edward," Meghan answered, "though he would like to think so, so you must speak of Llewelyn. Your own great modesty forbids you to speak so flatteringly of yourself."

"Aye, Llewelyn. Of mine own importance we do not speak. 'Twould gather every man in the land to our door and such a thing our larder could not afford, poor chatelaine that you are. Ah, let us go, girl," he said, his face serious. "The English speak ill enough of us as 'tis. Would you have them say we are also malingerers?"

Chapter 2

The English shifted in their saddles, speaking quietly among themselves, a raucous, ribald laugh occasionally bursting forth. At last the rains were gone. Their clothing was damp and chafing, their mail rusted, but the sun shone warm, lightening ill tempers. The supply wagons had reached them at last, filled with ale, flour, salted beef, and fish. Their bellies were full, their spirits good, and soon they would go home. All that remained was the taking of hostages and the pledging of fealty. After fifteen months in the field, they considered themselves well rid of Wales. There were only a few among the English who had longed to dig the Welsh out of their mountains. The others expressed their relief in crude jests and dour comments.

Hugh fitz Alan listened with half an ear. They sounded like washerwomen, he thought, and were equally opinionated. Nor did they discuss anything not touched on a thousand times before.

"They use their women," a knight complained. "I lost a sergeant—my best, but too easily led by his horn. Some Welsh slut offered him comfort in the underbrush and gave him a slit throat instead!"

There was a murmur of assent and other examples described, then a man cleared his throat. "A wench should recognize her master and obey. I mislike this contention they foster in their women. Such disgruntlement spreads."

11

"They all be contentious and their oaths mean nothing—from man or woman, even from their chieftains."

"They've no loyalty or honor," a third lectured. "Not even to their liege lord. 'Tis nothing but the clan."

"Aye," another agreed, "and 'tis no concept for a Christian knight. We are all under the Holy Church and the lord the church put over us; our fealty to them only! Anything else is unnatural—like frogs mating with toads."

"You should see," Henry Adney commented, his breath warm on Hugh's ear, his eye on the man who settled back, well satisfied with his oration, "all the toadish wenches on his estate. All fen, it is! On my oath, all the women within a league of his keep be wide-jawed, bugged of eye, and webbed atween the toes! Ugly, aye, and dark. 'Tis luck they don't have freckles like trout. Give me a plump, blond Saxon wench, myself!"

Chuckling, Hugh nodded in agreement. Then he frowned as another knight spoke.

"Your oath to the king, that's the thing! Let him do your thinking, and everyone in the place God gave him. A true knight fights, wenches, pays taxes, gives the king his due—nothing more, nothing less—and a tithe to the church."

"The Welsh be thieves." Adney laughed, enticing the conversation on. "Amongst themselves as readily as from others."

"Overbold of tongue and wit, they are," Hugh heard another man not noted for his intelligence complain. "They leave you bewildered as to compliment or ridicule."

"They are a queer, dark people," mentioned a man noted for piousness in a time when all were devout. "'Tis said they see the future in dreams and summon spirits. For all they claim to follow the church, they still believe in the old, dark gods. Their clergymen are no better—fornicating, even, and with concubines! Did they not accept excommunication to follow Llewelyn? They are a filthy abomination of God's sweet earth!"

"Filthy? By my oath," Adney baited, "not their women! They are the cleanest I've yet to bed."

"They do bathe often," humorless de Hart agreed, "several times a year, 'tis said. A bath be not worth the danger, methinks, with no wench to scrub your back—and more!"

"'Tis said they rub their teeth with hazel sticks and wipe them with a woolen cloth," another commented. "To stop the tooth rot. Yet everyone knows 'tis due to worms come up through the bones from the feet!"

"All the good that can be said of them," de Hart stated, "is that they be uncommonly melodious upon the harp. And they all sing—man, woman, child."

"As for me," a quiet, withdrawn knight blurted, "I mislike this treaty. We had them cornered and we should have gone into their mountains and dug them out, to the last whelp, no matter the cost! Aye, and their cattle and mutton with them! They be as lice, they breed as such, and now was the time to rid ourselves of them forever."

A hush settled over the lines. He spoke of sentiments contrary to the policies of Edward and bordering on treason. And few of the Marcher lords did not have a Welshman as friend, for all their talk. Many were married to Welsh women or carried more than a bit of Welsh blood in their veins. Men shifted in their saddles, stealing glances at each other.

"'Tis their mountains," Adam Patton said at last. "There be evil here. 'Tis verily in the air!"

Several knights glanced over their shoulders. There was something eerie in the air of Wales, but men did not talk of spirits and demons or the unaccountable lifting of hair at the back of the neck. To change the subject, Adney cleared his throat and mentioned a whore he had cheated in Chester.

Frowning, Hugh closed his mind to the gossip. The scene before him resembled a tournament or a fair. Pennants on the king's bright blue pavilion and on those of his nobles wavered in the breeze from the sea. Peddlers hawked their wares, meat pies, skins of ale and wine, sweets of fruit and honey, while dodging minstrels and jugglers. They had appeared from nowhere, like fleas on a sheet after the candle was blown out. There should have been dirges to meet the defeated race, and rain to witness their humbling; something more, certainly, than the long lines of armed and armoured knights.

Perhaps it *was* a fair. Perhaps all war was. Men rushed to them so eagerly, if only to put coin into the coffers of their estates, as he did Ainsleah's. And if Hugh was so frail-minded as to dwell on it, he should have been a priest, though it seemed the clergy was as avid as any man if souls or gold could be gained.

The stirrings of his neighbors roused Hugh and he swayed easily as his horse kicked out at another behind him. Leaning over, Adney jerked his chin toward Edward and his advisors.

"There they be, and none too soon. On my oath," he chuckled, "I'll be glad when this deed be done. I've a mind to seek a saddle more tender than this one I now ride—mayhap a Welsh saddle!"

Snickering, he rode off and Hugh smiled. Adjusting his shield with its bar sinister, he backed his destrier into formation and silently thanked the saints that the day's work needed no helm. As soon as they reached Rhuddlan, he promised himself, he would take a long soak at the bath house. There was a bath wench there, small and plump, blond and giggly, who would accommodate him in a sport that would relax him soon enough. It was said she spread her thighs for any man with coin and an itch, but she had yet to ask him for payment.

Briefly, Hugh wondered why women came to him so easily, the thought stirring flesh he had assumed had gone long since numb, as the rest of him had. For all his searching, he had yet to find a woman who fulfilled any need beyond a physical release. Perhaps they sensed he sought more than momentary satisfaction. Perhaps they sensed a void in him that nothing seemed to fill. Perhaps it was only that he enjoyed women for more than the easing of rut.

One eyebrow crooked and a small scar whitened at the corner of his mouth. Or perhaps they felt the vague loneliness holding him apart, a loneliness seldom admitted—the legacy of a bastard birth.

He jerked his mind away from this thought and to the notion of marriage. Edward had been pressing him harder of late to take a wife. God's word, but he had been offered half the women in England! Was he stubborn and set in his habits, as Edward accused? Perhaps, but he wasn't romantic, as Eleanor, the king's wife, teased. Marriage had nothing to do with romance. A man married for the land and position his wife brought him, just as a woman married for protection. Perhaps his pride was overweening, as Edward suggested, but a bastard learned early to value himself for himself and nothing else. And a king's favor, if you were fortunate enough, came from your own efforts and loyalties, and departed much more easily than it was gained.

Scowling, Hugh cursed himself for a fool. Other men were content with whatever face and form came with a hide of land and sought their happiness elsewhere. And he would probably do the same when Edward Longshanks's patience wore too thin. Yet there was a void in him as persistent as hunger, while all that was missing from his life, truth be told, was a wife. In the meantime, he wished only that the Welsh would come and end this day's work.

They came leisurely, a barbaric sight and seeming to revel in it, their casual line contemptuous of the ordered English formations. Their clothes were faded and ragged, their boots worn to the earth. The huge, drooping mustaches on all but the youngest male faces cast a fierce aspect to features a shade darker than the Normans'. Their Celtic blood seemed to press their bone closer to the skin, leaving the countenance open to the slightest emotion, yet now no face displayed anything more than boredom. Even their horses were skin, bone, and sinew, their hipbones sharp under dull coats.

They were, Hugh decided, indeed brought low. Never had he seen a more shabby escort for a ruler, not even on crusade, and the ruler himself not much better.

The Welsh knew how to dress; he had seen Llewelyn ab Gruffydd and his chieftains, Gavin ab Owen and Maddock ap Rhys among them, strut often enough in costly cloaks and calf-length tunics of linens and wools. The only thing to mark them as Welsh was their mustaches.

Perhaps the donning of their blood-red cloaks, scarlet plaid kilts, and sleeveless leather vests was an intentional display of defiance. Only the wide gold bands about their naked biceps declared a rank higher than the lowest Welsh warrior. Or perhaps they were harder pressed than Edward guessed.

Even the pennant lifted over them by the breeze was tattered and worn to transparency in the creases where it had been folded too long in a saddlebag. But the blood-red dragon on wool the hue of old ivory reared up defiantly. The dragon had been the symbol of Uther Pendragon six centuries before and of his son, the immortal, half-sanctified Arthur. It was apt, Hugh thought. The Welsh seemed to seek death like a dragon, a salamander tossed into flame, and were destroyed only to rise again from the fire.

The Welsh had halted and Llewelyn and his squire rode on alone to Edward, dismounting before him, ending a four-year battle for liberty. Alone of Edward's barons, Llewelyn had refused to do homage on the king's accession to the throne and now he and his people suffered for it.

De Hart's hoarse whisper caught Hugh's attention. "Ho, Henry, how is that for a Welsh saddle?" he asked Adney.

"Not bad, but I prefer a bit more padding, something to squeeze till it squeals! For all the trouble of a skinny wench, you might as well bugger your page. That one looks like she could have the balls off a man with a sneer and a word or two!"

Hugh searched for the face they discussed. He found her easily, despite her male attire and black hair cropped short like a page's. Although not beautiful, there was something about her that drew the glance back, then back again. But she was too dark, too vividly complected in a time when pink and gold beauties were admired, and too slim. There was, too, a temper in the lift of her chin.

Still Hugh studied her. She wore a war-stained surcoat wrapped twice about by a barbaric gold belt, and the coat's too-short length revealed inches of smooth, round thigh. The leather molded small, high breasts and left bare slender, well-muscled biceps encircled by wide gold bands. Her feet were shod in knee-high boots and she wore no hose. She was tall; her head would reach his chin.

She reminded him of a small statue of a pagan goddess he had seen on crusade. She had a hint of being tempered but never tamed. They didn't look quite mortal, the statue or the girl, more as though gotten on a water witch or a wood sprite. The taking of one, Hugh had heard, would leave a man mad and when she was gone, ever searching after her. Civilization's veneer was thin on her, this descendent of the Black Singers who had held even the legions of Rome at bay.

He had heard ab Owen's daughter rode with him, that she was either an Amazon or a witch. Though he knew now she was neither, she could well rob a man of his senses. She had an innocence more seductive than flaunted sensuality. And she *was* innocent. No awakened woman could ride as unclothed as she into a company of men and be unaware of the lust she roused. But Adney was right; she looked as though her tongue was sharp, her temper biting. And she was forbidden. She was the king's hostage, her honor his. It was worth a man's life to violate it. But even as Hugh argued with his rising lust and need, he noticed the girl searching the English lines for someone.

Llewelyn had warned ab Owen that Caradoc might be with the English. It was for him Meghan searched, although she knew that only Edward's most ranking lords and knights were there to greet and escort them to Rhuddlan. All others he had ordered on to Flint.

Sighing with relief, she studied the landscape. The mountains were at her back and she could see the sun shining on the Irish Sea. A ship, sails full and rows of oars lifting, was headed toward Conway. Far to her left was the headland that marked Penrhyn Castle and beyond it the Isle of Anglesey.

Something nagged at her and she shifted in the saddle, tugging at the hem of her tunic. Someone was staring at her. Her eyes found Hugh's. Lifting her chin, she returned his bold stare. She held his eyes a moment, then her glance flicked to the bar sinister on his shield and back to his face. Who are you, bastard, her arrogant features clearly read, to look on the daughter of Gavin ab Owen?

A cold smile betrayed Hugh's surge of fury. No woman had ever looked at him so before. This one had found his weakness without a word exchanged and was turning it into a wound.

Are you, in truth, so arrogant, wench? his eyes asked her. Are you as wanton as you seem and as immodest? Do you think you can quell my lusts so easily, you with your shrew's face and your indecent dress?

His eyes moved down her with a calculating appraisal, judging her, stripping her. His gaze climbed back, touching every inch of her before his eyes returned to her face. Lifting a scarred eyebrow dubiously, Hugh's eyes asked a question that brought a deep blush to Meghan's features.

Jerking her head away, she felt the heat of a flush and a foreign panic. Then she heard his gratified laugh, which lifted the fine hair on her forearms in instinctive fury. The rage itself frightened her in a curiously sensual way. Fighting her distress, she leaned over to touch her father's hand. He turned, his bushy eyebrow lifted, and she asked in a casual voice, "Who is he, that Norman knight, the dark one with the light eyes, the bastard?"

Ab Owen's eyes met Hugh fitz Alan's, and Hugh nodded a greeting. Then his gaze flicked to Meghan, touching her, claiming her, before returning to ab Owen. Their gaze locked and ab Owen recognized the lust and need in Hugh's. And something more, of which he sensed Hugh was not even aware. But he would be. It was the same thing that touched his daughter.

"Who is he?" Meghan asked again.

"Hugh fitz Alan," her father told her.

Her eyes demanded more than she realized, ab Owen knew, but that would pass. Her mother had reacted to him, a Welsh stranger come to Ireland, in the same way. But then she had softened, had accepted what they could not deny. She had followed him back to Wales, knowing she might never see home again except as a green haze across the Irish Sea.

Ab Owen's shoulders slumped and he wondered what he could say of the man who might take away the last thing he loved. He wished he could lie and paint the man black, but such words could not come. He regretted now that he had not allowed Meghan to marry Bran. She would be a widow, her holdings making her more desirable, true, but she might also be big with child. Yet fitz Alan's eyes told him that it was not her lands he wanted and that he could see beyond a bulging belly. Perversely, he was the kind of man ab Owen wanted for his daughter—strong enough to hold her, to arouse her to the intensity of need he felt vibrating now within her. A man like Bran would have turned her into a restless, unfulfilled, whining shrew.

Her voice pulled him from his musing and he shifted in the saddle.

"I've met him only at tourneys. We became besotted on wine together once or twice, but I still know little of him beyond what I sense—and what rumor says. He's a man who ever holds a part of himself aside and safe from others."

Ab Owen paused, his eyes squinting as he formulated the words. "He has no wife or mistress I heard tell of, though he be twenty-five or more, and Edward, 'tis said, urges him oftimes to wed. Yet he is no sodomite. Mostlike he's but as discreet as he is reticent. He has but one estate, near Oswestry. And 'tis his own, not held in fief, a rare thing with the Normans. 'Tis of fair size, though. He is a doughty fighter, one I would prefer with me than against me, and wholly trusted by Edward Longshanks, though no man calls him lick-spittle. Indeed, he's thought a friend. He's a bastard, aye, but not one to disguise it. His father was a Norman baron; his mother, I heard, an English blacksmith's daughter."

Ab Owen hesitated, then shrugged. "'Twas fitz Alan who deflected the assassin's blade from Edward's heart when they were in the Holy Land. There is gossip that Edward wished to grant him a boon, an estate, a position—a woman."

"I had heard that tale," Meghan mentioned.

"Then you know 'tis nothing but that—a tale."

She remained disturbed. Her father had said nothing but good of fitz Alan, but she still felt an unreasonable dislike for him. He was not ill-visaged; some would call him handsome, with his dark skin, light eyes, hawked nose. It was more the way he looked at her. He seemed to know all intimate things of her—so his eyes said. They seemed to tell her, too, that he could do as he would with her and make her like it, want it. But she couldn't find words to tell her father such a thing.

"I simply do not like him," she replied to his questioning eyes. "Methinks him insolent and bold! And he's Norman!"

To agree with Meghan, ab Owen knew from long experience, would only drive her to consider fitz Alan in another, more favorable light. To oppose her would intensify her dislike. Both her stubbornness and her sense of impartiality could be maneuvered and used against her.

"You forget your mother was Irish and foreign."

"No, I've not forgotten. But the Irish do not come to put our necks in a slave's yoke, nor have they for eight hundred years. Father, I would make no match with a man such as fitz Alan."

"Has he asked?" Ab Owen chuckled. "Yet he is such a man as I would have for you, would he not take you away from me."

Meghan's jaw tightened. Her chin jutted as he had seen it do too many times.

"You would choose for my bed the same man you would choose for the raidings!" she snapped. "You forget the purpose is different. But we talk of something never to be, and, as you say, he has not asked."

Meghan shrugged away a sense of unaccountable regret and added, "Look at me, sixteen and not even betrothed! Why should any man want me?" Her smile faded. "And I would mostlike be widowed now, had I married. Now, I would as lief never do so as to lose another I love. If I marry, 'twill be for an heir for Cleitcroft, nothing else. I'll give no man dominion over me, no matter how gentle the bonds."

"Aye," ab Owen said, "and that is why you fear him, is it not—that he could hold you?"

"An English bastard, sire? Methinks not. I dislike him because he is licentious and thinks each woman but a skirt to be lifted, nothing else! There's Llewelyn!"

She watched the Welsh prince ride toward them, his reluctant obeisance done, and she remembered their conversation the night before. He had not asked her to violate her father's oath to Edward. Llewelyn had only told her there was a groom in Edward's retinue who would relay messages to yet another man—and on to Wales. He had not asked that she spy; indeed, he had ordered her not to. But as a handmaid to the queen, perhaps she might hear something others would not. A man said things to his wife that he spoke nowhere else, forgetting her women. But she was only to send word of something extremely important. Let others ferret out lesser information; he but wanted her aware that such a system was available.

Frowning, Meghan decided she would go beyond his orders, if necessary. She could not stand by should Wales be threatened. Her father's oath did not bind her. The Welsh considered women capable of honoring their own pledge and not bound by one made for them. Let the Norman king issue proclamations as he would; he was not her lord, nor was her word the one given! Nor was a pledge given under duress binding.

Her eyes rested on Edward I of England and she compared him to his legend as the fairest prince in Christendom. He was no longer the slim, golden-haired man who had fought for his father's disputable honor, nor was he the handsome crusader, a lovely queen by his side. "By the Blood of God," he had raged on hearing that Phillip III of France had abandoned the Crusade, "though all my fellow soldiers and countrymen desert me, I will enter Acre with Fowin, the groom of my palfrey, and I will keep my word and my oath to the death!"

Edward had set out for Acre with a mere thousand men—and won. Allowing no rest, he had pushed on to Nazareth, then won again at Haifa. But his valiant example had not been enough and he had admitted at last that, though victorious, he had lost. It was a supposed envoy from the Emir of Jaffa carrying peace terms who attacked Edward with a poisoned knife, the blow deflected from the heart to strike him in the arm instead. Only a courageous and painful operation and the care of his wife had saved him. Still feeble, he had accepted a truce and sailed to Sicily, where he had received word of his father's death.

His hair had darkened in the five years since then, but his eyes still blazed as blue as legend described them. He had thickened about the middle, but his height, earning him the nickname "Longshanks," carried the weight well. He was said to be the tallest man in England, but Meghan had seen a man at a fair whom she guessed to be taller. The king's finely chiseled features were marred by a slight droop of his left eyelid, a blemish inherited from his father. War had left him no scars, but his position had marked furrows on his wide brow. His very presence seemed to diminish the lesser men about him. His wool cloak and russet-hued tunic, his few jewels, contrasted with the rich garb of his clergy and nobles, his plain dress more suited to his outdoor, active life. Yet his clothes only served to emphasize his masculinity.

He had changed, though, Meghan knew. He had once been a boisterous, rakish partner to the young nobles of the land. The Crusade, his assumption of the throne, and his love for his wife had matured him. The death of his son had grieved him. Too, he had little time now for wild friends and wanton wenches. Yet his charm drew men to him with an earnest ease. He could inspire loyalty with a glance and a smile, or be like a large puppy anxious for the attention and affection never denied him. But whatever manner of man he was, it would have been better for Wales—and for herself—if he had died under the assassin's knife.

She was wishing a man dead, a grievous sin, Meghan realized as she watched Llewelyn stop next to Bruce ap Howell. Their words were inaudible, but their faces were easily read. Then, with a slap on his shoulder, Llewelyn sent ap Howell on to Edward to deliver his son. Turning to ab Owen, the prince's eyes softened.

Hugh fitz Alan watched as Llewelyn clasped his chieftain's arm. Feeling like a voyeur, he saw the Welsh prince confirm something deeply felt as he stared into ab Owen's eyes. Then Llewelyn turned to Meghan. He kissed her lightly on the lips and Hugh felt an unreasoning jealousy at the customary greeting. The feeling deepened when Meghan returned it with more tenderness than convention decreed.

She darted a glance at him from the corner of dark-fringed eyes and smiled, sensing his discomfort. It was a victory she had not felt before and one she relished.

Then it was Meghan's turn to approach the English king beside her father. She kept her eyes forward as ab Owen kneeled in the dirt, his hands between those of Edward. This was but a ceremony, she reminded herself. The pledging of oaths would come later, after the Welsh had been freed of the ban of excommunication.

Rising, ab Owen stood aside as his daughter went to her knees. Then, touching her fingertips, Edward lifted her back up, kissing her brow. He turned to ab Owen.

"I've no woman to be with your daughter here, Gavin ab Owen. Would you ride with us to Flint where my wife awaits? There Meghan will be well chaperoned and instructed. My lady wife has need of a maiden skilled in music."

Ab Owen's mouth went dry at the thought of his daughter taken from him to sew fine seams for a foreign queen, to be chaperoned by prim-mouthed ladies and instructed in Norman ways. Yet he smiled inwardly at the thought of his tone-deaf Meghan playing to Eleanor on a badly tuned harp and of the clumsy stitches she would darn into Edward's hose. The joy of revenge, no matter how petty, lay in the thought. And they would know her temper and stubbornness. But the king required an answer, one couched in the courtliness his daughter must soon learn.

"My lord, I thank you for the honor you do my daughter. I pray she will please your most gracious lady wife."

Meghan swallowed hard, her gaze turned aside. Never had she seen her father so humbled.

Ah, Edward, she vowed to herself, I'll not soon forgive you that, unintentional as it may be. Even a flea in
your hose can vex, and I am more than that!

She tilted her chin, her slim body held straight as she
addressed Edward. She was well aware of the rudeness in
addressing him first and she gloried in it. "Sire, I do not
sing. I be a rarity—a tone-deaf Welshwoman. I was
trained in the longbow and in the sword, not in a harp.
But your wish 'twill be my pleasure!"

Without waiting for a reply, she turned on her heel and
strolled to her horse. Mounting, she rode back to her
people. Edward nodded at ab Owen's words of apology
as his gaze followed Meghan. Here was a woman who
could well prove a vixen, and, if he read her right, take
pleasure in it. He scowled, his eyelid drooping farther.
Then he put her from his mind as he greeted the remaining Welsh. He was unaware of how the ceremony fed the
hate and plans already growing again in the minds and
hearts of the people he so humbled.

Chapter 3

They rode along the Irish Sea toward Flint on a road cut through the forest by Edward's army. The day was warm for early November. The heat, the hum of insects, and the rattle of an army on the move dulled Meghan into a stupor. She had long since ceased to marvel and curse the labor it had taken to cut a road twice the distance of a longbow's shot through forests which had once been one of Wales' natural defenses. Her mind no longer dwelled on the ill treatment of the night at Rhuddlan.

Dinner, to the English, had been a banquet of elation. The Welsh had held their hauteur high, but their dignity sat ill on a stomach filled with defeat. To be sure, there had been no open gloating. Edward would not condone the demeaning of a guest. But even he could not check the slur implied in a glance or restrain a certain note of laughter.

Throughout the interminable meal Meghan had fought an urge to fidget under Hugh fitz Alan's gaze. Other men had stared, their expressions lecherous, but his had turned her fingers clumsy, spilling wine and skidding her knife across her meat. Compelling herself to ignore him, she had lifted her eyes to his but once from the trencher that she shared with her father. The deliberation of his survey had forced her to lower them again and heat had risen over her delicate collarbones, encrimsoning her features.

Before the meal had come the lifting of the excommunication and the giving of confession. To Meghan it had seemed a meaningless rite. She had not felt cursed by the English archbishop's anathema. The god the Welsh worshiped would give no man such power, no matter how holy or how regal his vestments, and her mind had wandered. It would be so easy, she had thought, to drift away, to close her mind, to let her soul be witched away. Then nothing could touch her, no insult, grief, or pain. The cord binding mind to body was thin. It could break so easily. But with such peace came insanity.

Confession had been brief, her penance light. She had anger to confess, and rebellious thoughts, hatred, the wishing of harm on another. Remembering the feelings provoked by Hugh fitz Alan, Meghan had admitted, in a small voice, to thoughts of lechery. The priest, his face hidden by his cowl and his thin fingers pressed against his forehead, had only sighed, waiting for her to continue. When she had not, he had asked, "What of the sin of giving succor to the King's enemy, child?"

Meghan had stared at him, unable to understand, but at last she spoke, her tone indignant.

"Father, I did but comfort and assist my people! Had I not done so, that would be the sin. Mayhap a sin more heinous than the one you would put on me!"

She had had an impression of shrewd eyes scrutinizing her. Then, finding no sacrilege, he had named her flippant and pronounced her penance.

Rhuddlan Castle, in the midst of construction, had been no place for a woman of rank. The room she had shared with her father had been small and cramped, with no door. Ab Owen had lain all night with his sword unsheathed by his side, guarding his daughter. What rancor disturbed his sleep, Meghan had not known and they had exchanged no words, both protecting the other. Meghan had resolved then that she would not, could not, pass the time of her exile conforming to the ways of her keepers.

There were certain advantages to being a hostage. She would be under royal protection and no one would dare harm her, only Edward. To do so would bring Wales to arms once more. Even the king had little control over her, as long as she avoided treason and did not leave his charge. She would take every advantage of her position.

Her future settled, Meghan had smiled and fallen into a deep, dreamless sleep.

It was this thought, too, which had straightened her slim back until she had been lulled into lethargy by the sound of men on the march. Nor did she notice a horseman coming down the line toward them until he wheeled to ride next to her father. It was his shield with the bend sinister and the single lion rampart that drew her head high again. Yet, as he pushed back his mailed hood and wiped perspiration from his forehead, Hugh fitz Alan ignored her, riding beside her father for a long, quiet while. That he was acquainted with her father through tourneys, Meghan knew, but she had not thought he would approach them. At last, Hugh addressed ab Owen.

"I cannot say, well met, Gavin ab Owen, but I would have you know I regret that my duty brought you to this pass."

"Ah, fitz Alan." Ab Owen sighed. "If 'twas not you, 'twould be another! I know the curtain wall at Ainsleah needs extending, as does that of every castle. My coffers, too, be empty."

"Aye, but it galls my pride to take the king's hire, especially against my neighbors."

And to do so, they both knew, could damn his soul. The line between soldier and mercenary was thin. The latter was subject to excommunication—unless he sold his skills to the church itself. Only Hugh's reputation and Edward's friendship held open the doors of his peers in hospitality.

"Ah," ab Owen answered, "you had scant choice— nor did Edward. He is a methodical man and we are a chaotic people."

Hugh grinned in agreement. He had heard Edward rant often enough against the Welsh and their laws, which treated civil war as a pleasant means of passing the summer, which preferred banishment to the death penalty— and so many thus exiled came to England!

"Aye." Hugh laughed. "Edward roared down the walls when someone mentioned that the murder of a bard was punished by a fine of a hundred and twenty-six cattle."

"But does he know if 'tis more or fewer for a king?"

"I know not, but he is aware that you feel the gift of music is God's blessing, while a prince is but a chance of birth and politics."

"Ah, but does he think on it?" asked ab Owen.

"No more than he thinks on the assistance Llewelyn gave Simon de Montfort against his father Henry."

"Aye," ab Owen mused, "'twas not wise of Llewelyn to defeat Henry so, not with such shame."

He seemed to have nothing more to say and they rode in the comfortable silence shared by men who understand each other, men of the same profession, religion, and temperament. Hugh fitz Alan was the first to speak again.

"I've not seen you since the tourney at Kenilworth, five years gone. You did well that day."

"Aye, fairly, and I took no falls. 'Twas a good day for you, too, if I recall aright."

"I fell three and the prizes sore needed. The bailey at Ainsleah needed thickening. Now 'tis in my mind to add to the keep—a room over the hall, mayhap. Something to give privacy should I take a wife."

"You did not marry, then?" ab Owen asked. "I remember you were considering Harry Morley's sister."

"'Twas more like Morley considering me! Still, I did think on it until I saw the woman. She was not uncomely but for one flaw. She was missing a tooth, this one." Placing a finger on one of his own strong white ones, Hugh said, "And well aware of it she was—and mumbled so well I did not note it for three days! Mayhap 'twould not bother another, but me, I couldn't go through life with the temptation to relieve her of the other—to give her symmetry!"

He shook his head at ab Owen's laughter. "Mayhap I am too much a granny when I would choose a wife, but once taken, 'twould be long years ere I am relieved of her."

"Caution is good, methinks," ab Owen answered, "but I am not the man to advise you. I was content in my wife, having choosen her for herself and nothing else. But such marriages are rare and you may never wed if you wait for the like. But what hear you of John fitz Williams?''

"I stopped with him not two years past. The leeches removed his leg below the hip after that fall. 'Twas too broke to heal. He took it well, blessed as he was to live. He has a cart pulled by a goat and he supervises his lands from it right well. He also finds it convenient in escaping his wife. There is a shrew! And 'twas not his leg's loss that turned her thus. She was ever so! But his crippling has not slowed him. I noted several brats who sported his red thatch. Aye, the shrew even had a toddler clinging to her skirts and her belly swelling with another!''

The men laughed in a male conspiracy that not only excluded Meghan but also insulted her.

"And Richard Pelton,'' Hugh gossiped, "no longer has a tooth in his head and is sore touched on the subject. He gums his food. His chin, on my oath, ofttimes rubs his nose and he frights the brats come All Hallow's Eve.''

Meghan had become increasingly irritated by the men's camaraderie and her father's defection. Too, fitz Alan's careless disregard of her pricked her pride. She had been prepared to defend herself from him, perhaps to find a weakness to turn against him. Then he ignored her! Leaning forward to peer around her father, she addressed him.

"You seem, my lord, overly concerned with the feelings of others, and with their appearance! What faults will you gossip on to others when you've done inspecting us?''

Both men turned to her, Hugh's eyebrow crooked, ab Owen frowning, his hand raised to stop her. But she rushed on.

"Aye, your leering eyes would strip me of what few rags your English army left—and my dignity with them. Leave us! We've no need for patronization masked in companionship!''

His scarred eyebrow lifting higher, Hugh allowed his gray eyes to sweep over Meghan in sardonic appraisal.

Her eyes are green, he told himself as he bowed with a courtesy so gallant as to mock. Her large and slanted eyes were marked by long, black lashes. Her skin was bronzed by months spent in the open but was so thin that veins showed at her temples. There was arrogance in her small, square-set chin and stubbornness in her well-defined jaw, but her mouth was full and red, the upper lip a trifle shorter than the ripe lower one. It was a woman's mouth, a mouth designed for passion. Pleased with what he saw, Hugh addressed ab Owen, ignoring Meghan once more.

"Methinks you've been neglectful in this woman's rearing. 'Tis said a properly applied birching to the tail corrects the action of the tongue." Turning, he studied Meghan's furious face, then continued. "Mayhap, though, she be too ripe for a father's hand. I would, however, recommend to her husband, God pity that unfortunate man, a sound switching once a month to keep her attention. Should she take a husband—some might think her too long of tooth for the altar."

Meghan drew a deep breath, fighting an urge to physically attack the smug knight. She tilted her chin while her mind searched for the means to most likely wound him.

"'Twill most surely not be you, my lord! I am not so doddering as to consider such as you!" Visibly relaxing, she smiled sweetly, then thrust with the only weapon at hand. "And tell me, sir lord, what know you of child-rearing, you who were denied a father's tender nurturing—every true born infant's right?"

Her aim was sure. Hugh stiffened and his eyes turned as cold as frost on granite, stirring a sudden panic in Meghan. She instantly, fervently regretted her words, thanking all the saints she had her father's protection from the man who stared at her so furiously, though her father, too, would make her pay for the shameful insult.

Hugh held her mesmerized gaze a moment more, then ran his eyes disdainfully over her, from her short-cropped hair to the insect bites on her bare thighs. As she prayed she might vanish, he rested his gaze on her face once more and his voice held both threat and warning.

"Tread carefully, my lady. Do not remind me of what I would forget, or question the affection of my sire. As for your suggestion of marriage, I advise you to wait for a proposal ere you reject it. Then mayhap you will be rid of your virgin state before you grow too haggard to tempt any man!''

Pausing, Hugh studied her, his wrists crossed on the pommel of his saddle in a gesture of insouciance, then he spoke again. "Mayhap your maidenhood constricts, accounting for a waspish tongue far beyond even your years!"

Her lips growing white, she started to reply when her father's voice halted the words in her throat. "Meghan, cease! You shame me. You shame us!"

Turning to him, she met a face carved in stone. His voice was the more ominous for its low tone. "Would you have yourself thought as ill-bred as you behave? You will hold your wanton's tongue and not speak again lest you are addressed. Do you understand me?"

Meghan nodded, anger choking her so tightly she could not have spoken. Yet her eyes flashed rebellion, throwing rage she could not articulate into Hugh's calm face.

"Be sure you do," her father commanded before he turned away, resuming his conversation.

Only Meghan's determination to give Hugh no satisfaction kept her head high and her tears unshed. Her father's rejection stung. He had not spoken so to her since she was a child. The English were even turning her sire against her, she grieved, and hatred for the tall, dark knight beside her produced an ache in her chest, making each breath painful.

Finally fitz Alan made his farewell to ab Owen. She shook with anger when he leaned over to smile mockingly at her, his voice insolent as he said, "Maiden, may we meet again," before sweeping her with one more glance of casual appraisal.

Meghan returned his greeting with her index finger raised in a lewd gesture. Hugh's eyes widened in surprise, then he threw back his head in laughter. He had seen the gesture employed by men amongst themselves and by the most degenerate of trollops but never before by a maiden of gentle rearing. His laughter still rang in her ears long after he had wheeled his destrier and returned up the line to Edward.

The warm day darkened rapidly as fleeting wisps of cloud gathered to form masses of gray slate across the sky, casting a pall over the sun. The wind moaned as it drove clouds into a tumbling, threatening horde above the army. The air no longer smelled of earth and salt but of the sulpher and brimstone of hell.

Frowning, Hugh stared up at the piling masses and drew his destrier out of line, turning back toward the Welsh. Meghan rode a small, scrawny beast who had carried her slight weight well enough in the narrow defiles and up the steep paths of Wales. But it was too worn to stand against a charging, panic-stricken war horse. And the Welsh wench's hands were slim. There was strength beneath her smooth skin but not enough to hold up the small brute should it be struck by another, larger animal.

Hugh glanced again at the ominous clouds, then into the anxious faces of the marching men. He imagined he could smell the acrid scent of panic about to break. Driven by an inexplicable fear for a woman he hardly knew, he urged his horse to a faster trot just as the storm hit.

The stiff pace set by the footmen changed to a disordered melee as a flailing wind suddenly flogged them with rain and hail, drenching them in seconds. The flashes of lightning and claps of thunder seemed to have no beginning and no end, filling the soldiers with a superstitious awe.

Meghan hunched forward in the saddle, the reins twisted in her fingers as she frantically fought to control her maddened horse. She could see no way to escape the insane rush of men and beasts around her. Her mount, frightened by the storm and the confusion of terror-stricken riders, resisted her commands, backing into the horde behind her. Her father's face disappeared in the throng, then reappeared. A large palfrey hit her, lifting her horse off its feet. Her mount struggled ineffectively, fighting her as much as the throng. Then suddenly the press eased, dropping her horse to its knees. Sobbing and cursing, Meghan somehow helped it find its unshod hooves once more and desperately drove it on over the slime-slick road.

Ab Owen's efforts to help only added to her distress, increasing her feeling of being pushed to a situation far beyond control. Cries of "There 'tis! There's Flint!" only increased the efforts of those around her to reach shelter from the devil-driven storm.

Meghan raised terrified eyes from the road beneath her horse's feet and glimpsed the walls of Flint through a veil of falling rain. Pressed by the masses behind and threatened by the ramparts ahead, Meghan felt an overwhelming need to escape. All fear of the mob around her was brushed aside by a deeper, more primitive terror and she swerved her horse to the side, away from the forces crowding and crushing her. She saw her father as he swept by, trapped by the mass. He turned, trying to keep her in sight, then she caught a glimpse of Hugh fitz Alan's hard features as he leaned forward to grab her horse's bridle, and her panic rose.

Her sudden veer caught Hugh by surprise, then her palfrey slammed against his warhorse as it came up behind her. Meghan screamed once as she felt her animal's feet knocked from under, then hands gripping like death snatched at her. They grabbed her rain-slick leather tunic, slipped, and frantically gripped again, jerking her into viselike arms. The impact jarred her. Gasping and retching, trying to drag air into her bruised lungs, Meghan leaned forward against the rocklike forearm supporting her.

Her panic redoubled as horsemen pressed close, crushing her legs, and men on foot shook fists into her face. Twisting above the insane mob, she tried to escape. Her feet pushed against the destrier as she struggled to break the grip holding her. Somehow she turned enough to aim a fist at Hugh's face. He dodged the blow, then spun her over until she lay face down across his legs. Her fists beat ineffectually at the warhorse as Hugh forced it through the maelstrom to the edge of the road.

Once free, he raised his hand with leisurely intent, bringing it down on her wet, round, wiggling bottom. The first two spanks brought renewed fight and spits of rage and curses fit only for the barracks. The third was rewarded with a wail of indignation that gave Hugh a curious sense of satisfaction. Flipping Meghan over, he sat her sidesaddle facing him, throwing his cloak over her head. He wrapped her close, letting her beat against the mail protecting his chest.

Finally he shushed her, gently moving his hand along her spine to her neck, then down again until her sobs slowed to gulps and hiccoughs. Staring down at his hand holding her hair, Hugh noticed blood welling up where his thumbnail had been. A dull ache throbbed in his wrist. He watched the hand shake spasmodically as he pictured what would have happened had its grip failed him. He saw Meghan's slim body broken beyond all repair by hooves the size of dinner plates. He saw her bright, proud face crushed beyond all recognition. Clenching his jaw in the sudden agony of the loss that had almost been his, Hugh pulled her closer still. He buried his face between her neck and shoulder, feeling her shudders as though they were his own, and he knew he wanted her. And he would have her, someday, somehow, this defiant woman-child with her innocent, proud eyes and her mouth shaped for passion.

Suddenly he grinned, with more pain than joy. How Edward would laugh! He had warned Hugh of just such a happening.

Angry when Hugh had refused a certain heiress, Edward had called him a fool and said love was a thing sung by troubadours, a game played by idle, seldom-bedded women. Any man who looked for it in marriage would find a wench who would rob him of his sense, make of him a jesting stock, and lead him about by his member. Hugh had reminded him of his own marriage and the king had waved the argument away. His wedding had been a political match and it had only been God's blessing that love had come of it!

Hugh's smile turned wry as he pressed his face into Meghan's dark, tumbled hair. Let them say what they would, and let Edward laugh, he would have this girl! His arms tightened, then he cautiously unwrapped the mantle. Meghan's face was tear-streaked, her knuckles pressed against her swollen lips.

"Are you all right, little one?" he asked, adjusting the cloak to protect her from the steady downpour of rain.

She nodded jerkily and gulped, trying to regain her composure. This man frightened her in a way no storm ever could and her voice was rough with tears when she spoke.

"I do not want solicitude or anything else from you. And keep your cloak to cover your mail that it may shine when next you attack your neighbor!"

Hugh grinned, one eyebrow raised.

"Would you go to Eleanor dressed like this?" he mocked. "And you tremble. I would not have you dead of the cold. Or is it my nearness that disturbs you?"

His eyes dropped to her nipples, standing erect through the wet, thin leather, and he wondered how they would taste, filling his mouth with sweetness.

"I would have you warm my bed one day and a corpse be poor company for the sport I think on."

Meghan swung at his face and Hugh, easily catching her tiny fist in his huge one, continued, "Ah, am I to understand you are not interested in my bed, only in my mail? But I will have you one day, though you may fight me. I *will* win. Then the victory will belong to both of us, for I will make you want me and you will know glory in it!"

Fighting again, Meghan muttered expletives as she tried to break his grip on her wrist. She'd heard such language from the rabble who follow every army and she threw every word she could remember into his face—every one but "bastard." That, she knew, would change his amusement to an anger she did not want to face. Hugh waited, a smile tugging at his lips, until she sputtered to a halt, her extensive vocabulary exhausted.

"You have the mouth of a gutterbrat," he commented, "and methinks you know not the meaning of half the obscenities you spit. Mayhap Eleanor can rid you of the habit. If not, 'twill be my pleasure to demonstrate their meanings once you are mine."

Meghan glared at him, opening her mouth to curse him, but Hugh shook his head.

"I would not advise you to revile me again. This time you might forget and speak the words you walked about so carefully afore. As for my armor, a barrel of sand will make it gleam as new and I would not quibble as to where defense becomes aggression. Let us save that when our juices have run dry and we be doddering crone and graybeard afore our fire.''

His words taunted her, yet Meghan read a desire in his eyes that stirred an unwanted, painful warmth in her belly and an ache in her groin. But Hugh did not see the fear in her eyes—or the bewilderment. He glanced about as though surprised to find they were alone.

"The rest are in Flint," he said, looking back at Meghan, his eyes drinking in her features. "As eager as I am to find a snug corner and pass the night in comfort and seduction, I am afraid they will be searching for you. And methinks ab Owen would not be pleased to find us in some villein's hut, me riding his fair daughter. Nor would Edward." His voice lost its mockery, becoming gentle and filled with regret. "And methinks 'twill be long ere I have this opportunity again."

Then his regret became concern.

"Are you ready now to face Eleanor and her harpies?"

Meghan nodded, refusing to meet his gaze. She lifted her chin and straightened her back, seeming to pull dignity about herself like a cloak.

"Aye, so you are!" Hugh whispered huskily.

Reading his intent in his eyes, Meghan fought to escape, twisting against his arms, but he held her immobile and his gaze pinned hers, trapping it with his need. His head lowered, his mouth pressing against the blue vein pulsing in her throat, and he felt it leap under his kiss. Suddenly Meghan could not move. She became aware only of the hammering of her heart, of the scent of the man who held her—leather, horse, the wet wool of his cloak—of his breath on her skin, of his mouth that seemed to draw all strength from her, shaking her with a sensation that frightened her even as she surrendered to it. Then his lips moved, drawing up her neck, burning as they traced a path under her ear, brushing her earlobe, sucking it gently, then moving along the line of her jaw.

Powerless, not daring to breath, Meghan waited, tears welling from behind her trembling lids, until his mouth claimed hers. She had known his lips would come, had wanted them, but his touch brought sensations she hadn't realized existed. His lips brushed hers as softly as a moth's wing, held for a moment, and Meghan felt a sob swelling her throat, heard it escape in a whimper. Then his mouth took hers fully. It caressed her tenderly and became demanding, as though he would drink his fill of a cup he knew could only inspire greater thirst. He turned her head to take her mouth more deeply.

She knew her lips softened under his, that they gave to him, that her mouth opened to his pleading tongue, was answering it. His hand released her wrist to accept the fingers she twined with his. Her hips twisted until her pelvis pressed against him, his manhood hard against her thigh. But she could summon no will to resist. An incredible warmth spread within her, a steady throb insistent in its demand yet refusing to burst.

As though aware he had awakened something that only he could satisfy, Hugh drew back, his eyes searching her features. Unable to meet his gaze, knowing he would read her response there, Meghan buried her face against his chest, sobs shaking her as she tried to defeat the desire he had awakened. His fingers softly traced the line of her eyebrow, her cheekbone, the shape of her jaw, as though to commit them to memory. Then he lifted her chin. His gaze intent, he passed a fingertip lightly along her passion-swollen lower lip until she lifted her eyes to his. There was anger in her gaze, and defiance, and something she could not hide that told him he had marked her as his woman, had awakened her in a way few women ever knew.

Hugh threw back his head and whooped his triumph to the skies, then he spurred his horse on to Flint.

Chapter 4

Horsemen led by ab Owen rode from the gates of Flint
in search of Meghan. As they met, ab Owen looked into
his daughter's set face. She would not meet his gaze and
a blush rose over her features. His eyes turned to question Hugh but found no answer there either. Turning to
ride next to them, he asked, fighting apprehension, "What
happened, Meghan? I saw you swerve when 'twas too
late."

Meghan kept her face forward as she tried to control
the turmoil Hugh's mouth had awakened. She told herself
she loathed him, hated her body for its betrayal. Yet her
senses were alive to the swing of his hauberk as its links
struck lightly against her back with his every motion. She
felt the strength of his arms around her hips. But her
father wanted an answer. Forcing her tone neutral,
Meghan replied, "My palfrey fell and Sir Hugh pulled
me from her. Was she injured?"

"She came in with the rest," ab Owen answered, "Are
you hurt? Did anything else happen?"

Her mind scurried about for words as Hugh's arms
tightened slightly. What is there to say? she wondered to
herself. That a man kissed me? That with that kiss he
violated me as surely as if he had raped me? And that I
responded as a wanton, wanting him, and, oh Holy
Mother, I don't want to!

"Nothing else," she replied at last.

Ab Owen studied her, finding no confirmation of the
lie he knew she told. He turned to Hugh, who rode with

his eyes on Flint, his body relaxed, the faintest of smiles breaking the hard, chiseled line of his features.

They passed the outer gates of Flint and entered the storm-deserted streets of the town. The outer ward of the castle itself was a mass of confusion. Slipping on mud and wet grass, pages scuttled around squires. Squires frustrated knights in the unsaddling and currying of mounts. Men-at-arms wrangled for the choicest place to spread their cloaks for the night's bedding.

Amazed, Meghan looked about. An eternity seemed to have passed in the last minutes. She had bridged the gap from maiden to woman when Hugh had awakened a desire she had not thought possible. Yet the army had only just arrived.

Dismounting, Hugh ignored Meghan's protests and lifted her from the saddle. Wincing at the pain in his injured hand, he let her slide down the length of him before releasing her with a grin at her flushed outrage. Handing his horse to a passing page, he pulled his mantle tight about her to cover what her wet clothes could not. A hand cupping her elbow, he guided her through the chaos, ab Owen following a stride behind. For all her contempt, Hugh was her only anchor in a sea of hostile, leering faces and she stayed close as he jostled and cursed his way through the outer ward. She found she hated him all the more for her dependence on him. Then he smiled down at her set features.

"First we find Eleanor. Mostlike she has clothes for you."

Digging in her heels, Meghan jerked back against his grip, halting them both. Ab Owen crashed into them. They both flashed him an indignant look.

"My lord," she spat out, "I mislike this concern for my modesty. 'Tis misplaced and misbegotten. My honor be mine own and does not need you to guard it. And your mindfulness implies a privilege that does not exist between us. I'll not have it!"

Gripping her arms, Hugh turned her until his back blocked her father in the press of people.

"My lady," he said from between clenched teeth, "if a wish to prevent you shame shows excessive solicitude,

I most sorely regret it! Nor would I care to suggest a relationship with you, privileged or no, that most wise men would run from as from death itself. But you are now the king's ward and, as I am his man, you are also mine. I do not abuse children or rape women but, by God's tooth, you dressed like that would tempt any man, and the sooner Eleanor raids her clothes chest for you, the sooner I'll rest easy."

"Aye, and you would have me take the castoffs from your English queen? Would the English give back what they take and expect Welsh thanks for it, too? Be you so very self-righteous?"

"You will find the queen a most gentle, generous lady. You'll take many a gift from her and never know it. Unlike what I would give you, were not the king's honor mine!"

Meghan's chin lifted higher. "Aye, and was it his honor," she demanded, "that you were thinking of back on the road? Could not such a lapse hang you, my lord?"

Hugh grinned down at her. "If I had thought you would tell, little one, I would have made certain the deed was worth hanging for!"

Hugh thought he saw her mouth quirk in a reluctant response before he drew her on. With ab Owen following, he hauled her down a narrow passageway thronged with shoving people and entered the castle itself. A glance showed that Edward was not in the inner ward and Hugh led her up the winding stairs to the great hall. There Edward stood near the far fireplace, surrounded by his barons.

The king's arm rested on the shoulders of a small dark woman with a lovely, gentle face and the long nose of Spanish heritage. His features were relaxed and his clothes, cleaned and brushed, showed a woman's loving touch. He laughed at something Eleanor whispered, bending down to listen as the queen stood on tiptoe. Hugh knelt before him, leaving Meghan to curtsy and keep the cloak about herself as best she could. His voice warm, the king ordered Hugh up as Eleanor greeted him, belaboring him with teasing words for his long absence from

court. At last she turned to Meghan, offering her hand as
Edward introduced ab Owen and his daughter.

"'Twill be lovely to have another young maid with me,
and you so comely!" Eleanor exclaimed.

Tilting her head to Hugh, the queen, ever the match-
maker, asked in her light Castilian lisp, "Think you the
maid lovely, my lord Hugh?"

Hugh leaned back on his heels, his arms folded across
his chest, and studied Meghan as though he had not set
eyes on her before. He grinned as she glowered back.

"Aye, my lady, her features bear a certain charm.
Unfortunately, her temperament and tongue don't match
her face. Mayhap," he added dubiously, "your gentle
care will teach her to be more feminine. Her apparel,
though, be no fault of her sire. She would play soldier
and is now dressed as such. Aye, and a warm bath would
help. She trembles from the damp, or mayhap 'tis something else unnerves her."

Meghan shook in incoherent rage as he affected a concern she knew to be false. She wanted to slap the smile
from his face. She barely heard Eleanor summon a maid
as Hugh took his leave, pleading a need to care for his
horse. Her mind scurried about for a means to wipe the
grin from his face. As she watched him stride away, she
called his name. He turned, suddenly wary.

"You forgot your mantle," she stated.

"Keep it, lady. I've another and you need it yet."

"Ah, no, my lord," Meghan answered, her smile
courteous. "I cannot keep a cloak so fine as this!"

She drew it off, holding it toward him, exposing herself in the short, clinging garment she wore. Lust rose in
Hugh as he noted how her wet kirtle and the barbaric belt
accentuated her breasts, the curve of her waist, the thrust
of her pelvic mound, and her long legs that any man
would want wrapped around him.

All the men in the hall stared, too, feeling the same
lust. Striding back to her, his jaw tight, Hugh was intent
only on covering what he strangely considered his and
taking it from under other itching male eyes. But before
he reached her, Meghan smiled again, revenge like honey

in her mouth. She dropped the cloak to the floor. Looking at it, her features dismayed, she feigned ruefulness.

"Ah, my lord, it did slip! 'Tis so heavy! And 'tis not a gift, is it, to press on a maid you've no claim to?"

Hugh halted in his steps. His eyes were steel gray with fury and Meghan's smile became mocking as she read his desire to possess her.

"You had best pick it up," she advised, her voice a bubble of satisfaction. "'Twill gather fleas if left and there may be dog turds to fragrance it for you!"

Her smile broadened, exposing small, white teeth as she savored her vengeance, her head tilted to better assess his impotent rage. Looking down, trying to tug her smile into a frown, she considered the cloak and nudged it with a booted foot, then turned on her heel to follow the maid. Her hips moved in a sweet sway, taunting Hugh, as she left her father to make what apologies for her behavior he cared to make.

Hugh watched her go, his anger abating, a faint smile touching his eyes. He shook his head at ab Owen's words.

"Nay, do not beg pardon for her!" Hugh said. "She is strong and now frightened, in a way she had not known afore."

Picking up the cloak, he tossed it over his shoulder. Then he shrugged, grinning as he asked, "Would I want her if she was a simpering wench?"

Meghan sat neck deep in the wooden tub, her knees tucked beneath her chin. She tried to enjoy the first warm bath she had had in months, but her mind refused. Her thoughts would run through the last few days from beginning to end, then over them again, no matter where she forced them. From the moment she had first felt Hugh fitz Alan's eyes on her, she had been pushed into committing the deplorable act in the hall. She turned crimson and her stomach tightened each time she thought of it, but she could find no way to rectify her deed. How could she wipe her immodest image from the minds of all who had seen her? How ease the shame she had given her father and make amends to Edward and Eleanor, whose hospitality she had violated? And how could she prove she was not the strumpet she had shown herself to be?

A public apology to Hugh fitz Alan would help more than anything else, but that she could not do! Yet even in her shame, she could not suppress a feeling of triumph. Just to think of the need in his eyes brought a restlessness and a yearning she could not reconcile with her self-esteem, and to watch it turn to rage filled her with satisfied glee.

Sitting straighter, Meghan ignored the water splashing over the edge.

"He is all I despise," she insisted to herself. "Insolent and arrogant! He would take me with or without my consent!"

A small voice whispered that she did Hugh an injustice. If fornication was his purpose, he would choose a wench of ill repute. And humility was a virtue allowed only women and priests. But she rejected these thoughts. Remembering his furious face, a giggle escaped her. Ah, but what he would have done had he been able to put a hand to her! Kindled by the idea, she stretched in the water, then curled up again, rebuking her own wantonness.

"And what do you find to laugh on, maiden?"

Meghan jerked around, sloshing water. The queen leaned against the door, disapproval marring her features. Yet Meghan thought she saw a glint of amusement in the stern eyes. Taking a deep breath, she forced her voice to remain level. That she was truly ashamed did not make the humbling of her pride any easier.

"My lady, I would make most abject apology to you and to your household for the disgrace I brought to it. I most truly regret my behavior."

"Do you? Is your contrition such that you would beg forgiveness of Sir Hugh afore the hall?" Seeing the set of Meghan's jaw, she snorted through her nose. "I thought not!"

Eleanor continued to appraise her ward for what was to Meghan an uncomfortably long time before she finally commented, "You've enough pride to respect it in others. You should, therefore, be aware of the hurt that willful damage to pride can impart to a man of Hugh's birth.'' Glancing at the tirewomen who dawdled about, Eleanor scowled. She ordered them from the chamber and sat on a low stool to face Meghan.

"He's not a man to injure without thought of consequence, maiden. That you are a woman would not protect you if my lord Edward did not. I do not say Hugh mistreats women, but no one has taunted him as you have done."

Eleanor gazed at the obstinate face before her for a long moment, her eyes astute. "'Tis not simply a matter of a proffered mantle, is it?" she asked.

Meghan shrugged and leaned forward, arms wrapped protectively around her knees. It seemed to her that another woman might understand her inner turmoil. Not since her mother had died had she had a woman to talk to, except for Glenna and she was such an ancient. When Meghan spoke, her voice betrayed her agitation.

"My lady, how do I tell of a tone of voice, a look in the eye? Sir Hugh strips me with his gaze, insults me with insinuation. When I fight back, he twists my words about. He makes of me a fool—and I am not foolish. His every deed is an affront, even to his ignoring of me. He makes me feel as though I am but a thing to be used." The kiss was, somehow, too private a thing to expose to Eleanor. "How do I explain how a man can convey lust and intent with but a lift of an eyebrow?"

"Ah, you say I would not understand." Eleanor laughed, an odd mixture of bitterness and love. She placed a hand on a belly rounded by early pregnancy. "How think you I came of this, and four others? My lord did lift more than an eyebrow, yet ofttimes I know his need ere even he is aware of it."

Meghan did not smile back and the queen grew serious.

"I can see how such desire in a man can be discomfiting, yet you must grow hardened to it. There is much lechery at court and you have made yourself vulnerable by your own behavior."

"I am not a stranger to would-be seducers, my lady, or to earthy speech. Except for a few whores, I was the only woman in the midst of fighting men for months! And I had six brothers once. Yet that bastard lord makes me aware of what I can well ignore from another! 'Tis something about the man himself.''

Suddenly she shivered. "I feel so naked afore him! Mayhap that is why I acted as I did, to show him what he cannot have, aye, and my scorn. But I do not offer excuse, do not think that, lady, only apology.''

Meghan's eyes held Eleanor's until the queen dropped her gaze in thought. Sitting on a stool, she ran her fingers over her kirtle, forming a pleat in the cloth. When she looked back at Meghan, her voice was that of one woman asking understanding of another.

"He is a good man, Meghan, no matter your feelings. There is nothing I would not give him, and my husband the same. 'Tis true he is a bastard, yet his parentage is of the best, at least that of his sire. His holdings are small yet profitable. You'd not want, nor your children. And Edward would gift him well, should he wed.''

Lifting her hand, Eleanor halted Meghan's protest.

"Listen to me! He is strong and methinks you need a firm hand. And 'twould not be a marriage of politics or of land. Do you know how rare that is? He has little to gain in the taking of you, much less than in other offers he has had. But if any man can hold your wild Welsh lands, 'twould be Hugh. Aye, and hold you!''

Eleanor paused, trying to read her words' effect. She leaned forward, her eyes intent on her ward's closed features. "I am fortunate that I have a marriage of love and respect. 'Tis rare! Sir Hugh has not displayed interest in a woman afore you. Methinks he wants you to wife, though he may not yet know it. A man does not show such rage at the spurning of a gift or in the manner 'tis rejected if the woman is not important to him. And methinks he would not affect you so if you did not care for him.''

"No!'' Meghan whispered, shaking her head. Biting her lip, she stared at the water swirling about her and reflecting the torches burning in brackets on the walls. Finally she raised her head, her eyes angry.

"I am Welsh, lady, and reared in the Welsh way, knowing I would have a choice in the man I marry and not be forced into a bed odious to me. I knew, too, 'twould be a man who would take me for myself, not for what I brought him. Yet you tell me to be grateful that a man is willing to take me in spite of what little I have? My lady, I cannot be so! If I marry a Welshman, my dowry would stay mine. And should I leave him, as I've the right, I take it with me, even should I marry another. That, too, is something you cannot do, you English— divorce and remarry. An Englishwoman can never leave a hated marriage in which she is raped night after night, or in which she is forced to birth brat after unwanted brat. No Welshwoman would stay, yet you English must."

Cutting off Meghan's words with a stab of her hand, Eleanor stood and began to pace. A scowl creased her forehead and she pressed her hands to the small of her back to ease a pain Meghan doubted she was even aware of.

"Do not," Eleanor ordered, knowing she was being pettish, "refer to me as 'you English'! I am of Castile!"

Meghan's smile was rueful.

"In truth, lady? Aye, mayhap were you to do something to anger the Normans they would call you 'that Castilian woman'! But your king and his lords would not have you anything but English—nor your clergy. When you wed, you became Edward's as surely as his horse, his armor, the tunic across his shoulder. His crimes are yours, his debts also. You are his chattel, to be used or misused as he wills. You are like a seed in an apple, an apple chosen for its flesh, not the seed. The seed is only used to grow another tree or is discarded on the whim of the man who strips its flesh. And should you be discarded, your kinsmen would not take you back unless 'twas profitable to do so.

"But in Wales," she continued, though Eleanor had drawn breath twice to speak, "married or not, I am a part of the clan, ever welcome at my sire's table. Even he cannot gainsay me that. My husband's debts and crimes are his clan's, as my clan's are mine. No matter where I wed, I am Welsh, and my children, no matter their sire, are Welsh, ever able to lay claim to my clan.''

Meghan set her chin in a gesture Eleanor had already come to know too well.

"I would be a fool, would I not," she said, "were I to wed anyone not Welsh, and that man a bastard?"

Eleanor only smiled. "I had thought 'twas not a Welsh prejudice to decry a man's birth, that bastards were as honored as true-born children. Do not your people extend this same courtesy to the by-blows of others?"

The rebuke's accuracy was proven by the flush rising over Meghan's features, but Eleanor did not pause to savor it. "And you would be a fool, would you not, to marry a man for his birthplace, refusing one who would teach you passion and give you the children of his love, who would want you as a woman to share his life? Aye, the Welsh are free, but what is freedom without someone to share it? Loneliness and unfulfilled passion are cages from which no liberty or privilege can free you.

"Think on marriage to Hugh, maiden," she continued. "You could always, should it be so odious, run away to your Welsh mountains."

Then she was gone, leaving Meghan crouched in a cold bath, her mind in turmoil.

Chapter 5

The dinner horn sounded. Ignoring the smirks of Eleanor's tirewomen, Meghan smoothed the soft wool of the tawny kirtle she wore and tugged down the pale gold sleeves of the undertunic so that they showed at her wrists. It had been months since she felt feminine, and knowing she looked well somehow gave her courage. Although Eleanor was shorter, Meghan was slimmer. The queen's skirts, worn so long that they had to be held up, lightly glazed the floor on Meghan. She only regretted her short crop of ebony hair which would not touch her shoulders, no matter how she tugged. Cutting it had once seemed necessary. Now she mocked the naiveté of the girl who had felt the sacrifice would aid Wales. Still, she told herself, her smile cynical, her shorn locks had made running through the underbrush far easier.

Taking a deep breath, she straightened her shoulders and lifted her chin. At least she could not be accused of hiding in her quarters. Smiling at the women, knowing they awaited her downfall, she preceded them to the hall.

Ab Owen met his daughter at the door and escorted her to the table, seating her with the Welsh hostages and above the salt. Meghan's carriage faltered for only a moment as curious onlookers stared and lewd ogling threatened to wilt her spine. That her father gave her no greeting and that her countrymen pointedly turned their backs on her hurt far more than the opinions of the English.

Yet, as the diners fell to their meal with more fervor than manners, she found herself ignored. The story of her humiliation of Hugh fitz Alan proved less interesting than their appetites. Wine and ale were poured freely and Meghan, too, addressed herself to the meal with more hunger than she had thought possible. The taste of bread after months of bannock, and the gamey flavor of swan stuffed with doves was welcome. She didn't raise her eyes again until she realized the knight opposite had spoken. His words were as innocent as his features were leering, and Meghan did not reply. She stared at him blankly until he blinked and looked away. Muttering a charm to his trencher, he furtively made a sign to ward off evil.

Smiling, Meghan glanced down the table for Hugh. She found him opposite and above her a short distance. He returned her cold gaze with a slight smile, giving approval to her rebuff of his fellow knight. Refusing to acknowledge him, Meghan let her gaze drift on, then return. He had turned and was now engrossed in conversation with his tablemates, drawing with his knife on the tablecloth to illustrate a point.

He was incredibly handsome, Meghan conceded. His rare smile changed his face to that of a small, mischievous boy, and only Edward dwarfed his height and the width of his broad chest and shoulders. Hugh's well-trimmed beard set him apart in a time when most men were clean shaven for comfort under their helmets. It molded close to his face, emphasizing the strength of his jaw and chin. Meghan watched his mobile mouth. His hands were emphatic in their gestures, his fingers long and slim. Her mind betrayed her with memories of that mouth covering hers, those hands caressing her body. When he looked up suddenly, meeting her eyes, a flush flooded her features. He seemed to read her thoughts, for his grin flashed.

Flustered, Meghan glanced up at the dais where Edward dined with his wife and the more honored guests. Llewelyn was on the king's right. On Edward's left and farther down the table, was a man she did not know. There were many people in the hall she could not name,

but this one held her curiosity; there was something
familiar about him. He was obviously Welsh, but his
clothes were as gaudy as a bishop's and he ate with the
affectation of a Norman dandy.

Bending toward her father, Meghan asked who he was.
Ab Owen scowled, his grizzled eyebrows meeting.

"Davyd," he answered, his voice harsh with distaste.

Meghan looked back at the man who was considered
the archtraitor of Wales. His resemblance to Llewelyn,
his older brother, had made him seem familiar. Traitor or
no, his behavior had been a catalyst for war. When Llewelyn had refused to grant Edward homage, the turbulent
Davyd had fled Wales, the accusation of a plot to
dethrone the pendragon hard on his heels. Edward had
given him sanctuary, claiming that the matter must be
settled by law—not by the ancient Cymry code of Wales
but by an English court. Not until the rebels were
returned, declared Llewelyn, would he do homage to
Edward, ignoring the order to meet his lord at Chester.
That had been a war ago and now Davyd was, after all,
a matter for the clan to settle and, therefore, not to be
discussed in front of foreigners.

Meghan could see no evil lurking beneath Davyd's nervousness. His mouth might be a trifle weak and his hands
fluttered in the way of court fops, but there seemed to be
nothing dangerous in the man—though weakness could be
as great a threat as strength. He was, Meghan decided,
more a pawn, as many claimed, and therefore, someone
to be pitied.

Still, when Davyd met Meghan's eyes, she lifted her
chin and let her gaze move on, not seeing his smile falter. Her eyes drifted over the hall, not really seeing anything, until they suddenly lurched back to a face she knew
too well, her stomach flipping within her.

There sat a grinning Caradoc, his red, sensuous lips
lifting as he raised his goblet in a derisive salute. His eyes
swept over her, defiling her in a way that the mocking
smile and strong hands of Hugh fitz Alan never could.
Meghan stared at him, the noise in the hall fading to a
murmur, her gaze snared by her half brother's like a rabbit's before a snake. With an effort, she jerked her eyes

away, her body shuddering. Her gaze flew to Hugh as she instinctively sought protection.

A frown knitted Hugh's brows. He had watched as she glanced about, had seen the way her gaze had leaped to fix on someone. Now her eyes held an appeal he did not understand. Then abruptly her fear disappeared, leaving her features impassive. Her disappointed gaze dropped. But her hands, he saw, still shook on her goblet, and he looked over to see what had disturbed her.

The man seemed no more sinister than many others. He was Welsh, with a sparse mustache. His hair was a matte black, seeming to absorb the light. The locks grew low on his forehead, giving him an expression of animal cunning. His large eyes protruded slightly beneath meager brows. Dark, oily skin was laid over flesh with seemingly no bone beneath. His body was big-boned with that deceptive softness of some extremely strong, agile men. He sat tall on the bench with a long trunk and proportionately short legs.

There was nothing to account for Meghan's revulsion. Indeed, his animal carnality would attract some women. But Hugh felt distaste, and decided the man appeared ungraspable, like a greased egg in the hands of an infant.

Then the man's gaze met Hugh's. His mouth curved conspiratorially before he looked back at Meghan. His gaze suggested an obscene knowledge and somehow tried to sully her in a foul, unnatural way. Glancing back to Hugh, he lifted an eyebrow, inviting him into some abominable complicity.

Hugh stiffened, his eyes narrowing as he unconsciously pushed himself halfway up from the table. His distaste twisted into loathing, into an urge to wipe the man from the earth as he would an insect that had crawled up from a cesspool. Then the man's eyes dropped, all insinuation gone from their depths, as though it had never been there.

Hugh stared at him, wondering if he had imagined what he'd read in the man's eyes. But Meghan's hands still shook. Ab Owen appeared undisturbed, gazing morosely into his goblet, yet Hugh felt he, too, would have been troubled had he seen the man.

Shrugging, Hugh slumped back to the bench, revulsion leaving him numb. He must, he decided, ask who the man was and what he had to do with ab Owen and his daughter. But when Hugh looked back, the stranger was gone and the opportunity lost.

Beneath Meghan's placid features, her mind raced. Even as a child, Caradoc had been somehow twisted. He'd fought in their games with a desire not to win but to maim, to give pain. So he had been on the raidings, astonishing and disgusting even the most war-hardened warriors. He'd lied not to protect himself but to create contention among others. He'd teased her with an obscene insinuation only she sensed. She'd quickly learned to avoid his hands, which had tried to pinch and probe her intimate places when he'd cornered her alone or under cover of a game. Now his presence both frightened and repulsed her.

Perhaps it was resentment that had warped Caradoc, though he had shared his brothers' rearing and had been treated equally, as was his right. Certainly he had had her father's love until he had proved himself unworthy of it. Ab Owen had paid fine after fine for his crimes, his rapes, his wanton destruction of property, not seeming to see the warped mind in a son he felt he had somehow wronged. But the murder of a bard was a crime even ab Owen could not excuse and he had not interfered when Caradoc was outlawed into exile.

Then he went to the English, as did Davyd ab Gruffydd, and they are fit company for each other, Meghan thought.

She glanced from under her lashes at Davyd, flicking him with scorn, then on to Caradoc. But he was gone! For a second, Meghan felt panic. But to fear even his absence was to give him the power he craved. She turned her mind to the minstrel, but was too weary to follow the Nordic saga he attempted. The events of the day had taken their toll and all she longed for was sleep. Cupping her chin in her hands, she dozed under the minstrel's convoluted lyrics.

The rest of the company, too, showed fatigue. The minstrel prudently stepped aside for a troupe of jugglers, who drew only derision from the more vocal knights. They performed in the hope of a few coins and were rewarded by a handful of scattered farthings from the more drunken lords, who were only glad to see them go. In the sudden lull, heads lifted from cups and red-rimmed eyes peered about to see what further boredom must be endured before they could seek sleep.

It was Hugh fitz Alan's voice that broke through their lethargy. All eyes turned to him. The entertainment he had provided earlier with the Welsh wench promised that this would be better. He was certain to set her on her heels. Fitz Alan had a way with words and wenches that could make this better than a bear baiting.

"My lord Edward," Hugh repeated, lifting his voice.

The king drew himself from Eleanor and nodded leave for Hugh to speak, his eyelid drooping in curiosity.

"I would ask a boon, my lord," Hugh stated, knowing the king could well refuse. But it was something he had to do. He wanted his claim known. His name and prowess were respected enough to protect where he could not, not yet. Briefly, he frowned, the unctuous, insinuating features of the unknown man crossing his mind. He was aware, too, of the eyes flicking from him to Meghan then to Edward and back again. This promised to be even better than anticipated and they all recalled the story of Hugh saving the King's life. Eager whispers hummed, then died to a hopeful hush. Edward's frowning glance, too, went to Meghan, who sat stiffly, her eyes wide on Hugh.

"What is it you would have of me?" Edward inquired, a subtle warning beneath his joviality.

Hugh's voice was low, yet it carried across the hushed hall as he said, "I would have the maiden, Meghan, daughter of Gavin ab Owen, to wife."

Expelled breaths hissed as Edward stared at Hugh. Then rage suffused his features and his jaw clenched, the muscles jumping beneath his ruddy skin.

"Hugh fitz Alan," he roared, "you are a fool!"

Only Hugh did not jump. He waited for the babble to calm. His lips twisted into a smile and he nodded. "Aye, mayhap," he answered, "but I would have her."

Edward half rose, his fists pressing on the table in front of him until the knuckles showed white. Eleanor placed a hand on his arm. Distracted, he stooped down and she whispered in his ear. The flush of rage receded, an expression of martyred patience replacing it. Then he shrugged, humor restored as only his wife could do, and he stood up again.

"You are aware, fitz Alan, that the wench is not the one I would have for you?"

Hugh nodded, his features unyielding beneath the faint smile he wore like a mask. Seeing his expression, Edward dropped his hands in defeat.

"Still, I had come to think you would never wed! Even a dowerless wench, and she is almost that, is better than a solitary bed and an heirless estate." Committed now, Edward leaned forward, regret in his voice, yet, consummate actor that he was, he was also enjoying the scene. "She is not mine to give, you know that, and I sore regret it. She is only mine to hold and protect. Her giving is in her sire's hands."

Turning to ab Owen, the king asked, "What say you, Gavin ab Owen? Methinks your daughter has need of a strong man and an iron hand. And fitz Alan is a good man, strong in his faith and his word. His lands are small yet yield well and I would gift him the estate of Eldon on his marriage. 'Twould please me to see him wed, with sons, aye, and you with grandsons."

Meghan turned to her father as he straightened slowly from the bench. The lines of his features seemed to have fallen since she had last looked at him. His hair seemed more grizzled, his shoulders more stooped. For the first time, she saw him as old and beaten. The sight brought an ache to her throat. Even with the death of her mother, he had not appeared so bowed and Meghan knew she could not refuse whatever he asked of her, not even marriage to Hugh fitz Alan.

A self-pity he had never felt before assailed ab Owen. His losses pressed on him, but he realized that his words, carefully spoken, his grief-dulled mind suddenly crafty, could bind his daughter ever more closely to him. It was to her he spoke more than to Edward.

"My lord Edward, I know Hugh fitz Alan. I like him, respect him. The praise you bestow is true. If my daughter should wed a foreigner, I would that it be one such as he, and I agree—she has need of a vigorous man to hold and bed her."

Pausing, his head lowered, ab Owen stared at the battle-scarred hands clenched before him on the table.

"I am long in years, my lord," he said. "Defeat lies heavy on me. For me there will be no more battles, no more raidings."

He lifted his head, his mouth hardening, and his bitter eyes met Edward's, his implacable hate deliberately exposed.

"I have lost much, including six sons, to you! Now you ask of me my daughter. Aye, and I would let her go should that be her wish. The choice is hers, no matter your contempt of our laws and customs. Nor would I force her, had I that right. Nor would I ask her to delay out of consideration for me."

Ab Owen held Edward's gaze a moment longer, then turned to Hugh. His voice was even, denying the plea in his words. "She is all I have left, this one. I loved my sons, aye, but Meghan is the child of my heart. I would have her with me always, were that possible. She held me back from death when I courted it these last months. It seems death evades those who seek her most ardently. Now I am condemned to die in my bed, with the wailing of women about mine ears instead of the clash of battle and the war cries of my comrades. 'Tis an ignominious death and one I would choose for no man save mine enemy. Yet if that is God's will, I would have the last of my loins with me to ease my passing."

A smile twisted his mouth and he chuckled wryly. "Meghan, for all her faults, is wise in the time best suited for the bestowing and withholding of tears."

Rearing his head back in a semblance of his old pride, ab Owen continued, "Although you, my lord, take her from me, she but goes to live amongst you, not to become one with you, as an English husband would demand of her. And I can hope that you, in pity, will return her to me ere I die.

"I love her well! She has ne'er brought me shame, though I did let your English ways persuade me so. Of her, I must ask forgiveness, but that is between my daughter and myself."

Ab Owen paused, his eyes lowered once more. "Bedded she must one day be, but I, in my selfishness, would have it be by a Welshman, that she may be ever close to me." He shrugged. "The choice is hers, to tell him aye or nay."

Meghan raised tear-filled eyes to Hugh and slowly shook her head. Perversely, she felt regret in the gesture. Yet her father was utmost in her mind.

Staring at her, Hugh knew he had not expected any other answer, yet still he felt an acute disappointment. Overpowering his anger was a longing to hold and comfort her. His desire for her in her grief was stronger than the lust he had felt at her challenge of him, than the triumph he had felt when her mouth had answered his command. He walked slowly to Meghan and ran a finger from her eyebrow to the line of her jaw. He touched her full lower lip and cupped her chin in his hand.

Addressing the king, although his eyes never left her face, Hugh said, "My lord Edward, I would add my protection of this maid to yours. Aye, over and beyond it. I would have it known that, should any man harm her, I would have him answer for it, unto death if need be! And if she is ever yours to give, I ask that you give her to me. Do you grant me so, my lord?"

Edward frowned then, leaning forward, nodded. "Aye," he reluctantly agreed, "I grant you so, and back it with my oath."

Hugh's gaze held Meghan until her eyes rose to read his expression, then he spoke again. "My lord, methinks the maid and her sire would take their leave. Gavin ab Owen leaves for Cleitcroft on the morrow and they have need to speak yet together."

There was no reflection of sun on the eastern horizon and the chapel bells had yet to ring for Lauds when Hugh entered the stables. Moisture from damp air and the exhalations of sleeping men and horses sprang up on the granite walls and seeped down into the rushes on chilled stone floors. The air was foul with the stench of urine on mildewed straw, of stale ale and wine on unwashed clothing. The cold was thick enough to dance teeth in their sockets. Hugh nodded to his squire, then stopped to aid ab Owen in the cinching of his mount's saddle.

"Would you ride with us to Hawarden?" Hugh asked. "We go to Ainsleah by way of Wresham."

Ab Owen shook his head. He felt no bitterness toward fitz Alan, who had only reached for something he wanted. Still, ab Owen refused. He was going back to Rhuddlan, then southeast to Cleitcroft. Hugh gripped the older man's shoulder and moved on to his squire.

"God's t-teeth, my lord!" Ralph Ramsden stuttered, "'tis a raw morning for a journey!"

"Aye, but I must see how things go at home now that Wales be done," said Hugh. "Godfrey is hard pressed to do all, you know that, and I've neglected Ainsleah for far too long. Nothing holds me here."

Ralph glanced at his lord's closed features and watched him check the destrier's fittings as was his habit, though he had yet to find fault with them. He started to reply, but there was a set to Hugh's mouth that told Ralph he would brook no questions—not of the Welsh wench. Finishing his inspection, Hugh took his cloak from across the saddle where he had tossed it and addressed his companion, Selig. "I have but one thing yet to do, then we go."

Dwarfing his horse by his own giant massiveness, Selig leaned against the mount, which shifted in protest. Smiling, displaying square blocks of teeth, the man flicked deep-set eyes to the cloak Hugh carried, then toward the king's hall, and back to Hugh. The bushy mass of his eyebrows rose in question.

Flinging his cloak over one shoulder to hook it on his thumb, Hugh laughed. Somehow the mute giant was able to take liberties no one else was allowed. Perhaps because Selig was his second shield, the sword ever at his back, and had saved his life on more than one occasion.

"Aye, I must go to see her before I depart." Hugh grinned.

The guard to the room of the queen's tirewomen was instantly alert when Hugh appeared. It took several farthings to buy entrance and Hugh knew he had aroused the guard's curiosity and increased his avarice. He would deal with that later.

The small chamber was colder even than the stables and ventilated only by a high window slit. Once in England, in the comfort of the many royal homes, Meghan would have warm rooms and the company of women her own age—other hostages or wards. Here at Flint only several widows and a bitter spinster or two attended Eleanor, not her usual chattering, bickering, giggling damsels.

Hugh's nose curled at the smell of unwashed flesh and stale wine and ale. Women so elegantly attired in the queen's castoffs by day—and so carefully mannered—now slept with their mouths agape in snores strong enough to shame vast Selig. Hugh's eyes moving quickly, he found Meghan's dark figure set apart from the others, on a pallet against the far wall. Cursing silently as he moved between the closely packed pallets, he wondered why everything always had to be done in the most difficult way. He moved with more care than on any battlefield, perspiration breaking out under his arms and between his shoulderblades. To wake one of those harpies would make him a jestingstock from Ireland to Normandy. At last, with a sigh of relief, he kneeled next to Meghan.

She lay on her side, her slim body curled snug for warmth and Hugh's mouth tightened as he saw her one thin cover.

"Those bitches!" he whispered, knowing they were well aware Meghan was too proud to complain to Eleanor. Resentful and prejudiced, they would take every opportunity to ill-use her. Unless she could win Eleanor's support, they would make her life a torment. Yet she would stand up to them, he thought, and well, giving measure for measure.

Hugh memorized each of her features, the dark eyelashes, the blue veins at her temples, the way she slept with her hand curled under her chin. He smiled when he noticed one front tooth jutting slightly out and over the other. Somehow the tiny imperfection added to her beauty, making her seem more obtainable.

When Meghan stirred in her sleep, she reminded him that he wanted to be well gone before the castle roused. He spread his cloak over her and she smiled in a dream, stretching out as his warmth enveloped her. Drawing a finger lightly down the side of her face, Hugh studied her for a moment more. Then he stood abruptly and made his cautious way from the chamber. It was the guard's leering face that reminded him of Meghan's need for dignity. Snatching the front of the man's jerkin, he lifted him off his feet and up against the wall.

"You will tell, when asked, how the maid came of my mantle and how brief was the time I spent with her!"

The face before Hugh alternated between fearful, furtive, and greedy. The forehead broke out in a sweat of indecision, though the greasy nose, too large in the narrow face, was blue with cold. Reading his mind, Hugh shook his head.

"No, not a farthing more, only the metal of my blade if I hear nothing but truth touching the maid! Hear?"

His eyes and fist still pinning the man to the wall, Hugh wondered how some men could walk upright and still wag a tail. At last, he released him with a shove of contempt and strolled rapidly back to the stables. With purpose in his stride and a set face that allowed no questions, Hugh joined his waiting men and rode with them from the keep of Flint. But for the first time in his life, he knew he was leaving a part of himself behind, wrapped in a dark green mantle.

Chapter 6

Meghan fit easily into court life. The king established his household at Windsor, the choice of his thin-blooded Spanish wife, although he spent much time traveling from one estate to another as duty and wanderlust called. His complete household, from Eleanor to the last serving wench, went with him. Edward was an adoring, affectionate husband and father. His wife and children accompanied him in hunting and falconry, on the royal barges, and in processions. He could as easily be found with them on a frozen river, skates of bone attached to his boots, as with his barons and advisors.

Meghan soon became a member of this household and a favorite of both Eleanor and her children. She was not above clowning with the royal offspring and Eleanor found her a companion suitable to her moods, with a quick, humorous mind. They were drawn together, too, as exiles in a foreign land.

Edward found Meghan stubborn and felt her rebuff of Hugh fitz Alan as if it had been his own. He felt a secret awe and mistrust toward women and thought Meghan must somehow be to blame for the contention aroused among his men. Yet he could find no fault in her impartial disregard of all of them. Edward, although often irritated with her, was fond of her.

With the royal family Meghan traveled from hunting lodge to castle to lodge, and on one pilgrimage to the next. She faithfully purchased a vial of the blood of the Holy Saint Thomas of Canterbury, though as a Welsh-

60

woman she disapproved of his politics—and of any church-dominated state.

She quickly lost the astonishment she had felt on first observing the royal household on the move. There seemed to be miles of wagons loaded with everything from clothing to mattresses to precious windowpanes taken from the king's halls and private chambers. Tapestries were taken from walls and rehung wherever the family found itself. Carts filled with pots and pans and apprentice cooks clanged and banged at the end of the procession, and over all was the raucous cry of birds of prey, for the lords and ladies must travel with their falcons at their wrists, ever set to toss should game be flushed. Only when Meghan remembered what a Welshman considered his only required luggage—a bit of cheese, mutton, or bread and his cloak and bow—did a whimsical smile touch her mouth. And sometimes all but the bow were left behind.

Although she loved the vagabond life, she liked less the weeks spent at Windsor or another of the royal residences. The press of people, the endless corridors and thick walls, the chatter of the other maids suffocated her. The endless monotony of women's work frayed her nerves. The diversions of court—dancing, mummery, blind man's bluff—seemed petty and frivolous. It was during those days that homesickness and worry over her father hit Meghan hardest.

There were too many days when the lords and ladies were left to their own devices. Edward was a man of multiple facets and interests and he did not take his position lightly. The laws of the land that he ruled interested him particularly. The systems of legislation and regulation so methodically set up by Henry II, taking the best of Norman and Anglo-Saxon law, had long been corrupted, abused, and ignored. Fearing the turmoil that had so disrupted his father's reign, Edward would spend days at a time closeted with his advisors, creating out of a hodgepodge of laws what would become one of the world's finest governmental systems.

Then, as the time for Eleanor's lying-in neared, the traveling ceased altogether.

Edward paced the small chamber, agitation in his every move. He spied a physician scuttling past and reached out, nabbing him.

"How does she, priest?" he demanded. "Why do I hear nothing? Why do you scurry by like an insect, with no word?"

He shook him as easily as a terrier shakes a rat, then released him, shoving the physician-priest across the room to land against Hugh fitz Alan. Hugh set the man from him and watched, amused, as the beetle of a man straightened his vestments, trying to restore his dignity.

"'Tis the maid, sire," he said, groveling, his eyes finding no place to settle as he searched for the best way to protect himself and yet answer. "She'll not permit your ladywife to cry out or struggle. 'Tis not fitting! Methinks your lady be bewitched."

Edward lifted an inquiring eyebrow and the priest plunged on, crying, "The wench but whispers, and the lady does but breath gently, as though not birthing at all. Nay, 'tis more as though the wench chants, my lord! Yet the queen will have her by her."

Hugh's smile faded as he straightened away from the wall. "Is it Meghan this man so maligns?"

Ignoring Hugh, Edward roared, "I asked how does my lady, and not of the wench with her! Of her I hear complaint enough! Aye, and too often!"

The priest's eyes flicked rapidly, then he grudgingly said, "She does well, my lord. The child may come soon. But there is no way to know," he added malevolently. "Methinks the wench slows the labor."

"Bah!" Edward snorted in disgust. "These priests will never give you an answer not twisting and turning unto itself. And the physicians be doubly cursed!"

Storming from the room, Edward scattered the people of his household before him as he stalked to the queen's chamber and threw back the door, letting it crash against the wall behind it. He had been through several accouchements with Eleanor, but this scene was strange in its very serenity. The chamber was lighted only by flickering candles, as it had always been. The naked woman on the bed lay calmly, her face smooth and uncontorted. The only jarring note was the cluster of priest-physicians in a corner, their animosity toward the woman kneeling by the bed evident in their malignant stares. One ran squealing to Edward, clutching at him. The king shoved him away, his eyes fast on his wife.

It was Meghan who moved, standing to curtsy on numb legs. "Sire," she requested, "would you uncover the windows? I've asked afore, but the others fear the air."

Edward stared at her, taken aback. Then he looked at Eleanor as she strained to see him over her abdomen.

"I beg you, my lord," she gasped. "I cannot breathe!"

Setting aside another complaining physician, Edward stalked to the window and pulled open the wooden frame, feeling the spring breeze before turning back to his wife. Sweat was beaded on her forehead and lip and Meghan dabbed her face with a damp cloth. Above her tender, ministering fingers, Eleanor smiled wanly.

"What do you here, my lord? 'Tis woman's work."

She licked her lips, then turned to Meghan who took her hand and whispered in her ear. As she whispered, Meghan's free hand lightly drew patterns on the distended belly. Edward watched for a moment, a frown creasing his broad forehead. Then he leaned over to listen to Meghan's murmur. His gaze held to Eleanor as she concentrated on the breath she slowly released with Meghan's words. He could see no pain, only the glaze of tension. Waiting until she relaxed once more, he teased softly, "What is this, lady? As you birth, do you hear talk of the scent of olive trees and oranges, of dry plains and eagles soaring and floating?"

Eleanor took a sip of wine and smiled. "Aye, my lord, it helps me to relax, then somehow the pain becomes less."

Edward studied her pleading face before bluntly asking Meghan, "Is this witchcraft?"

"No, my lord," she answered, holding his gaze. "It but gives her something to think on other than the hurt. How it works, I know not, but 'tis not unnatural."

His blue eyes held hers until satisfied. Then he kissed Eleanor. Before he left, he saw his wife take a deep breath, her gaze focusing inward once more, and he heard

Meghan begin to whisper once again. At the door, he paused, examining the physicians and midwives.

"The wench stays," he ordered.

His eyebrow quirked, Hugh looked up from an examination of his fingernails. Ignoring his unspoken question, Edward nodded toward a pitcher.

"Pour us wine, friend. I'm parched and have but left my lady sipping hers."

"Why is it," he asked, accepting a goblet, "that my most doughty knights quail at a woman's birthing and leave me to wait alone? Aye, the very ones who most seek battle and are most ardent in the beginning of the birthing process. Many are now attending errands left undone for years. Some have suddenly recalled that they have business as far distant as Cumberland and Cornwall and those with no estate needs must accompany another. I wager even you would be gone if given leave! And you have but just arrived."

"Not so." Hugh grinned. "Had I known, I would have but delayed at Ainsleah a week more, though all is in good order there after these last five months. I mislike the pain of a woman as much as any man, and feel as helpless afore it."

"Aye." Edward sighed and collapsed into a chair. "They weep and wail, speaking ever of their agony even as they spread their legs for a man's comfort, hoping, mayhap, to use their favor for some small trinket. Then they bemoan for the next nine months that they are caught! Do they ever lay their minds to the suffering *we* endure? Do they think it pleases a man to lie with a woman round as a barrel? They know it does not, for it hinders their pleasure as much as ours, yet they will cry and nag if a man's eyes but glance at another, more shapely form."

Edward demonstrated with his hands the shapely form he had in mind, then raised a finger at Hugh. "Nay, friend, do not laugh! You don't know of such matters. They think it easy to be a man, with nothing to do but wait and pace and drink. And only the most fortunate of us has a friend staunch enough to share our misery. And they think 'tis all our fault!''

He paused, listening, his head tilted.

"And this infernal silence is worse! At least when they scream you know they are still alive. But the man must ever be pushed aside, as though 'tis some sacred rite his sharing would cast evil on. Then, when all is done, you may have nothing but a little maid who must be clothed and dowered, with the wife ever nagging in fear she did not please you with a daughter. And all the while your counselors, aye, the whole realm, are at you to get a male heir!''

He stood and paced, glancing at Hugh from time to time. At last he halted and pointed an accusing finger. "Aye, 'tis your Meghan! Where else is the wench but in the midst of turmoil? A maid at a birthing! But Eleanor would have her, and how can I refuse? It seemed a paltry thing and my lady's carrying be harder than most dames'. She has no privacy. The eye of everyone at Windsor must measure and weigh her belly. Everyone—physician, charlatan, midwife, housewife—has a charm to guarantee a son or ease her travail. Had they their way, she would be burdened to her knees with bags of the saints-know-not-what noxious scraps and pieces, with vials of foul bowel-purging fluids. They'd have her eat all matter of strange things. And each day she has been poked and prodded, thumped and pinched!''

Edward shrugged at his helplessness. "Only your Meghan gives her ease. I think how it is for my Eleanor, with those physicians huddled about, black-garbed and sanctimonious. Aye, and they give no comfort but only censure for the sins of women and prayers for the life of the child—be it male! They'll not lay a finger on Eleanor, so vile they think she is, except to give her last rites! And the midwives are no better, with their coarse hands and vulgar tongues. Have you been at a birthing?''

Hugh shook his head and Edward scowled.

"Mayhap," he said, "'tis a cleaner thing with others, but with my Eleanor it needs must be a public fair, with all to bear witness to the authenticity of the child. And my lady is afraid, though she would not say so. Aye, and after seven births, who could hold her at fault? God's glove, so many times we've been through this hell! For what? For three little maids still living, and the clergy and my barons ever after me to get a son! Sweet Jesus, she's not their wife! If she should die they would but tell me to marry again. But, Holy Mother, what would I do should I lose her?''

Edward stared at Hugh, anguish in his eyes. Then he blinked and sighed. ''I can but thank the Holy Saints I was born male! Aye, and I know 'tis a plot between them, but if my Eleanor asks for the wench Meghan, if for nothing but comfort, I say aye! And 'twill be hell to pay when the bishop hears of it. Methinks he must be on the road here this same moment. Nor is it as though the maid is innocent. Eleanor did say she attended births in Wales. Aye, as lady of the clan, she would. Still, I wager the bishop won't be pleased.''

Edward studied Hugh, catching a grim smile tugging at the corner of his mouth. ''Friend,'' he told him, ''I am sore tempted to give her to you and risk ab Owen's wrath. Methinks it worth a war if only the wench were gone. I would only ask that you keep her ever from court and lock her away if ever I visit. God's blood, but our lives have been a tumult since her arrival!''

Edward shrugged. ''But I cannot. Besides, methinks there are times when a friend must stand between a man and his madness, to protect him from his insanity. You know,'' he said, lifting an eyebrow, ''there are those who say she has bewitched you.'' He ignored the anger in Hugh's face, continuing, ''And I would have to sacrifice my household's peace if she wed you. My Eleanor loves her and would never forgive me if I forced Meghan to marry you against her will. Still, it might be worth it if only to say 'I told you so' when she makes your life as miserable as she makes mine.''

Edward watched Hugh roll his cup between his palms, noting the set of his mouth. Then the king laughed ruefully. ''Ah, but I jest, Hugh. I wish you could have the wench, although I'm thinking you a lunatic. She's most opinionated and does not hesitate to correct whomever she feels is wrong. Aye, in the most humble manner, I give you that; Eleanor has not failed in all her lessons. But who would want a wife forever correcting, and worse, most times right? And stubborn, forsooth, the wench is stubborn!"

Edward shook his head, chuckling wryly.

"Close her from the front door and she'll come through the back. Block her there and you have her in the window! She gives a man no peace once she has set her mind to it. And she does not know the eye of a needle from the point. I wore a hose she mended and had a blister the size of my thumbnail for a week. I cannot say she darned the hole so badly with a purpose, though my complaints did amuse her but I swear, the darn was the size of a walnut, and as rough. I could have died had it festered."

Hugh looked up from the contemplation of his wine, amusement in his eyes as he watched his king pace. "There are maids to wield a needle," he said, "and stubbornness and opinion need only to be redirected. If I sought a deaf-mute sewing woman, I'm sure to find one in your vast realm."

"Redirected!" Edward snorted. "And what do you do when you would have it your way only because you wish it? There be those times, you know, and to give in will but get you a shrew for a wife. And I have but begun to list her faults."

Halting abruptly, he counted off on his fingers. "She is discontent with her woman's state and argues with everyone about it. Fortunately, the other maids mostly mock her and continue to be coy and simpering. She used to bait the priests and set them to pulling their hair. 'Because 'tis so, has always been so, and will always be so' means nothing to her. She wants answers to unanswerable questions. The priests came to me like crows to a cornfield!"

Edward made a rude sound of disgust. "I was forever mediating, and what know I of philosophy? I have my faith and I studied the ancients and have wit enough not to confuse the two. I finally threatened her with a nunnery and she has held from posing questions to the clergy since then. Remember this," he ordered, whirling to point a finger at Hugh, "if you are luckless enough to win the wench, she has an uncommon fear of walls."

Hugh started to reply, but the king raised his hand. "Hold, I am not done. She wished to practice archery with my nobles—and shamed them royally at the tuns. God's gown, but would I had a thousand men like her. And she is overly learned for a woman, aye, and for most men. Where she was schooled, I know not, but 'twas well done. And what good is a woman with her mind on Aristotle when yours is on bed?"

Folding his arms against the back of a chair, he eyed Hugh's downcast frown. "Now, I suppose you'll tell me you'll keep a mistress, aye, and hire a housekeeper when she neglects to change the rushes, being too engrossed in thinking to note the fleas. Ah, man, then there is her temper."

Hugh grinned sheepishly and Edward laughed.

"Aye, you know that quality in her. Provoke her pride, and she shows herself a true virago. 'Tis true she does hold her temper most times, wounding with words when a sword would suit her better, but I'd not like to have her loose on me! Her tongue is a deadly weapon and she knows well where a man is tender."

Hugh took Edward's goblet and poured more wine. Handing the king his cup, he said, "I know she's not gentle and all the faults you list are true, but, my lord, think of the sons I would get on her!" He squinted into his wine, his mouth twisting into a grin that did not hide the ache of his yearning. "And think of the battle to get them. I would rather have a fiery woman to subdue than one who but spreads her thighs at my nod, then gives and receives nothing. What are a few scratches and bites to the winning of such a wench? When tamed, my lord, will she not be a wife to have by my side? And, by all the saints, she would never bore me."

Edward threw back his head and roared his triumph. "Aye, and I knew it! You wear your balls where your brain should be."

"Aye," Hugh admitted, setting his goblet aside and crossing his arms. "I lust after her, but 'tis no itch an afternoon's play would satisfy. I lust to have her in my house as much as in my bed. I want her to wife, dammit! Aye, I lust after her but, strange enough, I like her, too."

"And I like her, friend," Edward admitted. "I do not mean to say I don't. Every bachelor who lays eyes on her likes her, and half the married men, as well. Hold there!" he ordered, seeing the rage in Hugh's eyes. "No one has dared touch her unless she's agreed, and she is not agreeable. She scorns them all equally. And if 'tis not the fear you and I inspire that stays their lust, then the thought of the wench herself gives them pause. Those who would try to get her alone find her guards along as added, interfering company."

Hugh quirked an eyebrow. "She has guards?"

"Aye, they arrived bringing her clothes and silver some few days after she came to me. Then they stayed, on ab Owen's asking. Hostages are expensive enough to maintain, methinks, without adding their household to the budget. But I let her keep them. There is something about her that arouses lust and I would not have her harmed in my care."

Edward saw Hugh's eyes narrow and he grew serious. "Ah, man, I doubt I can get her for you. I will give Llewelyn his demoiselle in October, though no one knows of it yet, and needs must then release all Welsh hostages, Meghan with them. Consider this, Hugh." He paused, conciliatory. "There is the widow of Reginald fitz Hubert, and with her go three manors in Strafford. She is comely and plump. She has borne three brats so there is no doubt of her fertility."

Reading refusal in Hugh's features, Edward cursed. "God's glove, man, be sensible! The wench brings nothing more than a croft in Wales that no Englishman could hold."

Hugh looked at Edward from under scarred eyebrows, his gray eyes unyielding. "'Tis not the croft I want."

Shrugging, Edward acknowledged defeat. His good nature returning as quickly as it had fled, he slapped Hugh's shoulder in a blow that would have taken other, lesser men off their feet. "Ah, Hugh, methinks the two of you deserve each other. If you get her, I only hope your whelps are as loyal as you—and as stubborn in my cause."

Edward poured more wine and studied his vassal as Hugh sat on the edge of a table, one leg dangling.

"Women!" the king snorted at last. "A man cannot live without them or with them. Mayhap the clergy are right to damn them as the source of all evil."

Edward considered Hugh, his silence disturbing his own hard-held ease. "Have you tried to compliment her?" he asked.

Hugh's laugh was curt. "And what progress has the flattery of your gallants made on her? My tongue would tie itself into a cat's cradle were I to attempt a fine-turned phrase. She knows well her worth. Aye, methinks she would but scorn such pretty words."

Edward shook his head at Hugh's ignorance. "They all like compliments. And the ones most worthy of praise need it most. They know their own value but must know that others, too, are conscious of it. What have you done to win the wench? You hardly play the fair lover. You say you cannot yet you saw her for only several days, just long enough to gain her animosity, and that five months ago. You asked me for her in a most forthright manner, afore all the hall, knowing I could do nothing but refuse, then you departed. You did nothing to soften the wench toward you. Man, I can speak a good word to her, I can give you her company from time to time, but I cannot court her for you!"

Hugh began to reply but was interrupted by a thin, high wail that grew into an angry cry.

"My lord," he said unnecessarily, "your babe is born!"

Hugh followed Edward to the birthing chamber and leaned against the wall by the door, his eyes searching. He found Meghan bending over Eleanor, her face soft as she laughed at the tightly screwed eyes and puckered mouth of the infant tucked into Eleanor's arm. Breathing deeply, Hugh fought the desire the sight provoked in him. She had changed little. Her hair was longer, her face more beautiful than he'd remembered. Suddenly, shifting where he stood, he wished the child gentling her features was his, theirs. The desire grew to an ache and he clenched his jaw against it as Meghan glanced up, her attention drawn by his gaze.

Joy lighted her eyes, then fled before Hugh was certain he had seen it. A flush rose to her high cheekbones and she dropped her eyes.

Drawing a full lower lip between small, white teeth, she knew she had betrayed her agitation, but Hugh's presence had startled her. She turned back to Edward and Eleanor, watching blindly as the king, cooing inanely, tried to chuck the infant's nonexistant chin. Her thoughts remained on Hugh. Perhaps he had only brought a message to the king, mayhap of trouble in the Marches. That would explain his travel-stained garments and weary features. Whatever his purpose, it was obvious he had come a long, hard way.

Yet he's no court gallant. Mayhap he'll not stay, she considered silently. She did not want him there with his mocking eyes and words, raising her carefully suppressed desires. She did have desires. He stirred something within her that ached to be answered, a promise, a threat, and she dared not succumb. Then she realized Edward was addressing her.

"I asked you, lady, what think you of my little maid?"

There was pride in his voice and Meghan smiled, thinking of Eleanor's fear that he would not be pleased with another daughter. She could not tell the king that his child appeared like all others—red and wizened as a newly hatched robin.

"She's lovely, my lord, and she was a good girl, giving her mother scant distress."

"So I was told," announced another male voice.

The voice was low, yet all eyes jerked to the Bishop of London. Several henchmen trailed in his wake, among them a beetle of a priest whose face twitched in smirking anticipation.

"My blessing on your infant," intoned the bishop as Edward kneeled to kiss the proffered ring. "'Tis a pity 'tis female, but you can pray yet for a son and know that 'tis the Lord's will. Daughters have their uses. Mayhap this one, too, you will dedicate to the church.''

His cold gaze turned to Meghan.

"What do you here, maiden?'' he asked, ''amongst midwives and physicians? Is it fitting and you not wed?''

Eleanor and Meghan both sought to answer, their words bouncing off each other's, but it was Meghan the bishop chose to hear. The queen was beyond his grasp. ''I would give her comfort and I've attended other birthings.''

The bishop's voice was sinister in its gentleness. ''What comfort has a maid to offer that the best of midwives and physicians cannot?''

Meghan met his fanatic gaze. ''The comfort of one who loves her and would ease her travail.''

"She chanted, Holiness!'' the beetle of a priest shrilled. '''Tis witchcraft! 'Tis common with the Welsh!''

"The Welsh,'' Meghan corrected, ''were Christian long afore your ancestors ceased dancing about stones and worshiping oak trees.''

The bishop ignored her indignation. His gaze not leaving Meghan, he asked, ''Did you chant, maiden?''

Anger flashed in her eyes. ''I did not! I spoke of pleasant things, helping her to breathe lightly. It but takes the mind from the labor and the pain.''

'''Tis true, my lady?'' the bishop asked Eleanor, his face set in feigned incredulity. ''And did you not suffer?''

Eleanor reached out to touch Meghan. '''Tis true, your Holiness; she said nothing amiss. And there was discomfort I could bear, nothing more. 'Twas not like the others.''

The chiseled features again turned to Meghan, the unctuous voice rising. '''Tis meet and proper that a woman suffer, and those who take that privilege and penance from her do sin most grievously. Who are you, then, to do so? The Lord God did command, for Eve's sin, saying, 'I will greatly multiply thy sorrow and thy conception; in sorrow thou shalt bring forth children'! 'Tis not meet that you deny the Lord God's word. Who are you to lead her from the suffering so justly imposed on her?''

Meghan stared at him. She had known she might be chastized for attending the birth; the English were strangely inconsistent when confronted with bodily functions. The tupping of a maid or the breaking of wind was treated with ribald humor while a woman's monthly cycle or the birth of a child was met with distaste. Now this sanctimonious celibate dared castigate her for relieving a woman's pain, a woman who was forced to give birth naked and before whomever cared to observe. Even animals sought solitude and quiet in which to deliver their young.

It was Edward who finally spoke. "Meghan, please go to your chamber. This matter will be discussed later."

She ignored him. Argument with the bishop, she knew, was useless yet she could not docilely leave.

"I am but a woman who loves her queen," she repeated. "Would God have given me this knowledge to comfort her if He had not meant it to be used? Did He not also order suffering for Adam? Do not the very alms you distribute then deny His word? Do these very physicians not deny His word with each wound they salve, each bone they set? If this is true, is not all alleviation of pain a sin, as is all man's striving to rise above the beasts?"

"See, my lord, see how she blasphemes!"

Meghan ignored the beetle priest as she faced the bishop, his features suffused with rage. He opened his mouth, but Meghan rushed on, anger drowning all caution. Her fury had been building too long, with each injustice and slight she had experienced as a Welsh woman.

"If you dare tell me I cannot ease a woman's pain, then next you dare judge how much pain a woman must suffer. Will you then carry rods and whips, scourging any woman whose agony you deem not harsh enough? What know you of women, you who have avoided them all your life? And what know you of pity? Do you suffer at your ladened table, in your well-heated chamber, in your rich and holy vestments?"

Meghan's words rang back from the disbelieving silence of the chamber. Suddenly terror weakened her knees, threatening to drop her to the floor in abject pleading for forgiveness. Only pride held her upright—and the knowledge that pleading would do no good.

"Silence!" Drawing himself to his full height, the bishop lifted clenched fists. His rage was so great that he stuttered. "Who are you, a woman, t-to question the will of God or me or any man? You have no mind, no intelligence beyond a simple animal cunning. Aye, I doubt you verily have a soul. Begone from me, witch," he ordered, "ere you foul the very air I breathe."

Her slim form rigid in defiance, Meghan was again ready to ignore the power of the man before her. She had forgotten everyone else in her fury, even Hugh fitz Alan. Alert and wary, he had stood away from the wall at the bishop's entrance, sensing trouble with which even Edward could not interfere. He now spoke Meghan's name, his tone harsh.

Shuddering as though the word was a physical blow, she whirled to meet this new threat. Hugh shook his head firmly. Her features hardened, then her eyes dropped. He was right; she could not win, not this battle. Turning back, her face blank, she dipped a disdainful curtsy then whirled back around, her knees suddenly trembling, her throat catching on a sob.

"Maiden!" the bishop ordered. "I did not grant you leave to go!"

Meghan stopped, her head high. "If a mere woman may correct you, you did order me to leave ere I foul the air. My lord Edward, have I your consent?"

The king glanced from Meghan to the bishop. She had, he realized, again put him between herself and the clergy. "You have my leave, but should his Holiness demand that you not attend birthings, you will obey. Should he demand an apology and penance, you will give that, too."

Meghan's shoulders squared further and she turned back, ready to argue, until she saw the set of the king's jaw. "Aye," she whispered, "but 'tis under duress!"

Edward held her stubborn gaze a moment longer, then his gaze moved to Hugh. "You may go now. Sir Hugh will accompany you. You will stay in your quarters until told otherwise."

Chapter 7

Turning on her heel, Meghan stalked from the chamber, missing the grin Hugh flashed Edward before bowing and following. She walked stiffly, her heels punctuating her anger on floors of heavy oak planks, her small chin jutting.

Hugh wore an amused smile as he appraised her. He noted the pulse beating at her throat, the way her high, round breasts trembled with each stride. The shape and length of her slim legs were exposed through the cloth of her kirtle with each long step. Aye, he admitted, glad he'd decided to come to court, she may have a temper but leastwise she's open in her thoughts and does not inflict pain on others.

"Maiden," he said, reaching out to grasp her elbow, "I would have a word with you."

Meghan spun about, needing someone, anyone, on whom to vent her anger. "And what do you want of me?" she demanded. "Would you have me close my mind to nothing but prayer on bleeding knee for my unworthy female soul, denying all independent thought, as does that most holy of bigots? Or would you have me simpering and biddable, as does Lord Edward? Tell me, Sir Knight, what in the name of the impossible would *you* have of me?"

Hugh's gaze touched lips tight with anger and he remembered their ripeness under his. Then he averted his eyes to her own, bright with unshed tears. Her refusal to yield challenged him and beneath he saw a plea for understanding.

"What I would have of you," he answered, "has nothing to do with priests or simpering."

His glance slipped down the length of her, his desire clear. Lightly running a finger along her hard-set jaw, he said, "I would have you beneath me, open to me in my bed."

Meghan was more disconcerted by a sudden surge of responding need than by his words, but anger got the best of her. She swung a raised hand at his face, only to have her wrist seized in a grip of steel. Attacking with the other hand, she aimed her fingernails toward his cheek. Hugh grasped both her wrists, twisting her arms up behind her. Tightening his grip, he held her pressed against his long length. His scent assailed her as she struggled—the smell of man, wine, and the outdoors.

Hugh jerked his head toward two men who were approaching with knives held in their skilled hands. "Call off those wardogs of yours!" he hissed, pulling her arm higher.

Meghan's gaze did not leave his as pain fought rage and neither yielded to the other. Not until her arm was forced higher against its socket did she speak.

"Back!" she whispered. "Rhys! Anyon! Back!"

They moved away, their eyes wary and resentful, and Hugh lowered her arm. Still watching them, he held her a moment longer, his features not yet softening. Releasing one slim wrist, he held the other gently, turning it, one finger lightly grazing the welts his grip had left. He studied her, noting her trembling lips and the tears of anger clinging to her sooty lashes.

"Maiden," he said gently, "you must learn that a frontal attack is not always the best or the most prudent, with me or the clergy. If you had been but meek and mild, you could have turned the bishop's wrath. If you had claimed ignorance or thoughtlessness or impulsive compassion, he would have faulted you little. You could have gone your way with only a small lecture, mayhap. As 'tis, I know not what he will demand."

Meghan shook her head, refusing to even hear Hugh's advice, and flung away her tears with the back of each hand. "I will not bow and cringe afore a fool just because he is a man—and a bishop!" Like a child, she lifted her chin. "You did not hurt me. I'm only angry—at them." She jerked her chin toward the queen's chambers.

"Aye, I know," Hugh agreed, a grin tugging his mouth. "I would not be one to urge you to learn guile," he said. "'Tis your very artlessness that appeals to me."

Looking at him with narrowed eyes, Meghan searched for insincerity in his expression for a sign that he was patronizing her. That she could not see it did not prove it was absent, and she began walking toward her apartments, her head down, dejection in every step. Hugh walked beside her, bewildered. Her temper he could deal with, but comforting came hard. Stopping in a window alcove, Meghan looked out, seeing nothing. She needed to express her confusion to someone, anyone. At last, she turned back to Hugh.

"What do they know of women," she wondered, "those men who spend their lives avoiding us? By what right do they define my life, my thoughts? By what means do they determine a woman cannot think and use my sex against me when I would earnestly seek knowledge? How do they find the Blessed Mother holy when she bore two sons after the Christ, yet judge me a vile thing, and I still a virgin? Do they hate life?" Meghan clenched her fists. "How can they lead us when they cannot see the faults in their own thinking?"

Hugh longed to soothe and comfort her. He gently pushed a stray curl from her cheek.

"Would you go with me to the parapet?" he asked. "All the others are at their meal, but I've no appetite."

Meghan didn't answer for a long moment. Although her fear and rage were now ebbing, there was still something about this man that weakened her knees. His nearness provoked a curious ache deep within her. To step into his arms would be to step into strength, into security, into the beat of his heart under her ear. But he had only offered a walk on the battlements, a stroll to view the river as any man might offer a maid. And he offered her

companionship for a short while. There could be no harm
in accepting that.

"To talk of priests?" she asked.

"Aye, to talk of priests or whatever else."

"I was told to go to my quarters," she reminded him.

"Edward did not say when." Hugh nodded toward her
glowering Welshmen. "And your lackies will come with
us."

Meghan's mouth tilted up. "You will explain to
Edward?" Hugh nodded and she laughed. "Aye, I'll go!"

Watching her as they walked, Hugh wondered at her
mercurial temperment; she was still so much a child yet
at the same time so much a woman—more than even she
realized. What was the source of his need for her?

Elbows resting on the parapet, they gazed down at the
river Thames, shining silver in the sun, and at the trees
along its banks, their new leaves a pale jade. Beyond,
fields green with the haze of spring stretched across the
land, and farther, the smoke of London could be dis-
cerned. A light breeze brought the odors of freshly turned
earth and rising sap.

Meghan sighed. "You're a man. Explain the way of
priests."

"Aye, I am a man, but I am no priest, nor have I
aspired to such. I like my life too much, and women too
much. Yet do not men insist that what they cannot have
is of no value, that it is repulsive, foul, and sinful?" She
nodded before he continued. "If they can convince the
woman of her sinfulness, then they can convince themselves. Fortunately, they usually fail!"

A blush rose over Meghan's features and she turned
away. Laughing softly, Hugh turned his back to the parapet, leaning his elbows against its edge.

"I wonder," he pondered, "who suffers more. The
priest who has known women afore he took his vows or
the one who was ever virgin. The man who knows what
he is missing or the one who ever guesses, and mayhap
builds the wonder of it to an ecstasy far beyond truth.
What think you?"

"'Tis not a subject I've thought on overmuch," she
admitted, picking at a piece of moss clinging to the wall.

"Mayhap you had best go to a priest for an answer." The corners of her mouth tilted. "The one who thinks oft on the subject. You will know him by his scraped and bruised knees."

Hugh feigned a grimace. "Aye, and be told, 'because 'tis so, always has been so, and always will be so'?"

Meghan laughed. "You've queried the clergy?"

"No, Edward. He told me 'twas the reply you always receive and I've no doubt 'twould be the same for me." Hugh ignored her curiosity, teasing it, and he turned back to the parapet, tossing over a stone.

"Why do men do that?" Meghan asked.

"Do what?"

"Throw stones. They are at it always."

Hugh considered. "Mayhap 'tis but done in idleness. Women have their spindle—all but you. 'Twas one of your faults Edward listed. He warned me about you and offered the widow of Reginald fitz Hubert instead."

An unaccountable surge of jealousy swept over Meghan and she tilted her chin. "Fitz Hubert's widow is fat!"

Hugh laughed. "Aye, so I thought when he described her as plump."

"He did flatter her. But she holds much land." Keeping her voice casual, Meghan asked, "And what flaws did Edward claim for me beyond the baiting of priests?"

"He told me you are forever in trouble, that you are opinionated, stubborn, ill-tempered, too alluring, and a poor seamstress. Your lack of a skillful needle seems to trouble him the most."

She propped her chin in her palms, keeping her eyes on the horizon. "He has never forgiven me for that blister on his heel and still wonders if 'twas deliberate. Those faults are all true, though he did miss many."

"I did not repeat them all to you for fear of wounding your pride, which is overweening. Or so Edward claimed."

"So 'tis," she admitted, her voice lilting. "I am of such conceit that a tally of my imperfections seems but flattery."

Hugh grinned then said, only half joking, "In truth, he deems you overlearned—for a woman."

"Why? He accepts Eleanor's education well enough!"

"Aye, but her station was set from birth. He wonders at your interest in subjects usually of concern only to priests."

"Mayhap I am overeducated," she answered bitterly. "I ask questions no man will answer. 'Tis because I was the youngest and the only girl in a family of men. My mother died when I was eight and afore that she was too busy to teach me of looms and spindles. I was left to be reared by my brother and the village herb woman, Glenna. I followed my brothers from the hunting to the tilting to the schoolroom. Usually they treated me like one of them. I think, mayhap, they spoiled me," she admitted, laughing but with a note of sorrow. "They were almost as baffled as I when I was forbidden to go raiding with them. From that time on they set me apart as different, as special. I hated it!" Her voice became quiet as she continued. "I lost three of them to the raidings, the others to Edward and his wars." Her face was drawn and pale. "Mayhap 'twas you who took them from me."

"Mayhap 'twas," Hugh admitted, his features calm. "I can not say for certain 'twas not, though I don't think so."

Their eyes held for a long moment, then she bit her lip. Drawing in a deep breath, she looked away. "But that does not answer your question. We had a simple priest to teach us our letters and a bit of Latin. After he died another came, a different kind of priest, an excommunicate. I don't know from where or how long Father Ambrose had wandered, though he spoke of Rome and Paris. He was English and it was the English clergy that had cast him out and named him heretic."

Meghan smiled to think of such a wise and holy man being so labeled. "Thinking we had won our freedom, we were none too pleased to have another teacher. But he taught us much. Mayhap I learned the most, since male activities had by then been forbidden to me. Bran, too. Father Ambrose even knew medicine and things taught only at the universities. He taught us to question, to look on something from one side and then the reverse. He left two years ago, mayhap to Ireland."

"Who was Bran?" Hugh asked, watching the dip and sway of a high-flying hawk.

"My foster brother," Meghan said, refusing to meet his eyes. Even as she added, "I loved him," she wondered if she had. "We were to be married," she said with more conviction. "He was too sensitive and gentle to physically compete with other men, but eventually he, too, died at English hands."

She turned to challenge Hugh, but he had caught the hesitation in her voice. Their gazes held. At last, she looked away. "How came you by Ainsleah?"

When Hugh did not reply, she noted his aquiline nose, deep-set eyes, strong cheekbones, firm mouth, and square chin. Her voice became soft as she placed a hand on his sleeve. "'Twas a frivolous question. 'Twas not meant to pry."

Slowly he traced the outline of her hand. His mouth tightened. He resented his own transparency as much as her sympathy. Then he shrugged. "No, lady, I did not deem your question more than light. 'Tis but something I do not speak of much."

Hugh hesitated, debating within himself. There was a quality about Meghan that opened thoughts and feelings in him that he had never exposed to anyone before. Perhaps it was her own sense of pride and self-worth that told him she would never violate the feelings of another person, not without cause. Only Edward did he trust as much, yet he had never talked to the king of such matters. And it was this openness, among so many other of her qualities, that made him want her so.

His mouth twisted into a rueful smile. One of those qualities, he told himself, was the way her breasts tilted to cup into his palm. When he spoke, his voice was hard.

"My father married a woman of wide lands, noble connections, and devious ways. She delighted in inflicting misery. If ever I hated anyone, 'twas the Lady Elga!" Remembering, his face hardened. "She closed herself to my father after producing two sons—her duty done, she thought. She didn't mind when he looked elsewhere for comfort. After all, she did. Aye, she verily flaunted her lovers! Discussing the attributes and shortcomings of his woman of the moment provided humor for her. Lady Elga did love to display her wit.''

Frowning, Hugh turned Meghan's hand over and examined her palm. "When he found my mother, the Lady Elga changed. Watching him horning from one wench to another was cause for drollery. To have him find a woman who gave what she wouldn't, something beyond the spreading of her thighs, who even provided him sanctuary from his wife—that humiliated Elga. So she redoubled her efforts to make life hell for him.''

"Why did he not rid himself of his wife? Other men do so. Such women fill the nunneries.''

"When her father and brother were amongst the highest barons in the land and her uncle a bishop? My father took me to her when I was eight for my training. Mayhap he thought my grandfather, who had been raising me, humored me too much. Or mayhap he realized that the life of a bastard is hard. Lady Elga mostly ignored me. My father took her abuse, but she dared not meddle overmuch with me. Yet she knew I preferred her vile attentions rather than watch her demeaning my father, and she took advantage of it. Her ire and spleen only increased when she found her sons would not join in the sport.''

The muscles of Hugh's jaw tightened, then, drawing in a deep breath, he let his next words out in a rush, as though if he did not say them then, he never would.

"My father died when I was fourteen, and she sent me away ere his eyes were closed an hour, forbidding me to attend his funeral. When I reached home, my lady mother told me they had arranged for me to win my spurs with Gilbert de Clare—and she gave me the deed to Ainsleah. She, too, died within the year. 'Twas then I discovered that my dame and sire had struggled for thirteen years to leave me an inheritance, to give me land which that wolf bitch Elga could not lay a hand on, though the saints know she tried! Yet she had no claim. 'Twas purchased in my grandsire's name with money earned through endless tourneys and countless battles. They used not a farthing Elga could claim as hers.

"As a child," he whispered, his fists clenching tighter, "I despised my father for his treatment of my mother,

thinking him weak. And I felt contempt for her, for
accepting him and the little he gave her, for the low price
she placed on her honor. I would have denied them if I
could have. I told myself I was a changling and, in truth,
the son of a wealthy lord who would one day find me. I
hated them each time I heard the whispers, the snickers,
the name 'bastard.' Yet they gave me my spurs and they
gave me Ainsleah.''

Hugh had turned away from Meghan and now, with
surprise, she realized that his body was shaking with silent
weeping. She stared at his back, feeling his pain. Aching
for him, she put her hands about his waist and lay her
head against his quivering back.

"Ah, Sir Hugh, do you not think they understood a
boy's pride? Mayhap they thought your scorn the price
they had to pay for their love of each other. Mayhap they
considered it their penance.''

Pulling away from her, he shook his head, leaving her
to plead to his unyielding back.

"My lord,'' she insisted, "they did what they wanted
to do in the way they wished to do it. Few people are so
fortunate. 'Twas a selfish choice they made, for whatever
they gave you, it was because they wanted to, not for
your gratitude or as a punishment. Mayhap they thought
you would become man enough to understand and to forgive the humiliation you suffered as a child.

"But that is not what you want to hear,'' she stated,
her voice cutting. "Would you have me say you are a
base ingrate? That you will suffer forever, that you
deserve to do so, your sin being most grievous? Do you
wish to hear that you should have held them in utmost
veneration, though your mother appeared the whore and
your father a craven who cowered under his wife's
tongue?''

Hugh flinched, yet Meghan continued, her scorn pelting him. "Shall I provide the lash so you can flagellate
yourself? Or a hair shirt, mayhap, with nettles to wear
under it?''

Ceasing her taunting, Meghan's tone became mildly
inquisitive. "Tell me, what did the priests demand to
expiate your guilt? A crusade, mayhap, or only a barefoot

pilgrimage to St. Davyd's? Did they double your tithe and demand a tenth of Ainsleah—or more? Or mayhap you were requested to join the priesthood—after, of course, signing over your lands. 'Twould give them delight, methinks, to watch a proud man brought low, scrubbing their pots, slopping their swine, and washing the wasted seed of their lust-filled dreams from their sheets! I am most curious,'' she mocked. "What mortification did they demand of a man who dared dislike being a bastard?''

Hugh whirled, his fists clenched, yet she stood her ground. Then he relaxed, seeing the tears that belied her sneer. Drawing in a deep breath, he shook his head, his shoulders slumping as though a great burden had been lifted from them.

"I went to no priest. I knew what they would say.''

"You went to no priest?'' she repeated, incredulous. "Nor does Edward know,'' she guessed.

Hugh laughed mirthlessly. "Would he then call me friend? Would he offer me the widow fitz Hubert, fat or no? I've told no one. 'Tis not a thing to bandy about the barracks or the hall.''

"Methinks you misjudge Edward. He's not a man to censure another so.''

Hugh only smiled and Meghan looked away, biting her lip. "Why did you tell me, then?''

He did not reply for a long moment, then he said, "You, I knew, would understand my hurt. And, like it or no, I wanted to hear your thoughts.''

The implication of his words struck Meghan and she reached up, touching the corner of his mouth. She shook her head, fear and regret flickering in her eyes. "And you would, in that way, tie me to you? Ah, no, my lord.''

He took her hands and held them to his mouth. He ran his tongue lightly across her palm and bit her fingers, his eyes demanding as Meghan tried to pull away.

"No, my lord,'' she whispered. "I cannot. I will not!''

"Ever refusing afore the question,'' he teased. Then he grew serious. "You must marry someone.''

"Aye, and I will. But I'll not be owned.''

"And I would own you more than another man?''

Her jaw grew firm in that obstinate gesture he had learned to know and regret. "More than a Welshman would."

Hugh shook his head. "But we speak not of legality, do we, but of something beyond, something given, not taken?"

She ignored his question, resistance leaving her as she laid her forehead on his chest. "I would have a man to give me children," she whispered, "an heir for Cleitcroft. Nothing more. He'll be a reasonable man. A man content to go his way and let me go mine. A man who would not possess me—not any part of me." Her eyes lifted and she whispered vehemently, "I'll not be owned! Do you understand me?"

"Aye, I understand," he said. "You are afraid of love and you would love me, for I could truly possess you in all ways, all of you!"

"It hurts," Meghan stated. "And it ends in loss. I'll take no more losses, no more hurt."

"Aye, it hurts," Hugh agreed, tracing the outline of her face, "but not as much as no love at all! Be aware, daughter of Gavin ab Owen, that I'll have you one day, when war comes again, if I have to slaughter every man in Wales to do so, including your husband, should you take one. Mayhap he'll be sore glad to be freed from the hell you're sure to give him. It will be a fight to the finish, 'tween you and me, winner claim all! And do you understand me?"

A small smile touched her mouth as Meghan nodded, then she frowned. "You think there will be war again."

"Aye, too much was left undone at Conway. 'Tis but a lull in the storm. Archbishop Peckham is already complaining of the laxness of the church in Wales and of the too-strong control Llewelyn has over it. Wales is the only place in Christendom where the church must do homage to the state for its lands. And many of the men around Edward are greedy. They will not be content until all Wales is under English rule." Hugh shrugged. "I cannot tell when, but there will be war."

Meghan gnawed her lip. Remembering Llewelyn's request for information, she felt a pang of guilt. She had sent no messages; there never seemed to be news important enough to relay. Now she knew there was. News far beyond what Hugh had told her. She had but to ferret it out.

At last, she raised her gaze back to Hugh. "Why," she whispered, "why can the English not understand us? They've driven us back into our little corner of mountains, mountains which are of no use to them, those men of plows and towns. Why can they not leave us to our own?"

"Mayhap because you shame us. When the Romans came, they forced us to become something different, but your people rejected those changes. 'Twas the same with the Norsemen and the Normans. Always we changed, accommodated, accepted, but you fought, rejected. By your fighting, you tell us we are wrong. You shame us and there are those who cannot live with shame, so they must change or destroy you."

"And they'll not change us. . . ."

Hugh studied her sorrowful face. At last he sighed, tossing another pebble over the parapet.

"Aye, there'll be war," Meghan agreed. "The Welsh may lose and you may seek me out. But there will always be protection in Wales for the daughter of Gavin ab Owen—and myriad hiding places. You'll not find me an easy quarry."

"I would not want you if you were. All said, 'twill be a game worthy of the players."

Glancing up at the sky, Hugh frowned. "'Tis getting late, lady. I will escort you to your quarters."

The people in the hall were still at their meal when Hugh guided Meghan, her elbow cupped in his hand, down the tower staircase. She felt relieved that she did not meet anyone, only servants about their duties, and she knew her guards would say nothing. It was unusual that she was escorted by a man; his possessive handling would be certain to cause gossip. Her treatment of Sir Hugh at Flint, his declaration of intent, even the clothes she had worn, would become common talk.

Somehow Eleanor's maidens had remained ignorant of his interest. There had been hints, but only enough to make them regard Meghan as something of a mystery. They would be avidly interested should the old scandal be revived. Her defiance of the bishop was grist enough on the mills of their idle tongues; the time she had spent on the parapet with Hugh would only add to it.

Frowning as she examined Hugh from the corner of her eyes, Meghan decided there was little she could do about it. The set of his jaw left no doubt he would do all in his power to fulfill his threat to win her. It was a face that could be ruthless. Yet his long, curling lashes gave his eyes a vulnerability that asked for the protection and love she would not refuse a child.

She watched the points of her dark green slippers appear and disappear beneath the embroidered hem of her surcoat as she walked, then returned her gaze to Hugh. His presence disturbed her. Even his hand on her arm, where a hundred other men had held her in courtesy, created an ache deep inside. She feared the power he held over her.

Her throat tightened as she thrust aside the thought that in gaining her wish to be free of him, she might find she had lost. Hugh, sensing her scrutiny, looked at her. His teeth flashed. "Do you think I will make a proper husband, lady? One who will give you strong, handsome children, and joy in the getting of them?"

Meghan's eyes glinted. "Aye, for some luckless wench and that wench not me!"

Hugh laughed. "Isn't it a pity we've no opportunity or quiet corner? I would give you a sampling of the pleasure you so vehemently deny."

"In what manner is the cod you hide beneath your breechclout so specially endowed? Has it some quality that other, lesser men lack?"

Hugh shook his head. "Eleanor has failed to control your wanton's tongue. But no matter, *I* shall. Or I'll teach you the purpose of what you taunt."

Ignoring Meghan's struggle to free her elbow, he turned her back to the wall and held his hard body lightly, firmly against hers. His features gentled as he began to lower his mouth to hers. He saw the unbidden leap of answering desire in her eyes and the softening of her lips, but suddenly the back of his neck prickled. Lifting his head, he saw her guards approaching.

"Even you, lady, are not worth a knife in the ribs when time will eventually give me what I crave."

Releasing her, he guided Meghan on without a backward glance. Only his grip told her of his need. Meghan did not face him at the door to her quarters. Her voice was flat as she thanked him for his courtesies. She started to enter her room, but Hugh took her hand. "Your guards, my lady?"

She knew what he wanted. What harm would it do, she wondered, just this once? She would have so little tenderness once he was gone, and she would never again allow him to take such liberties, of that she was determined.

She held his gaze as her hand moved, signaling her Welshmen back. Hugh's eyes softened as his fingers moved lightly along her jaw and his mouth descended. Meghan felt its gentleness, its warmth, and her lips parted, her tongue touching, holding his as a soft whimper quivered in her throat. He held her for what seemed an eternity, his mouth drawing need into her until her hands moved to his chest, his shoulders, blindly seeking his beard under her fingers, the features of his face, the silk of his hair at the back of his neck. She clung to him, letting the desire build and control her until at last he released her. Her head dropped to his chest and she refused to look at him. She knew he would gloat at his ability to arouse her.

But there was only concern in Hugh's expression as he lifted Meghan's chin. "Maiden," he whispered, "answer the priests softly. Do not argue. Let them think you agree, that you are contrite, accept their reprimand. 'Tis not a hard thing to say nothing."

"And is that what you would do? Would you follow your own counsel?"

Hugh laughed. "No, but the clergy's affairs and mine seldom meet. Thus I've not yet learned the wisdom of the caution I advise."

His features grew serious. "Go with care, lady." He pressed his mouth against the hollow of her palm and brushed his tongue across its softness, his eyes again mocking.

"About Edward, lady. 'Tis not common knowledge, but the church holds him in financial thrall—his father's debts, the crusade, then Wales afore his feet could touch ground. He'll give you what support he can, but he dares not antagonize the bishop. On the other side, the bishop knows he cannot condemn you as a witch, no matter how great his lust to do so. He, too, cannot yet afford another war with Wales."

Not waiting for an answer, he walked back along the passage with a lithe stride.

Chapter 8

Meghan closed the heavy oak door and leaned against it. Would God, she thought, I could as easily shut out the world! They'll be at me soon—the priests, Edward, the maidens—to harry, preach, question, demand, hector! Even Eleanor will be forced to go against me.

She fought an urge to run, to flee from Hugh and the confusion he aroused, from the jealousies and intrigues of court life, from the narrow ways and rigid deportment of the English. Pressing back panic, Meghan breathed deeply, easing the tightness in her chest and the dull headache that attacked her when she was confined to narrow, closed places.

"Oh, God," she whispered, "I wish I were in Wales!"

She stifled a sob. Holding her palm to her lips, she remembered Hugh's mouth pressed against it and the look in his eyes as he bent to kiss her. Desolation swept her as she realized he was the one person who would listen and understand, who she could go to for comfort. It would only cost her her pride and freedom to do so. His price was not unreasonable, just one she was unwilling to pay. And his advice concerning Edward and the bishops was sound, although the thought of assuming a submissive role sickened her. Otherwise, however, the bishop could send her to a nunnery.

Shuddering, Meghan decided she would think of what to say later. Pushing away from the door, she looked about the chamber. Flame from the torches sent flickers of gilt, amber, and ultramarine quivering against the granite walls, illuminated the beds folded against the walls, and gleamed against brightly painted clothes chests. Tapestries, hung over narrow windows, stirred in the remnants of breezes that passed through the eight-foot-thick walls. The vivid blues, reds, and greens of the undulating needlework were muted in the dim light.

A rodent disturbed the quiet then ceased, the hush descending again. Yet the walls seemed to echo the voices of invisible maidens, soft in gossip, light in laughter, shrill in quarrel. The aroma of spring rose from the lavender-strewn rushes on the floor, swirling in drafts to blend with the musky odor of young women and warm candles.

Frowning, Meghan surveyed the chamber's chaos. Clothes were tossed about in brilliant disarray—amethyst, gold, peacock; wool, serge, linen, fur. Scarlet undertunics with emerald hose hung over tapestry frames. Soft leather shoes were scattered through the rushes. Leaning over, she picked up a pointed, vivid blue slipper. Isabelle's, she thought, tossing it into a corner. Only she is vain enough to spend gold thread on something never seen!

Picking up a topaz-colored surcoat of fustian, she smoothed the velvetlike fabric and breathed in the foxy scent of the outdoors and roses. Someone had borrowed it, torn it, and replaced it unrepaired. She shrugged and went to look for a needle and thread to occupy her while she waited.

How low she had come that she would sew to keep busy. But her mind refused to be idle. Hugh was right—there would be war. It seemed the English wanted to eliminate everything Welsh—the language, laws, beliefs. They prated of law and order and railed against cattle stealing, yet cut down Welsh forests to build English roads on Welsh land. They used Welsh horses, carts, and wagons to build castles on Welsh soil. Yet they wanted more, and only the Treaty of Conway stood in their way. One day the indignities they suffered would again push the Welsh to the breaking point. Meghan could only pray she was in Wales when that time came. In the meantime, she would plan on how she could help Llewelyn.

Her candle had lowered a quarter and the tear sewn up two thirds when a timid knock sounded at the door. A slovenly maidservant entered with a tray balanced on her hip. "Be you Lady Meghan?" she asked. "If you be, I brought your supper. 'Tis cold, though. I've ne'er been above the kitchens afore and lost my way."

"Who sent you?" Meghan asked. Edward would usually banish someone from the hall, then forget to provide sustenance; Eleanor was confined to her chamber.

The maid giggled as she placed the tray on a stool and brushed back greasy hair with a rough hand. "A tall, dark man," she answered, surveying Meghan. "He gave me a coin to do so. Until you be back in the hall, he said."

The girl frowned. "I put the coin in my pallet, in a tear. Think you 'twill be safe? I've ne'er had a coin afore and no other place for it. I saw a red ribbon at a fair once and wanted one e're since. Now, mayhap, I'll have it."

"Aye." Meghan smiled. "And if you continue to serve me, mayhap more. What do they call you?"

"Yedda, lady."

"Did my lord give you word for me, Yedda?"

"Aye, lady," the maid answered, deciding she had never seen so fine a lady; certainly not in the kitchens. "He did say to tell you to heed his advice, then he pinched me. I've ne'er been pinched by a lord afore. What advice did he give you?"

Meghan frowned, nettled by Hugh's liberties with a serving wench—and such a grimy one who did not know her place. "What advice he gave me is no concern of yours, and aren't you too forward, slut?"

Puzzlement creased Yedda's brow, then, remembering her question, a cringing humbleness dropped over her features. Wringing her hands in her filthy kirtle, she became servile. "I be most sorry, lady," she whined. "My tongue runs away with itself no matter that the cooks do beat me."

Stealing a peek at Meghan, Yedda saw no softening and dropped to her knees. She would have clung to Meghan's skirts if she had not stepped prudently away. "Please do not complain of me, lady. The cooks do punish me something cruel and they'll not let me bring your

tray again. I be most quiet and proper when next I come.
I swear it.''

Meghan's face remained hard. The maid's sniveling
disgusted her and she was angry at herself for provoking
it. Yet beneath the pleading features she noted a hint of
resentment and anger. Placing the tip of her shoe against
Yedda's forehead, Meghan shoved her backward. ''I
know no cooks nor should I. Their position, as yours, is
far below mine. Oh, get up,'' she ordered. ''Your cringing sickens me.''

Yedda scrambled to her feet, tears streaking her grimy
face. Meghan was as offended by the sight of her as by
her own cruel treatment of the wench. An idea forming,
Meghan stalked about her as Yedda ducked, shifting as
Meghan circled.

Fastidiously lifting a braid matted with filth, Meghan
then dropped it and wiped her fingers on the underside of
her surcoat. ''Do you know who I am?'' she asked.

Yedda shook her head, rubbing her nose on a chil-
blained hand.

''Have you not heard of the Welshwoman who bathes
once a week, a habit which would serve you well? Surely
'tis you who heats my water.''

Nodding, Yedda watched Meghan, flinching when she
suddenly turned on her. The expected clout failed to come
and Yedda cautiously raised her head. Meghan tapped a
slim, well-shod foot. A finger pressed against lips pursed
in thought. Then she began to circle Yedda again.
''Would you like to serve me, wench?'' she asked.
''Would you like to be something beyond a scullery slut,
with more to think on than the next pile of garbage or the
next whoreson who wishes to bed you?''

Yedda shook her head, not understanding.

''Haven't you will enough,'' Meghan demanded, ''to
imagine a life without your arms to the pit in greasy dish-
water or yourself under any wretch who orders you so?''
She shuddered at the vision her words called up. ''Would
you like to be my maid?''

Yedda's eyes filled with tears. ''Lady,'' she accused,
''you jest with me!''

"I do not play games with those who cannot fight back. I've need of someone and methinks you have not had all the mettle kicked from you, though you hide rebellion well. I'm not wrong, am I? You do resent those who use you, do you not?"

Yedda's gaze lowered and she did not answer, afraid to acknowledge something she had not dared even consider.

Her voice irritable, Meghan repeated her question and Yedda's features brightened, only to collapse again. "Lady, I can't. I be a bastard and the priests say I must be content in my state for my dam's sin."

A curious expression crossed Meghan's face, then she laughed. "And if a bastard can ask a daughter of a chieftain of Wales to wife, why can I not have you for a maid?"

Her face puckered in puzzlement, Yedda decided Meghan's scorn was not for her and her features took on a glow. "Then you will have me, lady?"

"Aye, but there are some things I would have you understand." Meghan leveled a finger at her. "You'll never gossip of me and mine. I've need of someone I can talk to and not have the world know what I say. Have you a prudent tongue?"

Yedda's nod was emphatic. "And who would I be nattering to, lady? There be few friendships in the kitchens."

"You understand that this is not a short time thing, if you please me?" Meghan asked, wondering at her decision. "You'll not marry here, for I may want you to return with me to Wales, should I go. There you may wed if you so wish."

"Wales?" the maid whispered. "But there be monsters there!" Blanching under Meghan's scorn, Yedda timidly added, "'Tis said the people have tails!"

"There are no more monsters there than here, and like here, they all have human guise." Seeing Yedda's skeptical frown, Meghan wondered if she was taking on a more formidable task than she had thought. "Am I deformed? And who would know of monsters in Wales than one from there? Will you stay with me or no?"

Tears welled in Yedda's eyes as she fought her fear. With luck, the lady would never return to that place the priests so cursed. She nodded.

Meghan smiled, her eyes glinting. "There is one other thing, wench," she stated. "You'll bathe."

"Bathe, lady?" she asked, giggling. "But 'twill make me ill. I'll die of lung rot if I be not drowned first."

"Aye, bathe. And you'll survive it and many more. Tomorrow morn you'll be here directly after Tierce with a tub of hot water, a horse brush, and soap."

Yedda began to wail and Meghan turned casually away, examining skeins of thread on a tapestry frame. When Yedda's protests, failing, declined to damp sobs, Meghan turned back, her voice casual. "'Tis your decision. If you are not here, you will stay forever in the kitchens. I only ask that you not tell of my offer. There are too many who would gladly take it and I do not wish them forever at my door. Now go, I'm done with you."

Yedda envisioned the opportunity not only taken from her but given another. At last she blew her nose on her kirtle and shuffled to the door, dejection in her slumped shoulders.

"How old are you?" Meghan asked.

"I don't know, lady, though 'tis said I was born the year the rebel Simon de Montfort returned to England."

"That was twelve sixty-three," Meghan calculated. "You're fourteen or fifteen. And you've no brats. You don't, do you?"

Yedda lowered her eyes against the sting of tears. "No, lady. There was one, but he died in the birthing. I did not even give him suck."

"'Twas best. What would you do with a brat in the kitchens?"

Yedda's lip trembled against her hurt and anger. Her hands twisted. "Aye, Lady," she answered, "but I did want something of mine own. I'd never had such afore."

Meghan smiled, pleased at the girl's defiance, then she shrugged. "Aye, some need such. You may go. And Yedda, you will say nothing of the tall, dark lord or me to anyone. 'Tis not their concern."

Dismissing her, Meghan felt confident Yedda would be back. She sat on the rush-strewn floor to eat her cold meal from a low chest. The challenge of turning a scullery wench into a lady's maid enthused her. She needed such a project to fill her days with something beyond the needle and the penance the bishop would place on her. Also, it would give the court something to gossip on, distracting them from her efforts to aid Llewelyn. Yet Meghan found her thoughts dwelling on the injustice of a society in which women bore children out of loneliness and need.

Meghan was putting the last stitches to her mending when the other maidens returned from the hall. They entered like starlings descending on a wheatfield. Relieved and grateful that she was not the object of their gossip, Meghan listened, her eyes not leaving her work. She smiled to hear it was a man, as usual, who occupied their tongues, then frowned. The man was Hugh.

"Who is he?" Margaret Carrick demanded. "I've not seen him afore."

"Oh, but gray eyes and dark hair—'tis so unusual."

"And that scar at his mouth," Alice Beaufort prattled. "It twists his lip a little, as though he smiles, but his eyes don't. He could, methinks, be ruthless," she added, her eyes gleaming.

"And the king favors him," Kate Granville mentioned. "'Tis plain to see for he sat at his table."

"But he looks so stern," murmured Alice.

"Oh, but who would want a gentle man?" Kate giggled.

"But doesn't anyone know who he is?" wailed Maragret.

"I do."

All eyes turned to Isabelle Douglas. Her small, pale eyes flicked from one face to another as she savored the attention. She waited, her head tilted. "He's Hugh fitz Alan."

Alice's brow wrinkled. "Fitz Alan? Isn't he the knight who saved King Edward in the Holy Land?"

Isabelle settled herself onto a stool. "Aye, and 'tis said Edward would grant him whatever boon he wants, but he asks for nothing."

Kate shook her head and Meghan steeled herself. "Methinks he did ask for an undowered maid not so long ago, but she refused him. I can't remember who, though I know she was not English."

Meghan released her breath, thankful for the distortion of time and distance.

"Whoever she was," Isabelle said, "and I doubt the story, she was wise. For all his bold appearance and royal boons, he lacks ambition. If he had it, he would not absent himself from court as he does." Her smile arch, she added, "He did court me last summer, but I dismissed him, though the man is personable." She paused, playing her audience. "A Douglas would not wed a bastard, no matter how high placed. Some do say he is no fitz Alan but more rightly fitz Edward."

Meghan's anger rose at Isabelle's casual slurs, yet her voice held only idle interest. "What Edward would that be?"

"The king, of course," Isabelle answered, her caution overcome.

"Why do they say Edward is Sir Hugh's sire?"

"Why else would Edward give him a baronage and an estate? Sir Hugh is, after all, only the by-blow of a blacksmith's daughter. Surely you admit to a resemblance."

Raising her eyes from her needle, Meghan looked at Isabelle. "No, none beyond height. Edward is as noted for bestowing baronages upon those who serve him well as he is for seizing them from men who displease him. Is not Sir Hugh, as Alice said, the man who saved his life?" Isabelle tried to interrupt, but Meghan surged on. "His estate came not from Edward but as a gift from his sire."

"How know you so much?" Isabelle demanded.

"He told me. And methinks you lie when you say he courted you," she accused, the other's flush proving her right. "Why would he choose you when he can have his choice of wealthy heiresses?" Smiling, Meghan lifted an

eyebrow, adding, "And, Isabelle, mean you to insinuate
that all the tall men Edward esteems are his bastards? The
king is right young to be party to Sir Hugh's conception.
To say such a thing is a slur on his honor. Men have lost
their heads for less."

Suddenly Isabelle found herself not only mocked and
named a liar but also accused of treason. "How dare you,
you slut?" she whispered, her pale skin mottled. "You
twist my words. No one is more loyal than I to Edward
and to my father's oath." Isabelle pointed at the mending
in Meghan's lap. "What is that? A goatskin girdle, mayhap, to wear when you next go to battle beside your father's villeins?"

A hush fell on the chamber. Breaths were held. The
only sound was that of a stool knocked over by Alice
Beaufort as she backed along the wall, inching her way
to the door, hands pressed against her mouth to stifle a
sob.

With a sigh, Meghan pushed aside the surcoat. "Aye,
you are loyal, as only a lickspittle can be, fawning and
truckling. And you are right. My father would rather be
at English throats than under their heel, but he does not
posture, denying his hate, or smile when he would spit.
If your father is as loyal as you protest, why does Edward
hold you? Is your sire's pledge as empty as your head?"

Isabelle shook with rage as Meghan delivered her final
thrust. "No, the Welsh hold no villeins, and this is no
goatskin girdle. 'Tis a surcoat you borrowed for it still
bears your stink. Aye, I fought beside my sire and will,
mayhap, do so again. But when I do, I shall paint myself
blue and go leaping naked through the heather as do you
Scots."

The room erupted in a welter of shrieks and rustling
skirts. Alice rushed with a sob through the door and into
the arms of a gaunt visaged priest. He shoved her aside,
stalked into the chamber, and began pulling apart the
spitting, scratching, biting women. He jerked sobbing
girls from the melee and shoved them into corners with
a total disregard for their fragile limbs. When the battle
had subsided into hiccoughs of anger and sobs of humiliation, the priest looked about, his face hard, giving no

indication of the amusement he fought to control. He pointed at Isabelle with a long, thin finger. "Your gossiping viper's tongue is at fault here, isn't it?"

Not waiting for a reply, he whirled on Meghan, who sat crumpled against a broken tapestry frame. "And your temper must surely be of the devil! Isabelle provoked your overweening pride, did she not?"

The priest's eyes bored into hers and Meghan nodded. A faint smile twitched his mouth as he said, "You are to come with me. The bishop would have word with you."

Chapter 9

Meghan knelt before the altar and tried to force her mind into a proper state of contrition, but her thoughts kept returning to the last ten days. The tall, gaunt priest had not mentioned the fight he had interrupted in the maiden's bower, nor on the long walk to the bishop had he berated her for her defiance. Although Meghan had felt sympathy emanating from him, he had not spoken at all, except to repeat Hugh's advice, until he had ushered her into the bishop's quarters. A faint, sardonic smile had quirked his mouth as he introduced himself as Father Jerome. "I am Hugh fitz Alan's confessor," he'd said, then he left her to wonder just what Hugh had told him.

Meghan smiled as she recalled the interview with the bishop. She had played her role well. The bishop had been caught off guard by her humility, but he had not been able to cast aside his denouncement of her and had reviled her as a woman, had raved against her arrogance. His words had rung empty in the face of her meekness and penitence. It had been with a visible sense of anger and frustration that he had sentenced her.

All things as they were, Meghan assured herself, my punishment was light—a week's confinement and compulsory attendance at all holy services. The rising in the dark of night for Matins was the worst of it. Aye, my aching knees.

Shifting on the cold, hard stone of the chapel floor, Meghan frowned. Edward had not been so handily hoodwinked. The king had observed her apologies and remorse with an incredulous expression. He had mocked her repentance with a cocked eyebrow. He had enjoyed watching her grovel and had prolonged his questions and demands until her temper had been stretched to its breaking point. Only the sight of Hugh lounging against the wall and swirling wine in a goblet had held her tongue.

No, Meghan thought, scowling, I did not convince him. I entertained him.

Her mouth tightened. She had resented Hugh's presence more than Edward's condescension or the bishop's ranting. Hugh's attendance had greatly added to her humiliation. His casual interference had spoken of a relationship she did not want. Meghan sighed, thinking they had both delighted in seeing her humbled.

But Edward had given her Yedda. The scullery maid had come as ordered. Not until she had entered had Meghan realized how much she wanted the girl. It had taken several changes of water and a horse brush to strip away fourteen years of grime, but Yedda had emerged from her last soaking a pretty girl, well pleased with herself, with light blue eyes and soft, light brown hair.

Meghan had done well to choose her. For all her ignorance, Yedda seemed bright enough to prove loyal to those who treated her well. Meghan's guard Rhys seemed to be taken with her and Yedda had not been able to conceal her interest in him. Meghan smiled at the thought of Yedda, eager as a puppy, brightening when praised and cringing when slow or clumsy.

Meghan shifted painfully. Ten days of kneeling through seven masses a day had made her knees swollen and tender. She winced, blinking back tears of resentment and pain. Anger rose, followed by homesickness and the thought of the short, fat priest who served her father. Ah, but the English clergy would not have him. They, with their wide lands and love of opulence would accuse him of greed for his love of a well-done suckling pig. Aye, and Robert Burnell, Holy Bishop of Bath, with his bastard children, would be amongst the first to decry him for his sweet Gweneth and their children.

Meghan smiled, remembering, when a voice jerked her from her daydream. "Is it the contemplation of the sacraments that pleases you so, daughter? Are you in such a state of grace?"

She greeted Father Jerome warmly. "I was but remembering the priest at home, Father. He is a good man, aye, and a good priest."

"Yet you find him amusing?"

Meghan's guileless mind scurried about. "He's an honest, earnest man, Father, dedicated to the church, eager in his service, but he does have one fault—his greed at table. In truth, 'twas my knees did give me thought of him. In his eagerness to seek his repast, he makes his service short and strong. Yet he is well loved and respected, as much for his failings as for his piety."

"And does he have a concubine?" Father Jerome asked, then waved the question away, reading the answer in Meghan's face. "Aye," he agreed, "I ofttimes think the priest who is loved is of more value than the one who rules by fear. Is your contriteness suitable for confession?"

"Aye, for those sins of which I believe myself guilty. I cannot claim those that other people say I committed."

Father Jerome felt a stab of anger followed by grudging admiration; she was right in her belief that her sins could not be dictated by another. With a sigh, he blessed her and knelt beside her to listen.

Meghan sat as Yedda brushed her hair. The maid had learned to control her chatter and Meghan was lulled by the silence and the rhythmic stroking. She had confessed to Father Jerome what seemed a multitude of sins, including petty anger at Yedda and false humility toward the bishop. She had not included the easing of Eleanor's childbirth and he wisely had not demanded it. Yet Meghan thought he had granted her absolution reluctantly, as though he wanted to say more, but he only counseled her to be directed by those older and wiser than herself.

Now her penance was done, her limited freedom restored. I should be pleased, Meghan scolded herself, but

I'm not! I am but set loose from one cage into a larger one. Still, a cage within which I can learn much, she reminded herself, thinking of Llewelyn's request.

As though sensing Meghan's despondancy, Yedda slowed her brushing. "Tell me of Wales," she requested.

Meghan leaned back to rest against Yedda. "There are mountains there to break the sky and to rest the eyes upon. 'Tis green in the valleys, and the mountains are covered with trees of ash, oak, and nut. Up high grow the birch, which turn yellow in the autumn. It looks then as though a giant poured molten gold down the crevices, gold against green. The mists lie low about the mountains some days, moving like phantom smoke.

"We are a people who go when we want, stay when we want, with no man over us. We like to live apart from others, only coming together when we wish. The only towns are of the Normans and the Flemings. In the summer we go to the high pastures with the flocks to meet with other clans. At night we sing, tell tales, or listen to bards and harpers about the fire. In autumn, afore we bring the flocks down, we meet with others for feasting, courting, celebration, and council."

"In winter, we usually stay home. 'Tis hard traveling and visitors are most welcome. There is a custom there that, when a man enters a home, he is offered a bowl of water. Should he wash his hands, he'll stay but an hour. Should he permit his feet to be bathed, he will stay the night or more. To withhold water is deemed a grave insult. Men have been killed for such. The winter is spent in polishing and mending weapons. The women sew and weave and prepare for the spring raidings. There is always music and tales of valiant deeds."

Her face soft with memories, Meghan fell silent.

"And what of the spring, lady? What do you then?"

Meghan pulled away from Yedda and her voice was bitter. "I mislike the spring. 'Tis then the men raid the Marches or amongst each other. When I was a budding girl I wanted so to go with them. I thought 'twas only the lack of those inches of flesh men flaunt between their legs that held me back. I even prayed to grow one, promising all manner of impossible things. I even tried charms and potions."

Sighing, Meghan shrugged away the image of the child she had been.

"Then, one spring they brought one of my brothers home, slung over the back of his horse like a bag of meal. I wanted to kill those who had cut down my fine, tall brother for nothing but the taking back of cattle taken from us. Then I hated the spring and I cursed my woman state. In Wales, the men will raid and the women wait and weep. In the next two years, two more of my proud brothers came back over their horses, their hair trailing in the dust." She shook her head. "No, I do not like the spring."

Yedda began again to brush Meghan's hair, the black waves glistening blue and ebony. "Do all the ladies of Wales wear their hair cut so?" she asked.

Meghan smiled, remembering how young she had been a few short months before. "No, I cut it when I rode with Llewelyn. 'Twas a hard life and long hair catches on brush and trees and can be dangerous, or so I thought."

"You could have bound it, lady, and worn a wimple," Yedda suggested, dismayed that any woman would wantonly cut her hair for such a reason.

"'Twas simpler to cut it. Nor do I like my head bound."

Yedda pursed her lips. In ten days she had acquired many of the affectations of court. A lady, too, did not ride to war. Her mistress had told her of several who had, among them one who became queen of England, who had even gone on crusade. But that was many years before, not long after the Normans came, and nothing good had come of it, Meghan had admitted. Besides, people then were not so civilized.

"Have you other brothers or sisters, lady?" Yedda asked.

She couldn't see Meghan's face, but her stiffening told her the question was a mistake. "Aye, three brothers, no, four, for my father had a bastard, Caradoc. My brothers were killed these past few years, all but Caradoc. And I wished him dead, many times! I still do. Sir Hugh saw him once,'' she added, feeling that to mention Hugh's name with Caradoc's would somehow be a talisman against her half brother's evil. "'Twas at Flint.''

Meghan's head bowed and her fingers pleated the soft wool of her surcoat. Sensing she was lost in memories, Yedda searched for something she could say to bring her back. "My lady, Sir Hugh fitz Alan did ask of you.''

Meghan's head jerked up, but she made no reply.

"He did but ask how you be, if there be anything you need. I told him there was nothing, that I was not to speak to him, and he did laugh. Aye, methought he would make mock, but his face sort of closed instead.''

"Did he say anything else?'' Meghan's voice was soft, but Yedda sensed its angry confusion.

The brush paused and there was caution in Yedda's tone. "He did say you must be sore afeart of him.''

Whirling, Meghan clenched her fists at her sides. "Fear him!'' she cried. "'Tis only hate I have, and well he knows it.''

Her eyes flew to the opening door and her chin lifted when she saw Isabelle enter, followed by the others. "By all the saints, Meghan,'' she drawled, "I swear you did but acquire that slut of yours for nothing more than something to abuse!'' Pulling her surcoat over her head, she looked again at Meghan. "'Tis time for supper and you not dressed. I would think you eager for company. You've so much of ours these last days and 'twas something you never valued overmuch as is. Forsooth, you seem only to scorn it.''

Meghan gazed at her with disdain. "Do not provoke me, Isabelle. I do not waste my wrath on such as you.''

Isabelle shrugged. "I've not the time, anyway.'' She pulled another surcoat over her undertunic, then wrapped a band of slightly soiled linen under her chin and over the braids coiled at the sides of her head. She glanced at Meghan as she put her gold circlet over it. "You had best hurry. You, of all of us, should know Edward frowns on those who are late.''

"Would you save a seat for me?'' said Meghan to Isabelle's departing back.

The thin redhead turned and they measured each other, then Isabelle grinned and nodded. "Aye, I'll do that."

When the door closed behind her and the others, Meghan threw her brush at it. "Damn Hugh fitz Alan!" she whispered. "I'll show him I've no fear of him or any man, true born or bastard, lord or villein!" She whirled on Yedda "Am I beautiful?" she demanded. "The truth, and I'll not punish you for it."

Biting her lip, Yedda examined Meghan as she stood, her color high and head held proudly. The maid's voice was hesitant. "You be different, lady. Not like the milk-white ladies or the maidens who try so hard to be what they are not." She paused, fearful of her honesty. "I think, lady, though you be not like them, you could still take the eye of any man you should choose."

Meghan laughed and her tone took on the hard edge of purpose. "And I so choose! He wants me, so he says, and he will want me more ere I am done. And so will all the others who fawn and lust. I want my cream-colored undertunic, Yedda, and my green surcoat. 'Tis at the bottom of my chest."

"But I've not finished your hair, lady."

"And you'll not," Meghan decided, picking up a small mirror from Kate's chest. She held it at arm's length, the better to see her image in its ripply surface. A face with large, wide-set eyes and a mouth with an upper lip too short for the full, soft lower one gazed back at her. Ebony hair, parted in the middle, curved about her face and fell to her shoulders. Smiling, Meghan said, "I'll wear nothing but a gold band about my head."

Yedda started to protest, arguing that no lady wore her hair so, but Meghan only smiled. "If I am different, then I will make the most of it."

Hugh sat in the hall, listening to his companions with half an ear, his gaze wandering to the entrance. Meghan had not come in with Eleanor's maidens and he guessed she was either being punished for an additional infraction or perversely refusing to come from seclusion on her first day of freedom. Mentally shrugging, he turned to listen as de Hart described his new squire's clumsiness. The conversation drifted to their own days of apprenticeship. Loud guffaws greeted their always cruel, often ribald stories of earning their spurs. Gradually the gossip lessened as men gulped ale and wine and attacked the trenchers placed in front of them by pages.

"God's gown!" de Hart whispered suddenly, his whistle almost unheard amidst the table's gulping and chewing. "Is that the Welsh wench we took at Conway, ab Owen's whelp?"

Hugh saw Meghan at the entrance and his eyes narrowed. He felt the quick, demanding lust she aroused—and a desire to keep her away from the eyes of his companions.

She stood there a moment, her head high, her eyes drifting over the hall. Her glance touched Hugh's, then wandered on with no sign of recognition. Her slim body was encased in a surcoat of pale green that clung to her high breasts. The low, square neck was bordered by a band of green and gold, and the beginning swell of her breasts was visible through the thin fabric of her undertunic. Pulled snug by the gold-linked belt at her slender waist, the garment fell in folds to her feet, the band of green and gold repeated at its hem. Her black hair was uncovered and its soft simplicity put to shame the elaborate headdresses of the other women.

De Hart's breathing grew heavy. "She grabbed a man's eye afore, but I thought mayhap 'twas because I'd been so long from women, yet even here she puts a man's mind on bed." Glancing at Hugh, he frowned, remembering Hugh's claim. "Is it still in your mind to wed the wench?" he asked.

Hugh's gaze stayed on Meghan as she walked to her table and his voice was curt. "Aye, and my threats are the same, too."

Moving over on the bench, Isabelle made room for Meghan. Her voice was incredulous. "Meghan, your hair!"

Meghan shrugged. "'Tis too short to braid and the Welsh women need not hide their hair under wimples.

Nor do I. I am not here of my own will and who can rightfully gainsay me?''

Isabelle met Meghan's challenging eyes and smiled. ''You are plotting again, aren't you? Against whom?''

''Only one man, though I will use others, as well.''

Isabelle realized it would be useless to ask any more. Shrugging, she decided she would do best to wait and watch. It might prove interesting. Whatever else, Meghan was not dull.

Searching the hall, Meghan looked for the men most apt to suit her purpose. Her gaze touched de Hart's and she held his stare for a moment, then dropped her eyes in confusion. Peeking at him again, she watched his cautious interest change to avid attention before her eyes wandered on to Hugh.

He was rolling bread into pellets between his fingers, his frown telling her he had observed her coquetry. His eyes narrowed when they met hers, then her gaze moved scornfully on. He smiled ruefully, his jaw aching from clenching it. So that is your game, lady, he mused. And I had thought you softened to me. Aye, and 'tis a game two can play, for you must have an audience and I'll not give you one. You'll not enjoy that, will you—being ignored?

Scowling, Hugh watched Meghan bite into a swan's leg with small, white teeth. He knew she might come again to hate him, to believe the part she played. She might forget the time they had shared on the parapet. As though she had heard him, Meghan lifted her eyes to his and tossed the half-eaten bone over her shoulder to the hounds lying hopefully in the rushes. It seemed as though she flung away all he wanted to give her, all the soft moments between them. Momentarily an expression of sorrow touched her eyes before she lifted her chin higher and turned her face from him.

Chapter 10

Meghan dipped the quill into ink and paused, stroking the feather under her chin. There was much to tell Llewelyn and nothing she could omit on the excuse that someone else might have informed him. He had men who watched and listened, but no one so close to the king. Silently, she cursed Edward's love of the hunt. His sudden decision to leave Windsor for the lodge at Woodstock had upset her plans, forcing her to take additional risks. This afternoon she had pleaded a headache and returned to her quarters, dismissing Yedda. As for her guards, Rhys would keep Yedda occupied and Anyon was on guard at the door. Eleanor had excused her with a nod, her lips tight, and her eyes had held that bewildered expression she always wore now when she looked at Meghan.

In the last five months, ever since the birth of Eleanor's child, Meghan's role of self-centered flirt had convinced many people that she was brainless and shallow. Men who had once hesitated to speak before her now did not trouble to lower their voices at her approach. But her charade had also lost her Eleanor's friendship and esteem and Edward's respect. Meghan told herself they were less important than the messages she could send Llewelyn. But she missed the king's impassioned ravings and the verbal battles they had once waged. Even more, she missed Eleanor's friendship. But Hugh's withdrawal had been worth her efforts. The role she had assumed did have the disadvantage of keeping her surrounded by ardent and persistent admirers, however, which might have made it difficult to seek out the man who waited for her in the forest.

Thanks be to the saints, Meghan silently reminded herself, that the English do pursue the red deer as fervently, if not more so, than they do women.

Her thoughts moved to Hugh and she frowned. Although he no longer approached her or seemed to take notice of her, somehow he was always near and his presence disturbed her. He still had the power to make her feel awkward under his eyes, which seemed to both demand and threaten even as they drew her toward him. And he did pose a threat. Hugh was the only one who seemed to realize that her flirting was more than a game. He could see too much.

Meghan chided herself. He was just another man, and easy to hoodwink, but the unreasonable regret that Hugh had so easily given up his pursuit clung to her. *If* he has, a small voice whispered, and Meghan frowned, forcing her mind back to the parchment in front of her. Shifting on her knees, she leaned her elbows on either side of it, sorting through the information she had garnered.

It seemed always to be either the clergy or the attorneys, or both, who were at the center of all contention or covert behavior. Rumors, too, had reached court of a prediction made long ago by the wizard Merlin claiming that a man named Llewelyn would one day rule all of Wales and England under the dragon banner. Edward had laughed, but his eyes had held a speculative gleam.

So much could pose a threat. So much was like a canker, eating into English and Welsh alike.

Meghan brushed the quill between her lips, feeling the hidden sharpness of its edge on the tip of her tongue. Llewelyn wanted details—who complained, who demanded, who secretly corresponded. She organized her thoughts and began to write. Tomorrow there would be a hunt and the letter must be ready. Too much time passed between such opportunities.

The day was crisp and fair, although the morning mists deep in the forest had yet to burn away. There was a faint odor of smoke and earth, of trampled leaves and the approach of autumn. An occasional tree or shrub had turned to gold or bronze, a flame against the dark green of the forest.

Meghan rode toward the rear of the party, and the laughter of the others stirred excitement to a stronger pulse in her veins. The parchment, tucked securely in the top of her hose, added an edge of fear and she felt alive with a keenness almost painful. Although her nerves had been frayed by months of subterfuge, the danger appealed to her—perhaps more, she thought, than the needs of Llewelyn. She smiled at each of the men vying for her favor and wondered how she would get rid of them.

They are a sorry lot, anyway, she told herself. All younger sons with nothing to offer but themselves, or knights with little land and a flea-infested hovel they call a castle. Or widowers looking for a piece of flesh to warm their beds and rear their brats.

A few months before, it had been different, but many parents had long since interfered. A rash of weddings fulfilling betrothal vows had followed fast on her transformation from snob to flirt. Some had even sent their sons to school on the continent in preference to a possible Welsh daughter-in-law.

Turning in her saddle, Meghan located her Welshmen some ten paces behind, their eyes alert, their hands on their weapons. Her smile faded and she gave a faint nod.

Anyon dipped his head in answer. His broad, benign face wore its usual frown and Meghan grinned at him, hoping to ease his concern. My big bear Anyon, she mused, so slow he appears in body and mind. But she knew his appearance deceived. He was slow to anger, cautious and considerate, but swift when provoked. Any man who came within reach of his long, brawny arms regretted it.

'Tis strange that he and Rhys are so different, yet so close, Meghan considered. Anyon had her affection and esteem, yet it was the small, sinewy Rhys with whom she felt the greater kinship.

Rhys now gave her a quick grin, his dancing eyes stirring a new surge of excitement in her. She grinned back,

sharing his eagerness to once again fool the English. That
the English would, she hoped, never become aware of
their plot did not dim their pleasure. These were her father's men, more used to running at his stirrups than in
the escort of his daughter, and the gift of them proved the
value ab Owen put on her.

Her father had sent them to her not for protection from
the men who ever sniffed about her, as Edward thought;
there she could take care of herself. Her tongue drove off
the more easily intimidated and the knife at her girdle was
a warning to the few who might forget the king's protection. Her men were a guard against Caradoc. Her half
brother had attached himself to Davyd ab Gruffydd, casually ignoring Davyd's obvious dislike. And Caradoc himself had his toadies, sly-faced men who sniveled and
strutted within his shadow. He was now gone, and his
henchmen with him, but he was still a nagging worry for
the intrigue he must be weaving somewhere. He was in
Wales, she knew, as was Davyd, who Llewelyn had
invited back home at last.

Meghan's thoughts touched on Davyd and she smiled.
She still scorned him for his treachery to Llewelyn, but
she missed his Welsh voice and teasing eyes. The hands
that had gestured foppishly in the company of others had
become quiet when he was with her. Had he not a wife
and nine children, he told her, he would have asked her
father for her hand. He had laughed, tousling her hair,
when she had refused him. Of all the men at court, only
Davyd had seemed no threat to her.

But he was gone and missed. Others had found him
devious; she had found him shy and evasive only when
pressed too hard. But, she reminded herself, other people
had reason for their opinions.

Turning back, she caught sight of Hugh. He was a few
paces behind her and deep in conversation with a pretty
blond girl Meghan did not know. Damn him! she silently
cursed. Must he ever trail after me?

Suddenly the high yelping bay of hounds rang with the
ecstasy of the scent and the yelling of beaters burst from
the woods ahead. The horses surged forward and Meghan
urged her palfrey on. Then, seeing Hugh pass, she grad-

ually drew her mare in. But three of her companions turned back to canter toward her, Richard Oglesby and Edward Litton looking over their shoulders toward the baying with unabashed longing. As the three men neared, Henry Farold, a frown on his deeply lined and flushed features, flicked his eyes over her mount. "Has your horse gone lame, lady?" he asked.

Silently damning her luck, she considered how to send them on their way. Shifting in the saddle as though something chafed her, she settled back with a grimace. "I'm fine. But 'tis not the best of time for me."

Farold scratched the stubble of his beard, the rasp grating on Meghan's nerves. Clearly impatient with her female complaints, he glanced at Anyon and Rhys. "If your men wish to continue," he suggested, "I'll escort you to the lodge."

"No, thank you, I would not have you miss the kill, not so great a huntsman as you. They'll go with me. After all, 'tis their purpose."

Leaning toward her, Oglesby's callow face radiated concern. "Are you certain nothing troubles you, lady?"

Meghan smiled between gritted teeth. "I'm fine, Sir Richard. Only a bit cramped."

His concern turned to fear. "But 'tis dangerous," he explained, his voice cracking. "My sister had such in her side and she died within three days. 'Tis best you see a physician. And you need company beyond those louts of yours."

Farold guffawed and Litton snickered. Meghan could only stare at the man, astounded. Her voice was gentle when she spoke. "'Tis nothing but a woman's complaint, Sir Richard."

His eyes narrowed, then a deep flush rose over the pimples on his jaw. His companions' laughter soared to new heights. Leaning forward, Meghan put her gauntleted hand on his, but he didn't hear her soft voice. His eyes brimmed with tears and he wheeled his horse away into the forest.

Meghan watched him go, then looked at Farold and Litton, her green eyes flashing. She waited, her whip tapping her stirrup, until their glee diminished to an occasional chuckle under her withering stare. "Methinks, my lords, the hounds have cornered their quarry. May they be more gentle with it than you with the callow Sir Richard."

Both men flushed and turned toward the sound of the dogs. Their bay had changed to a sharp barking.

"I give you leave to go," Meghan declared. "Forsooth, I do not want your company. Your lack of compassion does not credit you with me."

Embarrassed and dismayed, yet eager to be off, they saluted her and rode off toward the hounds. Meghan's reprimand slipped from their minds as blood lust overcame them.

Anyon and Rhys watched the two men gallop from view. Waiting, they talked quietly, their ears alive to the sounds of the distant hunt.

When they heard the hounds set to new game, Meghan turned to Rhys. "Have you marked the tree?"

Grinning, he pointed to a tall pine in the distance. Meghan stood up in the stirrups, aligning it. Then laughing, her white teeth flashing, she spurred her horse toward it, Anyon and Rhys falling in behind.

Hugh sat easily, waving flies from his horse's head. The autumn sun felt warm on his back as he watched Edward approach the stag held at bay by heavy, snarling liams. The king's stride was as calm as his features were exaltant. He crooned to the terrified deer as he weaved through the pack of hounds, his voice lulling. Then he leaped, turning in the air to seize the stag by his antlers, twisting its head back and to the side with brutal force. His face contorted, Edward plunged his knife deep into the stag's throat. The animal leaped forward, his eyes startled as the knife released a fountain of crimson that sprayed all who had ventured too close.

The beast's eyes glazed with death, the soft brown turning to the color of earth as the king released him. Edward straddled the body, head down, jaws clenched, his face and shoulders spasming. Suddenly he shuddered in a parody of the stag's death quiver. He relaxed, his eyes clearing, and looked up at Hugh with a happy grin.

Smiling back, Hugh drew his horse away as the huntsmen pulled the salivating liams from the stag. The lords and ladies were already turning away, listening to the bay of brachets striking fresh scent.

Hugh searched the clusters of brightly dressed men and women scattered beneath the trees. Meghan loved the hunt, he knew, but she hated the kill. Her features were always flushed at the bay of the hounds, yet she held back from the sight of the cornered stag. Failing to find her, Hugh frowned, then noticed Henry Farold and Edward Litton and urged his horse toward them.

"Where is the Lady Meghan?" he asked, unintentional disdain creeping into his voice. "Her gallants seem scattered without her skirts to cling to."

Farold glowered, uncertain whether to take offense or not. His ponderous mind considered the bastard knight's friendship with the king, his prowess with lance and sword, and he thought better of it. "She returned to the lodge," he answered. "She is wearing the rag and claimed discomfort."

Not noticing Hugh's frown, Farold leaned forward, his breath foul. "Fitz Alan," he said, his tone implying more familiarity than Hugh cared for, "do you know Oglesby, the callow youth with the pimples?"

Hugh did not listen. Meghan was not one to be deterred by a female complaint and there had been an extra keenness in her face that morning, one which did not indicate cramps or a headache. If Farold was a sample of the men she surrounded herself with, he had either misjudged her or she was playing a game. "Did she return alone?" Hugh demanded.

Annoyed at Hugh's curtness, Henry Farold answered gruffly, "No, she had her lackies. I would have accompanied her, but she insisted there was no danger. 'Tis a hard choice—a pretty wench or the hunt."

Hugh silently cursed them as he asked where they had last seen Meghan. Farold puzzled over his concern; the man had shown no interest in the wench in months. He started to question the sudden change when Hugh cut him short. "'Tis none of your affair, Farold, but ask any man who was at Flint, and remember I tolerate you because I think you harmless. Now, where did you leave her?''

Henry's flush deepened, but Hugh's cold eyes quelled his tongue. ''In the clearing,'' he said sullenly, ''where we heard the hounds announce the stag.''

Without thanking him, Hugh whirled his horse away, nodding to Ralph Ramsden to follow. Watching him go, Henry Farold scratched his head in bewilderment.

Chapter 11

Hugh slowed his horse as they entered the clearing where Meghan had last been seen. "We look for three horses returning to Woodstock or, more like, off into the forest," Hugh told his squire. "One has a crooked left hind hoof."

Ralph nodded and they separated to the left and right to circle the clearing. Leaning forward over the saddle, they examined the ground. Hugh had almost finished his half when Ralph whistled him over. Hugh dismounted and studied the slightly twisted print of the palfrey Meghan rode. He sighed as he stood, brushing twigs and grass from his knee, feeling no satisfaction in the confirmation of his well-founded suspicions.

Lifting narrowed eyes, he searched the skyline for a landmark. "She meets someone, Ralph, and methinks 'tis best we know who." His gaze settled on a pine in a forest of hardwoods, a tree taller than the rest. "Mostlike there." He pointed with his chin. "But we best track her."

"My lord," Ralph said, "mayhap she'll not welcome our interruption."

"You think she has a lover?" Hugh asked. "Aye, mayhap, but methinks I would know if she did. And she is not one to seek hidden corners for such trysts. She would verily flaunt it."

Hugh mounted and urged his horse on, following the trail. Ralph rode behind, one arm raised to protect his face from the branches flipping back at him.

The forest seemed unusually quiet and Hugh realized that the hunt had veered away, its noise now a distant whisper. Still, his concern deepened. Though his features were impassive, questions whirled through his mind. She had to be meeting someone, but if not a lover, who? Someone who bore her enmity, perhaps. Had she made enough enemies for someone to wish her dead, to lure her out alone and harm her?

As Hugh increased his pace he remembered her guards. He had watched them one day at practice and realized she was well protected.

Ralph hissed at him and Hugh slowed. The tracks were now more shallow, the whole of the print distinct. His quarry had slowed. Then two sets went to either side and one remained to wait. The tracks became jumbled where the horse had shifted his hindquarters, then they led on. His eyes alert, Hugh kneed his horse forward, the soft mulch of the forest floor absorbing all sound. He silently cursed a chattering squirrel and stopped at the edge of a small clearing overshadowed by an enormous pine tree.

Meghan sat on her horse at the tree's base, the green of her surcoat and the cloak she wore blending into the foliage behind her. She was leaning over to talk to a thin man with a shaven pate and the rough habit of a monk. Her face was animated. Her soft laugh held a hint of sorrow. Her words were indistinct and she punctuated them with a flick of the parchment held in a gauntleted fist.

Hugh's heart sank to his stomach. Her recent interest in Edward's counselors, her attention to his advisors, suddenly made sense. The game she was playing was more dangerous than Hugh had thought and fear for her tightened his chest. He studied the monk and the horse he held. The animal, though hard-used, was too fine for a lowly cleric. The boots on his well-muscled legs, almost hidden by the long habit, were of Welsh design.

Hugh sought sight of Meghan's guards. Gone were their scarlet cloaks and white horses. Their earth-toned tunics melded with the brush behind them. They stood at opposite sides of the glade, both with longbows drawn and ready, their eyes constantly searching, their heads lifted to catch any sound. Hugh studied Meghan's face, more soft and eager than he usually saw it. He thought of the two bows and the men who held them, then of the hunting knife that was his only weapon. The gamble, he told himself, remembering the surrender of her mouth under his, was with Meghan.

Signaling a silently protesting Ralph to stay, he urged his horse into the clearing. From the corner of his eye he saw the smaller of the Welshmen whirl, arrow notched and ready, bow pulled taut. He knew the other had done the same, but he didn't take his gaze from Meghan.

Suddenly Meghan jerked around to face Hugh, her features instantly white and drawn. He heard her gasp and the whispered word of blasphemy she spoke in the abrupt hush. Then her chin lifted, a small smile curling the corners of her mouth. Her eyes flicked to Rhys and Anyon and back to him. The clearing seemed to vibrate with tension.

Hugh braced himself as Meghan raised her hand, her gaze never leaving his, and urged his horse closer. His voice was soft and caressing as he spoke her name, the command in it implicit. Her eyes challenged him as her gauntleted fist tightened once more. Then her defiance dissolved, her body relaxing. Her voice was thick with unshed tears as she spoke to the man in the monk's habit.

"Be gone. Tell my lord why you've no word from me. I cannot give you this parchment for they'll only search more diligently for you. Tell him the English will, with their law and dogma, push him to war once more if able. Tell him there are those within Wales who plot and to look to the clergy for dissenters there. Give him my esteem and assure him nothing will happen to me over this; they'll not dare."

Llewelyn's agent glanced at Hugh. "Come with me, my lady," he pleaded.

Meghan laughed. "And dishonor my father's oath more than I already have? Give the English a reason, no matter how flimsy, to attack Wales? No."

Finally tearing her eyes from Hugh, Meghan looked at the Welshman, forcing an assurance she did not feel into her voice. "They will not harm me. Edward, too, is not yet ready for war."

Unsatisfied, the man searched her face before reluctantly mounting his horse. With a salute to Meghan, he disappeared into the forest.

Frustration at her inability to order Hugh killed rose inside Meghan, and the taste of humiliation was bitter in her throat. Slowly she lowered her hand to her thigh. Rhys's arrow wavered in grudging hesitation, then also lowered; Anyon followed suit.

Releasing the breath he had not known he held, Hugh felt sweat running down his back. He clenched his hands to control their tremor and kneed his horse forward to Meghan. Her face was impassive as he studied her, noting the delicacy of the jaw and chin framed by the fur of her cloak—his cloak. The soft waves of her hair gleamed blue, ebony, and silver, outlining the width of her brow and the arch of her eyebrows. Meghan's mouth was set in a look of aloof disdain that somehow emphasized its seductive arrogance. Her eyes gleamed with a haughty defiance that challenged his very virility.

Hugh fought the desire that rose from his aching groin, angry that even now she could so affect him. The hand he held out for the parchment trembled and the knee pressing against Meghan's shook with lust. For the first time her eyes widened with fear and she drew back, her hand tightening on the reins, her body tensing as her knees pressed against her palfrey's sides. Terror fled across her face, followed by shame, and her eyes flicked away, searching for a way to flee.

"Do not try, lady," Hugh said gently. "I would be bound by my oath to Edward to hold you, and your men would kill me for my honor. If that was your wish, you would have so ordered it done ere now."

Silently she cursed herself for the control Hugh held over her. Despite the threat he represented, she could not deny the desire to feel his mouth on hers again. She held out the parchment. Hugh unrolled it and his lips moved as he read, a frown of concentration on his forehead.

Its details surprised him, as did Meghan's appraisal of them. Fury swept away his passion, fury at the men indiscreet enough to speak so openly, at Llewelyn who used her so, and at her father who allowed it, thereby forswearing his oath to Edward.

Hugh lifted his eyes to her calm gaze and tapped the parchment against the hilt of his hunting knife. His words were forced through a throat thick with rage and fear for her. "Is it for this trifle that you forswear yourself, that you play the whore?"

Wrath turned Meghan's eyes to green fire and she lifted a fist to strike his hated face. Then, abruptly, she lowered it and began to giggle, a giggle that soared to mounting, mocking laughter. Hugh's bewildered, angry features sent her into greater gales as tears sprang to her eyes and her laughter ascended into hysteria.

Hugh grasped her head, its delicacy under the masses of her hair surprising him, and slapped her sharply. Meghan gasped, her eyes disbelieving, his hand print rising crimson on her translucent skin. She fought for breath. "It disturbs you, then, my lord," she mocked, "that I play the whore."

Hugh's mouth grew taut and his eyes glinted ice until he saw her tears. Her trembling lips denied her smile. Slowly, he cupped her chin in his hand and wiped the tears from her cheeks with a gentle, callused thumb. "Aye, that it does, lady. I would not have you be what you are not, nor see you degrade yourself with such as those." He inclined his head toward the direction of the hunt. "And you play at treason."

He drew her to him, wanting to protect her from what he, himself, had to do. He sensed more than felt the soft teasing of her breath on the hollow of his throat. His hand circled her neck, the pulse below her jaw beating like the heart of a trapped bird. Her back relaxed slowly and she moved closer to him, though she shook with sobs.

Meghan let him hold her. Her loneliness pushing away all caution, she gave herself up to her need for comfort, a need she had denied for too long. His scent assaulted her with memories of her father and brothers. He smelled of morning ale, horses, wood smoke, and dew-damp wool, of the acrid, musty aroma of a young male and the spicy fragrance of leaves he had crushed in his hand. The sound he shushed her with was one from her childhood and she let him soothe her long past the end of her weeping, for the wonder of being a beloved child again. But the hands holding her and the voice whispering soft words were the hands and voice of a lover.

Hugh pressed his lips against the blue veins at Meghan's temple. His hands moved from her neck as he twined his fingers deep into her hair. Go slow, he told himself, breathing deeply. God help me go slow! I cannot rush her, not now! She is a maid for gentling and I must go slow.

He brushed his lips across her eyebrow. "Ah, lady," he whispered, "I mislike to watch you play the bawd, for whatever purpose. You thus besmirch your pride and honor—and mine."

Feeling her draw back, Hugh cursed himself for a blundering fool. Her eyes were swollen, her mouth blurred as though by passion, but her jaw was set firmly and her gaze again defied him. "What I do does not concern you. Nor do my deeds reflect upon your name. If they do, 'tis your own presumption that makes it so. As for that"—she nodded toward the parchment—"'tis to do with as you will. I'll not beg for it or ask that you burn it. I'll make you no bargain. Give it to Edward or no, 'tis your decision. Though methinks you'll not do so."

Hugh's mouth turned up in a bitter smile and his eyes were as cold as winter clouds. "Are you so confident of your hold on me, witch?" he asked.

Meghan smiled and tilted her head.

"Aye," Hugh agreed curtly, "'tis my decision." His laugh was short. "You say the affection I bear you is of no concern, yet you use it against me, forcing me to choose between my oath to Edward and you." His eyes were flecked with gold and glinting with anger. Not waiting for a reply, he pulled his horse around. "Come," he ordered, "I'll accompany you to Woodstock."

Meghan thought to protest, but Hugh's rigid figure warned her not to, and she nodded to her men to mount.

Chapter 12

Hugh straddled a chair, his elbows against its back, a goblet of wine forgotten in his hand as he watched Edward read and pace. He had requested an audience as soon as the king returned cheerful and jubilant from the hunt. Only Hugh's urgency had drawn Edward from the merrymakers in the hall.

Still dressed in clothes that were stiff with blood and gore, Edward was now deeply involved in the parchment. He held the letter delicately to save it from the grime on his hands. His normal ruddiness was purple with rage and his jaw clenched as he squinted in the light of the candles.

For the first time, Hugh doubted the wisdom of giving the parchment to the king. As vassal to my lord, he silently lectured his goblet, I had no choice. 'Twas my duty. To not do so would be a dereliction of the vows I made him—and of our friendship.

Hugh snorted and Edward scowled at him. Shrugging an apology, Hugh swung his leg over the chairback and ambled over to the table to refill his goblet.

Leaning against the fireplace, Hugh watched the flames lick at the logs. Aye, he told himself, I could have as easily tossed it to the fire and none the wiser. Only I would have known—and Meghan. 'Twould have been but a matter of watching her more closely. And not for long, for she'll soon return to Wales, if rumor is true. Only my self-respect would have suffered. Aye, and she would smile from those green, slanted eyes.

His hand tightened about the goblet and his jaw clenched. Ah, but she dared scorn me yet did think I would forswear my oath for her.

The memory of Meghan's face, soft and vulnerable, intruded on his indignation and Hugh glanced at Edward, noting the rage on his normally handsome, good-natured features. And if I thought he would hurt her? he asked himself. If I did not trust him and know him as I know myself, what then? Ah, but I do trust him—and I know him well. Aye, and love him as I love my right arm.

He grimaced at his wine. And if I love him so, why did I add this burden to his others? 'Tis something I could deal with myself, if she acts alone in this matter. Edward did grant me that right. I would have, but for my pride.

Gradually his rage fell away, leaving him apprehensive. I'll wager she is *not* alone in this. If Llewelyn would use her, there must be others. He is not a man to draw but one arrow to his bow. But does she know of them and would she tell?

Remembering the proud set of Meghan's head, Hugh knew she would not, not without persuasion. Frigid sweat sprang upon his brow at the thought of the methods employed by the king's executioners to obtain information. The thought of Meghan so misused twisted his gut into a knot that threatened to double him over. Pushing the thought away, Hugh watched Edward slap the parchment against his thigh in disgust.

"Why did you give me this?" the king demanded.

"It concerns you, sire, and is not something I felt myself able to deal with, not in justice." His voice held a hint of warning as he added, "Feeling as I do about her."

Edward held Hugh's stare before turning to pace again. "You read this?" he asked. "The wench is well informed, but there be nothing in this missive that could, in truth, harm me, although some things could well raise Llewelyn's rancor and in that I would not blame him. The advice she gives would benefit him if he paid heed to it, but 'twould do me no harm."

Halting, Edward grinned at Hugh. "Aye, and there is information here that I was not aware of. I always knew

I was surrounded by idiots, but now I know who will open his mouth at the smile of a pretty wench and who is indiscreet in his cups.''

Tapping the parchment against his teeth, Edward frowned before continuing. ''But a spy in my midst is not welcome. They are like vipers! Disturb one and he'll lead you to a nest of others. I always knew she took her father's oath lightly, but I would not have thought her capable of treason.''

''She never denied that her first allegiance is to Wales, my lord,'' Hugh mentioned.

''Does she know you brought me this?''

''No. Methinks she believes I am too enamored of her.''

Grinning in sudden good humor, Edward clapped him on the back. ''Aye, and so would I have thought.'' Ignoring Hugh's scowl, he poured himself wine. ''What do we do? I doubt that without pressure she'll name others who are involved. And pressure I cannot use without having Wales at our throats. Even if I were to hold Llewelyn by threatening his demoiselle, there is ab Owen, who could rally enough clans to be a painful thorn in my side.'' He shrugged. ''In any case I doubt she knows of the others who are involved. Llewelyn is not fool enough to put her into real danger; he knew we would not dare harm her. He also would not give her information to endanger others. I think we caught a very small bird who flies alone and too high, higher than Llewelyn intended. The problem is what to do with her. I cannot punish her severely because of ab Owen, nor can I let her go unscathed.''

Edward rubbed the stubble on his chin. ''I am tempted to let her go, to watch and see who she contacts.'' He whirled away, striking the parchment against his palm. ''Bah! She must work alone. There is nothing in this she could not hear in any corner and 'tis her mind I read in every word. I know that mind! I've tried to reason with it often enough. And it would take too many men to spy on her undetected by her guards.'' Frowning, he looked at Hugh. ''Unless one of her Welshmen is venal enough to be purchased?''

"They both ran at ab Owen's stirrups from the time their legs were long enough."

Edward sighed. "'Twas an idea. Mayhap, too, 'tis best if she does not think you so easily persuaded from your loyalty. 'Tis not good when a wench becomes too confident. For all the love songs sung by weak-wristed balladeers, a woman is best ruled by fear and a strong hand."

Hugh smiled mockingly and the king looked sheepish. "Ah, but my Eleanor needs only a gentle hand, not like that virago you wish to claim."

Edward paced the room once, then stopped in front of Hugh, hands on hips. "Friend," he said, "I am giving Llewelyn his demoiselle in one month's time and I must return Meghan to her father one month beyond that—in November."

Hugh's features closed, the skin tightening across his cheekbones.

Edward looked away, regret mingling with anger. "'Tis but one more reason this missive does not disturb me unduly. There is nothing she can do in that time, particularly if she knows we are aware of it. Yet I cannot let her go unchastised. The breaking of her father's oath angers me, though loyalty, as any priest will tell, is a concept women are too base to understand. I think I shall confine her under constant escort, whether riding or hunting or to the privy. That she'll find irksome! Anything more severe would not only call upon Llewelyn to redress but would attach more importance to the affair that it warrants. Nor will I say anything to Llewelyn. Let him wait and worry and wonder." Edward laughed, then scowled. "And you said she told the monk that 'tis not time? Time for what?"

Hugh met Edward's stare until the king snorted. "Bah! 'Tis nothing but brag and wishful thinking. For all his temper and stubborness, Llewelyn is too wise to challenge me again. I left him with as much as most of my vassals have. He has lands enough for any man and more freedom than most. What else can he want?"

Hugh lifted wary eyes. "He does not consider himself your vassal, my lord, nor do any of the Welsh. He'll accept no domination, and they'll accept no authority but that of a Welshman. Handle them lightly, my lord, and bid your underlings do the same. They do not brook insult easily.''

"Aye, so said the English afore William the Bastard showed them different in Hastings. Methinks you whistle up a whirlwind. Llewelyn is not stupid enough to defy me for this love of country or freedom the Welsh prate on overmuch. Aye, he complains of my lawyers and their methods and, though I chastise them, I cannot fault them. What thinking man agrees to a law withholding the rights of inheritance from a first born if he is a bit addle-pated or malformed; or agrees to the law allowing them to interbreed like rabbits?''

Hiding a smile, Hugh shrugged. Such a law made sense to him. Had he a weak-witted first-born son, it would be to the second he would look; a man without land seldom married and therefore did not pass on deformities or feeble-mindedness. And the marriage of second cousins held the land within the family, building it into a strong unit. But Edward was not seeking an answer.

"And the laws pertaining to women! God's blood! Do you know they have the right to their own dowries? And the right to divorce and remarry if their husbands are impotent, have leprosy, or fetid breath. God's gown! Fetid breath! Or if he is caught in adultery three times. What man doesn't rut after other women? And if the woman can get her foot into another man's bed fast enough, that man becomes her husband and the first loses all. How would you like to take your Meghan under such laws? If I know the wench, should you displease her in the smallest way, she would feed you garlic for a month, then be out the door!''

Hugh grinned and Edward crossed his arms and bounced on his heels. "Aye," he said, mind back on the main problem, "we will play it lightly and say nothing. Let it be thought she was caught in some minor misdeed. And I agree; the Welsh bear watching. Would you believe me were I to say I am the one man in England who does not wish another war with Wales?'' He cocked an eyebrow. "Do you still want the wench?''

Hugh's eyes grew dark as he thought of Meghan—of how easily she played the strumpet, of her mocking belief that he would not expose her. He had read the contempt behind her smile when she had left him at her door that afternoon. Then the remembered fragrance of her hair came to him and the response of her mouth when he kissed her, the bewilderment and fearful fascination he saw when her gaze unexpectedly touched his. He raised his eyes. "Aye, I still want her."

"And you are still a fool!" Edward snorted. He met Hugh's defiant stare and grinned. "Summon me a page, then, and I would talk with her."

Meghan sat curled up on her cot. Leaning her head against the wall, she watched Yedda brush the matted nap of her cloak. The thick wool sprang back to life, the dirt and stain disappearing under the carding. But for some reason the sight of it filled her with an intangible disgust and she turned to watch the other maidens prepare for dinner.

They barely tolerated her now, ignoring her when possible, speaking to her only when necessary. She told herself they bored her and always had, but their rejection hurt more than she would admit. To hold herself apart was one thing; to be excluded and reproved was another.

Isabelle was one of the few maidens who still acknowledged her, but the pale redhead needed intrigue to feast on. If there was no trouble, she would create it, if only to stand aside and enjoy the turmoil brought about by her manipulations. She shared Meghan's life vicariously by eagerly snapping up any suitor she discarded.

Watching the thin redhead primp, Meghan smiled wryly. Aye, she thought, she has had her uses and she has used me, but I've no more need for her. I do not trust her.

Meghan's gaze wandered to Eleanor de Montfort, Llewelyn's demoiselle, who was sorting tapestry silks. Raising her dark head, Eleanor's soft brown eyes met Meghan's and she smiled, her soft, gently pretty face lighting up. Keeping her own eyes cold, Meghan looked away, then chided herself for being deliberately cruel.

Aye, she insisted to herself, she calls me friend because I alone know Llewelyn. A pest she is with her questions. 'Is he as fair as ever? Was he sore hurt in the war? Does he still laugh with his head thrown back?' Aye, and what has he to laugh on? Foolish ninny! She cannot stay safely in France. Ah, no, she must sail to her betrothed and land in Edward's arms instead. What has held Llewelyn besotted is beyond my comprehension.

She was not being fair, Meghan knew. Eleanor was not so foolish or useless. She had seen her father die in his battle for the people of England, several of her brothers with him, and had had to flee to France, only to watch her mother die there. Separated from Llewelyn for years, she had tried to return to him, only to be captured and held hostage. Her last brother was still a prisoner at Crofe Castle and Eleanor was still no closer to a reunion with her adored Llewelyn.

Angrily, Meghan reminded herself that she, too, had lost brothers but her suffering had not robbed her of spirit. She rolled over to lie on her belly, her chin propped in her hands, but found Eleanor's hurt eyes hard to ignore.

Annoyed, she thought cynically, Ah, Llewelyn would be most proud of me if he could but know how I have flirted and lied to better do the task he asked of me. Surprised by her own resentment, Meghan shook her head. Ah, no, I cannot blame Llewelyn. He did not suggest I prostitute my soul. That was my game and well enough I liked it—then. But no more!

She frowned, her dark eyebrows knitting. Aye, and now I lie even to myself. 'Twas not for them I changed, but to thwart Hugh, to drive him away, and well my plan served its purpose.

Feeling a sense of dissatisfaction and loss, Meghan let herself remember the feel of his mouth on hers and a deep warmth curled in her. I had somehow thought, she told herself, that despite his words of wanting me, he would not put lust above honor.

Her brow wrinkled, unhappy with the knowledge that Hugh was as weak as other men. Still, 'twas fortunate 'twas Hugh who found me out, she thought. Another knight might have dragged me into the hall by my hair, yelling my treachery to the ceilings.

Meghan touched the cloak Yedda had set at the foot of the cot, her fingers light on the deep fur lining. Her face grew soft with memories of strong arms and a gentle, then demanding mouth awakening her desire. Such a silly little wench, she thought, to be so stirred by a man's touch!

She remembered waking up in a strange room, wrapped in the warm cloak and the smell of the man who had given it to her. She had kept the cloak because she needed it, but it had since become a talisman, a symbol of the man she could rely on if ever she needed someone beyond herself, if ever she wanted rest and comfort. But now, by choosing her over his oath to Edward, he had displayed his weakness and somehow failed her. The cloak seemed but a cloak, its nap growing thin and the fur matted. Picking it up, she tossed it onto her clothes chest. Yedda could have it, she decided.

A page was standing in the doorway, his face crimson and his eyes downcast at the sight of so many women in various states of undress. "Meghan," Isabelle called, "the king sends for you. What have you done now?"

Meghan felt a surge of fear intermingled with joy. Hugh could not have exposed her. Mostlike, Edward wished to tell her of Llewelyn's marriage. Nothing had been said, but the demoiselle had walked about in a deeper daze than was even her wont. There had been other rumors that Meghan had not passed on to Llewelyn for fear they were false. If true, though, she herself would soon return to Wales.

"I know nothing of it, Isabelle," Meghan said, "though, mostlike, you're correct. Aren't you always? There is much for Edward to reprimand me for, all told."

She followed the page from the room, hopeful thoughts of Wales rising in her.

Chapter 13

The page opened the door to Edward's chamber and closed it behind Meghan, leaving her to face the king alone. He stood scowling at her, his back to the fireplace, hands on his hips. His ruddy features were flushed and his eyebrows knit. He did not greet her, only stared, and she frowned, wondering what misdeed she was guilty of now.

Yet even as Meghan met Edward's stare, she felt other eyes on her. Apprehension building, she slowly turned to see Hugh leaning against the wall, a goblet of wine in his hand. His gaze was impersonal, as though he was looking at a stranger. A small, courteous smile played about his mouth and all at once she knew he had betrayed her. He had not forsworn his oath to Edward. He was still a man of honor.

Though a small part of her was relieved that Hugh had remained true to himself, Meghan's knees suddenly grew weak as she realized the implications of his presence. Pushing back her fear, she drew a deep breath, fighting an impulse to flee. Her thoughts skittered about, landing on the fact that Edward could not really harm her. Yet a nauseating feeling of shame assailed her. It was one thing to garner information, to dupe the English, to help Llewelyn. It was quite another to be caught in an open breach of honor. She had broken her father's pledge and her conviction that his oath could not bind her melted under Edward's gaze. She had used his and Eleanor's friendship. She had turned against them like a viper, had bro-

131

ken their trust, had insulted them with her wanton behavior. To have Hugh witness her disgrace only added to her humiliation.

Yet her face was smooth and her voice low as she turned back to Edward. "You sent for me, my lord?"

"Aye, I did." He lifted the parchment from the table. "This is yours, I believe."

Hugh watched Meghan. Her impassive face was set with a faint, affable smile. It faded, replaced by bewilderment, and Hugh's eyes narrowed, rage heating his blood. By all the saints! he told himself. She thinks to deny it!

Lowering her gaze, Meghan's eyes slid to Hugh, seeing his disgust, and the corners of her mouth curled up tauntingly. She relaxed as she faced Edward once more. "Aye, my lord, 'tis mine, or was until Sir Hugh did take it from me."

Edward stared at her, his anger dissolving at the sight of her wide eyes and firmly set mouth. "Are you aware of what you've done?"

Meghan flinched and dropped her eyes, then lifted them again. Her voice was tremulous. "Aye, my lord, and of the trust broken."

The king turned to Hugh, defeated by her sudden capitulation, and Hugh shrugged; it was no longer his problem. Finding no answer there, Edward's sharp blue eyes returned to Meghan. "There is little I can do to you. You know that," he said regretfully. "You will be confined to the lodge with freedom of movement within but under a constant guard. Inform your Welshmen and bid them not obstruct him."

He paused to add weight to what he next said. "'Tis not to my advantage to have your breach known. If it should become known, I will blame you and you will find yourself in a nunnery. Do you understand me?"

Biting her lip, Meghan nodded. Her voice quavered slightly as she asked, "Will the queen be told?"

"It does not concern her, nor would I have her so hurt. She once loved you."

Meghan bowed her head. "I thank you, my lord."

Edward waved her gratitude aside. "'Tis not for your sake, lady. Too many questions would arise should my lady wife treat you with even more contempt than she does now. You may go, lady, and I ask that you not offend my sight too often."

Meghan bit her lip as she curtsied and backed to the door. Her hand hesitated on the latch, then she lifted it only to turn back. But any apology she made would be meaningless. She started to open the door when Edward spoke curtly. "Lady, Llewelyn will be wedding the demoiselle in one month's time. You will be returned to your sire soon afterward." He paused, sarcasm heavy in his voice. "There is no need to inform him. A courier is on his way to Wales now."

Bowing, Meghan felt her face flush with shame and she stepped out, gently closing the door behind her. She leaned against it, her knees threatening to give way. A strange feeling of relief struck her and she wanted to laugh. "Thank God and the blessed Virgin 'tis over!" she whispered.

Hugh's face, closed against her as it had never been before, came into her mind. What must he think of her? And then she allowed a surge of elation and inexplicable relief to rise. He did not deny his fealty! she told herself. Fighting back tears, she pushed herself away from the door, her feet light, her head dizzy.

"Meghan."

She turned to see Henry Farold. His face was flushed, his smile fatuous. He's been at the wine butt again, she thought, but his actions no longer concerned her. Her smile was gentle as he stopped before her, rocking precariously on his heels before finally gaining his balance.

"My lady," he began. He paused, scratching his ear to collect his thoughts. He flushed and started again. "My lady, would you share my trencher tonight?"

Meghan touched his sleeve. "No, my lord, I will eat with the maidens henceforth. But I do thank you."

Smiling, she left him scowling in bewilderment as she continued to her quarters.

Meghan thought dinner would never end. Only pride had driven her to the hall from her room. Now she waited through the entertainment, her pride still too great to let herself be driven back to her quarters. Keeping her gaze focused on the minstrels and acrobats, she tried to ignore the barbed comments and giggled insults about her. Only Eleanor de Montfort had smiled when Meghan had sat down with the women. The other maidens had greeted her with exaggerated surprise and disparaging comments on the honor she dealt them. It was the first time she had eaten with them since she'd begun her flirtatious charade months ago.

Isabelle had been rapacious in her curiosity when Meghan had returned from Edward, becoming vicious when Meghan had ignored her. Now she attacked at each opportunity, Meghan's averted face and the sly laughter of the others driving her on. Meghan gritted her teeth, refusing to rise to their jibes, anger tightening her stomach.

Edward had looked at her only once when she entered the hall and since then he had treated her as though she didn't exist.

As he had all evening, Hugh was watching her, his features impassive. A small smile touched his mouth as he met her defiant gaze. His eyes narrowed in acknowledgment before he flicked them over her impersonally, appraisingly. They glowed with triumphant laughter when a flush rose on her face and anger squared her chin.

She knew there was much speculation about her in the hall. Let them think what they will, she thought, smiling, for soon I go home.

Meghan thought of the high mountains and green misted valleys, the people and way of life so alien to the English. It would be different now, with her brothers gone and her father grieving. Yet there would be too much work for loneliness to press too hard. And anything would be better than staying at court.

Feeling a sudden pain in her shin, Meghan jerked her gaze to Isabelle, who pointed behind her. Turning, Meghan saw Hugh standing over her. His slight smile was courteous. "Lady," he said, "would you dance with me?"

She stared at him in surprise. He had never approached her before, nor had she ever seen him dance. She had thought, too, that his discovery of her spying had quelled all interest in her, leaving only scorn and distaste. Abruptly she became aware that all conversation at the table had ceased. Angry, jealous eyes pierced her. Hugh, although considered unsuitable by most parents, was often the object of their daughters' whispers late into the night. Remembering the taunting and sly comments the maidens had dealt her, Meghan thrust all caution aside. Tilting her chin, she smiled. "I did not know you were accomplished in anything but war, Sir Hugh. I was not aware you were trained in the finer arts of gallantry."

"The Lady Elga taught me many skills I do not oft employ, and other ladies taught me more. Mayhap one day you will find advantage in my education."

Ignoring his insinuation, Meghan stood up and stepped over the bench, feeling Isabelle's stare on her back as they walked to the dance floor. Meghan knew she would be puzzling over Hugh's attention as he had shown no interest before. And Isabelle was clever enough to notice that theirs was not a dance of courtship. Surely she would see the animosity between them no matter how gracefully they moved.

Well, let her! Meghan thought as Hugh led her through the figures, turning her to sway gracefully before him. The tiny bells sewn in the hem of her surcoat to ward off evil spirits tinkled as she moved, mocking Hugh's grim features.

"I go to Ainsleah on the morrow, lady," Hugh told her, guiding Meghan in a circle around him, then turning her back, noting as he did the polite eyebrow she lifted. "When I return, 'twill be to escort you to Wales." He smiled at her. "Lord Edward granted me that privilege."

"You'll do as well as another, I wager," she answered coldly. "'Tis no journey of great peril."

Hugh's mouth quirked. "Aye, mayhap. The only danger are the charms of the lady herself."

"Ah, Lady Elga schooled you well," she complimented caustically. "Yet gallantry does not become you. I would as soon expect one of those painted monkeys to take up the lance, armor himself, and ride to war." She pouted, her lower lip red and gleaming. "My charms are of no great threat to you, my lord. I've unbounded faith in your honor."

"Aye." Hugh laughed softly. "Gallantry is as unnatural to me as flirting is to you."

Meghan smiled wryly as he turned her away, then back. His tone became hard. "I doubt, too," he said, "the danger of your charms. I shall but remember your waspish tongue. You'll find your trust justified, if you but take care not to taunt me too far."

She dropped her eyes, unaware of the violet shadows her lashes cast on her pale skin, then raised her gaze again, her voice derisive. "'Tis a pity, isn't it, my lord, that your duty is so limited? All that is required of you is that I arrive home safely, with no harm to my person or virtue. But it isn't my honor which most concerns you, is it?"

"Aye, but one day your person and honor will be truly in my keeping. I'm a patient man, lady, and I trust you to hold yourself unsullied until then."

He guided her through an intricate step before she faced him again. "If I thought that belonging to you was truly my fate, I would surely see you cuckolded."

He grinned, his confidence infuriating. "I do not believe so, lady. You do not remain chaste from any respect or affection for me but because you have too much pride to give yourself easily. "'Tis an asset of yours that goes to my advantage."

She glared at him. "Do not challenge me, my lord!"

"Ah, but I'll not leave you unprotected here, lady. I shall leave my word to guard your virtue."

Meghan quirked a puzzled eyebrow, but Hugh didn't answer, his mouth touching hers in the impersonal kiss that customarily ended the dance. He bowed as the music stopped. Drawing her up from her curtsy, he twisted her arm lightly behind her back and turned her to face the king. Suddenly his last words made sense and she tried to jerk free. Hugh only smiled, his grip tightening.

"No, my lord!" Meghan whispered angrily. "You'll not do it! Not again! I would return to my table!"

"My lady, do not force me to strip you of your dignity afore all the hall."

Helpless, blinking back tears of frustration, Meghan glared at him as he led her to the dias. Why did each encounter with him end in weeping for her, when she was not given to such weakness? She stood with her teeth clenched as Hugh addressed the king.

"My lord Edward, I would beg word with you!"

The king turned from his conversation with Robert Burnell. He looked from one to the other and grinned. "Methinks this a scene I witnessed once afore."

Hugh's features remained grave though his eyes laughed back. "Aye, my lord, 'tis so." He paused, giving weight to his words. "I wish to reaffirm a boon I begged of you at Flint and to state again that Lady Meghan is under the protection of my sword and my word. Any breach to her person or honor is accountable to me, as you did so grant."

Edward leaned forward, amused by Hugh's stubbornness and impatient with Meghan's. "I do reaffirm and wish, by God's gown, that she were mine to bestow so I could rid myself of her, you being determined to have her against all sense."

Hugh bowed his head gravely, although his gaze glinted silver. "I thank you, my lord."

"I, too, beg a boon, my lord," Meghan said. "I beg leave to return to my quarters and away from this man who holds me against my will."

Edward's eyes danced. "You may go. And," he added, "Sir Hugh will accompany you."

Meghan opened her mouth to protest, then realized its futility. She sank into a curtsy that managed to convey only scorn.

The rasp of gossip trailed after them as they left the hall. Meghan knew that by morning the story of her arrival among the English, much embellished, would be known by everyone from the lowest groom to the highest lady. Her stride lengthened.

At the door to her quarters, Meghan whirled, her hands clenched, her body rigid. "Damn you," she sputtered, stamping her foot in rage. "I have to live amongst those harpies! They'll know all about us, from the length of my tunic to the gift of your cloak. Everything! Aye, they'll even know what Eleanor said to me in my bath—or tell themselves they do. They'll not leave me alone, none of them. 'How came you by his cloak, Meghan? Is it true you were almost naked, Meghan?' " she mimicked. "God's teeth, the only place I'll find relief will be in the garderobe."

"Does it bother you, then, lady, to have our affairs so bandied about?" he mocked.

Unable to speak in her fury, Meghan aimed a fist at his face. He ducked the blow and caught her wrist, twisting it behind her, then grabbed the other as she swung. He felt her knee coming toward his groin and turned, catching it on his thigh. His eyes widened in surprise. "You little witch!" he cried, pulling her hard against him. "You'd have the very balls off me, wouldn't you? If not with your shrew's tongue, then in a blow that no one but a slut should know."

Meghan glared at him, her throat thick with frustration and tears. "Aye, I would! I hate you!"

Hugh stared down at her, his eyes dark, his fingers weaving through her hair. He watched the realization dawn on her face when she couldn't see her Welshmen, who were still at their meal—and unaware that she was not at hers. His eyes narrowed as he gazed at the challenging face she turned up to him, into her green eyes that refused to show fear. "I'll have you one day, little one," he whispered, "and you'll sore regret you tried that!"

Hugh brought his mouth down on hers. Meghan struggled against the arms holding her, fighting to take in gasps of air. He only held her tighter, opening her mouth with his and drawing in her lower lip to suck on it. The world began to tilt about her. She was aware of nothing but the steel hardness of his body and the mouth that drew an unwanted surge of desire from her. Suddenly he pulled her head back, his face that of a man in agony. His voice was a groan. "Damn you to hell, I want you!"

He buried his face in her hair. His arms encircled her, holding her closer still. His hand caressed her throat, shoulders, the line of her jaw, until she ceased to fight and heard only the hammering of his heart. He whispered her name over and over, aching want in his voice until his mouth found hers again. His kiss drew from her an answer to his love and need as she lifted to meet him. Then Hugh abruptly released her. He looked at her as though to engrave her features on his memory, then he turned and walked rapidly away without a backward glance.

Meghan watched him go, a hand pressed against her mouth. Her pride, her fear of loving, and the knowledge of her father's need for her fought with the aching desire to call him back. He turned a corner and was gone.

Chapter 14

Fog had settled over the world, blanketing the sky. It draped the hills and seeped among the trees. Over the rolling track, it shifted in sheets about the horses and their riders as they ascended the rise. It soaked everything it touched. Tall grasses bent under its weight. It collected on the branches of trees and ran in rivulets to the tips of twigs. Hanging there, it grew heavier, then dropped with a plop to the saturated earth. It gathered in beads on the eyelashes and whiskers of the horses, and was scattered in showers of fine spray when they shook their heads in agitation.

The mist muffled all sound. A doe and her fawn, startled by the ghostlike horsemen, leaped in silence into the shrouded forest. The rattle of sword in scabbard and the scrape of mailed hauberk on metal chausses were absorbed into the leaden air. The shifting of knights in the saddle was smothered to a groan of leather against sodden wool. Only the hooves of the warhorses could be heard, a moist sucking sound as the feet were pulled up from the mud of the road.

Meghan pushed back her hood and tilted her face, looking for a sign of thinning in the clouds. A drop of water struck her cheek and she brushed it off with a soggy leather gauntlet. Twelve days of travel had dulled her excitement at returning to Wales. Even the knowledge that she would probably see her father that day at Montgomery did not lighten her fatigue or stir her anticipation. Shoving the hood farther back, she let the moisture-laden air cool her cheeks. The November day was cold, yet she felt steamed in the soaked clothes she wore. She straightened her shoulders to ease the weariness, then let them drop again.

"Are you tired, lady?" Hugh asked.

Meghan thought to deny her weariness but shrugged instead. "Only a little. 'Tis the mugginess."

Hugh stood in his stirrups to ease a cramp. The humidity had formed a mist on his close-cropped beard, the gray of the fog matching his eyes. Removing a gauntlet, he wiped the damp from his face, then flicked it from his fingers. He glanced at Meghan impersonally yet noted the glow of her complexion, the drops of dew on her eyelashes. "Aye," he agreed politely, "'tis as though we ride through a purgatory with no beginning or end, nothing but the damp and fog. But it should burn off. 'Tis early in the season for the all day mists."

Looking ahead, he scanned the half-hidden road. Though his body was relaxed, his eyes were constantly alert.

Meghan studied the hawklike nose and high brow, the lips that firmly denied all emotion. He pulled back the hood of his hauberk and his thick, dark hair sprang from his forehead in waves. Hugh caught sight of Meghan's examination and raised a scarred eyebrow. Cursing herself for the flush heating her features, she turned away. He had treated her with utmost civility since arriving at Worcester to escort her home and she had replied with distant courtesy. Now she did not know what to expect from him—entreaty, demands, or incrimination. She only knew he had the power to hurt her if she lowered her guard.

Unobserved, Hugh studied her, as he had many times on the journey, noting the proud tilt of her head—so often averted from him—the haughty set of her back, the length of her leg under her surcoat. Her heavy mantle hid the thrust of her small breasts and the curve of her slim buttocks, but the knowledge that they were there teased his thoughts. He briefly imagined parting the cloak and cupping those breasts, the nipples hardening under his palms, his hands sliding over the tiny waist to the round bottom

and curving around it as he pressed her against the
demand of his groin.

Jerking his gaze away, Hugh forced lust from his
thoughts. He eased his hips forward, trying to relieve his
ache. Should he send Meghan back to ride in the safety
of the column? But no, he rejected the idea, as he had
many times before. To know she was behind him but
unseen would only tantalize him more.

His eyes narrowed as he again surveyed the road and
he shrugged, knowing he was being overly cautious. The
party of four knights, their squires, and fifty men-at-arms
was too strong for any band of outlaws preying in the
area. And the Welsh, their borders so close, were no
threat, not with Meghan along. The party would have
been much smaller if Edward had not decided to send a
badly needed troop to Montgomery, adding them to the
escort.

Hugh leaned forward, probing the mists. His four
men-at-arms were riding a quarter of a mile ahead.
Frowning, he searched for the source of his unease, then
Meghan's soft voice broke into his thoughts. "How far
to Montgomery, my lord?"

Her delicate features were framed by the fur hood, her
green eyes polite and impersonal. His gaze dropped to her
slightly parted lips, the lower one so full and round.
Turning away, he forced his words through a dry throat.
"We'll be there well afore dark, lady, should all go
well."

Silently he thanked the saints that the journey and his
torment would soon be over. Yet her absence would only
make him want her more, with a need no other woman
could satisfy. Her mouth haunted him. He wanted to put
his lips over hers, drawing that ripe lip between his teeth
to bite it gently. His jaw clenched in his frustration.

"Oh, look!" Meghan whispered, pointing toward
Wales.

A vagrant wind had blown the clouds away. But even
as Hugh glimpsed the far mountains, fog settled back over
them. Meghan slumped in the saddle, her face forlorn,
and his hands tightened on the reins, anger flooding him.
Suddenly he realized that it wasn't fear that disturbed him

but the knowledge that tomorrow she would ride into those mountains with their hidden paths and secret places and perhaps never emerge. The Welsh welcomed and protected their own and would reject any stranger who came to take from them a beloved woman of the clans.

And there is nothing I can do to keep her, Hugh thought. I was a fool to escort her. Would God I could take her, hold her, force her to my will! Once she got with child, no one could gainsay my right to her. Aye, and the pleasure would be short-lived, with the Welsh and Edward fighting each other for the privilege of hanging me from my own battlements, and me fighting both. Though, by all that's holy, 'twould be worth it to have her, to bed her, no matter how brief the time. And she would then weep to see me dead.

Shaking away such thoughts, he turned to Meghan. "Would you prefer to halt for the midday meal or push on?"

She drew her disappointed gaze from the now cloud-shrouded mountains. "I would go on. The journey has been overlong and I wish to be home as soon as possible."

His mouth tightened. "I will push the pace, then, lady."

Meghan frowned, bewildered by his abruptness, then shrugged. It had been a long journey. The rains had come early. The days had been spent helping tired horses through hock-deep mud and seeking places to ford swollen rivers. Through it all she had had to calm a terrified, saddle-sore Yedda.

The maid had lost her castle-bred sauciness in the face of a journey into a barbaric wilderness. Even now she remained dubious of Welsh civilization. She had ridden by cart when the court followed Edward in his nomadic life, but Hugh had refused her such a privilege this time. Her appeals to Meghan had fallen on deaf ears. A speedy journey was one thing Hugh and Meghan both wanted.

Was it Yedda's loyalty to her or to Rhys that drove her to brave the journey? Meghan wondered. She turned to see Yedda, her face wan and eyes wide, riding behind Rhys, her arms tight about her lover. I'll have to see them wed, she thought. That babe she thinks to hide will soon push through her kirtle no matter how tight she girdles it. 'Tis fortunate she is not due for a while or she could not ride and methinks Hugh would have left her behind, no matter how I entreated him. If her belly was much bigger, one kick of the infant and she would be over the horse's tail.

Amused, Meghan stretched to ease the ache in her back. As bad as the days had been with the rain, the detours, and Hugh's sullenness, the nights had been worse! They had slept in a series of nunneries, monasteries, and castles and she could not decide which she disliked most. She yawned, tired from nights spent entertaining hosts lonely for word of the outside world.

She felt dirty, as well. Hugh had been able to bathe at Ludlow, but she had refused. She would have been expected to share his bath water after he finished and help the women bathe him. As daughter of the house, she had scrubbed the backs of her father and brothers and of all important male visitors, but it would somehow have been too intimate with Hugh.

Lifting her face once more to the sky, she found a patch of blue. She smiled, the movement of the horse lulling her.

A hand shook her gently, and Meghan jerked awake to find Hugh leaning over her, a slight smile on his mouth. "You were sleeping, lady," he said, "and we near Montgomery."

She stretched and rubbed her eyes. The sun had forced its way through the clouds to reveal Montgomery on a hill, its fat towers glistening with damp. Sheep grazed, white flecks against the green of the slopes dropping away from the castle's high outer walls. Behind rose the mountains of Wales, touched pink and gold by the sun on early snow.

Pain rose in him as Hugh watched joy brighten Meghan's features. She breathed deeply, as though to hold the air of her home within her. Her lips were parted, her eyes glowing.

"I had forgotten its beauty," she whispered in awe.

Meghan wanted to share her joy with Hugh, but he turned away, his features harsh. A mirthless smile twisted his mouth and she blinked back sudden tears she could not explain. Perhaps, she thought, it was because she would never see him again, not after the next day, and something in her did not want it so.

Sighing, she leaned forward to run her fingers through her mare's mane, crooning softly. She stole a glance at Hugh and found him looking at her, his eyes intent. The muscles of his jaw were knotted and his face was filled with naked hunger. Her hand grew quiet, still wrapped in the horse's hair, as her body, her soul, responded to his need. An ache coiled in her, weakening her, cutting short her breath. Her sudden desire terrified her in a way she could not control. She shook her head, her gaze still locked with his.

"No, my lord! Ah, no."

Fear flashed across her features and without thinking she brought her riding crop down against her palfrey's flank. Hugh had ducked, but the whip's tip had nicked him, opening a wound at the corner of his mouth. He grabbed for her bridle but missed. The startled palfrey leaped away, then leveled out into a run. Spurring after her, Hugh felt rage and fear dry his mouth. The palfrey could fall at any moment, flinging Meghan from its back. It ran, head high and uncontrolled, its hooves missing their purchase in the mud, and it slithered and slid in panic. Once Hugh saw it stumble, legs tangled, and his heart lodged in his throat, but Meghan somehow held the horse up until its stride lengthened again.

Hugh's warhorse gained slowly. The animal's shoes, the size of dinner plates and heavy with cleats, found footholds where the mare could not. Yelling, Hugh waved away the men-at-arms who had turned back. To be attacked from the front or sides might send the mare into a worse panic, causing her to fall and crushing Meghan beneath her. Blinking against mud thrown by the palfrey's hooves, Hugh leaned over and reached for the small form on the maddened horse. A touch of the destrier's shoulder would send the mare spinning to the side in a roll, splintering her legs like jackstraws—and Meghan with them. Cursing his gift of the billowing cloak, Hugh glanced down to see that Meghan had kicked her feet from the stirrups. With her legs hitched up, she was ready to leap should the mount fall.

"Good girl," he breathed, then his arm encircled her slim waist and he lifted her to him.

Thrusting his boot under her groping foot, Hugh pulled his stallion to a halt, suddenly aware of Meghan's arms tight about his neck and of her gasping breath against his pulse. He held her there for a moment and breathed into her hair a silent prayer of gratitude. Then he peeled her hands from their grip on his cloak and held her away from him over the mud. She looked, he thought, like a long-haired kitten caught in the rain. He grinned, then anger born of intense fear drove his humor from him and his features hardened.

"You stupid little witch!" he whispered. He released her, flinging her away from him so that she fell face first into the mud.

He left her lying there. She was dimly conscious of dirt in her mouth and water stinging her eyes. Slowly she pushed herself to her knees, shaking her head to clear its ringing. She tried to stand, but her legs refused and she sank back, kneeling in the puddle.

The mare had slowed enough to be cornered and Hugh led her back. His face was still harsh and blood welled up from the cut on his mouth. Guiding his horse to stand over Meghan, he watched the rest of the party approach, surveying them until their babbling questions ceased. Yedda was crying and trying to dismount to go to her mistress. She hit Rhys with ineffectual fists then, sensing the tension, she quieted.

"My lady," Rhys said, "is she hurt?"

Hugh leaned over to examine Meghan. Concentration furrowed her begrimed features as she scraped dirt from the front of her surcoat. "Nay," he answered, "she's just a bit discomfited." Hugh addressed Humphrey Thorley. "She needs only a moment's rest to regain her dignity. Take the party on. Tell them she fell from her horse. We'll follow shortly. Ralph," he ordered his squire, "stay by me."

Humphrey stared doubtfully at Hugh. His lord had proved to be brave and never rash, but the man was addled when it came to the Welsh wench. Yet it was of no importance to him. The sooner he reached a bath and a wench to scrub his back, the better, and he put the column in motion. But Rhys held back, his gaze belligerent. Though he challenged Hugh, it was Meghan he addressed.

"Shall I stay, lady?"

Meghan shook her head. Whatever was to be said or done, it had best be said and done now. She was more aware of Hugh as he sat on his horse over her than of the party moving on. When they passed, he dismounted to walk to the palfrey. He ran his hands over her haunches and down her legs, calming her, then handed the reins to Ralph.

"Lead her slowly. I'll take the lady up with me. But first," he stated, glancing at Meghan, his eyes bright with anger once more, "I want a word with her. And tell them at Montgomery to prepare the lady a bath. She is in sore need of one."

Ralph grinned, then quickly scowled under his lord's stare before moving off.

Hugh stood over Meghan until she looked at him. Mud was packed into her hair and clothing. It ran in streaks down her face and her eyes gazed owlishly out at him from the white circles of flesh surrounding them. Tears had left streaks down her cheeks, giving her a clownish effect. Hugh tried to hold his features stern, but his mouth twisted into a grin. At Meghan's glare, laughter broke from him, doubling him over. He hung onto his horse, his sides aching from mirth, and still he could not stop. Blood dripped from the wound he reopened, but each time he tried to control his laughter, the sight of Meghan sitting solemnly in a puddle, mud-coated and sedate, rekindled it.

She waited expressionlessly for his glee to subside. Finally she said, her voice cool, "If you have yourself in control, my lord, would you be good enough to help me up?"

Lifting his face from his horse's mane, Hugh wiped the tears from his eyes. His mouth twitched as he took the dirt-begrimed hand she offered him and pulled her to her feet.

"You are the only woman I know who can sit in the middle of the road, covered from head to toe in mud, resembling nothing more than a drowned robin, and do so with dignity."

Meghan's eyes danced with laughter before she sobered, touching his bleeding mouth with fingertips as gentle as a breath. "My lord," she whispered, "I do most sorely regret the blow."

She pulled her surcoat up, revealing a fairly clean undertunic. Taking her knife from her girdle, she cut a swatch of cloth. Pouring wine from his flask into it, she cleaned the wound, her mouth tight with concentration. Then she pressed the cloth hard to check the bleeding, feeling Hugh's eyes on her all the while."

"Methinks 'twill scar, my lord," she said, looking up.

Hugh smiled behind the cloth. "'Tis but one of many, though the first dealt me by a woman."

Blushing, Meghan frowned as he took the cloth from her. He wet it again and washed the dirt from her ears, nostrils, and the corners of her eyes. Noticing her slight wince when he touched her jaw, he lifted gently mocking eyes.

"You hurt your jaw?" he asked and Meghan nodded. "Methinks 'twill bruise. Did your teeth loosen?"

Meghan pushed her tongue against them and bit down, wiggling her jaw. "I think not, though they are sore."

Hugh grinned. "'Twas a hard thing to resist—a troublesome woman and a mud puddle."

Hugh's smile faded as he ran a finger along her jaw and into the tumbled mass of her hair. His gaze caressed her features before he brought his mouth gently over hers. Meghan remained passive as his lips touched, held, moved, telling her of his need. When she tried to twist away, a whimper rising in her throat, Hugh continued to hold her until the drumming of her fists against his chest changed to a feeble flutter. Her mouth softened, swelling

as it opened to his demand. Her tongue reluctantly rose
to meet his, drew back, then rose again to cling sweetly.
Her hands moved to his shoulders, and around his neck,
drawing his head down, turning her mouth to fit more
closely, the taste of his blood metallic on her tongue.

Parting her cloak, Hugh's hands moved over her and
she gasped as he touched her breasts, the nipples hardening under his fingers. Her body twisted to meet his
hand more fully and he released her, his touch passing
down over her hips to her buttocks, pulling her toward
him, lifting her. A sob rose in her and she raised to her
toes, pressing against his hardness. With an agonized
groan, Hugh pulled his mouth from hers, his eyes desperately searching the bleak landscape.

Edward's constable at Montgomery had done his job
well, leveling all cover for miles around. No tree stood
to offer shelter to a man taking his way with a maid.
There was no shrub large enough for a man to place his
cloak under so he could lie down with his love. Hugh's
distraught glance fell on his warhorse, an animal trained
to stand immobile against all turmoil. Bragging stories
knights told of the taking of a wench, her back supported
by the motionless destrier, flashed through his mind. Then
the ignobility of the idea struck him. Grasping Meghan
closer still, he buried his face in her hair, breathing in the
fresh scent of it, his body shaking with need.

"Holy Mother of God!" he gasped. "Help me!"

Turning his hand in Meghan's hair, he gazed with
angry eyes into her upheld face. She stared at him through
passion-glazed eyes, bewildered at the sudden change in
him. Her mouth, swollen from his kiss, was lifted as she
offered it to him once more, a cup to his thirst. A smear
of blood from his wound was drying on her cheek.
Hugh's enraged whisper came from between clenched
teeth, striking out in his own thwarted need.

"I'll not take you this way, not in the mud like a villein!"

He drew her arms from around his neck and held her
from him, his hands tight about her wrists. His voice held
desperation. "Meghan, come to Ainsleah with me!"

She stared at him, aching with the need he had aroused, then tears filled her eyes. Her head fell back and she shook it from side to side.

"Ah, no, my lord, no! Do not ask it of me! I cannot leave my father when I am just returning to him. I cannot leave my people. I am all they have. And you, you would surely possess me, take from me my soul. I'll not watch you ride off to Edward's call time and again or wait for a man I love to come home to me tossed over his horse like a bag of meal. I'll not do it, not again, no matter how great my love. I'll not wash the blood from a beloved man's death wounds or sew his shroud. I'll not drop dirt into the face of a man dead in battle, not again. Do not ask it of me, Hugh, if you love me."

Her voice grew gentle as she read the pain in his features and she leaned back, trusting him to support her. "Someone else will do that, my lord—wait for you, watch for you, bury you. But not me! Aye, I'll ask after you from every minstrel and wanderer. Aye, and my body will remember and crave the release you now deny me. I'll remember you, pray for you, but my memories will dull and mayhap one day I'll realize I have not thought of you for hours, for days. Mayhap I will find I cannot recall the color of your eyes or the way the scar at your mouth twists with your smile.

"Time, they say, dims desire. Then I will be free of you. But I'll not love you, Hugh. I'll not marry you, wait or weep for you. Do not ask it of me."

Hugh's eyebrow quirked in amusement, but his voice was choked. "You are ever a maid who refuses afore the question," he teased. "Did I say anything of marriage?"

Meghan did not answer as he drew her back to him. "Aye, you'll not marry me, will not come into my house and live with me there, but you would lie in the mud with me, wallow with me in the fields with nothing but the sky to cover our shame. Aye, and after we had given and taken all we could of lust, you would rise, shake down your skirts, and mayhap carry my bastard away with you. But you'll not take the son I would give you in wedlock for me to nurture, to see grow tall and strong." His voice turned into a groan of anguish. "I would have you, Meghan!"

Her face had hardened and Meghan lifted her chin, her eyes gleaming with rage. "Aye, I would give myself here, with joy, with pride! And if I carried away a child, I would do so proudly, and he would be no better and no less than his sire. A bastard, aye, but a good man. And mayhap a fitting heir for Cleitcroft. In truth, you would do me service to lay me here and get me with child. Then I would need not take a husband to play the stud."

Fury shook Hugh, but he held her motionless, reading his own agony in her eyes. Her head fell forward against his chest and sobs tore her, ripping through him, too. His anger died as he took her into his arms again, cradling her, whispering her name until the crying eased. Then he tilted Meghan's grief-mottled face to his and smiled.

"Methinks there will still come a time when I will claim you and you will rejoice in it."

Regretfully, he released her and mounted his horse, reaching down to swing her up before him.

"There be nothing else to say, is there?" he said, then covered her mouth with his briefly, mingling his blood with her tears. She wrapped her arms around him, her head against his shoulder, the beat of his heart in her ear as he urged his horse on to Montgomery.

Margaret Stanmore stood on the steps leading up to Montgomery's keep, waiting for her guests and eager to see the Welsh wench about whom she had heard so much. Some said she was uncommonly beautiful, with hair so black that it gleamed and eyes that could steal a man's soul away. Others thought her complexion too vivid, her manner overbold. When Robert, Margaret's husband, had last returned from court, he had described Meghan ab Owen as a skinny, drab thing, too tall and not to be noticed in a crowd. In the next breath, he had said she made him uncomfortable with her quiet smile and a gaze that seemed to see too much, as though witching the very thoughts from him. He preferred fair, plump women with modest ways and downcast eyes.

Margaret patted the narrow strip of blond hair showing beneath her wimple and smoothed her surcoat over ample hips. Meghan ab Owen must have something to intrigue a man or there would be no rumors. It was said she had half the men at court in rut; though none would deny her virtue, many doubted it. Hugh fitz Alan had proclaimed his intention and protection toward her twice and had been rejected both times. Frowning, Margaret decided he would be a difficult man to refuse, then crossed herself against the thought. The queen, too, was supposed to have favored Meghan once, then suddenly withdrawn her esteem, though no one knew why. The king disapproved of her, as well, finding her indocile and too opinionated, yet his discipline had never been harsh.

Margaret glanced at Gavin ab Owen standing in tense conversation with Robert. Studying the Welsh chieftain from slanted eyes, she found it hard to reconcile the old, slack-muscled man with the tales she had heard of him. Stories of his prowess in battle still circulated. Margaret's childhood nurse had often frightened her into obedience with the warning that he would catch her, spit her on his sword, and eat her raw and writhing. The tales of his way with women must be exaggerated, too, Margaret thought, moving a step closer to her husband. If he had done half the things said of him, and if his daughter was like him in any way, then the stories of her must be true. Still, Margaret told herself, I can't believe a woman would go into battle, living like an animal with her sire's men.

Unconsciously she preened once more, then looked up at the parapet, wishing she could watch her guests approach from its height. But Robert would not approve and he was right; it was not the place for a lady. She frowned. How strange that Meghan and Hugh had not come in with the others. Sir Humphrey had said Meghan had fallen from her mare, but that was no cause for delay. There had to be more to it. The knight had not smiled, but his eyes had held a smirk. Then he had ordered a bath!

Margaret was pouting at this slur to her abilities as a hostess when she heard heavy hooves on the drawbridge. Stepping up the steps for a better view, she forgot her husband's admonishments on a lady's proper behavior. The destrier rode through the gate passage and Margaret sighed in frustration, unable to see the Welshwoman. Hugh fitz Alan held her sidesaddle, her face turned toward his chest, and a heavy green, mud-coated mantle covered her completely.

Hugh rode toward them slowly, guiding his horse through the crowded ward. He spoke to Humphrey, who argued briefly before nodding a grudging compliance, then Hugh rode on. Stopping at the foot of the stairs, he greeted Robert Stanmore, Lord of Montgomery in Roger Mortimer's name, and Gavin ab Owen. Margaret heard the gentleness in his voice as he spoke Meghan's name. He held his hand against her face, searching her features as though they were infinitely precious, then he bent his head, his mouth touching hers in a soft, regretful kiss. As he drew back, Meghan reached up, her fingertips on his mouth. At last, she turned to the group waiting on the stairs.

Gaping, Margaret couldn't believe this woman was the one she had heard so much about. Her hair was caked with mud and her eyes, though large, were puffed and dark, as though from weeping. The woven design of Hugh's chain mail hauberk had indented her cheek in red crescents through the cloth of his tunic. Though she bore no wound, her drawn face was streaked with dried blood, which emphasized its wanness. She stared back at Margaret, blinking in the sunlight before Hugh lifted her from the saddle. His hands clung to hers, and she stepped on his boot as he lowered her to the ground.

Turning to face the others, Meghan smiled shyly and flushed, embarrassed by her appearance and by the lie she had to tell. "I fell from my horse," she explained to her father.

Ab Owen stared at her, then he lifted angry eyes to Hugh, knowing as he did so that he would find no other answer there.

"You've not fallen from a horse since you were a babe."

"Or since Flint," she said, smiling wryly. "Remember? As there, the road was slick and my mare slipped."

Abruptly her defiance fled. Meghan saw how old her father had become and dismay struck her. "Oh, Father!" she whispered, moving into arms that folded around her, clasping her close.

Hugh's face was set in frustration and sorrow. He drew his eyes from Meghan only when Robert asked him to dismount.

"I thank you, Robert, but I can stay only for a short while. I hope to reach Ainsleah tomorrow eve, though I would beg fodder for my horses and"—he smiled at Margaret, who felt a blush rise,—"food for myself and my men. We've not eaten since Prime."

Hugh watched ab Owen lead his daughter up the stairs and into the keep. At the top, Meghan turned to face him, her back straight, her chin tilted. Their gazes held for what seemed an eternity, then Meghan's lips parted in a smile touched with the radiance of a woman who knows herself to be well loved. She lowered her head to Hugh in an unspoken acknowledgment and disappeared into the castle, Yedda fluttering and scolding behind her.

Part II

Chapter 15

Meghan was awakened by the shrill cry of Yedda's infant, but she kept her eyes closed in a vain attempt to hold on to the sleep she craved. Two babes in three years, she thought. Yedda has surely found brats enough to love. I'll have to send Rhys to the high pastures this summer to prevent another one's coming for a few months.

Hearing the gulp as the infant grabbed Yedda's nipple between toothless gums, Meghan smiled, ignoring her own hunger. The whisper of clothing being donned came to her, followed by a giggle and the closing of the door as the two other maids left the cold chamber. Rolling onto her stomach, Meghan snuggled deeper into the bedclothes, trying to find sleep. Finally giving up, she propped her chin in her hands and watched the vapor of her breath.

She sighed, thinking of her father. Even after several years, the shock of his appearance at Montgomery had remained with her. The tall, strongly thewed, straight-backed man she remembered seemed to have shrunk. His muscles had grown slack, his shoulders slumped. His long, vigorous stride had shortened and his great zest had gone, along with his booming laugh and roar of anger.

When Meghan came home, he had urged her to marry and get an heir, but he had seemed relieved when she refused. Now he no longer mentioned it, letting much of the household management slip into her hands. He seemed content to spend his days ambling over the fields and forests, going from household to homestead, cornering men in conversations of past battles and long-ago raids, or sitting by the fire with chance visitors, talking of the ancient glories of Wales.

Her father had also taken to passing his days, elbows propped on the table, staring into his goblet. Whether he thought of his dead wife and sons, or of the ignobility of dying by his own hearth, or of the defeat of Wales, Meghan did not know. Nor had he seemed concerned when she had told him of Caradoc's arrival during one of his absences, simply nodding when she said she had sent him on his way.

Caradoc had inquired of their father, yet an obscene insinuation had underlain his words, his protuberant eyes straying over her. His red mouth had curled in satisfaction when he had commented on her unwed state. Even with Rhys and Anyon behind her and her wolfhound under her hand, she had felt threatened. He had only laughed when she ordered him gone, leaving with a meekness that worried her. He still lurked in the hills, she knew, an unseen, haunting presence.

Scowling, Meghan thought again of her father. He had quickened suddenly, the spring of youth back in his step and anticipation in his eyes. The change had followed a visit from Davyd, the brother of Llewelyn.

He and ab Owen had talked as she went about her duties, their conversation halting when she or another maiden came within earshot. Their words they could hide, but not the flush on her father's features or their air of conspiracy. Yet when she had questioned him, he had put her off, telling her to mind the kitchens and to leave the affairs of men alone.

The months she had spent with him fighting the English had flashed through her mind and she had come close to hating him then. Sensing it, he had become contrite, complimenting her management, acknowledging the duties, rightfully his, that she had accepted. He had spoken of the days she had ridden with him under Llewelyn, but he had not told her what news or intrigue Davyd had brought. Then he had gone, calling in his men from hidden crofts and homesteads. Since then, the ward had rung with the thunk of arrows in the practice butt, of the crash of sword on sword, ax on ax. And more duties had fallen on her as her father trained men or sought out others of his clan.

War was planned, that a child would know, but she was puzzled. Why was Davyd, who had always aligned himself with the English, involved? If he planned to displace Llewelyn, he would not have come to ab Owen. The target must be England, Meghan thought, and, whomever plots, all Wales must be in it!

She rolled onto her back and stared at the high ceiling. Anger at the added responsibilities and her concern for what might happen should Wales rise again was mixed with the joy she felt when she watched youth and purpose return to her father. Mayhap, she told herself bitterly, he'll not die in bed after all. But I'll go with him whether he gainsays me or no. If he is killed, no one else will bring his body home. Nor will I wait for it here. Yet, if Wales should lose . . . Meghan knew Edward would not be merciful a second time.

She rose from her pallet. The cold raised goose bumps on her naked flesh and she reached for her kirtle, then paused, running her hands over her high breasts, their nipples taut in the frigid air, and down her waist to her hips. I am, she thought, the same as I was three years gone, though I am twenty now—an old maid.

Smiling ruefully, she did not care that suitors no longer came. Yet men's eyes still told her she aroused their lust. And there was time yet to marry, time to be demure and coy when she found a man she wanted, a man suitable for Cleitcroft. If he did not find her desirable, her lands and honors would secure the matter.

She pulled the kirtle over her head, trying to ignore the memory of a dark man with mocking eyes. Yet if Wales should lose . . . she mused, thinking of the rumors of Hugh fitz Alan's visit in Wales and wondering if he would come that day or the next or at all. Jerking a comb through her waist-long hair, she forcibly banished from her thoughts Hugh's promise to one day have her and she turned her attention to her duties.

It was time to check the kitchens for cleanliness, the salt meat for maggots, the flour for weevils, and to measure the supply of herbs. The laundry had to be done, the rushes changed, candles and rushlights replenished. She had to see if there was tallow enough, if the drains ran clear, if the well was polluted. She had to visit the sickroom; the number of wounded had increased since her father began his training.

Whether the men went to war or the high pastures, cloth had to be woven and sewn. Leather had to be cured and made into shoes. Food had to be prepared. It was close to Easter Week and a garden had to be planned, the size estimated and seed selected. The sheep were due to lamb and several of the earliest had already been lost to wolves. She would have to find women and boys to replace the men her father had taken from the flocks.

Meghan donned her surcoat and flipped her now-braided hair from under it. Morgant, wife of Maddock the tanner, was pregnant and due any time. She was frightened and it could be a hard birth, even with Glenna the midwife with her.

Mostlike, Meghan thought as she left the chamber, the wench will begin at night. 'Tis always so.

Her steps were firm and proud as she descended the circular stairs to the hall. She was the pivot the world of Cleitcroft turned on. The people were hers.

The day was unusual for early March. The sun shone warm, but the breeze was brisk as it licked old, rotting snow from the mountains and dried the fields and pastures. White wisps of cloud scuttled across the sky. Reining in his destrier, Ralph Ramsden beside him, Hugh stared at Cleitcroft.

"I'd not like to take that!" the squire whispered, awed.

"Aye," Hugh agreed. "'Twould not be easy without a seige—and that a long one."

The castle was of the simplest design. The keep was round and three stories high, the lowest floor containing the storerooms, the second the kitchens and the hall, the third the family sleeping quarters. It sat on a column of rock surrounded by a vertical drop of several hundred feet into a gorge. A tall curtain wall extended from the keep, circling the ledge. A narrow spit of land that had origi-

nally made a peninsula of the column had been removed
and a drawbridge, connecting the castle to the path leading to the village on the mainland, replaced it. A village,
Hugh knew, of a few widows, a couple of craftsmen, and
a priest. The rest of ab Owen's people were scattered
through the folds and creases of the mountains. How
many men he could call to war was known only to himself and Llewelyn. Beyond the village lay a few cultivated fields, most of the land being in pasture.

"Where do they get their water?" Ralph wondered.

Pointing to a long faint gleam at the base of the castle,
Hugh answered, "Mostlike they tap that brook."

Hugh had come to Wales at the private request of
Edward, without royal warrant, because the king was
concerned by rumors of unrest and unusual activity.
Travel had increased at a time of year when the chieftains
most loved to stay near their hearths. Forges worked far
into the night. And the Welsh, a cantankerous people, had
become meek, bowing passively to the laws laid down by
the king's representatives, laws they had blatantly diso-
beyed before.

It was not an assignment Hugh was comfortable with
and he had refused to come under pretense. His questions
were direct, his observations keen. He had heard and seen
nothing that spoke directly of preparation for war. The
many informers, the curse of the Welsh, were also silent.

Llewelyn had reminded Hugh of a great wounded bear,
cornered and dangerous in his baffled animosity, ready to
strike out at anything. His wife Eleanor had died in childbirth, leaving him numb with grief yet trapped between
the warring Welsh and English clergy, between the complaints of his people and the injustices of the king's
greedy, officious magistrates.

It was his brother who had maintained the conversation. Davyd had sat on the edge of a table, his foot idly
swinging, his eyes resting speculatively on Hugh. He had
shaken his head at Hugh's questions, a smile on his lips.
Yet it was Davyd, as elusive as mist and as private as a
closed book, who had said, "If we rose, fitz Alan, would
there be, in justice, any who could gainsay our cause?"

Hugh knew no one could.

In that way he was answered by all to whom he spoke. He was welcomed, offered ale and wine, bread, meat, and cheese. Friends were more reserved than their wont, those who bore him animosity showed disdain, but nowhere was hospitality denied him. Everyone disclaimed knowledge of unrest or plans for war. Yet the atmosphere was of the placid surface of a pond reflecting only sunlight back to the sky and concealing teeming life beneath. Behind the courteous eyes of all he met lurked derision and anticipation. He had detected an uneasiness among the chieftains, an evasiveness alien to the Welsh.

Frowning, Hugh knew he had discovered nothing that would give Edward an excuse to bring added troops to the Marches. Indeed, to do so would only offer the Welsh reason to rise. Yet there was something beneath the tranquil surface. . . .

He did not think to find an answer at Cleitcroft. Smiling ruefully, he thought, Aye, I'll find nothing except a maid three years older and mayhap no longer a maid.

Hugh had not asked about Meghan. Any questions of a favored daughter would only bring resentment—and no one had offered word about her to him. Yet when ab Owen's name was mentioned he had noticed a gleam in several eyes while others had appeared embarrassed. Her name had been most noticed by its absence. Hugh urged his horse forward, eager to see her yet apprehensive of what he might find.

The people went about their business as the small troop rode through, as villagers had done everywhere. They did not glare or mutter imprecations. There was no dashing of women to pull children into huts, no rush of snarling hounds. Too few men loitered about the ale house with the sheaf of moldy grain over the door advertising its wares. Hugh glanced at the sheep on the hillside. They were watched by two men, one who even at this distance could be seen to have only one arm. The few fields given to grain had been plowed earlier than usual. At Cleitcroft, too, the tranquillity was abnormal.

Studying the castle, Hugh sought weak spots in its defense and found none. The drawbridge was thick and the portcullis had recently been reconditioned. Only seige and catapults could take it, reduce it to rubble, and destroy the lives within. Yet ab Owen was practical enough to be aware that most enemies would simply devastate the countryside and leave the people of the castle to starve or survive as they would. The Welsh were experts at surviving. The castle, a recent Norman innovation, was perhaps an improvement on the older Welsh custom of fading into the mountains when attacked. Cleitcroft had not yet been tested. Perhaps it had been created only for the vanity and pride of Gavin ab Owen. Still, it was a symbol of strength and defiance to all who saw it.

In the outer ward, there were too many men going about too few tasks. Several well-used practice butts stood against the curtain wall and a battered quintain hung on the far side. There were no men using the targets, no spears or long bows visible other than those of the guards, yet the grass of the bailey had been trodden by the feet of men and horses. The livestock normally running free— the geese, chicken, and swine—were caged.

As Hugh dismounted, a squire took his horse and several men greeted him. Ab Owen emerged from the keep like a bear from his den, his welcome effusive. Hugh's anger and frustration rose. Whatever stirred, he told himself, it stirred here. He returned the older man's embrace.

Wondering where Meghan was, Hugh examined the hall as he entered and took the chair ab Owen offered. Although occupying over two thirds of the second floor, the hall was small by English standards, the castle having been built for defense, not comfort. Its three high, thin arrow slits cast little illumination and burning rushlights added a bluish tinge to the air. A blaze in the single fireplace failed to ease the chill in the far corners and there was a scarcity of wall hangings to control the drafts. Several animal skins hung there, a practice the English had abandoned centuries before. Yet the hall was scrupulously clean. The tables had been scrubbed until the grain of the wood could be felt. The rushes had been changed and the odors of basil and chamomile rose from them. The pallets used by servants and retainers were stacked neatly in a corner.

Yedda set down a pitcher of ale and three goblets. She smiled at Hugh, the first honest smile he had received in Wales. As she turned to go, ab Owen asked about his daughter.

"She's in the village, my lord," said Yedda. "There's a wench there soon to birth, but she knows Sir Hugh is here." Yedda cast a quick glance at Hugh before she left.

Hugh and ab Owen resumed their last conversation of mutual aquaintances and common interests, but the ease between them four years ago was now gone. Their laughter was forced, their reminiscences overlong, the pauses uncomfortable. Hugh told himself the very ease of his position was too casual. He sat scrunched down in the hall's second chair, his ankles crossed, his shoulders braced against the back, his buttocks against the seat. His wine was held low on his abdomen and he fought an urge to turn and watch the door through which Meghan would enter.

Facing Hugh, ab Owen sat hunched over, his elbows propped on the table, the goblet held tightly. His laughter was too loud and his eyes kept flicking to the door. His relief was obvious when he stood and said, "There's the wench—and about time!"

His throat suddenly tight, Hugh rose also.

Meghan stood in the passageway, ignoring her father's injunction to enter, the light from behind outlining her slim figure and shadowing her features. Word of Hugh in Wales had reached her days ago, yet she had not really believed she would see him here. He had lived in her mind for so long that he seemed unreal. He was a canker of emptiness she carried within her day and night, feeding on her unacknowledged need and on the demands of her virgin body. The sight of a woman swollen with child always brought a redoubling of the aching void within her. She longed to feel the weight of a child inside her, to watch an elbow or knee push against her belly. At the sight of a woman suckling a child, her own nipples itched to have a child at her breast. And always in her imagination that child was Hugh's. Yet still she resented his intrusion into her self-imposed purgatory.

As she stepped from the darkness, her expression was closed, the painful joy she had felt at word of his arrival deeply hidden. Two huge wolfhounds entered with her, great grandsons of the pair Meghan's Irish mother had brought as a portion of her dowry. One stayed under Meghan's hand; the other padded around the table to lie at ab Owen's feet. Meghan nodded toward the dogs. "I call them Rhys and Anyon," she told Hugh, her voice light.

"They are aptly named, lady," he answered, his smiling eyes studying her.

Three years had stripped away the last vestiges of childhood from her. Finely planed maturity had replaced her adolescent roundness. A hollow underneath each cheekbone accented her full mouth. Her jaw and chin had become more pronounced. Her eyes still betrayed innocence, but sorrow and loneliness lurked in their depths. There was strength and purpose in her features—and frustration. She was more beautiful as a woman than she had been as a girl, yet the need for fulfillment showed in the tight corners of her lips and about her eyes.

Hugh smiled to himself, noticing that, in her perverse pride, she had not attempted to improve her appearance for him. Her hair hung in thick braids over each breast and a tendril curled under her chin, tempting him to tuck it away and touch the cream of her skin as he did so. She wore a loose surcoat of dark wool, its full sleeves covering her hands, only the gold link belt at her waist giving it shape. Keys designating her role of chatelaine hung from the belt and a smudge of dirt was smeared across her cheek. The hand she held out to Hugh was rough and red, its nails split and broken. Calluses marred her soft palm, which smelled of basil, soap, and tallow when he raised it to his lips. Her own scent lingered, too—of earth after rain, of grass crushed in the hand.

Meghan's greeting as she rose from a curtsy was formal, her eyes cold. "Is there anything troubling you, my lord, that you stare so?"

Hugh grinned down at her. "No, lady, you've changed. You've become more lovely—and a woman." Eyes laughing, he added, "In most ways. And you are cleaner than when we parted, though there is a smudge on your cheek.''

His smile widened as her hand lifted. Then, eyes flashing, she turned on her heels and went to stand behind her father. Her voice was neutral as she asked Hugh to be seated, then she fell silent, her features indifferent as Hugh and ab Owen resumed their conversation. The fingers of one hand idly scratched the ears of the wolfhound leaning against her. The other she laid on her father's shoulder. The strength and confidence he took from her touch was visible in the straightening of his shoulders and the set of his jaw.

Meghan did not betray her anger and resentment. The years since she had seen Hugh seemed to have vanished. He had ridden up in his arrogant manner, sat down in her home with her father, and now talked of the same things they had discussed on the road to Flint. Meghan told herself his attitude toward ab Owen was condescending. Everyone knew why he was there and it was not to gossip. He was seeking information no Welshman would give him and he covered his business with the pretense of friendship. In honor, she told herself, ignoring the fact that it would have been a grave insult, he should ask after the information he seeks and be gone!

Meghan did not admit that most of her resentment rose from his comment on her dirty face. He treated her like a child, though he had once held her in passion. The sight of his bold face and mocking eyes brought alive again the desire smoldering within her which she had banked as she would a turf fire. He took the confidence she had acquired as chatelaine of Cleitcroft and reduced her again to an object to be used.

In the cold and lonely nights, she had warmed herself with memories of him that she chose to forget in the brightness of day. His presence now was a threat to the defenses she had built against the hurt he could bring her, defenses erected against loneliness and need.

Her father banged his cup on the table and Meghan jumped. A flush rose when she met Hugh's amused gaze. Leaning forward, she filled their goblets. "We had word of your travels, my lord, and of the information you seek,'' she said.

Hugh stared at her in surprise. She had broken a rule of Welsh hospitality by asking a guest his purpose.

Meghan's face flushed deep scarlet, but her eyes held his. Ab Owen shifted uncomfortably in his chair and tugged at his mustache, gulping his wine and scratching his head, but he did not admonish Meghan for her rudeness.

Straightening, Hugh leaned forward, his hands flat on the table, the bits of pumice used to scour it rough under his fingers. The atmosphere of the hall had been uncomfortable before. Now it was tense and expectant. He ignored Meghan, his gaze fixed on ab Owen.

''My lord Edward,'' he said by rote, ''has heard rumors of unusual activity, of unrest in Wales. He is concerned, wishing no discontent amongst his subjects, no disturbance of his peace. He asked that I verify or deny the reports and search for the cause of disquiet, if there is any, that he may rectify it.''

The bewilderment Hugh had met everywhere was reflected in the chieftain's features. Ab Owen scratched his ear. ''I heard, of course, that Edward's concern is the cause of your visit,'' he admitted, ''but I do not understand his worry or the rumor. What has he heard?''

Hugh sighed, the muscles of his jaw jumping. He spoke of forges used late into the night; of excessive winter travel; of concealed meetings among two, three, five chieftains; of the meekness of a people famed for rebellion.

Ab Owen's patronizing laugh raised the hair on Hugh's arms. ''Sir Hugh,'' he said, ''methinks you come on a fool's errand. Your lord seeks to find phantoms hidden under his own bed. 'Tis an early spring and the plows need repair. You know such tools always break at the same time and always men want their own fixed first.''

Hugh would have interrupted but ab Owen, suddenly wrought up, brushed his protests aside. ''Tis not only an early spring, but 'twas a mild winter. Is it amongst your English laws that a man cannot visit from Michaelmas to

Candlemas? Does your lord now tell us we cannot meet with friends without his permission? I think not, for even Edward would not dishonor the charter signed by your King John and reaffirmed by Henry. And would he prefer us to be hostile? Methinks 'twas due to our rebelliousness that he attacked us originally.''

Hugh ignored the fact that the Welsh had attacked first. ''Ab Owen, you and others play me for a fool. You speak with honeyed words of denial or you attack as a means of defense in your argument. You sit with bland faces and disclaim what is evident to an infant. Do you think I don't see fields planted early or not at all, boys with sheep where men should be, the sneers behind the smiles of your people? Your men are always at the practice butt; 'tis their pride and pleasure, yet in all Wales I've not seen one man with a bow and arrow set to a target. You seek to hide something and I want to know what it is.''

Ab Owen leaned over the table, Hugh rising with him. The Welsh chieftain's face was violently flushed. Veins stood out on his forehead, and he sputtered in rage. Meghan placed a calming hand on his arm.

''And do you think to carry tales of sheep and fields and unarmed men back to Edward?'' he demanded with a derisive smile. ''Do you think he would arm the Marches on such evidence? I think not, for then, in truth, Wales would rise—and no one would blame her!''

Hugh's face was set, his voice harsh. ''And do you think I am not aware of that?''

Ab Owen sat down again, Hugh following, and leaned forward, his manner beseeching. ''Hugh, my friend,'' he said, ''there are no plots of war, no intended uprising. I so swear it!''

Hugh's mouth was tight with frustration. He had noticed that ab Owen had sworn with a certain desperation and that he had not placed his oath on his honor or on God. Nor could Hugh ask that he do so.

Meghan poured herself a goblet of ale and sat on the arm of her father's chair, swirling the liquid about in the cup. ''And what did Llewelyn tell you, my lord?'' she asked.

''The same as I hear elsewhere,'' Hugh answered. ''He claimed ignorance.'' Looking down, he idly drew his thumb through a puddle of spilled wine and lifted his gaze to her again. "Yet he is a man who would strike out on any excuse, if only to ease his own pain."

"And Davyd?" she asked.

Hugh laughed brusquely and shrugged. "He knows nothing, of course, as ever." Meghan smiled in wry acknowledgment of Davyd's laconic habits. "He answered as had his brother, denying all knowledge or possibility of an uprising." Hugh turned his palms up. "Have you ever known Davyd to answer anything directly afore?"

Frowning, Meghan lowered her face and stared at the foot she swung. "Mayhap he but needed the proper question put to him. Would you stay the night, my lord? Shall I order you a bath?"

"No, lady, things have been said which would make my presence uncomfortable for you." Smiling derisively, he added, "And I know all you would tell me."

Hugh looked a moment more into Meghan's slanted eyes. His gaze roamed over her features and he smiled slightly as a blush rose to her cheeks. Reluctantly, he turned to ab Owen, gnawing his lip before shrugging uncertainty away. "Gavin, I would ask a boon of you. I would ask that, if there is fighting, you would send your daughter to Ainsleah that I may take her to the Lady Eleanor, away from danger."

Ab Owen sat stunned. When at last he spoke, his voice was harsh. "You come here without invitation, accept our hospitality, and ask me to betray my people! Now you have the insolence to tell me I cannot keep my daughter from harm! Think you I'm an addled gaffer with a sword arm as weak as an infant's? Think you the walls of Cleitcroft cannot protect her? You insult me, fitz Alan, and were you Welsh and not on your lord's deed, I would have your life for it—and none to gainsay me!"

Hugh leaned across the table, his eyes pleading. "And think you she would stay behind these walls if you go off to follow Llewelyn or Davyd or whomever it is who calls you to a fool's suicide? She would not! She would follow you whether you deny her or no! Do you think Edward would hold back from the spoils of war this time? He'll not, and well you know it! Think of what would happen to her, caught by men with blood lust! You've seen them, the women so used and mutilated! The lucky ones are either too weak to survive the countless rapes or killed by a sword thrust after the rape is done! Your Meghan is strong. She would live long hours—breastless, scalped, and ravished! Would you be there to put her from suffering? Can you rely on someone else with pity enough to deal her the knife of mercy? Send her to Eleanor, man, I beg you in the love you bear her!''

Ab Owen stood, his face suffused with rage, spittle about his lips. "Aye, I've seen such women, the handiwork of your English and your mercenaries! With or without the consent of Edward Longshanks, they rape. So you would have me send her to Eleanor and then, win or lose, you would have her there, to take with Edward's blessing. And you would rape her as surely as any soldier! You hide your lust behind concern for her safety and her honor when it is you who would strip her of both. Aye, you want her, that you never denied, and I tell you again the choice is hers. If she would go with you, then let her go now. I'll not hold her, but I'll not send her to you against her will.''

Hugh's laugh was bitter and he spoke from between clenched teeth. "Aye, you say you would not hold her but you do, old man, and well you know it! You hold her with the love and pity she bears you. You hold her with the loneliness she knows her leaving would bring you. She is the last child of your loins and you hold her to you with the deaths of her brothers!''

Hugh's voice lowered, becoming thick with desire. "Aye, I want her! But not as you do, old man. You look on her and she gives your life meaning and your losses purpose. As long as she is here, you do not question if it was right to send your sons to their deaths for Wales and for your pride. They died for the cause for which you reared them and she tells you the cause was just! She is a mirror, reflecting back your conceit, your infallibility. You feed on her, old man! You suck vigor from her and leave her a dry, childless, unawakened husk. You talk of finding her a husband, but you'll not do so. You'll hold her here because you need her. To lose her would be to lose the last prop that holds up your world."

Hugh leaned forward, spitting the words into ab Owen's stunned features. "But I'll take her, one day, even if it's over your corpse. Aye, I want her, but my wants are of life! I want her for passion, love, and children. And you think she does not want me? She does! You offer her memories to suck on, the pap of death; I would give her life!"

Straightening, Hugh forced himself to relax. He looked at the stubborn, wounded face before him and his voice softened. "Ah, ab Owen, you know I honor and respect you. I regret my words have caused you hurt. But you know I am right."

Ab Owen did not answer or lift his eyes. The hands holding his goblet shook with the palsy of age. Hugh's eyes were filled with sorrow when he turned to Meghan. She held her head high, her chin tilted. A faint smile touched the corners of her mouth and tears slid down her cheeks.

"Meghan, little one," Hugh whispered, "come with me!"

Her eyes lifted. "Why is it, my lord, that you speak of life but always bring me tears?"

"To weep is a part of living, my lady." His voice became a groan. "Little one, come with me!"

She smiled her regret, shaking her head. "I cannot and well you know it!"

Hugh studied her, seeking some means to persuade, but he saw only stubborn purpose written on her face. He sighed, the desire to fight gone from him, and smiled gently. "Go with God, then, lady."

Meghan stood motionless, her eyes on his back as he walked from the hall. She poured ale into his goblet and followed him out. He had mounted his horse and did not see her until he turned the animal for one last look at the keep. His gaze did not leave her face as he took the stirrup cup and emptied it in one quaff.

Meghan's voice was soft, a plea for understanding. "God go with you, my lord."

Hugh's eyebrow lifted and his teeth gleamed. "Aye, lady, though 'tis your company I would prefer."

She gasped at the blasphemy and hurriedly crossed herself as Hugh grew serious. Leaning over, he ran a finger down her damp cheek and under her chin. He tilted it up and lifted her to her toes until he could place his mouth gently on hers. When he released her, the mockery had returned to his eyes and he rode away with the taste of salt on his lips.

Meghan watched him go until he disappeared through the gatehouse, her eyes remaining for a long time on the passage he had entered. Then she turned back to the keep. Her stride gained purpose with each step that brought her to her father. Her gaze softened in pity as it rested on his bent head and hunched shoulders, then her face hardened. "Methinks, my lord father," she said, " 'tis time you told me of Davyd and what he would have of you!"

Ten days later a strange figure approached Cleitcroft. He dwarfed the heavy-boned, jug-headed horse he rode, his feet dangling far below its belly. His head was bald but for grizzled eyebrows that formed shelves of thick wool above small, deep-set eyes. The eyebrows looked startling against the tan of his head and face. A wide, dark brown scar split his head from crown to one high, knotted cheekbone. His face was broad and his wide nose was flattened from many breakings. The mouth was gentle beneath a huge, drooping mustache, with deep lines of laughter at its corners. In his ears were heavy loops of gold. His cloak was fur, and only a short, sleeveless leather tunic protected his barrel-thick chest. Under the tunic, front and back, he wore a large metal plate that conformed to the contours of his body. His feet were shod in rough, knee-high boots bound to his calves with strips of rawhide. Across his lap he carried a battle-ax the length of a small woman.

Riding unperturbed, he did not seem to notice the women who hastily pulled their children off the road and made the sign of protection from the evil eye. He grinned at a boy scarcely out of swaddling clothes who stared at him, round-eyed. The child grinned back just before his mother yanked him away. Astonished eyes gazed at him from the top of the curtain wall. In the ward, men put aside their spears and bows and stared as he cantered over the drawbridge and dismounted at the stairs of the keep. After withdrawing a parchment from his broad, brass-studded belt, he waited patiently for someone to relieve him of it, gazing about with childlike curiosity.

Meghan frowned when she saw him. She bit her lip, puzzled, before stepping down the stairs to him, stopping when their eyes were level. He grinned brightly.

Meghan kept her expression stern, although there was something about his smile that demanded a friendly response. In size he made her think of an enormous bear; in eagerness he was like a puppy. When she questioned him in Welsh, he shook his head. When she tried English, he scowled and pointed to a mouth devoid of a tongue and handed her the parchment.

Her frown deepening, she broke the seal bearing a single lion rampart over a bar sinister and began to read.

My Lady Meghan,
The bearer of this missive is Selig. I send him as a gift to guard you as I cannot. He was for long my right arm, the shield at my back. The love he bears me I give to you that he might keep you safe. All I hold precious, he deems sacred. Trust him as I do—with your life and honor. He cannot speak, his tongue having been taken from him for no fault of his own, but he understands English well and some little Welsh and French. May God go with you, lady, and protect you, as will Selig.

Sir Hugh fitz Alan

Pondering the letter, Meghan wondered how Hugh had come by such a man and why Selig offered him such loyalty. A scowl puckering her forehead, she met Selig's worried gaze. She smiled and held out her hand.

"Welcome, Selig, and may you serve me as you would your lord."

As he took her hand in his massive fist, his grip amazingly gentle, his face split into a huge grin.

Chapter 16

The morning of March 22, 1282, Eve of Palm Sunday, dawned cold and foggy at Ainsleah, but the mists burned off by noon, leaving the day clear and warm. It was a spring day that lured the castle-bound inhabitants outside into the fresh air.

Sighing, Hugh shoved aside the parchment he had been studying and, standing up, yelled for more ale. He stretched until his bones cracked, his arms clasped above his head, then strolled to the narrow window where he could see the mountains of Wales, their peaks still capped with snow. Muffled sounds came to him—the yell of villein to oxen, women laughing as they did the laundry in the ward, a page's cry as he was upset from his horse while tilting at the quintain. Hugh smiled at the laughter of the other pages and the oath of the squire. He heard the pounding of hooves a second time, the thud of a lance on wood, the *whoosh* as the weighted end swung about to knock the page from the saddle. Breathing in, Hugh imagined he could smell the rising sap and odor of freshly turned earth. He longed to be riding across his land, to be on campaign with Edward, anywhere but in the drudgery of bookwork.

Sir Godfrey Marwood watched Hugh. With his wasted leg and lurching walk, Godfrey understood how it was to be shackled to an unpleasant task when earth and spring called. He had known Hugh for a long while and had served Hugh's father. He had choosen to follow the bastard son rather than stay with the widowed lady. It was

Godfrey who had trained Hugh, had cursed him for clumsiness, had demanded perfection of skills already per-
fected. He had ridden with Hugh to his first tourneys,
celebrated with him when Hugh won prizes, derided him
as a weak-wristed woman when he lost. He had shared
Hugh's grief at his father's death and understood his guilt.

Godfrey had used work as a balm for Hugh's wounds,
driving them both to a point of exhaustion that allowed
no thought or brooding. He had watched Hugh emerge a
man, quieter and stronger, his scars well hidden. Godfrey
had come with him to Ainsleah and had worked with him
to make the small estate the finest in the Marches. He had
labored beside Hugh like a villein. It was at a tourney,
fighting for funds to put into the land, that he had broken
his leg. He had stayed at Ainsleah, managing it when
Hugh was gone to follow Edward. If any man knew Hugh
fitz Alan, it was Godfrey; and he bore him the love he
would have given a son.

Sighing, Godfrey arranged the parchments with their
lists of revenues, acreage, produce, and livestock; taxes
owed and paid; the number and names of each villein and
his family; the work week owed; the land used; rents and
other profits; the long list of debts. The remodeling of
Hugh's private chamber had cut into the returns and ways
had to be found to replace them. More land had to be
cleared and planted. The number of livestock had to be
increased. Godfrey silently cursed the Welsh wench who
drove Hugh to make such expenses, then forgot her in his
figuring.

There is profit in wool, he thought, then frowned.
Hugh hated sheep. Godfrey didn't like them either, but
the coffers were low and the wool the Flemings demanded
would fill them. Godfrey considered Hugh's suggestion
of raising destriers. The profits there were more uncertain
and it would be years before there would be a return.
Still, he though—since horses appealed to him, too—if I
agree, mayhap he will consider sheep to carry us until the
horses prove themselves.

Godfrey nodded to a maid who brought ale and looked
at Hugh, who was still gazing out the window. "My

lord,'' he said, ''we've drink to ease your agony while you labor.''

Turning, Hugh leaned against the wall. He accepted a goblet from the maid and grimaced at his bailiff. ''I must be daft,'' he commented. ''Why should I want a wife when I have you to nag me about my responsibilities?''

''Because, although I manage your estate, tend your wounds when vast Selig hasn't managed to kill you, aye, even run your household, there is one wifely duty I would balk at—even if you paid me enough, and you don't. Try as I would, I could never present you with an heir.''

Laughing, Hugh shook his head. ''Nor, although I love you, do you appeal to me.''

His face darkening as he thought of the woman he wanted, Hugh glanced back out the window and shrugged. ''Well, the sooner taken up, the sooner done.''

The hoofbeats of a hard-pressed horse on the draw-bridge drew his attention. The sound ceased abruptly and was followed by shouts and curses. He could hear no words beyond his own name called in urgent pleading. When he raised his head, Godfrey saw exaltation in his eyes. ''It begins!'' Hugh stated.

Godfrey lifted an eyebrow. ''What does?''

''War with Wales—and this time Edward will finish it!''

Striding back to the table, he lifted his goblet, his eyes shining silver. ''Drink with me, old friend,'' he ordered. ''To the woman soon to be mistress of Ainsleah!''

Godfrey raised his goblet. He had tried to argue Hugh away from his passion for a next-to-dowerless wench, cit-ing the need for funds, but Hugh had only set his jaw. When Godfrey saw Hugh's torment, he cursed Meghan ab Owen. When Hugh's face grew soft at the thought of her, Godfrey could only pray Hugh would one day have her. ''May the Holy Mother and all the saints bring her to him,'' he whispered before joining Hugh in his toast.

A smile lingered about Hugh's mouth as he turned to the young squire who stumbled into the hall, the men of Hugh's household in a torrent after him. The squire wore the badge and blue of Mortimer. His face was crimson with exertion and importance, his words tumbling over themselves as he kneeled before Hugh. Pushing him onto a stool, Hugh handed the squire a goblet of ale. "Drink this and compose yourself. You babble like a babe to his dame's pap."

The squire gulped the ale, then breathed in deeply, trying to calm his shuddering lungs. All eyes were on him and his chest swelled with importance. "Tell me who you are, beyond a man of Mortimer's," Hugh finally demanded.

"Edmund Audley, my lord," the squire answered, his adolescent voice cracking.

"You say the Welsh have risen. When, where, how many, and who leads them?"

The squire straightened. "I don't know," he admitted. "Montgomery is under seige and Lord Stanmore sent me out under darkness. He would have you join him, bringing your men."

Hugh lifted an eyebrow. "He would have me join him in his trap? What purpose would that serve? And he would have me strip Ainsleah, leaving it open to save Mortimer's estates?" Shaking his head, Hugh walked to the window. "I swore Mortimer no oaths!" Turning, he found Edmund Audley more composed. "Is it Davyd who leads them?"

The squire squinted in surprise at the guess. "So 'tis said, but 'tis also said Llewelyn joins him."

"What castles are under seige and which have fallen?"

Edmund's chin shook and he gulped back sudden tears. "Flint, Rhuddlan and Hope, under seige, my lord. 'Tis said Hawarden fell and Roger Clifford is taken."

Hugh gnawed his lip. "Then the rising is still in the north, but 'twill spread. Did you see any of the Welsh on the road?"

The squire's voice quavered with the realization of what he had seen, with the memory of Welsh pipes and voices lifted in war song. "Aye, my lord, I hid many times and there were hundreds together. They spare no one, but are killing, looting, and raping like wild beasts."

Hugh's smile was grim. "Aye, 'tis but a part of war the bards sing about and afore 'tis done, we'll do the same. Do you know where Edward is?"

"At Devise, Sir Hugh."

"Aye, the king passes half his year in the west, but the rising finds him halfway across England! Did Stanmore send him a messenger with word?"

"Aye, and he made it through the lines with me."

Hugh grinned. "You're fortunate to come to me; Edward does not like bad news. Are you to go to others?"

"Ellesmere, Chirk, and Dinas Bran."

"Go to the kitchens. Ralph Ramsden will get you a fresh horse. Tell those you see that I go to Edward, if they wish to join me. I'll wait at Oswestry until dawn, no longer, if 'tis not in Welsh hands. If they are all under seige, come to me there. There is nothing you can do at Montgomery but be another gut to feed, even if you break back through the lines. If Mortimer should question you later, you've my word and protection. Now go, I've plans to make."

Hugh watched the squire leave. In a few moments war had ceased to be a game of ballad and gallantry to Edmund Audley and had become the thing of blood and suffering it was. Hugh shrugged away his compassion, knowing it was something many men never learned until they met their own deaths. Godfrey's gaze was on him, and Hugh sighed, gnawing his lip. "'Tis best I go to Edward. He will know how to use me and I would be of no use here, beseiged or running through the Marches like a hare pursued by hounds."

Hugh hesitated, then began to talk as he paced. "I can leave you Humphrey, two squires, and five bowmen. The rest go with me. 'Twill leave you short, but there is no help for it. You can use the women. I doubt the Welsh will try long for Ainsleah, if at all, when they learn I'm not here. There are bigger fish who've done them more insult. Bring in the villeins and the livestock. Leave nothing outside, even if you have to burn it. Put the men on four-hour watches, alternating with women if you have to. Check the weapons, but I think there are arrows and bows enough to arm the more proficient wenchs. Start rationing. We've supplies enough, but rationing will convince the villeins of the seriousness of their plight. The roof is still damp, but if there is no rain in three days, wet it down.''

Pausing, Hugh became aware that Godfrey was regarding him with an amused smile. Hugh grinned back. "Aye, I need tell you nothing. I'm like a virgin telling a whore the ways of men.''

Reaching out, Godfrey grasped Hugh by the shoulder. "I will pray for you," Godfrey whispered and Hugh strolled from the hall, eagerness in his long stride.

Stopping on the stair, Hugh watched the activity in the ward. His thoughts took him back into battle. The odor teased his nostrils—the hot scent of blood, of excrement discharged in death or panic, the smell of vomit. The clouds of flies attracted by death, the buzzing of them trapped in his helmet, feeding on his sweat, tickling already abrased skin. The clunk of weapon on weapon, the thrum of arrows in flight, and the thump of them sinking into flesh. The moans, screams, and sobs of the wounded, the frightened, the berserk. All assaulted his brain. Hugh again felt the flow of sweat stinging his eyes, blinding him, the chafing of soaked cloth against skin rubbed raw from his baldric, his helmet, the weight of his hauberk, the numbness of a body and mind pushed to total exhaustion. His feet remembered the feel of blood-soaked earth, slick with gut and brain, the gift of the dead and dying.

All the battles he had fought condensed in his mind to the motion of wielding his sword at the end of arms long since numb, from earliest dawn until the dark was too deep to distinguish friend from foe.

His mouth twisted into a wry smile. "Aye, and the foe of one battle will ofttimes be the friend of the next!''

Shaking himself, Hugh drove away the memories. He started down the stairs, shouting instructions to his men, giving a command to Ralph Ramsden, creating order from chaos as he prepared to go to war.

The lazy feathers of snow that had fallen the night before had changed to a light rain, almost a mist. It hid the surrounding mountains and obscured the far reaches of the narrow valley down which the Welsh rode.

Meghan pulled her hood closer and tried to adjust her cloak over her hands. She was momentarily startled when Selig reached up and wrapped it snugly about her. Then she smiled her thanks. Selig had been with her for nine months, from the first days of March to this eleventh day of December 1282. He was unobtrusive but always there, sleeping next to her at night, walking at her left stirrup through the day as the hound Rhys did on her right. His presence had become such a part of her that she felt a sense of uneasiness when he was absent. Although he had come to her on horseback, he preferred to walk, one hand on her stirrup, the other swinging his huge battle-ax.

Shivering, Meghan cursed Edward for taking the campaign into winter, and herself for her stubbornness. It was all that held her with the army. She thought of Cleitcroft, of fire and food, warmth and dryness, a place away from all that war had come to mean to her.

Even riding with her father five years ago had not prepared her for this war. Songs and ballads did not describe the boredom and weariness of long days spent in the saddle or in seige, the nights spent on a hard bed of earth surrounded by raucous, brawling, blood-sated men. They did not tell of the wailing of women, the moans of wounded men, the sight of slain children. She had learned to avert her eyes from the bodies lying so incongruously among the ragged daisies in pastures or on hillsides covered with nettles and buttercups. She had learned to close her ears. The dead would be buried or would rot. The women might know rape again—and perhaps death. The wounded would either die or live to breed more sons for war. There was little she could do.

And the ballads also had not told of the waiting. Since the time she had been a child, she had waited in her home for her men to return. There, the habits of life had lulled her anxiety. The dawn-to-dusk activity had given little time to brood. There, she had not been within the sounds of battle. She had not been forced to sit within sight of war, her only companions a man who could not speak and a huge dog who whined in an attempt to comfort her. She had not had to try to keep sight of her father within the battle and she had not looked for a tall knight, a bar sinister on his shield, among the English.

She had not yet seen Hugh, but Meghan knew she would one day. She only prayed he would not be among the dead, and as she prayed, her resolve grew with her fear. However she found him, she would not be the woman to take him home—to wash his corpse or to live with him. The fear she bore was enough; to love him would take more than she could give.

With the cries and screams, the stench, the waiting, had come hate. It was a hate that seemed to have settled into her very bones, giving her strength yet sapping her, leaving her weak with a need for rest, comfort, a place to hide, for strong arms offering refuge. She hated the English for what they would take from her, and she hated Hugh even as she realized he was as much a pawn as she was. She hated it all—the damp, dust, marches, battles, the dead and the living. But her father and Hugh held her there in a way she could not understand.

Meghan shivered again, more from memories than from cold. It had been a summer of dust that sank into the skin, dust constantly aroused by the masses of men and horses. And of victory. Llewelyn now traveled south to take advantage of it, leaving Davyd and a part of the army in the north.

Tilting her face to the mist, Meghan wondered how much farther it was to Orewin Bridge and Llewelyn. He had ridden ahead with a few men, arranging to meet them at the Yrfor River. Meghan glanced back at the long line of horsemen and archers behind her, then forward to her father with Anyon and Rhys near his stirrups. She frowned at his broad back.

Ab Owen seemed to have regained his lost vigor, but it was a false strength. His arm swung with the old power. He showed no fatigue when younger, lesser men fell in their steps. But he no longer fought for love of battle or to drive alien feet from Wales.

He, too, searched for a bar sinister. Only Hugh's death would return his daughter to him and only his own would free her. Ab Owen went into each battle seeking the glorious death demanded by all Welshmen. He met the enemy with an animosity and recklessness that had not been his before. The enemy had become a fickle lover who denied him the death he craved. And, as with a scornful lover, frustration had turned him bitter. He moved in a solitude that neither his daughter nor Llewelyn could penetrate.

For all his grief and fatigue, Llewelyn, the Pendragon, led them well. But Meghan knew he, too, believed them destined to lose. He knew that the zeal of his people could hold only so long against the superior strength and numbers of the English. Edward had not only a country six times larger from which to draw troops but also the mercenaries of Gascony. He had enough supplies to carry him through a winter campaign which would only decimate a barren land blocked by seige. Llewelyn knew he could not win, but he fought a battle that would be long remembered. He fought so that his name and deeds would not be wiped from the minds of men. And he fought as a man who knew death awaited him, a death not sought but one accepted as a sacrifice due his people, one which would free him from the sight of the Welsh destruction.

Meghan's mouth drew tight. Aye, she thought, the English will win when all is done, but they'll not be able to say 'twas without a struggle. They'll not say we cringed or accepted their ignoble treaties easily. They'll not say we cowered. Aye, we are a stubborn, stiff-necked people, a thorn in Edward Longshank's royal arse!

Hugh sat easily in his saddle, studying the land before him through the screen of trees and underbrush. The low valley widened out from the narrow gulch of the Yrfor River through which the Welsh would come, then closed again at its lower end where Hugh was positioned. The men of Robert Estrange waited to close the trap when the Welsh entered. Low mists of morning had lifted and a light snow swirled with rain, melting as it settled on the waiting men.

One part of Hugh's mind heard the quiet, desultory conversation around him; the other continued with his thoughts. The scouts had reported that Llewelyn rode with the Welsh. They could only guess at his purpose in the area of Buith and assumed he had come to raise South Wales and take advantage of the death of Roger Mortimer, who had been in charge of military operations there. If so, Hugh told himself, 'twould be a gamble any man would take, though a gamble to be lost.

Briefly, Hugh wondered if ab Owen and his daughter rode with the Welsh prince, but he drove the hope away. The intrusion of a woman into a man's thoughts could kill him. He would find her one day, he knew. He shifted in the saddle, sighing. Around him were the sounds of men in ambush—the muted clank of a weapon, a quiet oath for silence, whispers followed by a raucous laugh cut short.

A frown creased Hugh's forehead, a sense of anger and futility haunting him as he thought of the men he fought. He remembered the friends—and the enemies—he had among those who rode toward him, men honest and direct in their camaraderie or animosity, men with a zest for war or a woman, men with a berserk desire for life and no fear of death. When Edward would finally decimate the Welsh and force on the remainder a foreign way of life, something superb would pass from the world.

The whispering around him suddenly increased, then stopped abruptly, a pall of expectant silence falling, broken only by the snort of an ill-trained destrier. Fear and exhilaration, panic and expectation became tangible, settling over them, pressing against them.

Hugh stood in his saddle, searching the entrance of the valley, and saw a ghost army emerge from the swirling snow. Drooping banners shone deep purple and white horses were dulled to a pale, shimmering gray. He sat back, thinking only of Godfrey Marwood's instructions, which had rung in his head through the endless years of his training. His mind and body became an extension of his weapons, his total being an instrument honed for the death of others and his own survival.

The blare of a horn ripped Meghan awake and she jerked her horse to a halt, holding it firmly as it stumbled. Her eyes grew frantic as she searched the valley floor and the forest rising in steep slopes on all sides. She could see nothing—then gasped as an arrow struck a man beyond her father, slanting downward to pin him to the saddle. Ab Owen turned and yelled something she could not hear. She whirled her horse to go to him, but he waved her into the forest. Indecisive, she stared at him, then Selig grabbed her bridle and forced the animal through the confusion of men and horses.

Turning back, Meghan's gaze clung to her father, foreboding gripping her as he watched until she reached safety, his eyes seeming to etch her features forever on his memory. The knowledge of death shone in his eyes until the underbrush hid him from view.

A tree limb slapped her and Meghan crouched low as Selig half led, half pulled her horse up the steep hillside. The sounds of the battle raging in the valley came to her above Selig's grunts of urgency, above her palfrey's harsh breathing and the sound of its hooves as it scrabbled for purchase on earth slick with moldy, half-rotted leaves.

Meghan did not raise her head again until Selig halted her horse. He helped her dismount, holding her until she steadied, then they sat down in the shelter of an overhanging rock. Curling herself into the crook of Selig's arm, her head against his chest, she tried to block out the raging clamor of war. He pulled his cloak over her bare head, her hood having been lost in the flight up the hill.

The wolfhound whined, his ears pricked, torn between loyalty to his mistress and a desire to join the battle for which he had been bred. Meghan drew him down next to her, soothing him, and let her mind wheel free as she had learned to do, willing herself into the security of sleep.

Dusk had fallen when she woke. She started up, confused and searching for Selig. She started to cry out, then remembered where she was and why. Fighting down panic, she wrapped her arms around the uneasy dog and hushed his soft howl. Tilting her head, she heard the shout of a man and the shriek of a woman, cut short. The wind whipped a swirl of snow toward her and with it came a harsh male laugh and an English oath. Meghan breathed in deeply to calm her pounding head. Jumping up, she took three steps down the hillside. Abruptly she stopped, clenching her fists until the nails bit into her palms. Standing there, she battled her own panic and fear for her father, then relaxed; there was nothing she could do. If he lived, she would find him. If not, he had found the death he craved. Selig was out there and he would return. Until then, she could only wait.

Hearing the whisper of cloth on bark and the growl in Rhys's throat, she stiffened, stepping into a shadow, the dog following her. Selig stepped into the small clearing. His features were stark and his eyes, filled with frustration at his muteness, searched hers, trying to tell her something.

Meghan touched his cheek. "They—the English—they won," she stated.

He nodded, sorrow etching his face.

"My father?" she asked.

Selig shrugged, spreading his hands to indicate he did not know; Meghan saw he did not believe ab Owen would have even tried to escape. Nor did she. He was dead. Her face was impassive as she sighed and shrugged, a faint, accepting smile at the corners of her mouth. "I'll not mourn," she whispered. "'Twould not be what he would want."

Then, suddenly, sorrow assaulted her, doubling her over, ripping sobs from her. Selig held her against him, supporting her, muffling her wails in his cloak. As quickly as it had come, Meghan's manifestation of grief ended and she drew back. She wiped the tears away with the back of each hand and lifted her face. "I'll have his body," she stated.

Selig shook his head in vehement refusal.

Meghan's features held only determination. "Selig, I will go down and find him and take him home!"

She lifted her chin, though her lips trembled. "I beg you, Selig, come with me or I will go alone."

He studied her a long moment, then nodded. The knuckles of his huge hand gleamed white as he gripped his battle-ax. He helped her mount her horse and Meghan looked down at him, the grief in her eyes eclipsed by unexpected exultation.

"But Llewelyn escaped them!" She laughed.

Hugh leaned against his destrier, his body numb and
aching. Shaking his head to clear half-deafened ears, he
accepted a flask of whiskey from a hand stained rust with
blood. After gulping the liquid down, he handed back the
flask. The alcohol stung his mouth and throat, which were
raw from the deep, sharp cries of battle, and burned away
his nausea. Wiping a dribble from his chin, he stared at
the dark circles beneath his own fingernails.

Mist had settled over the field, shrouding the corpses
that appeared slightly flattened, as though they already
sought to press themselves back into the earth from which
they had sprung. The torches of the men-at-arms reflected
light from the fog and touched with a gleam of gold the
scattered, discarded weapons of the dead and the knives
in the hands of the wandering men. They searched for the
wounded, whom they would release from suffering, and
for the dead who had not yet been stripped of valuables.

Accepting the whiskey once more, Hugh's eyes strayed
over the scene and the forest beyond as he half listened
to Robert Estrange speak of the ambush's success, of the
men's anger at missing Llewelyn. A shadow emerged
from the hillside and Hugh squinted. He watched,
unaware he was holding his breath, as the figure mate-
rialized into a massive man, a woman on horseback, and
a huge dog. He didn't hear the wondering oath behind
him as the woman dismounted. She took a torch from an
English archer, who stared at her and stepped back,
almost tripping as he crossed himself.

Meghan stared at the carnage with horror, unaware of
the men who watched her with awe and lust. There
seemed to be thousands of dead. Bodies, half or fully
naked, lay all around her. The snow that fell on the still-
warm bodies melted, not hiding their wounds, but the
chill and wet concealed the odor, making the scene
unreal, a gigantic, hideously staged passion play. Meghan
shuddered and bent, turning over a corpse, ignoring the
shattered bone and flesh where an arm had been. Selig
moved with her, holding the torch, helping only when a
body resisted her. This was something she had to do
alone. Soon, she became numb. She forgot that the dead
had once been alive and laughing, loved by women, chil-

dren, parents. She no longer recognized faces or put names to features. She moved undirected, dead to everything but her purpose. She did not feel the wolfhound move from her and his whining came as a distant buzz to her ears.

Jerking when Selig touched her, she dropped the leg she held. Following his gaze, she saw the dog nuzzling something, a whimper in his throat, then he raised his head in a howl that lifted the hair of all who heard. Near him, the impish face of Rhys stared back at her with white, unseeing eyes and a few steps beyond lay Anyon, also dead. Between them lay Gavin ab Owen.

As if in a nightmare Meghan walked to her father and knelt beside him. His mouth was twisted in a wolfish grin that bared his long teeth. One eye was half closed; the other strained in its socket to see something behind him, but Meghan could see no wound. Her fingers traced the cold, damp skin of his face. Her lips moved in a prayer that emerged half a curse, half a sob. Her hand slipped under his head to hold it from the earth and she felt the sharp bone of shattered skull, the softness of ruptured brain. Her head drooped to his chest, her body shaking with harsh, tearless weeping.

Purpose gained control over her tears, but still she knelt, unwilling to release the body of her sire. Then she felt the pressure of eyes on her. Carefully, she drew her hand from underneath her father, unaware that she wiped her fingers on her kirtle, and lifted her head.

A huge, dark horse stood before her. On his back sat a knight in full armor. His form loomed against the torchlight reflected on the swirling snow. Her body aching, Meghan stood, knowing him long before Selig lifted the torch to expose his features. A sense of helplessness, of being in a web she had so long avoided, held her rooted to where she stood. She was past caring.

Hugh watched as she rose, a part of him noting that she was dressed as she had been at Conway but for the cloak she wore—his cloak. Her uncovered hair gleamed black and gold, framing her face, and the heavy braids fell to her hips. As she lifted a hand to warily push back a tendril, he caught a glimpse of small breasts pushing against the tunic and of a wide gold band about her bicep, prizes for which any man would kill. The face she lifted was stricken with grief and blotched with tears. Her eyes were huge and her mouth looked bruised, as though by passion. She looked beaten down with despair and sorrow, defeated at last—and accepting it.

A surge of desire rose in Hugh and with it an urge to hold and comfort her. Her grief seemed a part of him, bursting through his weariness. And with the need to protect and console came a lust so potent it shook him. He ached with it. Leaning forward, he held a hand out to her, his voice hoarse as he spoke her name.

Meghan's gaze focused on him. Her back straightened and she lifted her head, gathering strength. She waved a hand over her father. "Did you do this thing?" she demanded.

Hugh shook his head. "I did not see him here afore."

Her eyes were impassive, measuring his words and finding them true. Her chin lifted. "I would take him home," she stated, "and his men with him."

He had thought that might be her purpose and his gaze narrowed. "I would have you go to Ainsleah."

Her jaw tightened. "I would take him home! I only ask that Selig go with me."

To deny her would be to lose her forever, Hugh knew. He considered the journey she would have to make and realized he would have to gamble on Selig and on Meghan's knowledge of her mountains. "I gave you Selig to keep. Take your father, if you must, but I cannot spare men or mounts for his men."

Meghan nodded. "Thank you, my lord," she whispered. Her eyes did not leave Hugh as she touched Selig. "We will take their hands, Selig, and their heads. 'Twill be enough."

Hugh's belly lurched. "That is a custom long dead, lady," he protested.

Meghan's lips quirked. "Is it? And what would you have me do? My sire will have them with him in death as they were here, at his right and his left." Spreading her hands, she shrugged. "Wherever it is he has gone."

Hunching his shoulders, Hugh swallowed and nodded. He urged his horse two steps forward until its breath blew hot on Meghan's chilled face. "I will meet you at Valle Crucis, lady," he told her, "in three weeks time."

Meghan's eyes dropped and her voice was neutral. "If you would have it so, my lord."

His mount moved closer. "Lady, you will be there!"

Her gaze returned to his and Hugh read her refusal there. His tone hardened. "You will be there. You are now mine by conquest, by Edward's word. If you are not there, if I have to come to Cleitcroft for you, 'twill be your people who bear my fury. If you think to hide behind your walls, I will hang a Welshman from the crossbeams of the church each day until you give over. And any Welshman will serve—man, woman, or infant. Do you hear me, lady?"

The determination in his features made Meghan lower her gaze and nod.

"Do you believe me, lady?"

She didn't, couldn't, yet she did not dare doubt him. "Aye, my lord," she whispered. "I will be there."

Hugh relaxed. "Will you stay the night with me, lady, to rest? I'll not take now what will be mine by right three weeks hence."

"No, 'twill be safer to travel through the night," she answered, her eyes mocking. "There are English about."

A corner of Hugh's mouth lifted. "If you would have it so."

A sudden shout down the valley interrupted them and they turned, Hugh with curiosity, Meghan with fear. A troop of horsemen galloped over the battlefield, heedless of the dead. Their leader bore a human head on the point of his lance. Meghan forced a whisper from between stiff lips. "Who is it?" she asked, then repeated the question louder.

Instead of answering, Hugh bent and drew her up to stand on his stirrup. He watched as she squinted in the torchlight at the grisly trophy. Her eyes widened in recognition and she moaned, her head dropping to his shoulder. Holding her close, he absorbed her shudders of inexpressable mourning until they became his own. He waited, knowing there were no words of comfort he could offer, no consolation for her final loss. His hands moved over her, caressing, as the shaking gradually ceased and Meghan lifted her tear-streaked face to his.

"Who is it," she asked, "the man who brought the pendragon down?"

Hugh brushed back a tendril of hair from her damp cheek. "Stephan of Frankton, a lieutenant of infantry."

Meghan's laugh was bitter. "A lieutenant, a leader of men-at-arms, brings down the prophesied of Merlin and bears his head on a lance. And we laughed at the audacity of the English when we heard it said that they thought God with them! Indeed, He must be with them, for He has, in truth, deserted Wales!" Her eyes dropped from his. "I would leave now."

He touched the silken waves of her hair and held his palm against her cheek, his thumb under her chin as he lowered his mouth to hers in a brief, gentle kiss. "Stay with me the night, little one," he whispered. "Then on the morrow let me send you to Ainsleah with your father. We can bury him there. When this war is done, we will take him to Cleitcroft. But stay the night with me. I would comfort you."

Meghan shook her head and Hugh reluctantly lowered her to the ground. He watched as she picked up a large, bulging bundle wrapped in Anyon's cloak. "Go with God," he whispered.

"And you, lord," she responded. She held his gaze briefly, then turned and began to walk north, a slim figure moving easily through the carnage, followed by a massive man leading the horse that carried her father's body.

Chapter 17

Meghan gazed down the hill to the monastery of Valle Crucis. From there, over a hundred years before, the abbot Enoch had run away with a nun, only to return a short time later, humbled and repentent. It was there she was to meet the man who would hold her in perpetual bondage. Had Enoch, in his brief freedom, looked longingly back to the security of his holy service as she would look back to freedom?

Sighing, she tried to reconcile the peaceful scene with her purpose there. The whitewashed abbey's walls gleamed silver from sun reflected off snow. The sound of its bells, ringing for Nones, drifted across the valley. The very peacefulness of the scene seemed a deception, promising peace and comfort. To her it was a snare set and waiting.

All she really felt was the ache of fatigue. The journey from Orewin Bridge had been long and hard, harder than anything she had done before. It had been a seemingly endless game of hide-and-seek with the English, a fight against the snow and cold. Even her mountains had tried to thwart them.

They had traveled by night and hidden by day, until they were deep in Welsh-held territory. They had shared their bodies' heat, the mute man, the grieving woman, and the huge hound all huddled together in a cave or under overhanging trees. Selig had led the way through unfamiliar terrain, along any path pointing north, over untracked country when they could not find a path. They had walked along the ridges, over rock-strewn slopes, along the edge of cliffs that dropped hundreds of feet to certain death if one was careless enough to slip.

Brush had whipped their faces. Thorns had torn through their clothes and skin. Both boulders and small pebbles had twisted Meghan's ankles. Rocks had torn her knees and laid bare her elbows when she fell. They had hidden a dozen times when English voices came too near, Selig's hand over the nose of the horse, Meghan's clasping the collar of the hound.

Why the horse did not do the wise thing and die, Meghan did not know, but she thanked God he did not. He floundered over trail and through brush, often falling on knees cut and swollen beyond the size of Selig's huge fists. He carried Meghan as she clung to him, her face inches from that of her father. He went where only desperate humans or mountain goats could go.

It was a nightmarish journey that had stripped her courage to the bone. It had tested her will and proved it dauntless. It was a journey only a woman uncommonly resolute and a man immeasurably faithful could have made.

Cleitcroft had tested her further.

Meghan had been greeted by grief and fear at the sight of Gavin ab Owen. She had stared at her people, so numb she could not, for a moment, grasp the reason for their keening. Hands had reached to her to offer comfort. Words meant to console had been flung to recoil from the wall of her sorrow. Pleas for word of men six days dead at Orewin Bridge had echoed against silence, building a pity she could not accept, knowing it would break her. Nor had she had the energy to answer. She had stood, head down, clinging to the last of her strength until the barrage of questions had ceased. When she had lifted her head, tears had wet her face. "Llewelyn is dead, his head impaled on an English pike," she had whispered. "Wales is lost, though we fight on. Do not look for your men to return. Few will."

The crowd had parted as she stumbled up the steps to the keep, her back straight, determination that she not

break holding her to her feet as she went into Yedda's
arms.

She had slept for a day and a half, but her mind had
refused to slumber, living over and over Llewelyn's degradation, her father's death. She had seen Hugh again as
he laid a claim she dared not refuse. Meghan's legs had
walked on a journey already completed and her lips had
formed protests already spoken. Only the need to use the
garderobe drove her from her pallet. Only the need to
bury the dead kept her on her feet.

Meghan washed ab Owen and wrapped him in his
crimson cloak. The head of Rhys she placed under his
right elbow, Anyon's under his left. His sword she
clasped over his chest and the hands of Rhys and Anyon
she put over his feet, where they had held to his stirrups
in life.

After the earth closed over Gavin ab Owen, her people's demands pressed in. She had but a few days to prepare them for survival in her absence, for any and all
contingencies. To leave them was to violate the trust put
on her; to stay was to gamble with their lives. And there
were so many contingencies. Even in her fatigue, she
thought of Caradoc and wondered where her half brother
was. His absence was as menacing as his presence would
be.

As she went about her duties, Hugh's words went with
her. She searched for a means to escape him and found
none. At night, her mind, thwarting sleep, circled like a
squirrel in a cage, not believing his threat but not daring
to challenge it. Beneath her fear and hate was a need for
the comfort and warmth he could give her. Under a need
to stay with her people was the desire to pass her burdens
to him, to surrender them as she would her body and
accept the sanctuary he offered. Beneath her pride's
refusal to yield to any man was her need and love for
him.

Now the bells of Valle Crucis threw their last notes
against the hard, cold sky and grew silent. The quiet they
left behind sounded as clearly as had their ringing.

Meghan shuddered as a small group of horsemen
appeared from the gates of the monastery, Hugh's banner

unfurled above them. The leader rode several paces in front, his horse forcing its way toward her through knee-deep snow. He was relaxed, his hair and face dark against a white world. Meghan's last hope, that he would not be there, slid into the pit of despair even as warmth enveloped her.

Turning, she looked at the mountains of Wales, their peaks forbidding to all strangers. Her gaze dropped to Yedda's tired, cold, pinched face. In front of the bulge of her belly rode her youngest child. Her older son sat proudly amid the baggage on a horse of his own. Meghan forced a smile at him and he grinned back from a face that could have been Rhys's, delighted at her attention and his adventure. Reluctantly, Meghan turned back to face Hugh, her hands unconsciously twisting in the reins, and she urged her horse forward.

Hugh watched the strange company. Selig, on foot, led a packhorse, on top of which perched a small boy. Behind them rode Yedda and her baby. Hugh's mouth twisted into a grin as he thought of what Edward would say if he could see the woman he wanted and the dowry she brought him—a pregnant wench, two brats, and a man who had once been his own. And Cleitcroft, of course, which no Englishman could hope to hold. Not yet.

His gaze shifted to Meghan and his love and need rose. Her ordeal was carved on her face, in the hollows of her cheeks, in the dark circles around her eyes. Her jaw was set with effort and her back was held erect by sheer will. Her eyes appeared even larger in the slenderness of her face and her gaze dropped as she stopped beside him.

Leaning over, Hugh drew his finger from the corner of her eye down her jaw and across her lips, a faint smile playing about his mouth. Briefly, he considered spending the night at Valle Crucis. Then, glancing at the sun, he decided that, pressing hard, they could be at Ainsleah soon after dark. He had waited too long to delay and he would not feel secure of his possession until she was in his home and in his bed. Having made his decision, he said, ''We go on.''

Hugh pushed them hard. By midafternoon heavy clouds had gathered across a sky that had dawned blue. A freezing wind teased through seams and gaps of clothing to find naked flesh.

Meghan rode in a stupor. The miles crawled by and the sun dropped with infinite slowness from the sky. It seemed as though the world moved past and they stood still. The fantasy of the earth in motion made her dizzy and her head ached as she tried to keep her eyes open.

Next to her, Hugh receded to a dark figure against a glowing sky. On the horizon the sun broke through the clouds and touched the snow with blue and gold, making the earth shimmer below her. The gold turned to orange as it danced into blue shadows cast by her mount, then brightened as it frolicked out again. The blue chased after the gold and darkened to purple, then all was black.

Catching her as she pitched forward, Hugh lifted her in front of him, her body weightless. Frightened, he looked into her pinched face. Lowering his head, he felt her breath stir against his cheek. Satisfied, his lips touched her forehead before he urged his horse to a faster pace.

The creak of a drawbridge, the drum of horse's hooves on wood, and shouted greetings penetrated Meghan's weary dreams. She stirred, murmuring protests, then drifted back to sleep. It was only when a torch was lifted, the light beating against her eyelids, that she roused and stared befuddledly down into a sea of faces. Instinctively she turned her face against Hugh's chest, closing away the light and clamor.

Hugh's proud whisper was soft in her ear. "My lady, this is Ainsleah. We're home!"

Fighting fatigue, Meghan straightened away from him. She forced a smile to the upturned faces and they responded with shouts to her health and welcome. Hugh introduced Godfrey and she focused on his grizzled, war-scarred face.

The gaze returning hers was noncommittal, the greeting formal. Meghan's reply sounded slurred as Hugh lowered her to the ground. Her feet touched earth that came up too fast. She stumbled, grabbing at Hugh's leg to right herself, and reached for the hand Godfrey offered. Meghan's fingers gripped desperately and she tried to smile, then whispered, "Help me!" His features swirled away as he caught her.

Godfrey stared into the face on his shoulder and ordered the people back to their beds. Relinquishing her to Hugh, he bit back his angry questions and followed Hugh up the steps to the keep.

Hugh kicked open his bedchamber door and laid Meghan on the bed. Gently, he removed her cloak. She muttered a protest and asked for Yedda. "She's with her brats," Hugh told her, "and I am able to play lady's maid. I will not rape you or even look on you. Not until the morrow!"

Meghan tried to get up, but he rolled her onto her stomach. She kicked out as Hugh pulled the bottom of her surcoat up and wrapped it around her arms and head, trapping her. He grabbed her flailing legs, removing her boots and hose. Holding her ankles, he jerked the surcoat off, her undertunic riding up with it to display a round bottom. Twisting, she tried to hit him and he laughed, drawing her undertunic back down. Meghan swung at him as he yanked the bedclothes up about her ears. He caught her wrists and leaned over. "You are more lively than I thought. Do you mean to tempt me, lady?"

Meghan glared at him. "Damn you!" she whispered. "I had forgotten you are such a swine! Aye, and but a part of one—the part which ruts, farts and—"

Hugh pressed a finger against her lips. "Tread carefully, lady," he cautioned. "You may forget yourself and say what you would regret!"

Eyes glinting, Meghan swallowed words of anger as Hugh laughed, running his finger lightly over her jaw. "Sleep well, lady," he told her, "for, by the saints, you'll not do so on the morrow!"

Meghan glowered as he closed the door, then fatigue replaced anger. Laying back, she surrendered to the bed's comforts and to sleep.

Hugh closed the door behind him and paused at the head of the stairs, a smile on his lips. When he had met Meghan at Valle Crucis, he had known she was exhausted. But he had also thought her resigned, all her spirit gone. The hauteur and courage that had attracted him had disappeared, leaving her empty. Without that, she would be but another beautiful, submissive woman. He had thought he had lost her.

Then she had fought back, her pride and will resurging despite her exhaustion. She would be no inert body to be taken without passion. His step was jaunty as he descended to the hall.

Godfrey was sitting at the table, two goblets and a pitcher before him when Hugh entered. Pouring wine, Hugh sat down opposite his steward, his feet up on a stool. He frowned, searching for a reason for Godfrey's disapproving mood. Godfrey returned his stare. Finally, Hugh shrugged, knowing his friend would explain his mood when he was ready, and he let his elation rise again.

"What think you of my lady?" he asked. "Think you she will make a proper mistress for me and Ainsleah?"

Godfrey's face did not alter and his voice was curt. "Ask me after she has had a week or two of rest, when her soul is back in her. You should have stayed at Valle Crucis."

Hugh's eyes narrowed, but he pushed aside his resentment. "Aye, I thought to, but I feared that I'd not be able to rouse her to ride on the morrow or to stand afore the priest the next day."

Godfrey scowled into his wine. "She is not well enough to be wedded or bedded, not yet."

Hugh frowned and straightened in his chair. "She will wed me on the morrow, and I'll bed her on the morrow, then she can rest. I've waited five years and more and I'll not delay now. Only when I have her before the priest, aye, and mine in my bed, can no one deny me of her."

Standing, Godfrey lifted his goblet. "Then I toast you now, my lord, and wish you health and happiness and many sons, for I'll not be here on the morrow to do you so!"

Hugh stared, trying to understand as Godfrey continued. "Methinks I'll not find it hard to find other employment, aye, and better pay. I'm known as an honest man and capable despite my injury. I'll not ask you for recommendation, nor would I take such. If asked why I left you, I'll but say I do not like the manner in which you treat your lady. There are gentle men yet who would understand me.''

Hugh's tone was incredulous, his words unconsciously cruel. "You would leave me after all these years because I would wed on the morrow and not three days hence? And you think to find another position, gimped as you are?''

Godfrey leaned over the table, his body off center as he supported himself on his sound leg. "Aye, I think to find another position and 'twas in your service I was injured. I care not when you take the wench, only how. I have watched you for five years, knowing she was at the root of your foul moods and excessive angers, aye, and I was ready to hate her for it. You asked me my opinion of her and I tell you this, I saw spirit and pride and great loss in her and the scars of an ordeal met and bettered! Now you have her and I'll not stay to see you destroy all that is fine in her. I'll not watch you turn her into a half-dead thing who does nothing but produce a brat a year for your precious Ainsleah!''

Hugh half rose, a protest on his lips, but Godfrey cut him short. "I am not done! You think of nothing but your prong seeking a warm, dark place to relieve itself. Aye, you waited five years but not chastely. There are bastards enough about the place carrying your proud nose. Now you have her, an object to be admired, shown off, and used when you feel the urge, with no thought or consideration. You would drop your seed into her as casually as you relieve yourself down the garderobe. Aye, use her, take her when she is too weak to fight! Grind her down now, my lord, afore she is able to give you battle. And when you've turned her into a dry husk of a thing, filled with nothing but dull resentment, cast her off. But I'll not be here to watch!''

Straightening, Godfrey looked at Hugh. "Aye, you would give her marriage, but 'tis for your own convenience. You can hold her no other way. You think to honor her, unwilling though she is, with the dubious privilege of bearing your brats and bastard name. And

with it you offer her more insult than ever your sire gave
your gentle mother when he made her his whore and gave
her his whelp.''

His face white, his body rigid, Hugh gripped the table,
fighting to control his rage. "If you were a whole man,
Godfrey Marwood, I would have your life for that!''

Godfrey laughed. "Would you, you piddling pup? Do
you think I taught you all the tricks learned by an old
dog? No man ever does. 'Tis wise to have a weapon
when the whelp turns, as they all do. So don't let my
gimp stay your hand.''

Hugh stared at the man who had replaced his father,
who had always stood by him. His fist smashed into the
table and he whirled to face the fireplace, his arms braced
against the mantel.

His words were a groan. "Ah, old friend, 'tis not that
way! I want her, aye, but at my side, not under my heel.
I want her to bear my children, not for heirs but to see
her bloom with them, a part of both of us. I need her,
Godfrey. Not as a slattern at my bidding, but as my wife!

"Aye, she is being forced against her will and she will
fight me, Godfrey, but 'tis a battle long between us and
of her choosing as much as mine. I will win, though I
swear to you, her defeat will not be bitter.''

Seeing the naked need in Hugh's face, Godfrey's
expression turned gentle. "Than wait, pup, a day or two
more, for the sake of the love you bear her.''

Hugh's eyes held his a moment, indecisive, then a
reluctant smile tugged at his mouth. "Aye, old friend,''
he agreed. "Because you ask it.''

Chapter 18

Refusing to open her eyes, Meghan snuggled deeper into the comfort of linen sheets and heavy robes, wrapped in a warmth she had not known for a long time.

Suddenly she jerked up, aware that she was in a strange room, and looked about the large, dimly lighted chamber. Rich tapestries covered the window slits and a thick rug in colors of gold, emerald, ruby, and sapphire lay over the rushes, a custom introduced to England by Queen Eleanor. Two chairs, each exquisitely carved, stood on either side of an empty tapestry frame near the large fireplace. In front of the hearth was a huge bearskin, its fur deep and soft. Against the far wall stood a wardrobe that had been carved in the design of the chairs. The bed Meghan lay in was deep and wide, its canopy covered with hangings to match the rug. It was a chamber a man would prepare for a beloved woman.

Meghan leaned back, her head still unsteady. Closing her eyes, she tried to remember how she had arrived there. She recalled Valle Crucis, a long ride with no end, and afterward, strong hands undressing her, Hugh's face above her.

When the door opened, Meghan jerked the covers up to her chin. But it was only Yedda, balancing a tray over the bulge of her belly. She closed the door with a swing of a hip and her intent face broke into a smile when she saw Meghan awake. "Ah, lady, we thought you would sleep the week away!"

Sitting up, Meghan asked, "Have I been sleeping long?"

Yedda set down the tray. "Three days and more. I woke you several times for broth and bread. Do you not remember?"

Shaking her head, Meghan eyed the boiled eggs, cheese, and apples on the tray as Yedda giggled. "Sir Hugh be storming about like a bull shut away from his favorite cow."

Frowning at the analogy, Meghan accepted a cup of ale and a peeled egg. "Tell me of Ainsleah," she ordered.

Yedda sat down on the edge of the bed, her face bright. "'Tis beautiful. Oh, not like Windsor or those other places we went with Lord Edward, not near so large. But 'tis clean and warm. There be seven fireplaces. Sir Godfrey says 'twas Sir Hugh's idea, that people need not be cold to work well. Sir Godfrey says—"

Irritated, knowing Yedda was comparing Ainsleah to Cleitcroft, Meghan interrupted. "How many towers?"

"Three, and it sits over a river. Sir Godfrey says it makes for a good defense; the men can cover all walls from each tower."

"I can see the advantage, addlepate," Meghan answered. "So could an infant! Who is this Godfrey?"

"Sir Hugh's steward. You met him when we arrived. He be a good man, methinks, and loyal to his lord. He likes my sons and did talk to me a bit. He asked of Wales and of my life afore. 'Twas Godfrey who asked Sir Hugh to delay the wedding. 'Tis said they did fight over it, a thing they ne'er do."

Meghan studied Yedda's blushing face, which clearly expressed hopes that Meghan doubted Yedda was even aware of yet. "And you think, mayhap, to bed Godfrey?" she asked scornfully. "Aye, mayhap to wed him? Rhys is not one month dead and you, slut, are thinking about another man?"

Yedda fought back tears, yet anger gave her courage. "Aye, and when I last had Rhys, 'twas but long enough to get another child and he was off again, following your sire with not a thought to me. I loved him with his happy, laughing ways. So did every other wench and there be bastards to prove it! Not all women be like you, lady. Some of us need someone to make us feel needed, to lean on. Aye, and a warm body to curl against in the night. 'Tis a comfort.''

Dropping her eyes, Yedda crumbled an eggshell between nervous fingers. "Not all of us be as you, lady, needing only yourself.''

Meghan studied her maid's averted face. The need Yedda spoke of stirred in her, but she pushed it back, unacknowledged. Her voice was soft as she asked for more ale.

They sat in silence until Meghan finished her meal. Sitting on the bed, her arms around her knees, she watched Yedda clean up. It was not, she decided, as much that Yedda required comfort as that she needed to bestow it. Though the younger woman, Yedda tried to mother Meghan, as she did everyone. When Meghan spoke, her voice was casual. "You say Sir Hugh is impatient?''

Yedda giggled. "Aye, he stomps about, cursing Godfrey and swearing that the guests will eat all the wedding feast long ere the bride awakes. He takes long rides—to cool his passion, he says—then returns angrier than before he left! He sent me to see if you be awake. He said there be time yet to wed today. I'll tell him you are up.''

Yedda started to the door, then turned back. "He bought you a wedding gown, lady,'' she said excitedly.

Meghan gave a mischievous smile. "I'll not wear it. My dowry is small, but my clothes are mine own! And, Yedda, tell my lord that I am still weak and must rest yet a while.''

Yedda stared at her then shrugged, knowing it was useless to argue. With Godfrey behind her, she could face Hugh, but there was no one to protect her from her mistress.

Meghan watched her leave before settling back to realize she was indeed drowsy. Hugh, she knew, would not come to pull her screaming from the bed, not with guests in the house. Closing her eyes, she drifted back to sleep, a small smile on her mouth.

Meghan stepped from the deep tub into a thick towel held by the waiting women, wives of the wedding guests. Their hands were unduly harsh as they wiped her and their comments were crude in a manner their husbands would not have recognized. Ann Clifford tweaked one of Meghan's small, rose-tipped nipples. "Would you not think Sir Hugh would choose a maid with paps larger than these, considering the size of the dowry?" she said.

"Mayhap," Elizabeth Grey stated, staring at Anne's ample chest, "he is aware that big-dugged women wear their tits about their waists after the first brat."

Anne glared at her. "Aye, but 'twould not be a problem plaguing you. I've seen more flesh on a hay rake."

Elizabeth shrugged. "Lord Grey says slim women give a better ride in the bedding."

Mary Berwick laughed, digging her fingers into Meghan's slim buttocks. "Then Sir Hugh will have a fine mare here, though there is little enough for a man to grip."

Anne's chuckle was forced. She was about to caution them to remember their own bridal nights, but the Welsh wench's proud face challenged her pity. "He'll fatten her, but 'twill be through *this* mouth," she said, yanking at Meghan's pubic hair.

"Aye," Elizabeth agreed. "That belly will bulge soon enough. And when she is full, he'll look elsewhere for pleasure—as do all men."

"He'll look for more than a comely wench to prong." Mary smirked. "Once he finds she is nothing but another slit, he'll have to look to Wales for the dowry!"

Sobering, Anne stared at Meghan, whose eyes shone dispassionate and proud as they gazed beyond the women. Suddenly ill at ease, Elizabeth giggled. "William did tell me he saw Sir Hugh leaving the miller's house this morning. And 'tis said the miller's daughter is comely, plump, and blond."

Anne frowned, remembering the brutal assault of her own wedding night. "Mayhap he thinks to assuage his lust that he might take his wife more gently."

Yedda met Meghan's eyes and saw a ghost of amusement in their green depths. She grinned back as Anne heaved herself up from drying Meghan's feet.

"Where are her clothes?" Anne asked.

Elizabeth nodded toward the bed. "There and I heard tell that Sir Hugh bought them for her, this one not having rags enough to stand afore the priest in. Too good they are, methinks, for a Welsh whore used to nothing better than untanned leather."

Anne fingered the rich cloth. "Aye, and she may as well enjoy them now. He'll not buy her anything else once he has her with a brat at her teat and one in her belly."

Gently picking up the soft undertunic, Anne turned, startled, when Meghan spoke. "I'll not wear those."

The women stared at her, then bombarded her with protests. Hiding a smile, Yedda savored the rare pleasure of seeing other women batter themselves against her mistress's stubbornness.

Meghan listened, her head tilted, her expression placid. A smile touched her mouth when they ceased their protests from lack of breath. "I'll not wear those. And if you insist, I shall scream. When my lord comes, I shall tell him of your rough handling of me, which I bear the marks to prove, and of your opinions of his choice of a wife."

She stared into each face. "While your spouse's opinions are no doubt yours, methinks they would be ill-pleased to share them with my lord." She surveyed their wary features. "Anything else to say?" she asked. "Then my maid will finish dressing me."

Yedda took an undertunic the color of new leaves from the wardrobe and pulled it over Meghan's head. The skirt was full, the long sleeves tight, the neck so low that it barely hid the rosy color of Meghan's nipples. Over it she dropped a surcoat of moss-green suede as soft as velvet. Its low, square neck was banded in embroidery of gold thread that repeated the pattern of the belt she wore. The band was repeated again at the cuffs of the wide-scooped sleeves, at the hem, and up the hip-high slits at front and back. Kneeling, Yedda fastened light green hose on Meghan's legs with garters at the knee, then buckled on suede shoes that matched the surcoat.

Satisfaction still softened Yedda's mouth as she painted a thin line of kohl on Meghan's eyelids and braided her silky hair a short three inches on either side of her face. Finally she stepped back, proud of her handiwork.

Meghan's voice was gentle as she thanked her maid and pressed a gold coin into her palm. Fighting back tears, Yedda impulsively embraced her mistress. Meghan's breath was desperate as she whispered, "Ah, Yedda, I wish I didn't have to do this thing!"

The maid swallowed her sobs, knowing tears would disgrace Meghan. When she released her, her mistress's features were calm. A smile curved Meghan's lips as she faced the other women. Her chin rose and her voice was mocking as she asked if they still scorned Welsh leather. Not waiting for a reply, she moved to the door, her back arrogant, her head proud, and began to descend the stairs to Hugh. The vows she was about to make would bind her physically to the man who waited for her, but she could still escape him, she told herself. No matter what he did to her body, no matter what her response, she would withhold the core deep inside her that could never be taken, only given, the gift that he wanted most.

Turning from Roger Grey and Harry Clifford, Hugh looked up the stairs and saw Meghan there, the other women clustered behind her. His throat tightened, then he noticed her dress and his eyes narrowed with rage. She met his gaze without flinching. All her fatigue was gone, replaced by hauteur and unyielding pride. Her eyes were clear and green. She was beautiful, proud, and barbaric.

Hugh felt his anger drain away, replaced by desire and triumph in his coming possession of her. A smile played about his mouth as he lifted his goblet to drink her a silent toast.

Her eyes shining in response, Meghan lowered her gaze briefly. When she lifted her eyes again, they were arrogant, all the mischief gone and only cold animosity remaining.

Godfrey Marwood laughed. "That one," he said, "you'll not break!"

Accepting the cloak his steward offered, Hugh tossed it over his arm. "Aye, but the saints know I shall bend her!"

He walked to Meghan and took her hand. He kissed it lightly and guided her down the remaining stairs. "My lady," he mocked, "the priest waits—as do I!"

His hands pressed against Meghan as he wrapped the cloak around her. To her they were like the bars of a cage closing in. The cloak seemed to wrap her in a life of its own, imprisoning her. For a second, darkness swirled and when it cleared the people pressing near had receded into shadowy figures among whom she walked untouched, unconcerned.

The village church was cold. Frosty breath rose to settle on the stone walls, condense and drip to the floor. The odor of stale incense and wet wool offended the nostrils. The acrid green and livid red glass of the two small windows cast light like bruises on the huddled figures of the guests.

The words of the rotund priest settled without meaning upon Meghan. A large droplet shimmered under his blue, bulbous nose, threatening to fall at any moment. Suddenly she realized he had stopped speaking and was looking at her. Hugh's hand tightened about hers and, disconcerted, she looked at him. His face, too, was expectant and apprehension creased his brow. Whispers rustled behind her. Hugh inclined his head toward the priest and Meghan followed his gaze.

The priest sniffed and repeated the words.

Meghan's voice was flat as she parroted him. "I, Meghan, daughter of Gavin ab Owen, take thee, Hugh fitz Alan, to be my wedded husband, to have and to hold, from this day forward, for better, for worse, for richer, for poorer, in sickness and health, to be bonny and buxom in bed and at board, till death do us part and thereto I plight thee my troth."

The priest's gaze moved to Hugh as he repeated the oath. The gold ring was warm from his hand against Meghan's thumb as he held it there before moving it on to each of her fingers one after the other, saying as he did so, "In the Name of the Father, of the Son, and of the Holy Ghost, I thee wed." He slid the ring up her wedding finger in a final, gentle gesture of possession.

Staring at the band, Meghan raised stunned eyes to him. He placed his hand against her cheek, his thumb under her chin. His mouth was tender on her unresponding lips. His beard tickled her chin.

Hugh was laughing as he lifted Meghan from before the altar. Congratulations buzzed about them. A man she knew was Godfrey Marwood spoke encouraging words into her ear before Hugh guided her to the church door and into the cheers of his people.

Meghan stood blinking against the bright light and let Hugh lead her to his horse. His laugh was exultant, his face victorious, as he lifted her to the animal's back and swung up behind her. Taking the bag of coins Godfrey offered with a blessing, Meghan tossed them to the excited children who darted under and in front of the destrier that Hugh turned toward Ainsleah. Her mouth ached with the effort to smile. With coarse jests and good humor, the guests fell in behind them.

The marriage feast was a haze to Meghan. She felt like a puppet responding to the countless toasts, each more vulgar than the last, only touching her lips to the goblet's edge. She leaned forward, attentive to words that made no sense. Smoke was thick and the smell of sweat heavy when the tables were at last pushed against the walls to clear the hall for dancing.

Rising, Hugh led Meghan into the first dance. His hand was firm, his step steady, and she smiled ruefully. He, too, had drunk little and she was thankful, though his purpose went counter to hers. After guiding her through several steps, Hugh led her down a tunnel of clasped hands and arched bodies, then he kissed her before Roger Grey could claim her first. Hugh's laughing face belied his concerned eyes as they followed her swaying figure.

Feeling lost and clumsy in a sea of drunken faces, Meghan was reeled from one stumbling man to the next. Sweaty hands groped at her breasts and buttocks, leaving damp smears on her surcoat. Men leered as they whispered what they would do if she was theirs. Their lips were slack and moist, their breath sour. Her knees turned weak with relief when Hugh claimed her again. He drew her aside, his eyes still on the dancers, but his scowl quickly cleared. "I will call the women to escort you to our chamber."

Meghan's eyes flew to his. "I want only Yedda."

"Why? 'Tis a custom that the guests prepare the bride and offer her advice."

"They will make a jest and an obscene thing of my disrobing." She paused, her throat tight. "And of my bedding."

Hugh studied her. All mockery fled his eyes, leaving only desire and understanding. "Go then. I will send Yedda. And, my lady, I will come to you alone."

Lifting her hand, Hugh brought it to his mouth. His tongue traced the deep love line in it before he turned her toward the stairs.

The door closed behind Yedda and, finally alone, Meghan flipped the bedclothes off and stood up from bed. Whatever happens, she thought, wrapping a cloak about her, I'll not wait placidly in bed like a cow led to the bull.

Walking to the fireplace, she stared into the flames, frowning. The smokeless air of the bedchamber had cleared her head and she felt alive and awake. She had rejected Yedda's compassion and her own self-pity. She felt no fear in Hugh's legal possession of her. That was his to take as he would, but the giving of herself in plea-sure-filled abandon lay in her hands. That she would not do, and she knew he would not settle for less. A sense of excitement curved a smile on her lips as strength flowed into her.

When the door opened, Meghan turned, her head high, her eyes disdainful. After dropping the bar over the door, Hugh leaned back, his arms folded across her chest. His gaze wandered over her as intimately as his hands soon would. Feeling the stir of desire his eyes always aroused, Meghan willed her mind and body to be apathetic. His smile became taunting. "I had thought, wife, to find you in my bed eagerly awaiting me."

Meghan did not answer and Hugh laughed softly. He had waited so long for this moment. Five years of need rose in him, yet he felt a sudden nervousness he did not know how to handle, an uncertainty he could not admit to himself. Moving away from the door, he tossed his belt to a chair, his tunic following. His eyes did not leave hers as he removed his shoes and hose and stood there naked except for his breechclout, his well-muscled male body a silent declaration of war. He leaned back again, the fire's light flickering over his long legs, broad shoulders, and narrow hips, his scars standing white against the darker hue of his skin. The laughter in his eyes departed, leaving them intent with need.

"Come here," he ordered.

She walked slowly, meeting his gaze with a haughty stare. He closed his fingers about her thick braids and pulled her closer. "Unbound hair, lady, denotes a virgin. You are a virgin, aren't you?"

Lazily, he separated the ebony strands, combing them with his fingers, then set her back from him. "Drop the cloak," he ordered.

Meghan's eyes flared before she let the mantle fall in a pool of green about her high-arched feet. She stood indifferent as his gaze roamed from her high, round breasts to her tiny waist which flared into curved hips above long, slim legs. Hugh drew a circle in the air and she turned to display a proud back and a small, rounded bottom. Touching her shoulders, he turned her to face him again. Sinking his fingers into her hair, Hugh drew her closer until her breasts grazed his chest. His eyes became hooded with desire and the mouth that touched Meghan's was gentle, soft. Then his tongue thrust into her yielding, unresponsive mouth.

One hand turned her head under his kiss, his mouth seeking the passion she denied him. The other drew her closer, lifting her against his swelling manhood. His fingers twisted harder in her hair and Meghan gasped as he jerked her head back.

His eyes were narrow and his lips curved into a sardonic smile. "So that is the game you play, wench. You think to hold your passion from me." Laughing softly, he ran a finger from her jaw to her collarbone and down to touch a nipple, lifting an eyebrow. "'Tis a game I know and one I will indulge, lady, for I know well the heat I can arouse in you. I've already tasted it."

Meghan gazed back, impassive, and he frowned before carrying her to the bed. He removed his breechclout and lay down, covering her body with his own. His elbows enclosed her as he took her face in his hands and ran his fingers over the fine bones of her face.

Meghan stared at the canopy above, shutting him from her sight, sending her mind away, willing her senses dead. The hands that caressed her touched a body she did not acknowledge. His mouth that pleaded with hers and roamed over her closed eyes, his lips that caught at her nipples, his tongue that teased the delicate convolution of her ears, circled her navel, and tasted her soft, inner flesh—his body loved a woman whom Meghan watched with apathy, a woman who felt nothing.

Suddenly Hugh yanked her head away from his, jerking her spirit back from where she had sent it. He pushed her away from him and stood up. His face was white, his manhood flaccid. He leaned over her, the scar at the corner of his mouth twisting. "You bitch!" he whispered hoarsely.

Shaking with anger, he whirled to stand before the fire, his arms braced against the mantel. The flames touched his muscles with bronze and cast shadows into the hollows of his body.

Pushing aside her growing pity for him, Meghan refused the words which would call him back. Sitting up, she wrapped her arms around her legs and rested her chin on her knees. "I do not please you, my lord?" she asked derisively.

Hugh turned and the fury in his eyes seared her. She regarded him triumphantly, a cat's smile on her mouth. Gradually his scowl turned to a smile that unaccountably chilled Meghan. As his impersonal gaze traveled over her naked body, Meghan felt exposed as she never had before. She fought an impulse to pull the bedclothes over her.

"No, my lady," he answered, "you do not please me—but you will!"

The gleam in his eyes acknowledged her sudden fear. He walked back to the bed as though stalking her. He pushed her back and leaned over her, pinning her wrists. Dropping one knee between her legs, he watched her try to control her panic and laughed softly. "My lady," he whispered, "you mistook the battle for the war. Aye, and your error puts the game in my hands."

Hugh watched Meghan's vain struggle to escape, his mouth twisting into a grin before he brought his lips down on hers. She forced her body rigid as his mouth moved from her cheek to her ear. "Afore, lady, your mouth was soft, denying me nothing, giving me nothing. Why is it so resisting now?"

Hugh's chuckle was triumphant as his lips moved down her neck, nipping at her skin, his tongue creating tremors of excitement despite Meghan's will to fight him. His lips touched her breast, his tongue tracing its roundness before his open mouth brushed over the nipple, his breath hot and moist.

"Why is it, my lady," he asked, "that your nipple was soft afore and now it fills my mouth, as sweet and hard as a cherry?"

Meghan tried to twist away and he laughed as she cursed him. Her body grew heavy and aching and his mouth at her breast seemed to pull invisible cords to her womb, tugging it into a desire so acute that it hurt. She half relaxed with relief when his mouth drew away, only to be jerked back into stiff resistance as his teeth bit the flesh at her navel. Her fists clenched as she fought the desire his tongue aroused as it traced the pattern of her pubic hair. His breath was searing against her thighs as his lips bit at the tendons there and she waited, her body taut, with fearful, yearning anticipation for his mouth to press once more against her soft moistness. Instead, his hand ran over the smooth curves of her body to the joining between her legs, stroking her into waves of need. He grinned at Meghan's closed, angry face, his gray eyes mocking. "My lady," he said, feigning surprise, "afore you stayed cold and dry, but now you are fairly wet and swollen."

Hugh's smile faded and his expression became intent. His eyes held hers as he moved up between her legs. A flicker of amusement danced across his mouth when she recoiled from his hardness pressing against her. Meghan stared back at him, her jaw clenched, challenge flaring in her eyes, until he lowered his mouth to hers. She tried to jerk away, knowing he would take her and that she would respond, but Hugh's mouth refused to let hers go. Though he felt her sobbing protest, his tongue took hers, demanding a response as his body pressed even closer. Even as Meghan fought, her hips lifted to him.

Then his mouth was gone and he was staring down at her, his eyes demanding, beseeching. "Meghan," he whispered just before she felt a tearing, like a knife through parchment. Hugh moved once more, fully taking her.

He held himself quiet, deep within her, his lips soft on her averted face before his body began to gently stroke away her hurt, caressing back her passion. Moving slowly, he watched as she struggled to control her body's demands. Her lips whispered protests even as her breath came faster. Even as her head turned from side to side in denial, she moved under him, lifted to him, drew him deeper yet. Her wrists escaped his hands, her fingers twining with his as she used his strength to brace against his thrusts and to drive back against them. Hugh watched as her mouth parted. Her eyes, still defiant, closed as her head fell backward in mute refusal as she moaned with the rising waves of heat. Throbs of agonizing pleasure shook her as she felt Hugh plunge deeper. He groaned her name, his spasms jerking him as he sent his seed flooding within her. Then she spun away into darkness. . . .

The touch of a hand gently brushing damp hair from her face aroused Meghan and she stirred, opening her eyes. Hugh smiled and ran a finger over her passion-swollen lips, then bent and kissed them lightly. Her eyes filled with tears of anger and scorn. "Damn you," she whispered bitterly. "Are you well pleased with me now, my lord?"

Hugh laughed wryly, not knowing if he mocked himself or her. "Aye," he said, "you please me well."

Meghan knew she had somehow won, but the pain in his voice stunned her and she dared not respond to it. Then degradation overwhelmed her and she shook with sobs. He drew her to him. His hands tenderly stroked her until her weeping slowed, her breathing relaxing as sleep claimed her. Hugh drew her closer and curled his body around her, listening to her breathe, feeling her heart beat. He gazed, unseeing, at the reflection of the fire on the stone walls of the chamber as they flickered lower.

He had possessed her. He had driven her to meet him passion for passion, need for need. She belonged to him in the sight of God and man. It was his right to control her, to hold her ever to him.

The knowledge that she had somehow escaped him tasted bitter in his mouth.

Chapter 19

Meghan woke aware of where she was and of the events of the night before. The presence of the man next to her was somehow less strange than his absence would have been. She had slept on the edge of consciousness, listening to his breathing and, for a short time, the groans of a nightmare. She had hushed him, soothing away his dream until he had fallen back into peaceful sleep.

Her body felt sore and abused, her nipples swollen and itching. The hurt between her thighs stung with the pressure of a full bladder and she stirred against the ache. Hugh's arm was flung over her hip, his breath feeling warm on her shoulder. His leg was wrapped around hers, the coarse hair on his calf pricking her. Slowly, carefully, she eased her leg away and lifted his arm, slipping from under it. On her stomach, she slid from the bed to her knees on the floor. Trying to rise, she felt her hair being pulled. Peering from the corner of her eye, she saw that thick strands were caught in Hugh's hand.

"Are you deserting our marriage bed so soon, lady?"

Startled, she jerked around to meet Hugh's grin. His silvery eyes danced at her undignified position and the blaze in her eyes.

Meghan's jaw tightened. "I would like to go to the garderobe, my lord."

His grin broadened. "The garderobe is cold, my lady, but there is a chamber pot under the bed."

She refused to answer. Laughing, Hugh drew her to him by the hair until her face was a hand's breadth from his. "Is your concern for my slumber such that you slip from my bed as silently as a Welsh thief in the night?" Her gasp of indignation at the insult made him smile. "Your modesty ill befits a married woman. 'Twould betoken a coldness to me. Are you cold to me, lady?"

A blush rose from Meghan's round breasts to her face. Then his eyes lost their derisive anger and his features hardened. "You have my leave to go, lady," he said, his fingers tightening in her hair. His breath was hot on her mouth and his lips grazed hers as he spoke. "But do not linger for I have need of you."

"Mayhap," Meghan answered, regretting her words even as she spoke, "the miller's daughter would be more willing."

"What is this? Are you jealous of my favors and so soon wed to me?" Pressing his finger against her lips, he hushed her. "Little one, you'll not find me remiss in my attentions. Cleave to me, give to me, and I'll not look elsewhere. You please me well."

He brushed her lips with an open mouth, the tip of his tongue teasing the corners, but when he released her, the need in his eyes had turned to mockery. He grinned as she slid from the bed and wrapped a cloak about herself. His pose as he lay stretched out and relaxed, his manhood half erect, taunted her as she closed the door to the chamber and stepped over Selig, who lay snoring in the passageway.

The rushes on the garderobe's floor did not keep the stones from numbing Meghan's feet. A cold wind blew up the privy hole and, once finished, she pulled the cloak back around herself and leaned against the wall, indecisive. Lifting first one foot then the other, she pressed them against her calves for warmth.

The desire to run back to Hugh and curl into his warmth warred with her pride and anger. She felt trapped, knowing she had to return but determined to delay as long as possible. The thought of his complacent possession of her shook her with fury and the cold clattered her teeth.

Slow tears welled in her eyes at the humiliation of having to ask like a child to go to the garderobe. Then, wiping the tears away, she smiled, realizing she was indeed behaving like a child. Straightening her shoulders, she returned to the chamber. Hugh had the right to take all he could, and she had the right to withhold the part of herself that she had to keep inviolate for her own self-preservation.

Hugh lay sprawled on the bed, although another log had been added to the fire. He had been studying the flames but turned appraising eyes on her when she entered. A small smile curled his lips. "Is your pride sufficiently cooled, my lady?" he asked. "You were gone so long I thought mayhap your bottom had frozen to the privy hole."

Going to stand before the fire, Meghan refused to acknowledge his eyes that made her so aware of her sleep-tangled hair, of her fingers blue with cold, of her naked feet. Hugh watched as her discomfort grew. When he spoke, his voice was hard. "Come here. I've need of you."

"Am I your dog that you would so call me to heel?"

"No, you are only my wife. Indeed, a dog I would pay for; you came to me for nothing. Though, in truth, I esteem you more than most women, for I took you with nothing but a barren stretch of land of no value to an Englishman. You are mine, to do with as I will, and you cannot gainsay me. And you've no man left in your family to call me on it."

Meghan's mouth trembled, although she regarded him blandly. His grin disappeared. "I can, lady, order you tied to my bed and take you as I will. Do not play games with me. Come here!"

Meghan dropped the cloak and walked to the bed. She lay stiffly on its edge, her legs straight, her arms at her sides, her eyes on the canopy. Turning, Hugh pulled her to him. Catching the fist she swung, he wrapped his arms around her. Doubling up, she thrust icy feet into his groin. "God's blood, woman!" he swore, "would you freeze the very balls off me?"

The lump of humiliation in her throat dissolved into a giggle. Meghan's eyes blurred with hurt laughter as they met Hugh's angry gaze. His scowl relaxing, he smoothed her hair back from her face, recognizing the hysteria beneath her glee. He rubbed her feet with rough hands, then tucked them between his calves for warmth. He waited for her laughter to die as he untangled her hair with gentle fingers.

Gradually Meghan's mirth ceased. Her eyes met Hugh's and she let him read her abasement and fear. His fingers gently touching her face, he traced her eyebrow, the curve of her cheek and lips, which trembled slightly. The mouth he lowered to hers was incredibly tender and drew a response from her that was painful in its need to give and take. Her lips opened under his. Her tongue drew him in, offering him her mouth. Its sweetness filled Hugh, hurting him with the knowledge that he did not truly possess her. Jerking his mouth from hers, he buried his face in her hair. "Ah, little one," he groaned, "I would have you love me!"

His words seemed to reverberate from the walls and taunt him with his weakness, with his need of this woman's love.

Her fingers were gentle as they stroked his hair and rubbed his temples, then moved to caress his shoulders. The pity Hugh imagined he felt in her touch shook him with shame and rage. His hands clenched into the flesh of the woman who had seen his need, had heard him speak of his frailty, the woman he loved. But her voice was soft. "My lord, I cannot love you," she whispered. She paused, feeling his hands bruise her shoulders. "But, in truth, I do lust for you! 'Tis like a weakness in me, this need I feel."

Slowly Hugh relaxed, lifting his eyes to meet hers. "Methinks," she continued, "mayhap the other will come, for you do draw me somehow, my lord, though, by all the saints, I intend to fight it."

Hugh's mouth twisted into a grin. "My lady," he mocked, "I must confess your body is of more use to me now than your heart."

Meghan forced an answering smile, weeping inside at his pain. She passed her hand over his eyes, closing the hurt from her sight. She smoothed away his crooked grin with a soft finger, then drew his head down to her. Her sorrow became a sob of passion as his mouth touched hers. It pressed against her lips with a demanding hunger, as though to draw her soul from her. Her hands moved over his face, touching his eyes, his cheekbones, following the scar on his eyebrow. Her hands moved to his shoulders and under his arms. Her fingers dug into the muscles of his back as she pressed against him.

Hugh's lips clung as his hands roamed over her. He touched her with the fingers of a blind man, seeking to know the texture of her skin, shape of her breasts, hardness of her nipples above the softness of flesh. He heard her gasp as he pressed against her, felt her recoil from his hardness, and he drew his mouth away to look at her. "Do I hurt you, little one?" he asked.

Her voice husky, Meghan passed the back of her hand over his lips. "Aye, but not as much as the need I feel."

The teasing fled her eyes, eclipsed by want. Her lips grew soft. Tilting her hips, she slowly pressed against him, easing him into her, her wide eyes never leaving his.

Hugh groaned and his mouth claimed Meghan's again as he felt her fingers dig into his back, driving him to her. He moved gently, fearful of hurting her. He heard a moan begin deep in her throat, a moan that became a croon as her need grew, the croon becoming a sob as she found release. He felt the rhythmic throbs deep within her, her hands fluttering over his back, helpless as passion shook her. He drove into her once more, a groan bursting from him and his body shuddering in the ancient act of worship of man for woman.

Meghan's breathing slowed and she opened her eyes. Hugh was heavy on her, yet she did not feel trapped. He roused to move, but she held him. "No, my lord," she whispered, "do not leave me yet."

Hugh put his mouth against her throat, tasting their mingled sweat. He rolled over, taking her with him, and caressed her with knowing hands. His fingers sought secret places where nerves jumped, where skin quivered. He moved his hand to press between her thighs and Meghan moaned, opening to him. He stroked her, watching her face, reading her pleasure. He watched her expression change to one of surprise and he held her when she would pull away. He waited for her to relax, then caressed her until she gasped, her body shuddering under his hand.

Curling into a ball, Meghan hid her face against his shoulder. ''That cannot be new to you,'' he said. ''Have you not done it to yourself?'' She shook her head and he laughed. ''There is no shame in it, no matter what the priests tell you.''

'''Tis not the sin of it,'' Meghan confessed, giggling, ''but that I did not know the way to do it.''

Astonished, Hugh threw back his head in laughter. When his mirth subsided, he whispered her name, wonder and affection in his tone, then drew the bedclothes over them. He drowsed, letting his hand wander over her, feeling her nibble at his neck. Meghan put her head on his chest and blew the hair that grew there, tickling him. He slapped her bottom and she laughed before snuggling against him, drifting into a light sleep.

The whisper of his name roused him sometime later. ''Hugh,'' Meghan repeated, ''when do you go to Edward?''

He twined her hair around his fingers. ''He gave me three weeks. That leaves sixteen days, although he may call me back sooner. Are you so eager to be rid of me?''

''I wish you did not have to go at all, my lord.''

His hand drew still and he frowned. ''Is your concern for me or for Wales?''

Meghan's eyes pleaded for understanding. ''Both, for I've no wish to be a Welsh widow in a Norman castle, with, mayhap, a babe within me. Edward would leave me scant time to mourn you. He would give me another husband afore the year was out. He loves you, true, but is ever practical, and your widow, holding Ainsleah, would be a convenient prize for any loyal knight. I came to you, my lord, unwilling, yet I would not lose you. In truth, I would grieve deeply. Nor would I want another man after you—not in this bed, not using me so.''

Hugh lifted her chin, smiling at her, and the corners of her mouth tipped up in answer before she grew solemn again. ''My lord,'' she said, ''what will become of Wales?''

"Do you not know? Must I speak of it?"

She blinked tears away and nodded. "Aye, I know, but I must have you speak of it. Defeat is not mentioned in Wales and I need it said."

Hugh stared up at the canopy. "Aye, there'll be defeat and 'twill be bitter," he said at last. "Edward is not one to abandon a cause and he is sorely angered. He'll not rest until Davyd has gone the way of Llewelyn—and his men with him. He loved Davyd well and his defection deeply hurt him. There'll be defeat and hunger and hardship. And there is nothing I can do, little one, except make the end come sooner."

"And my people?"

Hugh smoothed the frown from her brow. "They'll be secure. Your father built well. You left them food enough, did you not, and orders not to leave, no matter the provocation?"

A brief vision of Caradoc's unctuous features touched Meghan's mind before she nodded. Hugh laughed at her fears and kissed her gently. "Do not think on it or brood," he ordered. "You've done what you could. They'll soon be under my care and I'll succor them as I would you."

He closed her eyes with his hand and moved to enclose her breast. Molding her body to his, he said, "Sleep now, lady, for, by the saints, you fatigue me with your chatter, aye, and your lustfulness."

Laughing, Meghan wiggled against him. "What time is it?"

"I heard the bells for Tierce some while ago."

"Will not the guests be coming soon?"

"Methinks they are still abed or retching over a chamber pot. And they'll not disturb us with Selig at the door. Go to sleep. Yedda will wake us afore noon."

Meghan closed her eyes, then opened them again. "How came you by Selig, my lord?"

Hugh groaned. "I had not known you chatter like a jackdaw. I did but preserve his vast hide for him."

"But how?"

"If I tell you, will you cease your questions? I have not passed the last four days abed as you did."

"Yedda did say you rode a lot." Meghan giggled.

"Aye, though 'twas not the mount I wished for."

His hands roamed significantly over her and Meghan snuggled down as Hugh began his story. "I found him on crusade," he told her. "He had been captured by the Saracens three years afore and they put him to mining salt. 'Twas a miracle he survived. Few lived out the year, especially those as rebellious as Selig. When we found him, he was scarce able to crawl, but the infidel were sore afraid of him and kept him shackled though he was out of his head, speaking gibberish. He came to his senses when he set eyes on his lord, Otto of Ludenscheid. He railed against him, telling of how the lord had led his men into a trap, then deserted them. Otto had been too involved with his lover, Manfeld of Stuttgart, an angelic-faced youth with a viper's soul, to send out scouts. He had relied on the word of others, being too lazy to seek out the facts for himself. 'Twas Otto's way to let others do the labor, then he would fall on their heels, reaping glory for the fame of his name and an assured place in heaven."

Scowling, Hugh looked at Meghan. "You are aware that this be rumor and Selig's word? I was not there except at the end."

Smiling, Meghan touched the scar at his eyebrow. "How came you by this?" she asked.

Hugh bit her fingers, one by one. "I'll tell you another time. Do you wish to hear of our brave Selig or no?"

"Aye, I would hear of our brave Selig," she whispered, finding a strange, frightening satisfaction in his use of the word "our."

"Anyway, Otto's information was either deliberately false, for many hated him, or only carelessly garnered. He led his men into a trap; then, realizing his error, he left them to be slaughtered or enslaved. The story he told was of his desire to fight to the death and of his followers forcibly removing him from the field, leaving only the dead behind. 'Twas a tale few believed, but none could prove it false until Selig was found. His rage overcame all discretion and he told everything. His lord was sore angered and he would have had Selig put to death, but gentle Manfeld suggested 'twas more fitting to deprive

him of his tongue, thus ending the slander, and to sell
him to the galleys. Manfeld was ever one to see the value
of silver, no matter what the source.''

Ignoring Meghan's teasing fingers, Hugh remembered
the Crusades—the insects that burrowed under a man's
skin, creating wounds that would not heal; the heat that
roasted a man in his armor; the fever and chills that shook
him until his teeth ached.

"I had been to El Arish," he said, "and returned too
late to save Selig's tongue, but I challenged Otto for his
person, more from dislike of Otto than to save Selig's
skin. Otto, not being a man to risk his life, feigned illness and took to his tent, selecting a knight to stand for
him. Mayhap the knight was weakened by the flux; we
all were, or his heart was not behind his lord. Selig
became mine. Nor has he given me doubt until now. He
sore loves you, little one. Methinks, had you called last
night, he would have cleaved me to the bed.''

Meghan smiled. "No, my lord, he would have but
restrained your passion.''

Hugh chuckled. "Aye, a swinging battle-ax does that.
But his loyalty now is not something I would put to the
test.''

Rising onto one elbow, he cradled her face in his hand.
"But you did not call to him.''

"No," she admitted, her eyes dropping. "I did not.''
Turning her face into his palm, she tasted the mingled
salt of their bodies' love. "Go to sleep, my love,'' she
whispered. "I will have need of you later.''

The fire had lowered again when Yedda knocked. She
entered on Hugh's command, balancing a tray as she
swung the door closed. Her eyes were hopeful as they
sought her mistress, but Meghan refused to meet them,
keeping her flushed face hidden.

Hugh winked. Yedda blushed and her answering smile
was bawdy. Sliding glances at Meghan, she arranged the
ale, cheese, bread, and meat and added wood to the fire
before addressing Hugh. "Your guests be grumbling, my
lord—those not still abed. They complain that you do not

permit them to bring the morning cup or to examine the marriage sheet.''

Shrugging, Hugh accepted a goblet of ale. ''They may eat my larder empty and drink my casts dry, but I'll not have them make sport of me and my lady wife. In truth, they are welcome to leave. They came as a diversion from the war and not by invitation. If they complain, direct them to Godfrey.'' He paused, scowling. ''Aye, and direct the cooks to serve well-watered ale, dry bread, and salted mutton. They'll leave when their bellies are poorly served.''

Yedda was turning to go when Hugh called her back. ''I would have a bath brought and you may then take the sheet and hang it for all to see. Though, by my faith, my lady's virtue should concern no one but me.''

Curtsying, Yedda left. Before she closed the door, she saw Meghan accept a kiss and a cup from Hugh, her eyes laughing at him over the brim.

Chapter 20

The days melded one into the other, then they were gone. Meghan had buried all concern for her people and Wales deep within, lulled into a sensuous lethargy and refusing to think of Hugh's approaching departure. She lived in a fairy tale of love that would soon end and she stored the memories to hold against the future. She knew, too, that she did not want this idyll to continue; she was coming too close to making a total commitment, each day building the love she denied into a stronger force. She refused to acknowledge a sense of foreboding that haunted her.

Their guests departed amid grumbling and complaints, leaving them alone to explore each other's minds, emotions, and bodies. Meghan watched Hugh, followed after him, searched for him when he was gone, met his eyes in smiles that excluded all others.

In their bed she reached for him, opened to him. She brought to their lovemaking the innocence and exuberance of a child newly introduced to a joyful, exciting game. Her face sometimes grew intent and sometimes teased as she explored his body, seeking how best to please him. Her mouth moved over him, nibbling, caressing, until he reached for her, groaning with need. She would answer with a passion that equaled his or she would elude him, tormenting him until her own desire drew her to him, to take the joy he gave. Their bath became a time of touching, a time that ended with long, tender love in their bed; or bathing became an opportunity to tease, to splash, to soak themselves and the floor, heedless of Yedda's scolding, until they came together with a playfulness that quickened to an intense yearning.

Their bed became a haven where they would lie quietly, touching, each absorbing the essence of the other. Or they would talk for hours of inconsequential things—their childhoods, people they knew or had only heard of, court gossip.

They rode the lands of Ainsleah together, for it and its people would become Meghan's charge when Hugh returned to Edward. Godfrey Marwood was steward, but the final decision in all things would be hers. Her responsibilities went deep, into the very lives of Ainsleah's people—into their beddings, their birthings, the christening of their newborns.

Hugh took her to each hut and introduced her to each villein living there, from the youngest child to the oldest crone. He listened as she spoke to each, her smile warm, her words drawing them from their self-consciousness. As they rode to the next hut, he told her the most significant facts about each tenant. And, although her eyes teased him, although she touched his wrist and his mouth, although her hand accidentally brushed against his manhood, although he grabbed that hand and sucked her fingers until passion leaped into her eyes, he knew she stored away all the information he gave her. He knew it even when they forwent the next hut and returned to the castle instead. They would race their horses back, Hugh allowing her to pull ahead. To watch her look back at him over her shoulder, to know that he would catch her and lay her down and part her thighs while her face grew rapt with need, teased him, excited him. They would race over the drawbridge, ignoring the squealing swine and squawking fowl. Tossing their reins to any available hand, they would run up the stairs of the keep, Meghan's hand secure in Hugh's, only to halt at the entrance of the great hall. Composing their features, moving sedately, desire curling warm within them, they would walk across the hall to the stairs and up, only to meet in their chamber, straining to each other, at last giving in to their passion.

Hugh took her through the fields, naming the villein who worked each one, naming the crop to be planted there come spring. And she would remember, though it seemed she, too, was a fertile field, a warm, dark earth to be plowed, to be planted by him. Once, she watched him, her face intent as he pointed out a plot to be sowed in barley, its dark plane already prepared in deep, dark furrows.

"I want you," she whispered, when he turned back to her.

Hugh stared at her, his face reflecting her need. He led her to a copse of alders and helped her dismount. Leaning her against his destrier, he loosened his hose and breechclout. Then he pulled up her skirts and lifted her up, his hands cupping her buttocks, and impaled her, driving deep within her, while her back was supported by his motionless destrier. Her eyes went wide with surprise; her mouth became a circle of pleasure from which a gasp escaped as he drove into her, as he carried them both to a moaning climax. Somehow it did not seem ignominious at all.

Hugh watched Meghan—as she lifted a child, as she scowled over some needlework, as she listened, smiling, to Godfrey—and he knew she could make him content. He would feel, then, a glow deep within and try to ignore the whisper that taunted, telling him that she was not yet fully his.

They knelt at mass, the priest's words droning over them. They responded from long habit, yet were ever aware of the other, their hands and bodies awkwardly straining with the need to touch.

They went about their separate duties, Meghan accepting the household keys Godfrey gave her. They issued orders, settled quarrels, yet they were like puppets until they came together again. Their preoccupation excluded everyone who tried to enter the circle they had drawn around themselves.

Yet the barrier Meghan had erected against him was still partly there. Even as she contorted in ecstasy, Hugh felt her withdraw. She gave herself in joy but willed away the love she might have felt. He saw the barrier in the

sorrow lurking in her eyes at odd moments. He heard it
in her brooding silence when the household laughed and
jested in their cups, when their people danced in the eve-
nings or listened to the minstrels.

Hugh knew, too, that he withheld something from her,
afraid of losing her completely, of smashing the chamber
within which she had locked herself. Fear held his tongue,
fear that words of love would put bonds on her she could
not bear.

Hugh gazed at Meghan as she lay in his arms, her head
on his shoulder. Selig had tapped on the door moments
before, but Hugh had been awake for a long time, reluctant to awaken her although his arm ached. He watched
dreams chase themselves across her face, a smile curving
her mouth, a frown creasing her forehead. She tossed in
her sleep, disturbed, then settled back at his whisper.
Bending his head, Hugh whispered, "'Tis time, little
one."

She woke slowly, lifting her mouth to him, and turned,
her hands reaching for him. Hugh started to put her from
him, knowing their time was short, then succumbed,
needing her one more time. He held her, caressing her
with hands that memorized her curves, wanting to make
this time last forever. Suddenly a need to take her, to
stamp his possession on her, seized him. He entered her
and Meghan responded, her hips raised to him, her fingertips pressing on his back. She tossed her head, sobbing, then her eyes flew open. Her body grew quiet and
her whisper held an accusation. "You leave today," she
stated.

His features hardened, defying her to try to hold him.
"Aye," he said casually.

Meghan searched his face, reading his regret at leaving
her and his eagerness to go to Edward. Her gaze grew
shadowed and she drew his head down and moved under
him, drawing him from himself while she stared at the
ceiling. If she was never to see Hugh again, his features
would fade in time. But she would always remember the
arrangement of planks high above her, the twists of the

wood. She lifted Hugh to the peak of ecstasy, but for the
first time he went alone. Nor did she feign a response.

Hugh stared at Meghan as she knelt before him, fas-
tening his chausses. Her smooth hair shone, ebony glistening into deep blue. She wore it pulled into a heavy
knot low on her neck and held there with ivory skewers.
No single strand escaped. The severity of the style seemed
to be a silent rebuke.

Hugh pushed away the desire to loosen the tresses, to
let them fall, to turn her once more into the wanton girl
who had romped with him, to banish this austere woman.
He watched her slim fingers tie the mailed leggings to his
underbelt. Her hands were sure on the points, knotting
them tight, then tugging to secure them.

Standing, she lifted his hauberk, her gaze avoiding his.
Its heavy, shining links slipped and she caught the mailed
shirt on her knees. Hugh knelt and she pulled it over his
head, covering the quilted tunic beneath, and guided his
hands into the loose sleeves. Over it she drew his outer
tunic, then clasped his heavy, silver-studded baldric about
his waist. His sword was heavy across her palms as she
knelt before him, kissing its cold blade and offering it to
him.

Taking it, Hugh slid it into its scabbard, his gaze never
leaving her lowered features. Lifting her to her feet, he
took her face between his hands and held her until she
lifted her eyes. Her mouth was cool under his. She felt
his anger in his kiss and she called on pride to stifle the
plea in her throat.

She was the daughter of Welsh chieftains, of countless
generations of women who had armed their men and sent
them into battle without tears. But she had seen the
weeping when the men returned dead. She had keened for
her own and had vowed she would not weep so again.
Yet she prepared this man for battle against her own people. She handed him his sword just as she would soon
offer him the stirrup cup, her face set. So she had been
trained, but she raged silently against this senselessness.
Were this man to stay with her, she might dare love him.

Ignoring a whisper that told her she would only scorn any man who did not honor his oath, Meghan inwardly rebelled against a system that demanded a man fight, a woman wait. She fought against the fear that had teased her happiness for the last few days. Lifting her eyes, she stated, "I wish that you would not go, my lord Hugh."

He frowned, wanting to comfort her, to offer promises he could not keep. To stay would weaken him. She should not ask it of him.

"'Tis my duty," he told her. "And you'll not stand between me and my lord, nor will your coldness turn me from him. See that my homecoming is warmer than the leave-taking you offer me."

Meghan lifted her chin. "Others give scutage, my lord, and their loyalty is not questioned. Why can't you?"

Hugh's features became harsh. "I'll not pay men to fight or die for me, to accept the duty I owe my liege."

Seeing anger flaring in her eyes because of her fear, he softened and drew her to him. "My lady," he pleaded, "nothing can keep me from coming back to you—not death itself—if I go with your blessing."

"You've my blessing, my lord, and my unceasing prayers," she answered stiffly as he released her. "'Tis well past Prime, my lord," she reminded him, "and you must travel far today to meet with Edward."

Hugh's mouth tightened at her coldness. He turned on his heel and stalked from the chamber. Picking up his helm and cloak, Meghan followed him to the hall where he accepted his household's blessing. He did not acknowledge her as he took his cloak and led the way to the ward, where his men-at-arms and knights waited. His hauberk jangled as he walked. His sword clanged with each long stride. Pausing on the steps, he breathed in the cold, sharp air and glanced up at a clear sky. He descended the stairs and swung into the saddle, his destrier steady under his weight.

Finally he looked at Meghan. He accepted his helm, then the stirrup cup of mulled wine that she held out. Turning it to the spot where she had kissed the rim, Hugh drained it in one draft. He tossed the cup to Godfrey, his gaze never leaving the proud face of his wife. Extending his hand, he grasped Meghan's and pulled her up to him. "This," he whispered, "is my stirrup cup."

His mouth lowered and he felt her lips, at first stiff, then soft and yielding. She clung to him even after he released her, her face buried in his neck. Her words were desperate. "My lord, I am sore afraid! 'Tis like a portend. 'Tis ominous!"

Grasping her thick hair, Hugh pulled her back and stared into her distraught face. His features were all flat planes and sharp angles as he loosened her grip. Lifting her, he held her out and dropped her to the ground. Meghan stumbled, clutching at his leg to keep her balance. Placing a foot against her chest, he leaned over, his words hissing into her face. "Pray for me, lady. Pray also for trust in my prowess and pray that you learn your place. Do not dare demean me further or hex me. And control your humors and your Welsh fancies! If you should now carry a brat within you, I'll not have him marked by your savage megrims!"

Hugh held her gaze, his eyes unrelenting, then he wheeled his horse around. His men followed him out the gates. Meghan watched him go, her eyes glinting with hatred, tears welling in them. The sense of foreboding rose again, stronger this time, bringing with it a vertigo and nausea that were new to her.

Only when the last man had ridden from sight, only when the pigeons, disturbed by the men of war, had settled back on their perches on Ainsleah's walls, did she turn back into the castle.

The sense of foreboding clung and grew stronger long after Hugh's departure. Meghan tried to taunt it away, laughing at herself for a woman plagued by her body's humors. But her fear refused to leave.

She tried to reason it gone and to find its source. It did not touch specifically on Hugh. Nor did she fear for her people. Her fear went beyond the defeat awaiting them. That she had felt this presentiment before and knew it always brought grief made it all the more terrifying.

Kneeling on the church floor, she felt the rough stones cut into her knees. The aching cold creeped up, pricking her legs with tiny red-hot knives. She had come again at earliest dawn, as she had for days, seeking through the faith she had so long neglected an answer to her dread.

She had avoided Ainsleah's chapel and sought instead the village church. She held her eyes on the crucifix with its crudely carved, disproportionate figure of a misshapen serf. The nails in its hands and feet, the thorns at its brow, were huge. The blood from its wounds was too vibrant to have ever flowed in human veins. Meghan stared until the figure seemed to writhe, its face grimacing a malignant hatred.

She forced a prayer from her lips. Her fingers, stiff with cold, twined through her rosary. She sought the state of grace she had achieved as an adolescent when, seeking to delay her body's growth toward womanhood, she had turned to the church. Despite her brothers' teasing and the impatient grunts of her father, she had moved about her chores with downcast eyes, her fingers clasping beads, her lips moving in prayer. Her brothers' ridicule and her father's smile were but crosses she had to bear, the means to martyrdom, and their souls had become the objects of her most fervent prayers.

Then her mother had become ill and Meghan's faith had been the only means of helping a woman who was beyond all aid. The hours spent on her knees in prayer had multiplied. Her mind had turned to the suffering of the saints and she had tried to emulate them. She had placed nettles against her skin from chest to hip. She had worn stones in her shoes until her feet bled. She had fasted until she seemed to float. Her father, grieved by the illness of the woman who had been his life's center, had not noticed Meghan's emaciated body or glow of martyrdom.

Then her mother had died, leaving Meghan with a cynicism that was painful in one so young. Yet she still clung to the rituals of her faith—there was no alternative. Although her unquestioning faith was gone, she remembered the ecstasy of sanctification and the visions. It was that state she sought, hoping to find in it an answer to her fear.

While she prayed, a small voice in her mind jeered, tempting her to turn her face from God. It filled her with hopelessness and a sense of isolation from Christ. The voice convinced her of her unworthiness.

Bending forward, Meghan struck the floor with clenched fists. The pain of her bruised hands, the futility of any offer she could make against fate, drove her anger deeper. It mocked her as she lay shaking with sobs. At last she grew quiet, unable to sustain her painful emotion any longer. She let her mind go free, swinging above her, and she dozed.

A voice called her. A hand gripped her shoulder and she sat up. The light from the narrow doorway framed a bulky figure. The face lay in shadow, yet it was familiar.

"Anyon," she whispered, realizing in the same moment that he was dead and buried.

Kneeling, bringing his features into view, he shook his head. "'Tis Gower, lady."

Returning her stare, he gave Meghan time to know him. Gower, son of Anyon, and so like his sire. His hands were steady as he lifted Meghan to her feet.

Her head against his chest, Meghan allowed relief to sweep over her. The foreboding, she realized, concerned herself and whatever it was Gower would lead her to. It was the life she had begun with Hugh which was threatened. The fight Wales waged was still hers, denying her peace and rest. Yet this knowledge lay deep within her; her conscious mind still sought the reason for Gower's presence. At last she lifted her head. Even as she spoke, she was aware of the inane pride in her question. "How long were you there, watching me?"

Gower's features tightened at the implication that he had violated her privacy. He did not want to be there. It had not been his decision. "Only a moment," he answered, "and not without purpose. Glenna sent me."

"Glenna?" Meghan repeated, remembering the old woman who had pulled her from her mother's womb, to whom she had run for comfort, who had taught her medicine and her people's folklore. Glenna, grandmother to Anyon, father of Gower.

"Why?" she asked, ignoring her apprehension.

Gower studied her, needing to know where her loyalty now lay, if he should follow her once more. He watched her face grow taut and saw her pale as he said, "Caradoc is back. He took the people into the mountains."

He gave no further explanation. She had left them, had married a foreigner. She did not yet deserve a full recounting. And, like his father, Gower was a laconic man.

Now there was a face to Meghan's foreboding and she cursed herself for not at once putting Caradoc's name on it. She had thought him behind her, no part in the life she had begun with Hugh. Now she mocked her complacency; he had always been there. His cruelty had stained her girlhood. He had been at Flint; Hugh had seen him there. He had haunted her first days at court, playing lickspittle to Davyd ab Gruffydd. The knowledge that he was in the hills around Cleitcroft had shadowed her return from England. Even in his absences she had felt his sinister presence, knowing he was plotting somewhere and that she was somehow woven into the design of his intrigues.

The fear aroused by mention of Caradoc gave way to rage, to purpose. He had taken her people, knowing she would have no choice but to intercede. And in so doing, he threatened a love and a life she suddenly wanted very much.

"How many went with him?" she demanded.

"All but the far crofts. They went to Davyd long afore."

"The women and children?"

"All but Glenna and Wynne—and he wanted Wynne."

"He would." Caradoc's insinuating face leaped into her mind. For a moment a feeling of helplessness assailed her, but she pushed it back, puzzled that he had not stayed at Cleitcroft, where he would be safe from enemies and in possession of much wealth. But there he was but another of her people. The very soil and walls were to them the clan. Only away could he control and debase them enough so that they would willingly return with him one day to truly take Cleitcroft. He knew a confrontation at Cleitcroft would weaken him while giving her an advantage, but she could not understand why he wanted her there.

His twisted features returned to her. Unable to acknowledge their meaning, she drove the picture from her mind. Cleitcroft could not be his under English law, and, were Davyd to defeat Edward, Caradoc would be outlawed once again. The people knew him. They had all felt his cruel jesting, twisted lies, and violent temper. They had scorned him, had expelled him as surely as had his own sire and the courts of Wales. Only with Cleitcroft leaderless had he dared return.

"And why," she asked Gower, "did you not go with them?"

"Had I been at Cleitcroft," he answered, "I would have, mayhap but for a short time. But I went to Davyd from Orewin Bridge. 'Twas by chance I went to Cleitcroft—to recruit men for the pendragon."

Meghan's mouth quirked at his honesty, then she sobered. "How many came back from Orewin Bridge?"

"Thirty-eight. Thirty-three went to Davyd. The others are with Caradoc," he answered, naming them.

Meghan shook her head, unable to believe such men would desert her. "But where is Caradoc now?" she asked.

As Gower told her, her blood began to quicken. Her skin seemed to tingle with purpose. Gower's coming had cast her into a situation which, to her, left only two choices—to stay at Ainsleah or to go to her people. She was going, she told herself, because Hugh could not. She was going to protect the dowry she had brought him, knowing as she did that she was lying. Once her decision was made, set firmly in the rock of her rage, she used Hugh's demeaning words of farewell to drown the memories of their days of love.

Meghan gnawed her lip, the corners of her mouth lifting in angry laughter. Silently, she thanked the fates that Selig, ever vigilant, had gone with Hugh.

"Can you meet me here at Nones?" she asked Gower.

Chapter 21

Sir Godfrey Marwood rode into the ward of Ruthin Castle on an errand that he regreted with all his heart. He urged his horse among scurrying pages, shouting squires, and cursing groups of men-at-arms. He swung his maimed leg over his horse's back, staggering as it struck the cobbled courtyard. His face contorted, sweat breaking from his forehead. Clinging to the saddle, he conquered the pain and turned to the stairway, its height presenting another obstacle. Handing his horse to a page, he started up. His leg shot agony into his teeth with each swing. A brusque shoulder struck him and a knight cursed all cripples who hindered the passage of a sound-limbed man. The blow knocked Godfrey off balance before unknown hands steadied him and helped him up three more steps. Godfrey leaned against the door of the hall, his breath coming in gasps, sweat drenching him from his armpits to his waist.

The huge chamber was in chaos. The air was thick with smoke and noise rose and fell like the beat of surf. The shouts of men at dice punctuated the roar of conversation. Every foot of space was occupied by men talking, cursing, drinking, eating, gambling. Pages intent on their errands weaved through the confusion. Maidservants laden with trays avoided grabbing hands with swinging hips and taunting laughs.

Stopping a squire, Godfrey asked where Hugh was. The man gestured toward a far corner and hurried on. Frowning, Godfrey forced himself through the mass of men, his dreaded purpose dragging his heels.

Hugh was sitting with four other knights, his eyes on a diagram drawn with charcoal on the table. Pointing, he asked a question, scowled at the answer, and suggested an alternative. His mind on the problem, his gaze passed over Godfrey, then flicked back. Surprise turned to apprehension as he excused himself and came to meet his steward. "What do you here?" he demanded, fear filling his voice.

Godfrey forced his eyes to Hugh's, knowing there was no way to ease the blow. "Your lady wife is gone," he stated.

Hugh's eyes bored into his, first incredulous then cold with disbelieving anger. "When?"

Godfrey shoved a shaking hand through his thin hair. "Three days gone. She left in the early afternoon, but we did not miss her till dusk and the dark hindered the hunt."

Hugh's features became deceptively calm. Only the twitching muscles about his mouth betrayed his agitation. "Did she go alone?" he demanded.

Godfrey hesitated, then answered with a sigh. "She met someone at the church, a man wearing Welsh boots. They took two horses."

"My horses?"

Hugh's eyes grew cold at Godfrey's nod. His voice was heavy with sarcasm. "God's blood, and how is it my lady came by, not one, but two of my horses?"

"She said she wanted to take food to that slut in the village whose husband ran off last summer. She took a page and left him tied in the church, taking his horse. She had been broody, Hugh, missing you, I thought, and I rejoiced to see her occupied."

Hugh's mouth twisted. "Aye, she laid a simple plan for a simple fool. And my errant wife took not only two horses but food for her journey as well!" His next question was foolish, but he asked it anyway. "Where do you think she went?"

"Wales, Hugh. She left you this."

Taking the parchment, Hugh frowned, finding no salutation or signature.

Word came, my lord, that my people left Cleitcroft to follow my half brother Caradoc. I am concerned and must go to them. 'Tis a thing I've no choice in. May God bless and go with you.

"Have you read this?" Hugh demanded. "By all the saints, she writes little! Aye," he whispered, his words mocking both himself and his wife, "and methinks she had but little to write, knowing well I would reject words of love or apology! Do you know anything of this Caradoc?"

"Only what she told Yedda—that she does not trust or like him."

Scowling, Hugh bit his lip and laughed. "Do you know," he admitted, "that for a moment, when I read this, I credited the slander concerning the incest of the Welsh? Do you know I thought she had gone to a lover and that lover her brother? But she goes to her people! Damn her and them with her! A man I could destroy—I could take her from him—but her people? How can I hold her from them and from Wales?"

His fist lashed out against the granite wall. He leaned his head against the stone's coolness, tears streaming unheeded down his face, blood welling unnoticed from his hand. Godfrey moved to shield him from curious eyes.

Hugh's weeping ceased as abruptly as it had begun. Godfrey turned back when his lord addressed him. "There is nothing I can do. My most devoted wife must wait for my attention until this war is over. May God and the holy saints protect her, for I cannot."

Hugh dropped a forgiving hand on Godfrey's shoulder. "We must find you food and a bed in this rats' warren. Methinks there's room by my pallet—if no one else has yet claimed its dubious comforts."

Meghan rode up the trail to Cleitcroft, Gower behind her. The light February snow swirled, obscuring then revealing the castle across the valley. Even at that distance, its desolation touched her. Shaking off its spell, she rode through the village, her horse's soundless tread adding to the eeriness. The village, too, lay deserted except for one small hut that flaunted a plume of smoke. Glenna lived there, but she could wait.

The drawbridge was down, mounded with snow. The ward was empty and wind-blown. Icicles hung from the eaves of the outbuildings; there being no small boys to knock them down. A shutter hanging askew from a stable window was caught by the wind and slammed against the wall, the sound echoing from the parapets.

Meghan dismounted and gazed at the wide front door of the keep. "I'll go in alone, Gower," she whispered, glancing at him. Her feet were heavy as she mounted the steep stairs. Snow had blown through the entrance and lay in drifts over the filthy floor. Meghan imagined she could smell the feral stench of Caradoc mingled with the dank odor of mildew and smoke.

The walls had been stripped of their hangings. Those tapestries not taken had been trampled by muddy boots. The massive tables, so often ladened with food and drink, and the benches, where bard and begger had rested, had been set afire in the middle of the room. Meghan pulled a leg of her father's chair from the pile of ashes. She traced its intricate carving and tossed it aside, wiping her sooty fingers on her cloak as she gazed about in disbelief. She looked at the ceiling eighteen feet above; the planks were blackened but intact and solid.

On numb feet, she went into the kitchens. They, too, had been ransacked and now stank of stale urine. Utensils had been scattered over the floor, pots and pans smashed and dented. Meghan's hoarded herbs and spices and her medicines had been flung about the rushes, their irreplacable bottles now useless shards. Bones gnawed by rodents lay strewn over the floor. Rats, grown bold, backed into corners, their eyes red with malice. Meghan ignored them and entered the larder. Its stench drove her back. Covering her nose, she went in again.

Casks of salted meat had been chopped open, their contents spilling rot and maggots. Barrels of flour had been turned over, the white powder sullied by rat droppings.

Meghan leaned against the door, sickened by the hatred reflected in such violent destruction. Fighting nausea she returned to the hall, only glancing up the winding stairway to the private chambers, and continued outside. Her feet were steady as she descended the steps to the keep, then her knees buckled. Kneeling, she vomited away her sense of personal violation and a deep hurt and rage. Cleansed, she wiped her mouth with fresh snow, then went to Glenna.

Meghan rapped on the rough-hewed door. A dog barked once, then whimpered with joy. A voice, wavering with age, addressed her by name, bidding her enter.

The sudden warmth burned her face. She glanced about the single room as she shook the snow from her cloak. It was a room as familiar and comfortable as her own skin. The fire in the center, the pallets rolled up against the mud and wattle walls, the cow and pig stabled at the rear, were all as she remembered them. Even the stew simmering in its pot cast off an aroma that spoke of home.

At last her eyes rested on the figure standing before the fire. The face peering back at her had not changed since Meghan's infant eyes had first seen it. The skin was as fine as parchment and creased with deep wrinkles. The black eyes were as wise and impudent as ever. In her arms Glenna held a huge wolfhound who squirmed and whined. Meghan whistled for Rhys to come to her and fondled him, warding off his lapping tongue. "How did you know 'twas me?" she asked.

Glenna chuckled. "'Twas the Tylwyth Teg told me."

Meghan smiled back. "Aye, mayhap 'twas the fairies and mayhap 'twas the dog. Mayhap you heard the horses and peeked. Or mayhap you saw the hoofprints and guessed."

The old woman snorted. "Aye, mayhap 'twas that way." Sobering, she studied the sorrow under Meghan's smile. "Come to me, child, and tell me of your woes."

Meghan kneeled and put her arms about Glenna. She held her for several moments, letting the woman comfort her. But when she drew back, her features held more rage than despair. "How dare they do this to my home, *their* home!" she demanded. "How dare they so defile the clan!"

Glenna stroked Meghan's hair. "'Twas not your people," she answered gently.

"Then who? Caradoc? His perverted lickspittles?"

"Aye. Wipe your nose, child," Glenna ordered, "while I pour ale and tell you of it."

Meghan wiped her nose with her hand like a child. Her teeth still clenched, she dried her tears on the hem of her kirtle. Sitting on a pile of furs, she drew the dog to her. Glenna handed her a cup of ale and poured another for Gower, who had also entered and was stomping snow from himself. He winked at Meghan as the old woman shooed him into a corner like the child she still thought him. Then Glenna settled herself next to Meghan.

"'Twas not the people," she repeated. "'Twas Caradoc and those with him, those outcast mongrels," she said with the Welsh scorn of foreigners. "They took all they could carry and destroyed the rest. They killed the livestock or all they could find. Methinks 'twas in his mind to leave nothing for the people to return to, should they desert him, should you come for them."

"He expects me," Meghan stated.

"Aye, he knew your fear would draw you. But you have put fear away and come with hate instead, haven't you?"

Reading Meghan's answer in her slight smile, Glenna nodded in satisfaction. "He was a strange child, cruel and furtive. He is a worse man. I would you had not come alone, that your lord was with you. Take care with Caradoc, child."

Meghan nodded, then asked about Wynne, the young girl who was even now hiding in the shadows of the hut. "How was it they did not take you or Wynne?"

Glenna chortled. "I told them I would put a curse on them that would wither their poor pizzles! I cackled and waved my arms and neither Caradoc's threats nor that one's budding body was enough for them to come within a tall man's pissing distance of us! Caradoc is still afraid of me, though he does cover it with boasting! He caught the grippe once, after killing a puppy of mine, and he believed 'twas my evil eye did sicken him.'' Her ribald features grew serious. ''Take care with him, child,'' she repeated.

Meghan smiled, but her eyes were hard. ''Aye, I've experience with Caradoc! Gower and I will seek him tomorrow.''

Her fingers caressed the hound as she gazed into the fire, a scowl marring her features. Yet she was content. Then Glenna broke into her musings. ''How went your journey?''

''Not hard. I took food and horses. To the English I became a woman in search of her husband with a deaf mute servant. Only once was I questioned. 'Twas my lord's name did gain me release, though I hate to use him so,'' she confessed. ''Twas luck the knight did not know fitz Alan's wife is Welsh.''

Pausing in thought, Meghan sighed then continued. ''But the Welsh still guard the passes. They have nothing left but rags, dignity, and determination.''

Meghan took the bowl of stew Glenna gave her. ''How was it the people went with Caradoc?''

Glenna shrugged. ''He is sly, that Caradoc, butter not melting in his mouth. When he came, he did praise your sire, aye, and your brothers. But his praise did turn back on itself. 'How is it,' says he, 'that a man of such prowess and wisdom as ab Owen would leave you unprotected?' ''Tis true,' he says, 'he is dead, and valiantly did he die, but why did he not put someone beyond a woman here to lead you? And my brothers, they were brave men, none braver, none their equal. Isn't it sad they were so brave, so eager for the fray? For had they been lesser men, would not at least one be with you now?' ''

Glenna laughed. ''He did not at first lay tongue to you. When he saw they agreed with his praise but not with the faults, he became more blunt. He railed at them for hiding behind walls while Wales fights. 'For do not Welshmen,' says he, 'scorn walls as a device of men afraid to meet their foe face to face? Be not the trees, the mountains, the valleys shield enough for our valiant breed?' Then he called them craven, men in skirts for sitting safe

while others fought, for hiding behind a woman who
deserted them to live in unsanctified fornication with an
English lord.''

Pausing, Glenna's sparse eyebrow lifted, her eyes asking questions of her mistress.

Meghan put down her bowl. ''I am properly wedded,
aye, and bedded,'' she answered. ''I did not go to him
of mine own will. He had ever wanted me and he was
there—at Orewin Bridge. He told me 'twould be the clan
who would suffer should I not go to him. He is gentle,
most times, but blind when roused. I did not dare defy
him for, methinks, Wales will be forced down and Cleitcroft will become Hugh fitz Alan's.''

''Aye,'' Glenna agreed, '''twill end in suffering, no
matter had you gone or no. I, an old woman not stirred
from here in forty years, can smell the rot of it. I saw it
in your sire's eyes before he last left. And when animals
such as Caradoc run the land unhindered, 'tis a sure omen
of hardship. I fear, child, for those fools up in the mountains. Still, I would not have sent for you had I known
you were breeding.''

Meghan's hand dropped to her belly. ''You can tell? I
was not certain of it, myself.''

Glenna chuckled. '''Tis in your eyes and the way you
walk, as though you carry something precious. Is it precious?''

Meghan smiled. ''Aye, though I would not have
thought it so afore he bedded me. In truth, methinks I
love him, though 'tis not a thing I want. Mayhap, if I did
want to love him, I would not be here, but Caradoc
threatens my child, even my lord somehow, and I'll not
have it so!''

Glenna poked at the fire, her features softening. ''Love
weakens some women, child. It turns them into clinging
babies ever afraid of losing what they love. Others, like
you, it strengthens even as it binds them to a role no better than a slave's. Take care, though, that you are not
stronger than your lord!''

Meghan shook her head. '''Twould not be possible. No
woman and few men can match his strength.''

Glenna gazed at her dubiously, then sighed and turned her eyes to the fire. "You were speaking of Caradoc," Meghan prompted, rousing her from her musings.

The old woman blinked. "Aye, I was," she agreed. "Well, he did shame them. Aye, and those men back from Orewin Bridge were bitter, their need for revenge strong. They listened to his talk of your desertion, of the glories to be gained, of English to slay. I doubt they believed him, but he gave them a banner to march under, and men ever need that. And the youths panted to prove themselves, to offer Davyd unbloodied weapons. Methinks the others went in fear of Caradoc and his wolves. So they left, taking the women and the brats. But 'twas not for the women's protection, as he said, but for his lusts. Nor did they go to Davyd. They are up in the mountains, wenching, drinking, preying on the people around them."

Puckering her seamed lips, Glenna paused. "I mislike sending you, but methinks the people will be sore glad. Aye, and you have Gower and the hound. With the people not against you, and mayhap for you, you'll not come to harm."

"Did you burn the hempseed for me?" Meghan asked. "What visions did they give you?"

Glenna's eyes dropped. "Aye," she admitted. "I burned the seed. You will win the people back."

"Did they tell you anything else?"

Glenna sucked in her lips, her gaze avoiding Meghan's. "They told me nothing else."

Meghan knew she was lying but that she would tell her nothing more. "Do you still have the weapons I left with you?" she asked.

Glenna nodded and Meghan smiled. "Then I will win my people back," she agreed.

The hut was dark when Glenna woke Meghan. She sat up and watched the old woman stir the fire, feeding the embers, chanting an ancient charm. Satisfied, she settled back and placed wood in the hearth. Though she had gone through the same ritual every day of her adult life, though the fire was older than she was, Glenna threw Meghan a grin of triumph. Darkness had again been banished—and the sun could rise.

Muttering, Glenna roughly shook Gower and roused Wynne with a cuff. She fed the cow and milked it, crooning as she did so. She put gruel on the fire and handed Meghan a mug of mulled ale.

Meghan stroked the wood of the cup, breathing the odor of ale and spices as she watched Glenna dish out the food. The gruel was good, sweet with honey, the milk still warm from the cow, the heat of the hut comforting.

Still, the meal was over too quickly and Glenna pulled aside her pallet. Her eyes sparkling, she produced a long, narrow bundle and unwrapped the hides. Meghan took the fur-lined leggings and boots and tied them on her calves with strips of hide. After pulling the knee-length tunic over her shift, she secured it with her father's belt. Then she took the longbow the old woman proffered, a bow as tall as she was. Kneeling, she held it across her lap, examining its slender arc of yew, searching for flaws. Standing, Meghan leaned against the bow, bending it to attach the gut. With her fingers, she plucked it to a low hum, inclining her head to listen. She smiled with satisfaction and accepted a handful of yard-long arrows, sighting down each, finding them true.

Glenna drew a cord from around her neck and untied the ivory archer's ring she wore on it, dropping it into Meghan's hand. Meghan slipped it on, then drew the bow to its full extension. Her body seemed to sing with the same taut vibrancy as her weapon. The smooth, round flesh of her arms bulged with muscle concealed by flawless skin. She and Glenna exchanged a grin before Meghan drew on her cloak and ducked out the door.

The sunshine's reflection off the snow blinded Meghan for a moment and she closed her eyes. Opening them, she saw Gower with the horses. She listened to Glenna's last words of advice and accepted her blessing, then mounted. Turning her gaze to the mountains, Meghan urged her horse forward.

Chapter 22

Dusk found Meghan and Gower deep in the Berwyn Mountains. A soft wind had warmed their journey. Running water trickled beneath rotting snow and gargled in rivulets under ice-bound riverbeds. But night brought the cold again, coating the snow with a sheet of ice that cracked as the horse's hooves broke through it.

Halting beneath a huge tree, Gower lifted a hand to stop Meghan. He pointed across a gentle ravine. "There," he said.

Leaning forward, she peered in the direction he pointed. The glow of a campfire could be seen.

"Tell me again of their camp," she ordered. Six men and Caradoc, Glenna had said.

"'Tis a cave, lady, not large enough for all. The path leads up from that slope below us between two rocks my height or more, with room for only one man to pass at a time. The rocks are some fifteen strides from the fire."

"The rocks are shadowed?"

"Aye, and the only other escape is the path into the hills. There is a guard on each path, mostlike drunken."

Meghan smiled and slid off her horse. She watched Gower until he faded into the shadows, then wrapped her bow inside her cloak for warmth. The string she fed into her gauntlet. Leaning against the tree, she waited, the wolfhound beside her. Gower needed time. If he failed, so would she.

At last the voices from the camp grew drunken and boisterous. Leaving the horses, she moved toward the fire's glow. Her calm face belied the excitement and fear coursing through her.

A guard was squatting on a rock near the trail, his face turned longingly toward the roistering. Meghan brushed her fingers together, the rasp of the cold leather gauntlet jerking the man around to face her. His features, Meghan saw as his eyes flicked from her to the wolfhound, were unknown to her. She smiled, mocking his wariness, her head tilted coyly. Standing with feet apart, she drew her cloak aside and put her hands on her hips in challenge. His tiny eyes widened and Meghan jerked her chin toward the fire. "Might that be Lord Caradoc's fire?" she asked.

His gaze flicked from her breasts to her pelvic mound and back. "Aye," he whispered, licking slack lips.

Meghan shifted her hips once before turning on up the path, the guard swiveling with her. She heard him stumble, felt his hand. His face leered into hers, displaying black stubs of teeth. "Ah, wait, now!" he chuckled. "There be none better at pleasing a wench than Walter here!"

Meghan stepped into his arms with her eyes squeezed shut. A sob blocked her throat as she thrust her knife up between the man's ribs and into his heart. It was, she thought in surprise, no different than administering the mercy knife. But this was done in cold blood. She stepped away from the dead man and shoved him from her in horror. He swayed on his feet then crumpled. Her stomach roiling, Meghan stared at him. Never before had she killed a man as she would a rat in a cellar, and she knew she must do so again.

Pausing in the shadow of the looming rocks, she assessed the scene before her. The faces of Caradoc's men were flushed with drink. In contrast, her people's features were calm behind their laughter, their eyes occasionally searching the darkness. So Gower had done his job. But how well or with what result, Meghan did not know.

Only one man was on his feet, stalking about the fire on short legs, the flames casting his shadow into that of a grotesque gnome. His pale, hairless hands gestured as he exhorted the few who listened. While Meghan watched, a man rose unsteadily and pulled a protesting woman into the cave.

As she slung her bow, Meghan's eyes never left Caradoc. She waited for the familiar sensation of fear but found only a cold, sustaining hate. She slipped an arrow into her bow and drew, centering the shaft on the man who paced about the fire. Then she stepped from the shadows and waited.

Slowly the drunken conversation ebbed. One by one, faces turned to her in surprise or gratification.

Caradoc's steps grew hesitant. His hand dropped to rest on his knife. His gaze flicked over the faces intent on something behind him. With a show of nonchalance, he turned. Surprise flared in his face then was gone, but not before Meghan saw it and felt satisfied. Never before had she startled him.

Then he relaxed and a leering smile lighted his protruding eyes. His thick tongue flitted over red lips, wetting them. "Ah," he mocked, "'tis my fair sister come to join us. But sooner than I thought or I would have prepared for you. Did you bring others or only your most welcome self?"

Meghan ignored his question. "You may lower your voice," she said pleasantly. "Your guards will not wake, not from the sleep now holding them."

Caradoc feigned surprise. "'Twas not you, sister, who treated poor Edgar and Walter so, was it? You've not size or stomach for it."

Meghan smiled. "'Twas Walter's lust killed him. Ask Gower of Edgar."

Caradoc whirled as Gower stepped from the shadows, an arrow aimed on Caradoc's men. Shrugging, her brother turned back to Meghan. His eyes flitted over her, touching her obscenely. He waited for the flush such a glance always brought to rise on her face and was not disappointed. For a second her gaze dropped, refusing to read his insinuation, the point of her arrow wavering. Then it steadied and her anger-filled eyes met his.

Caradoc laughed. "And I welcomed you, thinking you wished to join us! I hoped for such. But I had not thought to meet you in such a manner. We are the last of ab

Owen's seed, we two. As such, there should be love between us.'' He paused, something obscene in his eyes. "Why, then, do you bring contention? Why do you insult us with your weapons?''

Meghan did not answer. Her smile widened as she saw hesitation and sudden doubt in his eyes.

"Why is it, sister,'' he asked, "that you left your bastard lover's warm bed to come to cold, struggling Wales? Did word of our plight stir you? Or did you find he would not make an honest wife of you, would not cherish you?''

The unspoken words "as I would'' reached out to touch Meghan, their suggestion strengthening her resolve where once they would have weakened it. Caradoc saw the effect of his words and his jaw tightened, genuine fear rising in him for the first time.

"Did he find you brought him nothing but a worthless croft?'' he taunted. "Did he tire of your fleshless body and waspish tongue? Some men do not find it to their taste as it is to mine. Or mayhap you tired of only one man in your bed, after rutting with every man in the Welsh army and half the English besides? Or so rumor has it. Why did you come, sister, and desert your comfortable bed of fornication? Were you perhaps seeking another?''

Meghan's smile did not waver. No stain of shame darkened her features. She knew, though, that Caradoc sensed the ache on her arms. He was aware that her draw was as strong as a man's, her aim as sure. Kay had taught her well. But he knew, too, that she lacked a man's endurance. He hoped to keep her talking until her strength failed.

"I was sent for,'' she stated, "by one who said my people needed me. And why are you here, Caradoc, you who hovers over strife as a vulture over death?''

A scowl curled his lip, then he grinned. She had left a chance for him. "You left your people, sister, with no one to follow. You deserted them. You locked people who love freedom behind walls and walked away, leaving them unprotected. They would fight the English, but you would not lead them. They would go to Davyd, but you

forbade them, preferring to lie in rut with a Norman than
to fight against him.''

He shrugged, triumph in his cunning eyes. "I came
because they needed me, wanted me, as they no longer
want you. But *I* want you!" He dropped his eyes over
her. "Together we could lead them. Together we could
do many things!"

Meghan tilted her chin, though pain squirmed in her
back. The tension among the people around the campfire
was near its breaking point. What he suggested did not
surprise her. His desire for her had always been there,
only its vileness preventing her from seeing it.

"Do you suggest incest, Caradoc?" she asked. "Are
you so foul? And you are not with Davyd. Or am I mistaken? Is that an English corpse I see turning on its spit
over the fire? It smells of mutton to me—stolen Welsh
mutton. Or am I mistaken again?"

Caradoc felt rather than heard the people's pent-up
breaths. He did not need to look to know that their faces
revealed their shame. He saw, too, the tremor of Meghan's arm and knew he had but to hold her for a few
moments more. She could not kill in cold blood—not her
brother.

One of his men saw it, too. The fear he sensed in Caradoc filled him with contempt. His hatred for women now
centered on the one who dared challenge him, dared hold
him immobile with a weapon that only a man should bear.
He leaped up, his knife flashing, its blade between his
fingers. Suddenly his eyes widened. He fell back, borne
by the weight of the wolfhound, his throat ripped in a
wound that sprayed blood over the snow.

Meghan had seen him leap. The dog's lunge threw her
off balance and as if in slow motion Caradoc moved
instantly behind his man, then leaped forward and to the
side toward Meghan. She released her arrow, knowing as
she did so that her aim was gone. The shaft entered high
in his shoulder, spinning him around, and Gower's arrow
flew harmlessly past as Caradoc fell to one knee, swaying.

He remained there, facing Meghan, disbelief on his
features, time halting as her stiff fingers pulled a second

shaft from her quiver. She fitted it with shaking hands, her purpose still clear despite her body's trembling. Before she could draw the string, Caradoc became a blur, lunging up and toward her. His shoulder struck her and she stumbled, the arrow whirring away into the dark. Then he was gone.

Spinning back, she sent a third arrow a finger's width below Gower's in the back of a man who scurried to the cave. Her fourth flew past a man fleeing into the dark. Gower fired a second later and he fell, the shaft pinning him to the earth.

Lowering her bow, Meghan pulled her shoulders forward against strained muscles. She stared at the corpse of Caradoc's man, his throat ripped by Rhys's teeth. The blood still flowed though it seemed hours had passed. Her only sensation was amazement that she felt no remorse.

Turning, Meghan's eyes flicked over her people. Her gaze fell on a grizzled warrior who sat, not in shame, but in amused anticipation, his eyes on her. Meghan jerked her chin toward the cave. "Rid me of the carrion who ruts with your daughter, Kent ap Evan."

He stood, a faint smile on his face. Meghan watched him until he ducked into the cave, then she sought the men she wanted to draw once more under her control. Her voice was expressionless as she ordered them to kill the man grunting with pain beyond the fire. They calmly went to take the bodies from the camp and drop them over the ledge to the wolves. Meghan returned to the fire and cut a piece of meat from the sheep that sizzled over it, handing it to Gower and carving another piece for herself. Her gaze wandered over the apprehensive faces as she ate, her rage hidden as she waited for the men to return from their tasks.

Only when they had seated themselves again did she speak. "So you would go to Davyd," she stated. "Aye, and mayhap 'tis better to die in valor than to be cursed as cowards who hide behind a woman, than to watch your children's eyes grow hollow with hunger, to watch your women raped, your lands despoiled. Aye, to die is easier than to build again under the foot of the conqueror, to watch the old ways change, the customs die. Aye, for you 'tis easier. But not for me. So go, and I will go with you, though I carry the child of an English lord in my belly, a lord I honor. I will fight beside you against him, if that is your wish."

Pausing, Meghan frowned, fighting fatigue, then shook her head. "No, you've no choice! You will fight and I will see you fight well! But your women and children will stay. They return to Cleitcroft. In truth," she continued, weariness making her spiteful, "they will know hunger, aye, and mayhap starvation, but they can feed on the sheep lying frozen on the hills. They can eat of the flour littering the floor of the storerooms, once 'tis cleaned of rat turds. You wish to go to Davyd and we will go!"

Staring at them, Meghan knew they doubted her sanity. They knew nothing of the desecration of Cleitcroft, but it ached in her and she thought it only just that they suffer it with her. She shrugged, suddenly not caring about them, even hating them, feeling bone weary and deeply lonely. "I go to bed now. Eat, then do the same. There is much to accomplish on the morrow. Women, say farewell to your men. There are many you'll not see again."

Her eyes touched on Kent ap Evan. "A word with you," she requested sarcastically, "most trusted man of my sire."

A smile quirked his lip as he rose and walked with her to the edge of the fire's glow. They stared out into the darkness, wondering the same thing. "Do you think he will live, ap Evan," she asked, nodding toward the night. "Out there?"

The grizzled warrior shrugged and shook his head. "Wounded as he is, with the wolves eager for flesh? I doubt it. Were it another, I would say no and know my words as truth. But Caradoc is a weasel, with bolt holes unknown to others, with ways of squirming from deaths that would end most men. I will try to track him but"— he glanced up, large flakes of snow falling on his strong, lined features—"methinks all trace of him will be gone by the morrow. Still, the snow falls on him as it does on his tracks. I'd not like to be out there, wounded and unarmed and friendless."

He turned, studying Meghan's face. "Lady," he said gently, "consider him dead. Put him from you."

The old fear of Caradoc rose up and Meghan wrapped her arms about herself, trying to control her shaking. Her gaze met ap Evan's and she saw the same doubt in his eyes. She considered asking why he, too, had deserted her, but she was too weary. Her mind flew to Hugh and suddenly she wanted his arms about her, his support and protection. But she had lost them forever.

"Thank you, ap Evan, but I think he will live and that he will be back. Nevertheless, we go to Davyd."

She turned away, her feet leaving small prints in the snow.

Part III

Chapter 23

A May mist fell, veiling the stunted trees and huge rocks pushing up through the thin topsoil. This high in the mountains the nights turned chilly even after the hottest days and Meghan pulled her cloak closer.

She followed the page through the dusk. Even he, so young, walked with the heavy tread of hunger and fatigue. He carefully avoided men who lay in sleep, men who had fallen where the end of the march had found them. Some lay curled like infants, seeking a security remembered only in fitful dreams. Others sprawled on their backs, their mouths open to the rain, the drops settling into the hollow sockets of their eyes. Meghan looked at each as she passed—youths whose mustaches were still a faint down, old men marked by the fear they hid in their souls. Old or young, they appeared strangely similar. So few men were in their prime. Most of those had been left long since in graves scattered across the length and breadth of Wales.

Not all the men slept. Some, gathered into uneasy groups, greeted Meghan as she passed. She smiled in return and tried not to see the fear and questions lurking in their eyes. They, too, felt the tension teasing the night. They sensed an enemy that lurked beyond the edge of their vision, ready to slip among them, dividing and destroying them. Fear seemed to ride the faint, resin-scented wind. Terror whispered in the rustle of leaves and many a man turned to listen, hearing only his own pulse in his ear.

Meghan tried to blame her own disquiet on hunger. Her stomach growled and her hands flew to her slightly rounded belly. Feeling the child stir, she smiled then frowned, her anxiety growing. She wondered again why Davyd sent for her. That it had to do with the restlessness in the camp she did not doubt.

Meghan smiled as she thought of Davyd, a smile tinged with sorrow. He had gratefully accepted her and the men she had brought over three months ago. Since that time she had learned to love and respect him. The traits that had plagued his youth—vacillation and envy of his brother—had left him. He had become a quiet, forthright man whose smile seemed to mock himself or comfort others. He loved his men. His compassion for the wounded, the hungry, and the dead had hardened his features and etched deep lines on his face.

Davyd had changed, Gavin ab Owen had once insisted, and Meghan had smiled, doubting him. But he had changed. He had found strength and determination in his attempt to deny the stepping of foreign feet on earth he considered his. He had earned Meghan's respect where once she had had only her scorn. Her respect had grown to love for the man who fought so hard against odds no one could defeat.

Still, the change had come too late to earn him the loyalty of the chieftains. Though his leadership was good, though he had brought them through battle after battle, out of one seemingly undefeatable trap after another, all but the staunchest allies had gone. With each English victory, with each foot of earth they gained, more men were lost to Davyd, too many to death. But more left him to go to Edward in an attempt to save their lives and land. Only the most faithful now followed Davyd.

Meghan had stayed. She was held by the man who, it was said, had begun the death of Wales. The responsibility had been Davyd's, as much as any man's, and he shouldered guilt with his other burdens. And with his burdens he accepted a love of Wales he had not known before. It was his desire to preserve his country as separate from England that had driven him to this spot deep within the mountains.

Now he stood alone. Bere Castle's fall to the three thousand men of Robert Estrange and William of Valance in April had driven him deeper into himself. The loss of the men and supplies there had depressed him, but the castle's loss had meant more. It had signaled the beginning of the end and he knew then that he had failed. He fought more for time than against the enemy—time to live a day, an hour, a minute longer, time to engrave his deeds and those of his brother a little deeper into the people's memories, that their honorable intent might live on in tales told around the fires in the night.

Deep in thought, Meghan stumbled over a tree root. The page steadied her and pointed to Davyd's small pavilion. She frowned. He had not used the tent in months and his sudden need for privacy puzzled her. He had preferred to sleep in the open with his men, to confer with his chieftains within earshot of everyone. Hiding her concern behind a smile, Meghan ducked under the flap that the page held open.

Davyd motioned her to a stool. A smile touched his eyes before he returned to his quill and parchment.

Studying him, Meghan knew she would not now recognize him for the fop he had been at court. His mouth was hard, a mouth held firm against a daily diet of sorrow in a belly often hungry for more solid nourishment. His skin was no longer soft or unlined. The huge, well-groomed mustache that had once been his only display of Welsh heritage had grown scraggly. One end was shorter than the other. When deep in thought, he chewed on it. It was a trait that drove Meghan mad, yet it was one she loved and would always associate with him. His dark hair had grown gray at the temples and he no longer wore it long in the Norman style.

Meghan's eyes dropped to the long hands driving the quill over the parchment. The white, soft hands that had once gestured almost effeminately were now hard. The nails were torn and calluses marred the palms. They were hands now more familiar with lance and bow, sword and knife, than they had ever been of a woman's body.

Tearing her gaze away, Meghan looked at the pine torch he had wedged between two rocks on the table. It spit and sputtered sap with sudden sparks and smoke. Glancing up, she saw he had cut a jagged hole in the tent's roof to release the acrid fumes. Letting her gaze return to the flickering light, Meghan thought of the last months. They telescoped into endless attacks and retreats, an aching body—and Davyd.

He had been a part of every moment. He had never insulted her with proffered help when she had stumbled and grown numb with fatigue. But he had always been there should she need him. Somehow his nearness had helped drive her on. He had shared his meals with her. He had offered the same fare as his men, but his gossip and their shared laughter had improved the food's taste and texture. His company had filled the nagging void in her belly when there was not food enough to do so.

In the last weeks, too, Meghan had slept close to him. Her nearness had given him comfort. She had listened to his plans and worries when he could not sleep, understanding the thoughts he could not speak. His sorrow, the compassion he shared, had eased her pain when she had tended the wounded. The words of comfort she had whispered to men who cried out in agony were the ones he would have spoken had he been able to play the role of mother or wife. His hand touching her shoulder had spoken of shared remorse and guilt when she had had to order the mercy knife to men beyond healing.

Suddenly Meghan realized that the quill no longer scratched across the parchment. The only sound was the wind blowing over silken ridges and whistling down the smokehole. Smiling, Davyd nodded toward the torch. "I've no more candles," he explained needlessly. "That is a crude device, but it works."

He sighed, his fatigue visible. Absent-mindedly, he rubbed his high forehead, his eyes on the parchment. "I ofttimes think on this as a war of improvisation," he mused. "Of making something out of nothing."

Davyd lifted his eyes that were suddenly bleak. "'Tis the end, Meghan, daughter of Gavin ab Owen. There are no more places to run, no battles to fight, not for you. I'm sending you away from me with your men, or what is left of them."

Meghan stared at him, dumbfounded, the pain of his words twisting her heart. "Why?" she whispered.

Standing, Davyd began to pace. All the anger, grief, and despair of the past months welled up and was unfairly directed at Meghan. "Why? You of all people ask me why? Can you not see? Have you not known from the beginning that our cause was but a fool's venture? Do you think I can produce food from pine and pitch as easily as I do flame? Do you think I can cut clothes from the sky or boots from the earth to protect the men bleeding now for my sake? Do you think I should drive them on, expecting them to subsist on the hope in their hearts when I have none in mine? Aye, and do you think I should lead them, staggering with hunger and fatigue, once more to the English girding about us and strangling our souls?"

Laughing curtly, he leaned over Meghan, the rage at his failure flaring in his dark eyes. "And with what do I arm them? Methinks there are no more yew trees in all of Holy Wales tall enough to make a bow for a puling infant."

Davyd snorted his disgust and wheeled away, his fists clenched. When she did not answer, he turned back. A small, sad smile was on her lips. "I meant, my lord," she said, "why do you send *me* away? I would stand by you."

Never before had Davyd mentioned her pregnancy. Now he spoke of it. "The life I now lead is not one for a woman with child. You need food, warmth, comforts I cannot give you. 'Tis not only you I think of, girl, but myself as well. You can do nothing but hold me back, make me more vulnerable. And 'tis not only you. In the next days, most of the others will go. You are but the first. I keep only those whose loyalty is excessive of their sense and those who prefer to die in defiance than cringe in some corner."

Davyd's voice became pleading. "Think of your child, girl, and of me, if you love me!"

He watched as Meghan's head drooped. Seeing her tears, he went to her. Lifting her chin, he forced her gaze to meet his. His whisper was tender. "Do you think I will forget the months you stood by me? That I will forget your support or the comfort you gave me when no one else could?''

Sniffing, she shook her head.

''You will go, then?'' Davyd asked.

Meghan nodded, though anger and regret flared in her eyes.

Laughing softly, Davyd wiped away her tears. ''Had I not a wife and nine children, girl,'' he teased, his banter ill-concealing his grief, ''I would have long since asked your father for you. Aye, even when you first went to Edward. Remember? I saw you there at Flint and you did scorn me.''

Meghan smiled back, forcing her words to match the lightness of his. ''I would not have had you then, Davyd ab Gruffydd, Norman fop that you were!'' Her eyes grew tender and she bit her lip. ''But now, had you not a wife and nine children and had I not a husband and a babe within me, aye, I would have you, if only to stay by you here.''

Davyd's smile grew tight and his voice husky. ''Do you know that I love you, Meghan, daughter of ab Owen?''

Nodding, Meghan saw his eyes fill with need. His lips touched her forehead then her mouth, holding it briefly. When he drew back, his gaze was veiled. ''I would have you, girl. I would ask of your comfort, but 'tis not in you to give where you do not love, nor could I take it from you.''

Meghan traced his lips with her finger. ''But I do love you, my lord.''

Smiling ruefully, Davyd nodded. ''Aye, but not as I would have you, not the way you love your Norman lord. I would not take a woman for the pity she bears me and respect is a cold bedfellow. Aye, you love me, but with the love you give each man who comes to you hurt, sick, afraid. You would give me comfort with your body as you give them comfort with your words. Mayhap my need is greater and your love for me more, but I'll not take you for the comfort you would give from pity. 'Twould sully you, and the love I bear you, to do so.''

Lifting her chin, Davyd brushed away the tears that flowed once more. "Shush," he whispered. "Do not weep because you cannot give me what you do not have."

"But I have it!"

"Aye, you do but, girl, do not ask me to bear the worry, too, of you and your lord. You could not lie to him about us and methinks he could not bear it if 'twas true."

He held her tightly, burying his face in her hair, then released her. "I've some wine. 'Tis thin, sour stuff, but still wine. Would you share it with me?"

Meghan nodded and Davyd filled the goblets, giving her time to compose herself. When he turned back, her face was calm once more. Accepting a cup, she sipped and grimaced.

Laughing, Davyd lifted his goblet. "But 'tis wine! Mayhap the last, the best in Wales!" Sobering, he asked, "Will you go to Cleitcroft?"

"No, I must return to Ainsleah. 'Twas there I left him and 'twill be there he'll find me, if but for his pride's sake. I would not have it said he must carry his wife home against her will."

"Will he harm you, Meghan?"

She smiled and shook her head. "Methinks not. I hurt him and his pride, though I would not have had it so. He'll not easily forgive me that, nor will he trust me again soon, but he'll not hurt me, if but for the babe's sake."

Davyd chewed on his mustache and smiled. "You love him, do you not?"

Meghan dropped her eyes, then met his gaze again. "Aye. 'Twas not a thing I wished, but 'tis there."

Davyd read the pain in her eyes—and the fear that she had hurt him. Taking her face in his hands, he gazed into her eyes. "Your love of him robs me of nothing, girl. I would not want you to have no other but me. What can I offer you? There is nothing left to give. And 'tis for love of you that I send you from me."

Meghan turned her face into his palm, her lips soft on his calluses. "What will happen to you, my lord?"

His jaw set and he avoided her eyes. "I will run. I will hide. And I will fight." Drawing a deep breath, Davyd shuddered slightly. "And I pray God grant me the death that was Llewelyn's: to be killed by one blow from a man who does not know me. I pray God spare me an ignominious death, that He will not allow me to be taken, to be caged, to die on alien earth. But methinks He will not have it so. Methinks I will be taken, aye, and mayhap by Welsh hands. And methinks Edward, in his rage, will devise for me a death no man has yet suffered."

He looked at Meghan, his eyes pleading for understanding of his fear. "Pray me an easy death, girl, if you love me!"

Davyd's voice was gentle as he shushed the words that reached in vain for hope. Holding her, he felt her shudders. When they subsided, he pushed her gently from him. "'Tis late, lady, and we but confirm the gossip said of us." Meghan lifted her head and he laughed. "Aye, I heard it, too. Soldiers prattle worse than crones and their words always reach the man who leads them. There was nothing I could do. I only hope your lord does not hear of it."

Gazing into her face, Davyd strived to memorize each of her features, then he turned her away from him. "I would have you gone by morning. There is nothing left to say and to look on the woman I would love is too hard for me. Now, go!"

Turning back and leaning against him, Meghan lifted her lips and touched his mouth gently. "I love you, my lord Davyd," she whispered, "and I will pray for you!" She walked to the door, then hesitated.

"Go!" he whispered hoarsely.

Meghan ducked under the tent's entrance and was gone. Outside, she waited for Davyd to call her back. He knew she waited and she knew he would not relent. Still, she stayed. At last her head drooped. Weeping without sound, she walked back to her men, men to whom she would have to admit defeat.

Chapter 24

The sun was warm on Meghan's back. A soft breeze stirred the newly unfurled leaves of the trees. The drone of bees and the whir of grasshoppers seemed clamorous after the eerie silence of the mountains of defeated Wales. The odor of sap and of crushed grass were strong.

After leaving Davyd, she and her men had traveled by night and hidden by day. The English had seemed to be behind every tree and rock. Each village and croft had held the threat of English sympathizers. Starvation in a child's eyes turns a man's loyalty to the heaviest purse, the sharpest weapon. Then her men, Gower and ap Evan with them, had left to go to Cleitcroft and she had traveled on alone.

Now she neared Ainsleah. Less than two days' journey, she thought; its proximity lessened her caution. The major part of the English forces were behind her, controlling Wales, holding Davyd cornered like a fox in a den.

Pushing back her cloak, Meghan lifted her face to the sun. Her foot brushed a rock, dislodging it to strike another. She stopped instantly, her head lifted like a cautious wild animal, but she could see no one the noise might have alerted. She went on.

The clatter made Arvel raise up to peer over the bushes concealing him. He gripped the arm of the man next to him, silencing him in the middle of telling an obscene story. Trehern, raising sparse eyebrows, rolled over and followed Arvel's stare. He grinned, displaying broken teeth, and whistled softly. Breath hissed from his nostrils.

"Aye, I see her," he whispered, "and she be breeding. I like breeding bitches! They fight more. And she wears gold enough that we could leave the lords to fight their own war. With her throat slit, who would be the wiser?"

Arvel only squinted, a frown furrowing his low brow, then he laughed soundlessly. "Aye, and that slut would fight. I saw her at Dolwyddelan and she fought like the bitch she be. If you want her gold, try for it. Me, I would rather have the dozen whores a purse of gold would buy than that one, the bitch! She opened her legs fast enough to Davyd, but it was a knee to the balls for the likes of me when I tried to be but a bit friendly!"

Arvel didn't meet Trehern's stare but continued considering the possibilities. "Aye, Edward Longshanks would pay dearly for Davyd's whore. And that lord she ran away from—he would pay and plenty. Methinks he would reward well a man who returned his bitch to him. Once he knocks that bastard out of her, she'll be good as new. Methinks he'll make her pay dearly for her rutting ways."

He relished the thought, nodding. "But we'll take her carefully. I've seen her with that knife. She can take the balls off a man, aye, and like the doing of it."

He watched Meghan pass beneath them, ducking as she glanced their way, then he lifted his head again. At last he turned to Trehern.

"She's a mean bitch, she is, but she'll not ignore a wounded man. I've seen her—that uppish face too good for the likes of me but all soft for a man with a knife in his side. I've a plan, and after we've taken her, you go for the limp-pizzled Edward Litton. Tell him who we found and bring him back."

"Aye, after I've played a few games with her."

Arvel shook his head. "Not with that one, breeding or no. Methinks the king and her lord would both be sore angered to receive damaged goods. All we'd get for that would be a day on the whipping tree. Unharmed, they'll pay dearly."

Trehern grinned, his mind eagerly counting the coins he would receive. Then he scowled. "Would Caradoc want her? Isn't she his sister—the bitch he curses so oft?"

Arvel's eyebrow puckered then cleared. "Aye, and 'tis more than revenge he wants. He ruts after her, does our Caradoc, and well would I like to see him have her. But Edward and that stone-faced lord of hers would pay more. And we'll be gone to London long afore Caradoc gets wind of it."

The sun was now dropping toward the west, Meghan's shadow falling in front of her, its radiance behind her. In the distance, she could see the farmlands of the Marches and smoke from a distant village. Ainsleah was near. She would be there tomorrow. A smile curved her lips and started to move on, then halted again. The sense of something wrong assailed her and she lifted her head, suddenly wary.

Faintly she heard a moan. She waited and it came again from the deep brush at the side of the path. Hesitating, she drew her knife from her girdle and moved cautiously toward the sound. A man lay face down in the grass, a knife protruding from under the arm clenched tightly to his side. What appeared to be blood stained the cloth around it. All caution gone in her concern, she thrust her knife back into her belt and knelt down at his side.

A twig cracked behind her and she half rose, realizing at once that it was a trap. A sinewy arm snaked around her neck, cutting off her breath, and her arm was jerked behind her. Twisting her head, she sank her teeth deep into her captor's biceps, his acrid scent harsh in her nose, while her free hand fought to reach the knife in her girdle.

"Help me, Trehern, you useless bastard!" Arvel grunted in her ear and Meghan saw the man who had feigned being wounded rise up. His eyes gleamed with a feral joy and his broken teeth were displayed in a mindless grin.

"She is breeding." He chuckled. "And the breeding ones do fight best! But Trehern'll tame her!"

He lifted his foot, but its import didn't reach her until he swung his heavy boot back and sunk it deep into her belly. It took a moment for the pain to reach her, a moment more to realize that the groan of pain was her own. She felt herself falling to the dirt, being dragged into the brush at the side of the road. For a brief second she saw a face through her agony that was vaguely familiar.

"Arvel, Arvel," she heard a man moan, "I'm most sorry, Arvel, I am in truth! I know you wanted her unharmed! I know that, Arvel! But she shouldn't have fought, she shouldn't have! And she be breeding, Arvel! Trehern likes the breeding ones!"

There was a curse for silence and she felt a tug as her gold link belt was taken from her. The wide gold bands about her biceps were yanked away and her wedding band was jerked from her finger. Her body rolled as her cloak was taken.

"Arvel, Arvel!" she heard, "what do we do now? He'll kill us, Arvel, he will, that lord of hers, aye, and Edward Longshanks!"

"He won't, because we won't be here. We'll go to Chester and from there to Ireland. 'Twill be safe there until this dies down. She'll not live long, bleeding like that and with luck 'twill be months afore anyone finds the slut!"

A heavy boot sank into Meghan's side and everything went black. . . .

The sun had sunk low when Meghan awoke. For a moment she watched a small red bug crawl up a twig, then the pain assaulted her. She curled into it, remembering what had happened, and realized she was losing the baby, Hugh's baby.

Fighting the grip of agony deep inside, Meghan crawled inch by inch through the brush to the road, each movement seeming to rip her apart. She lay there resting, husbanding her strength, wondering which way to go. Whatever she did, it would have to be before dark because she could not live out the cold night, not like this.

Then she heard the fall of a horse's hooves and the clink of harness.

In the stables of Castle Rhuddlan, Edward's strong-hold, Hugh held his destrier's foot over his knee. His head was bent as he gently probed around the frog, but he was aware of Ralph Ramsden leaning over the top of the stall, his freckled face apprehensive. Finding a stone, Hugh cursed the rocky soil of Wales and carefully extracted it before glancing up. His eyes narrowed against a surge of emotion when he saw Ralph's face. He knew what his squire was there to tell him and his hands grew still as his heart quickened.

"What news, Ralph?" he asked.

The squire hesitated, then blurted out, "She's here—your lady! She was brought in but moments ago!"

Frowning, Hugh looked at the huge hoof on his knee. Picking up a small, curved knife, he carved at a bit of the horny material. "Who brought her in?"

"Edward Litton. He found her near here, less than a day from Ainsleah. Methinks she was returning home."

Glancing up, Hugh scowled. "Aye, mayhap. What is it that you don't tell me?" he asked.

Ralph's eyes looked everywhere but at his lord. At last he sighed and gritted his teeth. "She was breeding, my lord," he said, "but she was attacked where Litton found her. She was sore hurt, my lord, and Queen Eleanor thinks she'll lose the babe, if she hasn't already, while we talk."

Hugh dipped his fingers in a pot of odoriferous ointment and smeared it on the cut in the horse's foot. He washed his hands, dried them carefully, and stood up. His face was stark as he asked where Meghan was.

"In the queen's chambers," Ralph answered, taking the halter Hugh handed him.

"Take him to the smith and curry him," Hugh ordered, slapping the destrier on its haunch as he left.

Strolling toward the keep, Hugh looked neither left nor right. He acknowledged no greeting but was acutely con-scious of the whispers and stares, of the snickers and smiles. The glee in the eyes of many at the sight of a high-flown bastard brought low tightened his jaw and drew his mouth taut. The sudden fear and love he had felt at Ralph's message, the sharp need, gave way to fury at the humiliation being dealt him.

But Meghan was hurt and he, baffled in his impotence, could do nothing about it, he who had sworn always to protect her. His raging thoughts turned to whoever had dared harm her, to whoever had dared harm anything of his. And his child—if it was his child—they had dared destroy the child he had not even known existed until moments ago.

It seemed hours passed before Eleanor let him in the chamber, hours during which he paced and listened to Meghan's muffled groans. The door opened and closed, maidservants, midwives, the queen, and her ladies all came and went in a flurry of skirts while he stood and paced or sat, only to stand again. A priest went in and Hugh turned his face to the wall to pray, his head buried in his arms. The priest came out again, Eleanor after him, smiling encouragement.

When at last he was allowed to see his wife, it was all over. The chamber was dark and smelled of sweat and blood and, strangely, of sex. Meghan lay in the center of a large bed, her damp hair spread out around her. Dark shadows smudged her closed eyes, her lips were gnawed and bloodless, and hollows like thumb prints sank beneath her cheekbones.

Sitting down next to her, Hugh took her hand and turned it over in his. Her hand seemed too small, too fragile to bear the strength he knew lay beneath its smooth muscles. Rubbing the archer's callus that marred her finger, he looked at her again. She was studying him, her features expressionless, yet she seemed to wait for some word from him, what he did not know. He stared back, aching with a need to hold and comfort her.

But perhaps it was Davyd she wanted and Davyd's child she had lost. If it was so, then he had truly lost her. He had wanted to protect her, but it was too late. She had already been injured, violated. Still, it was not too late for revenge; that was something he understood. That was a gift he could give her.

"Who did this?" he demanded.

An intense sorrow flitted across her face. "It does not matter, my lord. I would have it done, finished!"

Hugh's jaw clenched. "Did you know them?" he demanded.

Meghan wearily shook her head. "One only looked familiar. Methinks he was briefly with the army months ago."

Hugh did not need to ask "What army?" and he dropped her hand to begin to pace, his doubts driving him. When he turned back, his face was filled with a rage for revenge. He could not hit out at Davyd, not yet, but the ones who had harmed her, those he might take.

He sat down on the bed, his arms on either side of her like a lover, his mouth inches from hers. "Tell me what you know of them!" he ordered.

Her eyes soft, Meghan reached up to touch his mouth with gentle fingertips. Then her eyes closed and slow tears flowed from beneath her dark lashes.

"They called themselves Arvel and Trehern," she whispered. "They go to Chester, thinking to sail for Ireland. . . ."

Her voice murmured on, giving what descriptions she could, answering Hugh's questions. When she was finished, Hugh smiled, though his eyes were grim. He kissed her softly, lightly, as though in thanks for her information, and stood up.

"Do you go, my lord?" she asked.

Hugh turned back, surprised at her question.

"My lord," she whispered, "I wish you would not go!"

"My lady," Hugh rapped out, "something of mine has been hurt, damaged. I cannot suffer such insult."

Meghan watched the door close behind him and touched her belly for comfort, as she had so many times during the last few months. But this time her stomach was flat and she closed her eyes, weeping for her loss, for all her losses.

She was not to be left alone in her grief. Eleanor came the next day and Meghan drew herself from her sorrow to greet her. Meghan's voice was warm as she asked after her lady's health and told her of her happiness in seeing her again.

"You've another child, I've heard," Meghan said.

Eleanor stared at her, startled that she would ask about another woman's child so soon after losing her own. But Meghan only smiled back.

"Did your Edward puff and strut as though 'twas his doing only and you merely favored?" she asked.

The queen returned the smile. "Aye," she answered, "and I kept silent, being not fool enough to think I could convince him otherwise. He is easier to live with so."

Meghan giggled, then a shadow crossed her face. Her hand pressed down on her flat belly. "I had hoped," she said lightly, "that this would be a son. I thought mayhap he would soften my lord toward me." She shrugged away the hope and asked, "How does my lord? I saw him but briefly last night."

"He has good health," Eleanor said slowly, her worried eyes on Meghan's calm features. "He was wounded once, in the shoulder, and that healed quickly." But it was not Hugh's health that concerned Eleanor. "He is bitter, Meghan, and stern now. He seldom laughs and has no thought for anything but the next battle. He was sore hurt by your leaving and methinks 'twas more than his pride was hurt."

"Ah, my lady." Meghan smiled. "I most sore regret that I hurt Sir Hugh. 'Twas not my intention. I only did my duty—as he does his." She paused, her smile still in place, then said, "I'm tired, lady, but you'll come back, won't you? And bring your son. I would so love to see your son."

Eleanor returned many times, but she never brought the baby; there had been too much pain in Meghan's smile. Nor did Meghan ever ask again to see him.

Edward came, too, his need for information stronger than his aversion to female sickrooms.

"Well met, my lord Edward," she said and he snorted.

" 'Well met!' says the wench," he mimicked. "And I thought myself well rid of her! God's blood! When I gave her to that fool, I hoped she would plague me no more."

Meghan smiled back at him, her eyes curiously vacant. Edward shrugged, suddenly uneasy. "Why did you leave Davyd?" he asked before he had intended to.

"He sent me from him," Meghan answered calmly. "My belly had begun to hinder me."

A ribald comment rose to his lips and he swallowed it back as a glimpse of defiance and hurt touched the blankness in Meghan's eyes. "How many men has he?"

She shrugged. "I do not know."

Edward snorted. "You say you do not know, yet you've been with him close to four months? My spies are better informed than you."

"'Tis a hard thing to guess, my lord," she carefully explained. "The spring is a difficult time to hold men. Davyd lost many to the plowing and planting, but 'tis finished now. Most will return to him," she lied, past her indifference.

Edward grunted his disgust. "Plowing and planting, have you? The Welsh plow nothing but their wives and any other wench they can hold down long enough! And plant? They plant nothing but more Welsh bastards to harry me and mine. The only husbandry they practice is the stealing of their neighbors' cattle."

His banter struck an answering chord and her voice held laughter. "But we do grow corn enough for our bannock, my lord—'tis hard to always know if the English will have harvest enough to share at summer's end."

His eyes glinted in appreciation of her wit. He had missed her impudence. Then he grew serious.

"There are things I must know, Meghan," he stated.

But she told him nothing.

In the days that followed, Meghan's depression deepened. She forced her mind to remain empty, let her thoughts float free, remembering the relief from pain such dullness brought. When faced with any small decision, such as which clothes to wear or what to eat, she would burst into tears. To move was an effort she could seldom make. Once she learned to send her thoughts from her, to escape herself, she found she could not always summon them back at will. At first the discovery terrified her. Then she found peace in the sanctuary of mindlessness.

Eleanor brought needlework to occupy the days during which Meghan was bedridden, but she often found her with idle hands, gazing at nothing or weeping over what color thread to use. The friends Meghan had made four years before came to visit. When she saw them—Isabelle Douglas, Kate Granville, and Alice Beaufort—Meghan searched for Eleanor de Montfort. But she did not ask and only later, waking from sleep in tears, did she remember that Llewelyn's wife had died in childbed and that he was dead, too, his head on a pike on London Bridge.

Meghan tried to summon interest in her visitors' gossip, but her mind drifted and she brooded through their prattle. Her thoughts ran in endless circles—Wales defeated, her child lost, her father dead, her brothers gone. Hugh was gone, too, chasing revenge, when all his rage could be calmed with a question he would not ask. And he would not ask it because the child was dead. She could find no end to the circles in her mind.

Her visitors left. They did not return despite Eleanor's urgings. Nor could she blame them, for Meghan was poor company with her vacant eyes and her sudden, unprovoked flow of tears.

Sixteen days later, Hugh returned, his features stark with purpose. He found his wife sitting in a high-backed chair staring into an empty fireplace. Only when he repeated her name twice did she turn to look at him. She looked so thin, so apathetic!

For an instant a small smile of joy tipped her mouth. Welcome and love shone in eyes the color of new leaves. Then she scowled, as though trying to remember why he made her happy. Yet she still regarded him politely, as she would a stranger.

A feeling of cold fingers walking up his spine assailed Hugh. He shook it away. "My lady," he said, and her eyes regarded him more courteously, "I return these to you."

He laid her gold link belt across her lap and slipped her wedding band back on her finger. She stared at the band a moment and slid it up and down on her knuckle as though it felt foreign. Then she touched the belt.

"You found them?" she asked, sounding glad. "You found Arvel and Trehern? They took my father's belt from me, you know. And they killed my baby."

Goosebumps leaped up over his flesh. His hands reached for both of hers and he buried his face in her lap, his shoulders shaking with grief.

"Where is he?" she asked, and Hugh jerked his head up at the coldness in her voice.

"Where is my son? Where did they bury him?"

Hugh drew her hands to his mouth. "Outside the churchyard, my lady. I marked the spot."

Her mouth tilted in a smile. "'Tis fitting, isn't it?" she asked. "Where else would they put the unbaptized son of an excommunicate mother and a bastard sire but with the murderers, the thieves, the rapists? And mayhap they say he, too, was a bastard?"

Hugh's heart leaped in hope that she would deny it, but she only laughed. "He'll have much Welsh company there, will he not? Aye, but I would have him brought to Ainsleah!"

Hugh's eyes held her green ones, which stared back at him, determined, demanding an answer. He nodded and she smiled.

"I thank you, my lord," she whispered, and her mouth dropped to press against his fingers. Abruptly her eyes jerked up to his, panic stricken. She mouthed his name, a soundless plea, before she drew away to regard him as a stranger. Yet she should know him, she knew. And she loved him, loved him more than life, that she did know. She wanted him, wanted his mouth on hers, his body pressing her down, possessing her. But to acknowledge those desires brought pain. To give way to love brought only grief. How could she love a stranger?

It was Eleanor who gave Hugh comfort. She spoke of despondency after childbirth as a common thing, especially when the child was stillborn. Many women temporarily lost their minds then, especially ones with as many losses as Meghan had suffered. Some even blamed themselves for the child's death; perhaps Meghan did. That would account for her extreme grief. Perhaps she even felt she had lost Hugh. But it would pass, she assured him, it almost always did. All he could do was be patient, to give Meghan time. And Meghan had her good times, Eleanor reminded him, times when she was just lethargic. If he could but draw on those, encourage them, expand them. She advised him to take her to Ainsleah, to a place where she could be busy, to a place that was comfortable and known to her.

Hugh thanked Eleanor, but he knew Meghan's despondency went deeper and suspected the queen knew it did, too. What lay at its core, he could only guess at.

They left Rhuddlan twenty-one days after Meghan's arrival. She accepted the move with apathy. Only for a moment did she come to life, vehemently refusing a litter, declaring it a contrivance for old women and members of the clergy who were too fat or too lazy to straddle a horse. The mocking light in Hugh's eyes, and his unspoken hope that her stubbornness was a sign that she was healing, quelled her resistance and drew a pall over her features once more.

The litter swayed with each step of the horses bearing it. Through parted curtains, Meghan could see the village below Ainsleah. The priest stood near the church to welcome his lord and lady home. Children ran beside the litter, their skinny legs flashing brown. The flowers they threw had been hastily plucked; dirt still clung to the roots. Their avid eyes belying their bland features, women stood beside their doors or in small, gossiping groups, clutching infants. A toddler released his mother's skirts and staggered toward the gaily hung litter, his chubby legs set wide, a grin of triumph and delight exposing his few teeth. Meghan smiled back, momentarily sharing his joy, then her features closed and she leaned back, shutting the curtains to hide his face.

Resting against the cushions, she closed her eyes and yearned for the sleep she would have at Ainsleah. She heard sounds of their entrance into the castle, the creaking of the portcullis and the thud of hooves on the drawbridge. The litter entered a shadow cast by the castle walls, then came out into the sunshine of the bailey and swayed to a halt.

Stepping out, Meghan gazed blankly at the surrounding faces—Yedda's beaming welcome, Godfrey's reserved smile, the other faces. They all seemed alien, as though they were puppets playing the roles of people she loved. Nor could she summon affection for them. Forcing a smile, Meghan greeted them and thanked them for their condolences. She stared dully at the keys Godfrey offered, the keys she had left behind in her flight to Wales. She touched them, then drew her hand back empty. Lifting her eyes, she saw Selig staring at her, a scowl knitting his brows. His concern touched a nerve deep within her and her mouth curved slightly before it fell into sorrowful repose once again.

She gazed at Ainsleah's three towers. Their white-washed walls dazzled her eyes. A flock of birds lifted from the parapet, circling into the sky, and her gaze followed them into freedom.

A sudden sense of vertigo blackened her vision and she clung to Godfrey's arm, closing her eyes. She swayed, then breathed deeply. "I would go to my room," she whispered.

No one moved, all eyes turning to Hugh. He sat on his horse, surveying the scene—an uninvolved spectator. When he made no move to go to his wife, the people surrounding Meghan turned back to stare at her, wondering at the turn of events.

Finally Selig growled and, pushing people aside, went to her. He lifted her in his arms and effortlessly carried her into the keep. Yedda followed. Looking back over Selig's shoulder, Meghan flinched at the scorn in Hugh's eyes and she dropped her gaze.

When Selig closed the chamber door behind him, Meghan rose weakly from the bed and tried to undress herself, her fingers fumbling. Yedda helped her and stood back, eyeing her with distaste. "I'll order a bath and food," she stated. "Do they not eat or bathe at Rhuddlan?"

"Aye, they eat at Rhuddlan—but not in Wales!" Abruptly her shoulders slumped and she leaned back against the bedpost. "I'm too tired to bathe, Yedda, and food sickens me."

Yedda frowned. "I know 'tis hard to lose a babe, but you're filthy and you must eat for strength."

Meghan's hand tightened on the bedpost. It seemed as though everyone was pushing her. Shaking her head, she muttered, "I'm too tired to argue so don't nag, Yedda, not now or you'll find yourself back in the kitchens!"

"I won't nag, lady, but I won't go back to the kitchens, either. I married Sir Godfrey!"

Meghan merely looked at her. "My best wishes," she said at last. "I'll give you a gift someday, but now I must sleep."

Meghan's hair on the pillow looked too heavy for her pinched face and slim neck. Her eyes were enormous above her hollow cheeks. "Mayhap I could drink a little broth," she conceded; she could always pour it in the chamber pot as soon as Yedda left.

It was late when Hugh came to bed. He had stared for hours at the fire, his hands clenched around his untouched goblet of wine as he sought the words he knew he must say to his wife, words that would force her mind back from wherever she had sent it. As he sought the strength and cruelty to say them, he knew that they might also drive her further away. But he had to do it; he had to do something!

The slam of the door jarred Meghan awake and she lay rigid, listening to the sounds Hugh made as he undressed. She pictured his movements from behind closed eyes, pictures from a happier time when she had watched him disrobe in joyous anticipation. She heard the grunt he made when pulling off his tunic and imagined him standing on one foot then the other to remove his chausses. She saw him again as he scratched a wide chest, down a hard belly, and into his pubic hair, his lustful, laughing eyes holding a promise of a night of passion and love. Then he came to her, in those times, triumph in his eyes, knowing her need was as great as his.

Sighing, Meghan forced the pictures aways and felt him ease into bed. Her breathing deepened, but she shuddered away from the hand touching her shoulder. The fingers tightened, jerking her over, and Meghan stared into Hugh's eyes, eyes that were grim in the firelight.

"You were not asleep, lady," he stated. She reminded him of a cornered rabbit, but he refused to feel pity.

"My lord," she pleaded, "'tis too soon!"

He laughed, then his features turned hawklike. One brow crooked and his eyes were hard as they flicked over her. "The lady thinks I would seduce her," he mocked. "The lady has a poor opinion of my taste. God's glove, but she would insult a swineherd to offer such stuff as she is, all dirty hair and skinny shanks and jutting hipbones."

Hugh's nostrils flared, his mouth growing taut. "Aye, and your stink offends me! You are as odious as a slaughterhouse with your unchanged rags, the filth of your hair, the grime of your flesh."

Abruptly all merciless glee fled his eyes, leaving only ruthless cruelty. His voice became relentless. "I did but wish to speak to you, you who have been so assiduously avoiding me. I did but wish to tell you how things will be here and, lady, you had best heed me."

Pausing, Hugh let silence add weight to his words, his eyes piercing the veil Meghan tried to maintain around her mind. "You will no longer stay hidden away, seeking sleep. I married you to control my household, to warm my bed, aye, and to breed my children. You have duties and you will fulfill them. I'll forgo the dubious pleasure of bedding you, out of pity and because you do not arouse my lust. But I expect you to relieve Godfrey of the duties that are yours. Tomorrow, you will take the keys you so discourteously refused today and you will become, in truth, mistress of Ainsleah. You will no longer hide behind tears, feeble gestures, and downcast eyes. You will answer when addressed. You will issue orders and have them obeyed. How you do it, I don't care. I only care that it is done. If you should fail, there is many another wench, prettier, stronger, and with a better dowry to take your place. Aye, and many another more worthy of my pride and trust. As for the duties which so repulse you, I'll find my ease elsewhere until I judge you well enough to bear a child. If you should choose to fight and deny me, I will not hesitate to place you in a convent. And methinks you have given me cause enough for annulment should you think to thwart me by denying me another woman to wife and the brats I would get off her. Think on it, lady. You would never see Wales again. I shall see to it.''

The anger in Hugh's eyes changed to disgust. "And you will bathe. I need not partake of your body but I do, for appearance's sake, have to share your bed.''

His eyes flicked over her one more time, aversion plain as he read her hurt and anger, her plea for understanding. Then he rolled away from her and fell into a deep slumber.

Meghan stared at the canopy. His words had pierced her shell of apathy and touched the core of pride that was still intact within. He had ripped away her last support— the love she thought he still bore her—leaving her to stand or fall alone.

Whimpering, dragging herself to the far edge of the bed, Meghan fought the urge to run from the chamber, go to the parapet, look to the mountains of Wales—and jump. The thought of the brief fall and the quick end that would join her to her child drew her and slow tears flowed down her cheeks, streaking the grime. She wanted it so badly, but the seed of anger at Hugh's challenge, the need to hurt him as he had her, held her back. Her jaw tightened into a hard line of resolution before she finally slept.

Chapter 25

The grip on her shoulder was rough. Meghan moaned, trying to turn from it, but she was only shaken harder. She stared up at Hugh, remembering his words of the night before, and the bewildered look in her eyes turned to hostility. Sitting up, she held the bedclothes high and returned his mocking stare.

"By the saints," Hugh jeered, "had I seen your filth by light of day, I would have preferred to bed with the hounds! Yedda will bring your bath. See that you take it. And get rid of that," he ordered, pointing to the cloak thrown over a chest. "Give it to a beggar, if you can find one so humble as to take it, or burn it. It reeks as much as you do."

His voice grew derisive as he added, "Methinks I can well afford a cloak for my lady wife. I would not have it said I do not honor her—whether or not I do."

"No," Meghan stated, her jaw suddenly stubborn. "I'll order another cloak, my lord, if you will have it so, but I'll not rid myself of that."

Tilting her head in a proud gesture, Meghan ridiculed what he had once meant to her. "I want to keep it for sentimental reasons and as a reminder not to repeat the mistakes of the green girl I once was."

Hugh's features remained dispassionate though he inwardly grinned. "As you will. But I would prefer that you not wear it. There are things I, too, would prefer to forget."

As he left the chamber, his lips puckered into a sound-less whistle and his steps were light on the stairs.

Meghan glared at the door Hugh closed behind him, then her eyes grew dull again. She wrapped her arms around her knees and rested her head on them, afraid that if she lay down she could not rouse again. She dozed until Yedda entered, carrying a platter of breakfast. Following her were two men with a bathtub. The smell of food filled Meghan with nausea. Yet, as she thought of Hugh's words, her anger grew, building an appetite she had not felt for weeks. Suddenly ravenous, she ate quickly and watched the men fill the tub with countless buckets of steaming water. When they were gone, she climbed into the water, gasping at the heat.

Yedda only smiled. "It has to be hot, lady, to remove the grime."

Ignoring her, Meghan inched into the water. Leaning back, she savored the heat and the sensation of floating.

Yedda let her soak as she cleaned the chamber, lifting Meghan's garments with fastidious fingers, clucking over their disgrace. That done, she attacked Meghan with wood ash and a stout brush, ignoring her mistress's howls, scolding, and muttering.

"You cluck like a hen," Meghan accused when at last she was out of the bath and wrapped in a towel. "I remember when it took three tubs and more to clean *you.*"

The hands drying Meghan's hair grew still. "Aye, but I did not know better," Yedda retorted.

Meghan chuckled and took one of Yedda's hands to pull her around. She touched her cheek and asked, her voice teasing, "Who is the maid and who the mistress? Who is the older and wiser?" Abruptly she frowned and cast Yedda's hand away as her eyes darkened with pain. She wandered about the chamber, her gaze on the bed, yearning for the oblivion of sleep. "Aye, I know," she whispered, her words coming through a sudden assault of tears. "You are mistress, for you have more to say of your life than I ever could. I am but a pawn to be pushed about by politics and by a man's whim. Though your years give lie to it, you are older, wiser. Have you not loved two men of your own choosing? Aye, and borne living children of your own will? And soon another, if my eyes do not play me false. While I have but carried one child five months, a weak, stillborn thing, too small, too unformed to draw one breath of God's good air!''

Her head dropped and her voice came so softly that Yedda strained to hear. "But I loved two men, too," she stated. "In God's most holy truth, I did. Once. 'Tis gone now. One sent me from him; the other left though he holds me still."

Her head jerked up at a knock, but it was only the serving men come for the tub. Forcing herself to her feet, Meghan wiped away her tears. When the men left, her features were composed. "Tell me the gossip, wench," she ordered.

Yedda talked as she combed the tangles from Meghan's hair. She prattled of the affairs of this neighbor and that, and Meghan let the hum lull her into lethargy. Only when Yedda spoke of Meghan's furtive departure from Ainsleah did she rouse.

"Sir Godfrey was sore angered and hurt, lady," Yedda told her as she carefully pared Meghan's toenails.

Meghan shrugged. "'Twas not to distress Sir Godfrey that I left."

Yedda's red face spoke of the anger she dared not speak. "Aye, I know that," she admitted. "Sir Hugh did say you went because your people needed you. He said Caradoc had taken them. But he did not tell of how you won them back."

Meghan frowned, the idea of Hugh defending her puzzling her. "How does he know what happened?"

Finished with the pedicure, Yedda hunkered back on her heels. "He spoke with Glenna. She told him. Not that you were with child, but only what happened. But he'll not tell us. He only gets that tight line about his mouth and will not say. He shakes his head, though Godfrey thinks him half fearful for you, half proud. What did you do there?"

The curve of Meghan's lip was enigmatic. She pulled her undertunic on and asked, "Who did my lord send as steward to Cleitcroft?"

''Sir Humphrey Thorley, the knight who rode with us to Montgomery.''

Meghan nodded. ''He's as good as another and better than many. He'll do little good but less harm, mayhap.''

Slipping on a surcoat, she looked at Yedda, her eyes teasing. ''What happened at Cleitcroft? I did but kill a man, nothing more.''

Yedda's eyes grew round as Meghan clasped her belt about her waist. ''In truth,'' she said, looking at the hanging folds of fabric. ''I am too thin! I had not noticed it afore.''

Her smile flashed as she left, leaving Yedda to straighten the chamber, her curiosity unsatisfied.

Hugh was talking to Godfrey when his wife entered the hall. The knight rose from the table, but Hugh regarded Meghan with shuttered eyes. Though she resembled a child dressed in her mother's clothing, he forced down a grin of relief to see her up and about.

Meghan returned his nod and continued to the kitchens, not seeing Hugh's pleased smile as he eyed the arrogance of her back, the proud tilt of her head. But in the corridor connecting the family tower to that of the kitchens, Meghan felt her strength crumble. In a rising tide of panic, she tried to hold on to it, but it slipped away like water through her fingers. Her knees grew weak and tears of frustration spurted from her eyes as dizziness overwhelmed her. Clinging to the wall, she lowered herself to the floor and settled into a heap on the rushes, her thin shoulders shaking with sobs.

It was there that Yedda found her. She tried to lift Meghan, but her bones seemed to have melted. Rising, alarm in her placid face, Yedda gasped. ''I'll call Sir Hugh.''

Meghan clutched her skirts, her face white, eyes terrified. ''No! He'll be sore angry.''

Yedda stared at her, her eyebrows gathered in disbelief. ''But you be ill. He must see that.''

Meghan's fingers tightened in Yedda's surcoat and she pulled herself to her knees. ''No, he'll think I complained. He told me I must fulfill my duties or he'll send me to a nunnery. You know I cannot abide walls.''

Pondering this, Yedda nodded. "Aye, he's become hard. You made him so." Then her face brightened. "Come and rest in the kitchens. 'Tis a place he never enters and I can do what needs to be done there. In truth, I've done so since you left—and no one will tell him. I know of certain vices of the cook and a whisper in his ear will hold his tongue. And the maids and spitboy will not tell for fear of the cook. But you must help. As skinny as you be, I cannot carry you.''

The fear ebbed from Meghan's eyes and she smiled gratefully. With Yedda's help, she rose and continued to the kitchens.

So began the conspiracy that drew all the household into its web, fear of Yedda holding them there. Her granted authority was scant, but she had held the reins when there was no one else to do so and she liked the taste of power. As Godfrey's wife, she had only to whisper a word in his ear. Having been of the lowest of servants, she knew their minds, their tricks, the wiles they employed. She ruled with a strong hand and soon everyone joined in her protection of their lady.

Yedda said nothing to Godfrey, but he knew. Though he refused to become a participant, his silence suited her as well. He would say nothing to Hugh, nor would he lie should Hugh question him. Yedda knew she could ask no more of a man so loyal to his lord.

If Hugh was aware of the conspiracy, he gave no indication. All he demanded of his wife was done and he seemed satisfied. Meghan bore the keys, though Yedda wielded them, and Hugh appeared none the wiser. But when he met his wife, the lines about his mouth tightened and his eyes narrowed. He noticed the flesh slowly filling in the hollows of her cheek, the color that tinged her transparent skin. The eyes that met his were no longer dull and glazed. That it was anger and hate that lent them sparkle only seemed to amuse him.

Anger and hate gave Meghan strength to be at his table and attentive to his every whim. She used those emotions to hold back in his presence the tears that still welled up unsummoned. Anger and hate lifted her head with a pride that belied the ache in her throat. They tilted her mouth and steadied her steps when her heart and soul screamed for the oblivion of sleep, when the blackness threatened to melt her into helplessness.

Her rage grew each time she felt Hugh's eyes strip away her clothes and mock her slack breasts and the sharp bones of her elbows and knees. Her rage did not rest when she lay stiff and resentful on the bed's far side during the nights Hugh choose to sleep there. Her anger rose still higher when he slept elsewhere; where, she told herself, she did not care.

Forcing back the dark curtains in her mind became easier each day that Hugh's presence demanded it. Through the end of spring and into summer, her endurance grew. The times she spent huddled in a nook in the kitchens, her mind numb, lessened. The attacks of tears became less frequent and slowly, reluctantly, Yedda began to relinquish the household's management.

Yedda found Meghan in the garden one afternoon in late June. Her eyes hardened at the sight of Meghan sitting against the wall, her head thrown back, her body sagging as tears flowed down her face. Whether her anger was at Hugh's treatment of her or at Meghan's frailty, Yedda did not wonder. Drying Meghan's tears on her undertunic, Yedda crooned as she would to a hurt child. Then she whispered that which would rouse Meghan, a certain pleasure in her tone. "My lady, your lord has need of you. There be guests."

Meghan shuddered. Her nails dug into her palms as she forced back the darkness. Gradually, the world formed about her again: Yedda's frown, the warm lichen-covered walls, the rows of herbs—fennel, bryony, campion, rue, rosemary, basil, St.-John's-wort, gillyflowers and violets, lavender and roses, the good and the dangerous. The veils shrouding the edges of her mind remained, but she had learned to function through them so well that no one suspected they were there. Her motions seemed puppetlike, but it was the fashion for highborn ladies to move so.

Sometimes the pall hung thicker; sometimes, occasionally, it disappeared altogether.

Meghan stood, one hand on the wall. She breathed in and the veils parted a bit more. "Who gives us the pleasure of his company?" she asked.

"Sir Humphrey Thorley."

Frowning, Meghan tried to put a face to the name.

"Sir Hugh's steward at Cleitcroft."

"Aye, I recall," Meghan answered, wondering why an Englishman was at Cleitcroft. Then, remembering, the pall deepened before she pushed it back. Forcing her steps steady, Meghan went with Yedda.

Hugh sat in the hall, his body stretched low in his chair, a goblet of wine in his hand. A smile curved his mouth as he eyed Humphrey mumbling over the parchments spread before him. The knight's stubby finger passed over each line of crabbed script as he tried to decipher words and figures.

Looking up, Hugh watched his wife enter the hall. An almost imperceptible hesitation broke each step, as though she doubted the floor would be there when she set her foot down. Her back was stiff, lacking its former supple grace, the tendons in her neck were strained, and her face was taut. Hugh could feel the effort it took that held her on her feet.

His own body tightened in an effort to send strength across the space separating them. Where had Yedda found her this time? Seeing the dirt clinging to her surcoat, he guessed the herb garden. He mentally questioned for the thousandth time if he had been right to try and drive her from her despondency with taunts and demands he knew she could not fulfill. But she did seem better. He sensed the intense anger and hate that was driving her and hoped that someday love would return. But a Meghan fighting him he could win, he thought, he hoped.

Glancing up, Meghan met his stare. The line of concentration on her brow cleared and her gaze was cold as she inclined her head. Hugh nodded in return and swept her with a gaze that was deliberately ridiculing, then he returned his attention to Humphrey.

The knight's voice was overloud in his eagerness to escape the bookwork. "I've not told you, my lord," he said, "that Davyd was taken. Have you heard anything of it?"

From the corner of his eye, Hugh saw Meghan falter. He watched her slowly, carefully, turn back, her eyes stricken. Her face rigid, she crossed to the table. "I would hear of it," she stated, her level gaze defying him.

Hugh shrugged his indifference, pushing out a chair from under the table with his foot and motioning her to sit.

Not noticing his discourtesy, Meghan sat, her eyes on Humphrey. She automatically took the goblet Hugh offered, not looking at him.

The flustered knight's gaze twitched from Meghan to Hugh. A flush deepened his ruddy complexion as he remembered a rumor of adultery between Davyd and the lady before him. He scratched the bristles of his beard and looked at Hugh for a hint of what to say, but found no response in the bored face that watched several puppies fighting in front of the hearth.

Briefly, he wondered at the state of affairs between Sir Hugh and his lady. Clearly, they had settled into the position of most wedded folk—an armed truce constantly violated. Sir Hugh had been so set on her, but she had proved to be like all the rest—untrustworthy. Sir Hugh didn't even have a worthy dowry to comfort him now that his lady no longer did so. And she had lost much of her beauty. She had always been too skinny, but now she was like a rake. Smugly he congratulated himself on his wisdom in staying a bachelor.

Meghan drew him from his musings. "You said my lord Davyd has been taken," she prompted.

Shifting in his chair, Humphrey gulped down wine and wiped his mouth with the back of his hand. "Aye," he said, "nigh on a week past."

Meghan forced down the frustration the tongue-tied, bumbling man provoked. "Where was he found?"

"Near Cader Idris, 'tis said."

"And who took him?" she asked, knowing the answer.

"Welshmen. 'Tis said he was betrayed by one, taken by others. There be truth in the saying you can't trust the Welsh. They can't even trust their own. Why, I remember . . ." He stumbled to a halt under Meghan's gaze and the flush rose again.

But she only smiled ruefully and gazed into her cup, seeing the reflection of her sad eyes in the ruby liquid. "Aye," she whispered, "he said 'twould be his own."

Lifting her gaze to Humphrey, she asked, "Did he fight well?"

Humphrey's eyes flicked to Hugh, but his lord studied his wife, seemingly unemotional. "Aye," Humphrey said, "'tis said he fought like a cornered man, for he was. They were sore put to take him. He was bent on fighting to the death, as though he truly craved it."

Meghan nodded, her mouth soft in thought. "He would do that, though he knew 'twould be to no avail. And they took him alive," she repeated to herself. Breathing in deeply, Meghan let her breath go in one shuddering sob. "And I forgot to pray for him!" Looking up, she explained, "He asked me to pray for his death. For an easy death. And I forgot. I, who loved him, who would never have intentionally betrayed him, did so."

She lowered her eyes and ran her finger around the rim of the goblet until the silver purred. Her jaw clenched in an effort to contain her grief. Now was not the time for it. It was, somehow, too private and intense a thing to expose to anyone else and she was too weak to bear it just then. It must be held until later.

Staring at her, forgetting his doubt, Hugh longed to draw her to him, to comfort her until her sorrow gave way to passion. With passion he could draw the grief from her. He thought briefly of her body beneath his, giving to him, her mouth clinging to his, a moan deep in her throat.

As though sensing his turmoil, Meghan lifted her eyes to his. She saw a need beneath his impassive gaze that was somehow familiar, that somehow stirred her. It flared in his eyes, warming her, then fled, leaving them shuttered once more. Her hands shook and she thrust the answering need away. Turning to Humphrey, her voice calm, she said, "Tell me of Cleitcroft, how it goes there."

Muttering, he shuffled the parchments and wondered what his lord would have him say. But Hugh waved a hand over the papers. "Forget those," he ordered. "We would hear of conditions beyond the number of sheep and how many weevils are in the corn."

Leaning forward, Humphrey placed his forearms on the table. His frustrations poured from him in a gush. "'Tis bad! I've few people and they'll not survive the year without provision. I've no food and too few people to grow any. Those I have be mostly women and children or crones and gaffers, too old to do anything but eat. I think there be men in the mountains, though, coming down at night to their women, to get more brats, to eat what little we have. Most of the ground lies fallow. There be no men to plant it. I've no smith, nor can I find one. There be no furniture in the keep; you saw that, my lord, and no hands I can spare to make new. Most of the men be ancient gaffers or half-grown whelps with nothing but wenches and their empty bellies on their minds. Those I've put to watching the sheep, yet I still lose lambs to the wolves."

"They tell me the roads of Wales teem with homeless men and women," Hugh said. "Can you not recruit them?"

Humphrey shrugged. "Aye, they come, some alone, most with women and brats. They stop for a few days, listen to my offers, talk to others, then leave. When they go, they carry one of my pigs under their arm, though I've yet to catch them at it. 'Tis as though they look for something lost. God knows what it be. I've never understood the Welsh."

Helplessly, Humphrey stared at his broad, capable hands, hands more suited to a sword or battle-ax than to people. "No, they'll not stay, not and serve an English lord. And there be nothing I can do without them. Get me Englishmen, my lord, for I cannot get the Welsh. And could I work with them if I did? They be a stubborn, perverse, contentious people who will be neither pushed nor led.'' Glancing at Meghan, he bit his lip. ''Forgive me, lady, but by God's blood, 'tis true!''

Meghan smiled and touched the hand he had slammed on the table. ''Aye,'' she answered proudly, ''I know.''

Hugh leaned forward, his elbows braced on the table. ''No, no Englishmen. I would try the Welsh a while more. 'Twould be a red flag in their faces to put my villeins on their soil, nor can I spare men to guard our people there. And I mislike this planting of foreign people on alien earth. Later it may be necessary, though I hope not.

''In truth,'' he continued, ''I hope one day to make a Welshman steward there. 'Tis the only way I can hold it, and then I'll give you Renshaw. As for now, methinks I can feed you through the winter.''

Meghan smiled slightly. ''I thank you, my lord.''

Hugh only scowled. He could not speak of his respect for the Welsh or of the love he had borne for so many now feeding their flesh to the sparse earth. He had seen the qualities he loved about them die in Meghan and it had frozen something in him. He would not aid the killing of it in Wales any longer, not at Cleitcroft. He would not make of his Welsh people villeins with flat faces and dead eyes, as he had somehow made his wife.

''Twould not be politic to do otherwise, lady. An English estate would not survive long in the middle of Wales.''

Meghan flushed, her eyes dropped, and her features grew hard again. Needing a distraction, she fingered the parchment littering the table. ''What of these, Humphrey?''

Soon their heads were bent over the accounts, deciphering, questioning, explaining, suggesting.

Chapter 26

The next few days passed in a frenzy. There were storerooms to be examined, casks of salted meat and fish and barrels of flour to be counted. The amount that could be spared must be figured down to the last barrel, for Ainsleah had to survive on what remained until harvest. The village was combed for surplus provisions and a careful account kept of what was taken from each villein. Clothing was collected and wool and linen woven.

The castle reverberated with the gossip of women busy at looms and needles and with the cries of their children. The ward rang with the shouts of men, the clangs, bangings, and hums from the smithy and the carpentry shop. Livestock added their distress to the racket. Yelping dogs, and the curses of men who stumbled over them, added to the din. Plowshares, furniture, and crates of poultry were added to the wagons.

Meghan spent each day in constant motion. So much had to be done in so little time. No black moments threatened her and she came to each meal ravenous. Flesh seemed to spring back to her face and figure, rounding her contours. At night she went to bed exhausted and slept soundly. For the first time in months she did not awaken in tears from haunting dreams.

It was Hugh who now lay awake and rigid. Their paths crossed many times each day and each time he grew more aware of her swaying hips, of breasts which once more pushed provocatively against her surcoat. Her eyes were alert and bright. Only when he spoke to her, his voice light and mocking, did her gaze flare with its old animosity.

A hundred times a day thoughts of her flashed through his mind and Hugh felt again the ache that only Meghan could satisfy. Each time, he told himself he would go to the miller's daughter, but he found himself instead climbing the stairs to the chamber he shared with Meghan. There he would find her asleep, frowns and smiles chasing themselves across her features. Her hair, escaping its braid, half covered a naked shoulder that tempted his hand as much by its frailty as by the strength he knew existed beneath the smooth skin.

He would lie down next to her, counseling himself in patience, assuaging his need with the knowledge that soon she would be his again. Three nights, two nights, one. When Humphrey left, he would lead her up the stairs to their chamber and claim her once more. She might fight him, but he had felt her anger and hate turn to passion many times before under his mouth and caressing hands and, he told himself, he would feel that again.

On the eve of Humphrey's departure, Hugh found himself almost hating the rough, honest face of the knight across the table. He wanted Ainsleah back to normal. He wanted Meghan in his bed, no longer exhausted from the work Humphrey's mission demanded. He wanted her as his wife once more.

Frowning into his wine, Hugh told himself he was behaving like a petulant child. He tried to listen to the talk about him but resented the light voices, the laughing faces. He glanced at Humphrey's usually solemn features, now bright as he described with broad gestures his one great jousting feat. It was a story Hugh had heard too many times.

Meghan sat next to Hugh. The gold-colored surcoat she wore brought an amber glow to her green eyes. She wore her hair pulled into a loose, heavy knot low on the back of her neck and a tendril of ebony had escaped to curve in punctuation under her chin, tempting him to tuck it back, to feel the velvet of her skin.

Meghan was listening to Humphrey with rapt attention, her lips parted and moist. As she questioned the knight,

Hugh scowled and recalled that, although she loved tournaments, she loathed their recounting. Now her eyes danced and her features were animated and Hugh felt an unreasoning jealousy. Laughing at a point in Humphrey's story, Meghan glanced at Hugh's glowering face. The gaiety fled her features. She seemed to be assessing him. Her lips parted as though to speak, then, with a slight shake of her head, she returned her attention to Humphrey.

Hugh's eyes narrowed on her profile. Under her vivacity, he sensed an expectation, as though she waited for something, and he knew it concerned him. He saw her hand as it rested near the trencher they shared. He covered it with his own and ran a finger from her wrist to the tip of each finger and back. Feeling her tense, Hugh held her hand imprisoned before lifting it to his mouth. His eyes still on her, Hugh ran the tip of his tongue over her palm. Gently he bit her knuckles, then drew the ball of her thumb between his teeth, sucking on it.

Her movement brittle, Meghan turned, her jaw set. She leaned toward him, her mouth inches from his. "My lord," she whispered, "you mock me!"

Smiling lazily, Hugh allowed his gaze to touch the red mouth, the stubborn chin, the pulse beating at her throat. He touched her neck with a languid finger, then placed his mouth where his finger had been. The pulse seemed to leap under his lips. Idly, his mouth traced the line of her jaw to her lips. He held it there for a moment, then drew in her full lower lip, touching its ripeness with his tongue. Finally he drew back. His eyes held hers as he asked, "Do I, in truth, mock you, lady?"

A flush rose over Meghan's features then fled, leaving them white. Hugh watched the hauteur in her eyes turn to fear and heard her sob before she turned away. Her voice was high as she recounted to Yedda the mischief of her oldest son. Her words tumbled over themselves as she fought the memories Hugh's kiss had released, memories that threatened her, that awakened a desire long dead. Fear dizzied her, fear not of the mocking promise in Hugh's eyes but of the need she had seen beneath it, fear that he would use it to hold her.

Hugh stared at Meghan's averted head for a moment, her chatter like the sound of angry wasps in his ears, then he carefully placed her hand next to the trencher and picked up his wine. A scowl blackened his features as he leaned back in his chair, a silent, glowering guest at his own table.

Meghan was waiting when Hugh entered the chamber that night. She heard his uncertain step, his fumbling hand on the latch, and knew, dismayed, that he was drunk. Sitting in her chair, she gazed into the fire, her psalter in her lap, until she heard the door close behind him. Then she stood.

Leaning against the door, Hugh stared at her, an eyebrow lifted in derisive surprise. His eyes took her in, from her proud face to the white chamber robe falling to her feet. Their high arches and slim toes seemed strangely sensual beneath the hem of the concealing robe. Her hair hung in two dark braids to her hips and Hugh wondered what it reminded him of in the flame's glow. A raven's wing? Or coal? A fresh piece of split coal, black yet iridescent, shimmering blue, gold, and amber. He hummed softly to himself. "My lady fair, with raven hair, so like the coal . . ." He laughed, bemused by his poor attempt at minstrelsy.

Abruptly the sight of her sank in and his inebriated thoughts reeled to a halt in instant sobriety. For a second, Hugh wondered if Meghan felt the same need that surged through his veins. Reading no softness in her face, he put the hope aside. Shoving himself away from the door, he inclined his head, asking, "My lady, to what purpose do you so honor me?"

Meghan swayed into a curtsy, her braids sweeping the floor. "My lord, I would but talk with you."

Hugh's eyebrows meshed with suspicion. She was not one to give obeisance to any man. She wanted something and foreboding crawled his spine. Casually, he leaned against the door, a smile curling his lips as his gaze swept over her, stripping her. "My lady," he drawled, "you would but speak with me and I had hoped for a more lively entertainment!"

His eyes, his words, wound about Meghan, caressing her. For a moment the chamber echoed back the croon of love he had once brought her to. His voice, soft with endearments or triumph, reverberated from the walls in a whisper of passion. In panic, she shook her head, pushing the sounds back to the oblivion from which they had come. Her cutting words were aimed as much at herself as at Hugh. "Have you tired, my lord," she said, "of the miller's fair, fat daughter?"

"So you've heard of my mistress? No, I've not tired of her. Many a man would envy me her favors. She is ever warm and willing, laughing and giving."

The words "as you are not" hung unspoken between them and Hugh forced a smile at Meghan's flinch of pain. He strolled to the table where there stood a pitcher and two goblets. "You, too, I see, consider talking dry work," he commented. "I thank you for your thoughtfulness but, by God's blood, I wonder what it is you would say that makes you provide refreshment. Do you think I will need fortification?"

He poured one cup and glanced at her, questioning, then tilted the pitcher to the second. For a moment, her words did not touch his consciousness.

"I wish to return to Cleitcroft with Humphrey."

Hugh's features did not alter when at last he heard, but his arm jerked, spilling wine in a ruby pool on the white cloth. He watched stupidly as the puddle spread and wine dripped into the rushes. The face he turned to Meghan was stark, with white lines twisting his mouth. "You wish to return to Cleitcroft?" he repeated. Laughing, he shook his head. "You would return to Cleitcroft!" he shouted incredulously. "You, my lady wife, who deserted me once afore, who gave aid and succor to the enemies of my liege; you who befouled my name by putting the horns of cuckold on my head; you who, in your folly, lost my son and heir—you have the insolence to beg my leave to go to Cleitcroft!"

He whirled away and paced the room three times, four. Then he leaned against the bedpost and stared at her. "Why, my lady, do you not just run away in the night like the Welsh thief you are? Why do you, who have never showed my courtesy, show me such now? Why do you ask my leave?''

Drawn by his pain, Meghan stepped toward him, then halted, warned back by the rage in his eyes and by his raised hand. She shook her head, searching for words, and Hugh's voice cut across her flying thoughts. ''I wait, lady!''

Meghan's words came in a rush. ''There is much I can do there that Humphrey cannot. The men will come, will stay for me. I could go into the mountains and seek them out and bring them back. I know the people and they know me. They trust me! I could—''

Her tongue died under his stare. There was no way to explain that Cleitcroft's responsibility was hers, that she could not desert it, that she needed the clan's strength as surely as the clan needed hers.

Hugh studied her as though he had never seen her before. Then he picked up a goblet and asked, ''And then, lady, when you have done all you say you will do, what then? What will you do then?''

''I will return,'' she whispered. ''What else?''

No joy or warmth remained on Hugh's face. ''Why?''

Meghan spread her hands. ''You are my lord, my husband. This is my place.''

Hugh laughed. ''Is it, lady? Then why do you leave it and me? And are you my wife? Do you come to me eager for love? Do you share my bed? Do you bear my children and willingly grace my table? Is your face soft toward me? If you, in truth, are my wife, why do you ever slip through my grasp? Why can I not hold you to me?''

Meghan moved toward him once more, but he waved her back. He did not want her touch, her concern—her pity. Slowly rage and despair flowed from him, leaving only futility. ''Go, then, lady,'' he said, moving toward the door. ''Make more worth of your dowry than you, yourself, have ever been.''

''Where do you go, my lord?'' she whispered.

He turned back, his smile mocking her. ''I go to tell Humphrey that you join him. Methinks he'll be ill-pleased, bachelor that he is. 'Tis one thing to face a simpering woman across a table, another to accompany her on a venture such as you propose.''

Shrugging, Hugh laughed mirthlessly. ''Then I go to my mistress. I have neglected her of late and methinks her welcome will be warm, her demands few.''

Numbly, Meghan shook her head and her words pushed past her pride. ''I would have you stay by me the night.''

Hugh's mouth crooked in a joyless smile. ''And may-hap send you off with another brat to drop, stillborn, on some Welsh mountain? No, lady. And I have never been a man to make use of whores. To give yourself in grat-itude, lady, would make of you a whore; enough men call you that already. A lady awaits me who gives in love and sport.''

Hugh courteously bowed and left. Staring at the door, Meghan sank to her knees on the rushes, beating at them with clenched fists. Hugh's granting of her request was poor balm to her wounded pride. Telling herself she hated him and did not want him was no solace to the pain of his rejection.

The sun had not risen when Meghan descended to the deserted hall. The great fireplace was still banked, the furnishings looking forlorn in the dim light. Meghan's soft boots sent back no echo from the vaulted ceiling as she hurried to the stairs. Fear that Humphrey had left without her nagged at her heels.

The wagons were gone, but Humphrey had waited, accompanied by two guards and Selig. With them were Godfrey and Yedda, Ralph Ramsden and three others, but not Hugh. Ignoring their disparaging stares, Meghan drew her shabby cloak closer against the chill. Yedda and God-frey parted for her, not speaking, and Meghan lifted her head higher, swallowing a lump of guilt. Glancing at Humphrey, she saw his eyes take in her knee-length tunic and high boots.

''You're late!'' he accused.

''Aye,'' she agreed, ''I'm late.'' Her stare dared him to reproach her further, and she felt a sense of satisfac-tion when his gaze dropped.

''I sent the wagons ahead,'' he stated gruffly.

Not replying, Meghan mounted, then glanced at Godfrey and Yedda. Yedda stared back, her pale eyes hot with censure. Godfrey simply turned his face away. He would not, she knew, forgive any hurt to his lord. Nor was there anything she could say to Yedda to make her understand. She had become too proper, too concerned with propriety and the opinion of the neighbors. Her chin tilted, Meghan wheeled her mount out the gate and over the drawbridge, leaving Humphrey to follow as he would.

The village was beginning to wake and smoke curled from the mill's chimney. The door was shut, but as Meghan watched, unable to look away, it opened and Hugh stood framed in the passage. He was clad only in an underclout and the rising sun burnished the bronze of his shoulders and chest. Yawning, he surveyed the passing group with seeming indifference. A short, plump woman came up behind him, dressed in a simple kirtle, her long blond hair falling in disarray to her heavy hips. Smiling, Hugh drew her to him, the pressure of his arm pushing her full breasts to greater prominence. Standing on tiptoe, she whispered to him and he laughed, hugging her closer, then followed her back into the mill.

Staring at the closed door, Meghan felt anger and humiliation drown the last vestige of shame and guilt. She realized, too, that if he had stayed with her the night before, she might not have been able to leave him. Turning her face toward Wales, she forced her thoughts to the people and problems awaiting her, driving away the memory of Hugh's voice accusing her of running from him.

Chapter 27

The village appeared to be deserted. Many of the houses were empty, the doors ajar on leather hinges, displaying forlorn interiors. A few chickens scratched dispiritedly in the roadway. At the approach of the men and wagons, dogs slunk away through the weeds, their tails between their legs.

The few villagers were subdued and sullen as Meghan had never seen them before. Ignoring the horsemen, they stared at the wagons. There were no men to be seen. A few women stood at their doors, silent, with runny-nosed children at theirs skirts. Some old people, so ancient it was difficult to guess their sex, sat in the sun near the well in mute resignation.

The castle's drawbridge was up, offering warning instead of welcome. The keep's unpainted walls had been darkened by rain and the squat tower stood ponderous against the blue of the storm-cleared sky, the crenelations of the parapet gaping like rapacious teeth. The massive bulk seemed not to protect the village at its base but to hold it in thrall.

The keep had ceased to be home to Meghan. Caradoc's vandalism had defiled it and, with Humphrey as seneschal, it was no longer her responsibility. Hugh owned it now, passed to him through Meghan and, to insure his full ownership, gifted to him by Edward when it fell into English hands.

Meghan stared at it a moment more, willing it to become no more than the pile of rock it was. A lone figure appeared on the parapet and waved, his shouted greeting lost in the wind. Sighing, Meghan turned to Humphrey. "I leave you here, my lord."

"But Sir Hugh did not order it so," he argued.

"Nor did my lord order that I stay with you. He did but ask that I accompany you. He gave me Selig for protection and I can do more from the village. If I stay at the keep, I am but Sir Hugh's lady. Here I am of the people."

Humphrey tried to appear thoughtful but felt only relief. When Hugh had informed him that Meghan was to travel with him, he had been thunderstruck. A woman had no place on such a venture. The pace would be hard, the trip dangerous, and a woman, with her complaints, demands, and foolish questions, would only hold them back. But Meghan, he had discovered, had spoken little. She had asked for no privileges, eating as they ate, stopping when a halt was called, sleeping wrapped in her cloak as they did. In all, she had been as easy a traveling companion as he could want and Humphrey had to admit a grudging respect for her. If she had been a man, he would have found no fault at all.

Still, traveling for four days was not the same as living under the same roof. It was not that he was attracted to her; she was too skinny and her wit too sharp and, as his lord's lady, she was sacrosanct. It was that the company of a gently reared lady, even if she did not always behave as such, embarrassed him. He wanted to belch, scratch, and fart when he felt like it and if he had wanted to share his house, he would have married. And he would have chosen a plump, silent wench who would cook his meals and mend his clothes and wouldn't look at him with laughing, knowing eyes.

Humphrey's gruff voice was affable when he bade her good-bye. In his expansive mood he told her to call should she need anything, unaware of the many times he would regret his words. Returning to the column, he looked back once and saw Meghan watching him, a small, slim figure that looked strangely alone, although Selig stood beside her. Under her hand was a huge dog that seemed to have appeared from nowhere. The sight touched him and he sourly reminded himself that she would not be alone now if she had stayed by her lord.

Meghan watched after him for several moments then, turning away, she went in search of Glenna. The old woman was kneeling in her garden, her gnarled fingers digging at the resistant weeds. Her frail figure, her twig-like limbs, resembled those of a starving child and when she lifted her head, she blinked in the sun like an infant. Recognizing Meghan, she settled back on her haunches.

Glenna studied her for a long moment, seeming to see into her very soul, and Meghan opened herself to the old woman's vision. She felt Glenna's healing touch as she examined her pain, rage, and grief.

At last, the old woman patted the earth. "Come, child," she ordered, "I need help and the weeds are bad this year."

It was late summer when Meghan walked with Humphrey in the pastures above Cleitcroft. The sheep dogs warily watched their approach and trotted in a circle around the flock, drawing it into a tight mass of squirming sheep.

Meghan and Humphrey spoke in low voices and she pointed to the earth. What appeared from the village to be thick pasture proved on close inspection to be many tufts of grass too tall for the sheep's teeth. Kneeling, she separated them with her hands, displaying the unprotected, overgrazed soil at their roots. The summer rains had washed away the thin layer of topsoil. Tiny gullies had been created that, in time, would strip the hillsides of all pasturage.

Letting the grass fall back, Meghan told Humphrey, "The skin of the earth is thin here, my lord. We have little soil and I would not like it to wash away to England. They have taken so much of ours already."

Humphrey squatted next to Meghan and, refusing to look at her, tugged at the grass with nervous fingers. His stomach churned. Never before, not until he had had to deal with his lord's lady, had he suffered such disquiet. "And you would have me send the flocks to the summer

pastures?'' he asked at last, mentioning the request he had
denied her for so long.

He studied Meghan's averted face. She had been apathetic since the letter from her lord had arrived, informing
Humphrey that Hugh had gone to court. Hugh had not
asked after her, nor had he sent her greeting, hurting her
more than Humphrey would have guessed.

Scowling, he thought of how their relationship had
changed in the last months. She had involved him in the
problems of her people, unwilling though he had been.
When he had refused to attend a council meeting, telling
her his authority came from her lord, not from a gaggle
of senile crones and gaffers, she had brought the council
to him. She had caught him at his evening meal and he
had been forced to listen, wondering if she would have
followed him to the garderobe, her bevy of ancients after
her. It was the first of several councils and the only one
he had sought to avoid. All introduced problems he had
been unaware of and he came to consider the solutions
his.

He had fought her, had stomped and cursed. He had
argued and raged at much of what she had proposed,
aware as he did that he would give in at the end. She had
maneuvered him, he knew, yet he could never rouse himself to the anger he felt her actions deserved. That, too,
had irritated him. Tears had become her last line of
defense; she knew his weakness there. And despite all her
stratagems, she respected him. That he saw through her
games only added to her pleasure in them. Frowning,
Humphrey told himself that, should she have wished it,
she could have manipulated him to do anything she
wanted and he would never have been the wiser. But to
do so would have taken his authority and make him a buf-
foon.

Humphrey turned from Meghan to gaze down at the
village. Remembering how she had tricked him into taking the blacksmith, he smiled. She had come to the keep,
her face bright and eager, to tell him a smith had come.

''You'll try him, won't you?'' she had asked and, not
seeing why not, he had agreed. Only much later had he
seen the man and realized he had but one leg. Yet it

worked; the smith's lout of a son became his legs. The skill, after all, was in the man's hands.

Together, Humphrey and Meghan had made Cleitcroft a living thing again, taking the best from the Welsh and Norman ways. She had been able to persuade men to stay. He had offered the incentive to keep them there. The cattle the men had brought with them now grazed in the meadows. If some bore English brands, Humphrey chose not to notice. After all, bygones were bygones and the English possessed cattle of Welsh markings. It would be impossible to return them to their lawful owners and they did look fine in the lower pastures, sleek and fat, their bellies deep in grass. And he chose not to notice Meghan's smile when she saw him admiring them.

Still, he was no steward; he was a man of war. He had always been landless, as his father before him, and had never aspired to own property. He liked his freedom. He knew little of farming and had never thought to learn more.

Take the sheep. He had been right in the spring to refuse to send them to the upper pastures. But the flock had tripled since then because two men had brought some down from the mountains, unable to keep the wolves from them. The chieftain who had owned them was dead, fallen at Bere, and none of his family was left. The men themselves were the last of the clan. They wanted to add their flock to Cleitcroft's. Humphrey had stared at the mangy, insect-infested flock and decided that sheep were sheep and he didn't care for any of them. Too, the men who gazed at him with hopeful eyes were two more that he sorely needed.

Then the flock had doubled again when Hugh sent Ainsleah's sheep. Now there was the matter of the soil to consider. He returned his gaze to Meghan, who continued to stare out over the valley.

"You would have me send the flocks to summer pasture?" Humphrey repeated.

Meghan blinked to rouse herself. "Aye, there is nothing else to do. If we send them now, they'll have over a month there, time enough for this land to heal. And we have men enough now to guard them."

Humphrey stared at her, a line of worry between his eyebrows. She was merely going through the motions because someone had to. He had not seen her so apathetic before and he felt awkward and helpless. It was this more than her argument that influenced him. "Then they'll have to go, will they not?" he agreed.

Meghan touched his hand lightly. "Thank you," she whispered. Pausing to weigh her words, she frowned, then added, "I, too, must go, not only to the pastures but farther. There are men there I want to see, men once loyal to my father."

"But I cannot spare men for you, lady," he objected.

Shrugging, Meghan smiled. "I've Selig, I need no one else, and where I go no one will harm me."

"'Tis not the Welsh who worry me but the troops Edward left behind."

"The English dare not touch me, not with Selig and with the name I bear. Sir Hugh is well respected and, in truth, should anyone harm me, he would know you were blameless."

His facial muscles tensed in sudden anger and his eyes refused to meet hers. "'Tis not your lord's opinion that concerns me," he burst out, "but your safety!"

Meghan smiled. She slipped her hand into his. "I thank you, Sir Humphrey," she said softly, "for your regard. Strange as it is, we've become friends, haven't we?"

He dragged his eyes to meet hers. His lord's lady, a lady such as he had spent his life avoiding, and she called him friend. And such they were. He just had not put a name to it. Grinning, his grip tightened on hers. "Aye!" he agreed. "We are that."

They sat in quiet companionship for several moments, then he rose, suddenly ill at ease. He had to leave, to be alone to examine their new relationship. "I return to the keep, lady," he announced. "Will you come with me?"

"No, I would like to stay here a while yet."

Staring at her drooping head, Humphrey felt angry at Hugh. Hesitantly, he put his broad hand on her sleek head. "Sir Hugh, lady," he gulped and stammered, "he did lust after you as I've never seen a man lust afore. Methinks he does still."

Meghan laughed, her voice soft and catching in her throat. "Aye, he did that, did he not?"

The crimson flush staining Humphrey's features ebbed with the knowledge that he had made her laugh. He grinned then nodded farewell and lumbered to his horse.

Meghan watched him ride away, a stout figure too large for the small palfrey. Smiling, she thought of what he had told her. She lay back in the grass, a hand raised to shield her eyes from the sun. Humphrey's words had brought back memories Meghan had held at bay too long. Now she allowed herself to remember the way Hugh's eyes had warmed her, the way his mouth on hers had melted her with its lightest graze, the way his hands caressing her body had made her tremble with need. She welcomed the desire her thoughts awakened.

Turning to her stomach, she thought of Glenna. In the days following Meghan's return, the old woman had plumbed the depths of Meghan's despair and rage. She had forced Meghan to speak of her life with Hugh, of the first time she had seen him, of his demands at Orewin Bridge, of her marriage, of Davyd and his rejection. She had jabbed painfully into memories of the child's death and demanded that Meghan tell of her feelings—her grief, anger, humiliation, need, desire. With her questions, Glenna had pricked the pustule of shame, hate, and pain that Meghan had hidden deep within herself, draining it, healing it. Somehow, in the telling, Meghan had relived the anguish and found relief and understanding. The wound healed slowly. No longer avoiding the hurt, she touched her wounds with her thoughts, at first hesitantly, then with growing confidence.

Frowning, she gazed at the mountains she soon must enter. She thought of how Glenna had turned around the things Meghan had told her, showing them from Hugh's point of view. The old woman had showed her a man who was reluctant to expose himself to hurt but unwilling to take less than what he wanted—and he had wanted her. He had taken her the only way he could—with force. But he had tempered that force with tenderness. He had sensed the desire Meghan felt, the need she denied, and used it to arouse her, to bind her to him. Then, trusting her, he had ridden away and she had not only failed him, but had given him every cause to doubt her.

Scowling Meghan watched a beetle climb a blade of grass, inches from her nose. With misplaced vengeance, she flicked it to its back. She observed its futile efforts to right itself, then flipped it back over, wondering how it viewed so chaotic a world. Then her brow creased again.

Glenna believed Hugh still wanted her; she was his and to denounce her would be to dishonor himself. In such a way did the Normans bind themselves with their codes of chivalry, codes that the practical Welshman with his less romantic view of human behavior scorned.

Meghan could not understand Hugh's sense of honor, but she wondered if he still thought of her, needed her. "Aye," Meghan had told Glenna, "and what of his mockery of me, his ridicule, and what of his mistress, the miller's overblown whore of a daughter?"

"What was Hugh to do?" Glenna had asked. "Plead? Show his hurt and needs? Would she want him so? Was she still woman enough not to want a humble, begging man?"

Tossing away the blade of grass she had been nibbling, Meghan shrugged. No, she only wanted to know what he wanted of her. In answer, she heard again his urgent whisper, "Meghan, I would have you love me!"

Yet if he were to ride up the hillside to me at this very moment, she told herself, nothing would be changed. We would circle about as warily as afore, each searching the other for signs of need, refusing to show such need in ourselves.

Looking down at the village, Meghan saw the blacksmith come to his door, leaning on his crutch. She smiled wryly, remembering how she had duped Humphrey. "Cleitcroft," he had cursed, "is nothing but a place of cripples! You force on me every gimp who crawls to our door. If they were with you at Orewin Bridge or at the fall of Bere Castle or at the battle of Dolwyddelan, if they but say they were, you must find a place for them!"

He was right, Meghan admitted as she walked to her horse. All Wales was crippled, herself as much as anyone.

Chapter 28

Amused, Meghan watched the daughter of Kent ap Evan light the small fire, using the same motions and incantations that Glenna had used for as long as Meghan could remember.

Standing up, the girl rested her arms over her huge belly. Her eyes met Meghan's and she flushed. Meghan remembered the night she had taken the people from Caradoc. She wondered who had sired the child and doubted the girl knew.

The girl handed her a mug of thin ale and a bit of goat's cheese. What comfort could Meghan offer? It was worse to think that the child was likely sired by a foreigner than that the girl was still unmarried.

Meghan waited until the girl left, then began to eat, her thoughts on the last few weeks. The time she had spent in the high pastures had been brief. She had stayed with the clans for only two weeks, unable to find the peace she had hoped to recapture. The clans had huddled close together, their numbers greatly diminished. The faces of men she had known since infancy had held only distrust, resentment, and guilt. She was the wife of a Norman lord and they doubted her purpose there. They dared not insult her for fear of forfeiting the little left them, nor would they call on their relationship with her dead father. The men who had not answered Llewelyn's call and had deserted Davyd hated her for her loyalty and for keeping her lands by selling her body. They called her a whore behind her back, remembering the rumors of the love she had shared with Davyd. She knew their women spat behind her back in fear of the lust she might arouse in their men.

Impatient, Meghan watched the smoke of the fire waver and finally escape through the walls of the brushwood hut. Kent ap Evan would come in his own time, when he had reached his decision. But he had made her wait a long time already.

Leaving the herds, she and Selig had sought and found the hidden glens where fugitive men had welcomed them. In these secret camps lived the dispossessed, the proscribed, those who refused to submit to English law and to confess to foreign priests, those who had lost everything except freedom and their hatred for foreign feet on Welsh earth. With them, too, lived men who preferred the company of those they had lived and fought beside to the unknown foreigner; men who bent their knee to none. These were the men who had been courted by the chieftains since the days of Arthur Pendragon. It was here that Gavin ab Owen would have come had he lived. It was here that Meghan would return to live should Hugh refuse to let her come back to Ainsleah. And it was among these men that she had searched.

She had searched for her father's men, those who at Davyd's command had turned their backs on him and walked away. Of them all, it was Kent ap Evan she needed most. With him on her side, the others would come, too. It was ap Evan Meghan had thought of when Hugh had suggested a Welsh steward for Cleitcroft. Ap Evan was a quiet, steadfast man who kept his own counsel, yet there were few who would stand against him. For all his laconic habits he had been the one most trusted by her father. He had never failed him and only once had he disappointed her—when he had gone to Caradoc. Only later had she realized it was the only way he could have held the clan together.

For weeks, ap Evan had evaded her, while each autumn day brought winter closer. Somehow, for honor's sake, and because she had told Hugh she would come back, she wanted to be at Ainsleah before winter.

At first, she had not understood why it was so important to her that she be there before winter. Then thoughts
of being locked in Ainsleah by piling drifts of snow had
brought visions of the warmth of its hall and its people—
and of Hugh.

The door Glenna had opened in Meghan's mind
allowed too many memories in. Images of Hugh came to
her—the laughter and affection in his eyes; their long,
close hours of bedtalk; the way his gaze followed her
about a crowded room, claiming her, bringing the two of
them together, no matter how physically apart. She found
she missed him and needed him with an intensity that was
marrow deep. She thought of being snowbound with him,
the two of them forced to turn toward each other, to find
each other again in a much deeper way than they had ever
allowed before. Images came to her of what they would
do—of their closeness, their passion, the hours they would
spend in bed, exploring each other, teasing each other to
a desire that, surely, could not be as gripping and fulfilling as she remembered it. But she knew it would be
as wonderful, and that knowledge created an intense and
ever-present need in her.

Sometimes she doubted they would ever again have that
passion; perhaps she had driven the wedge between them
too deep. Yet, she would never know until she was back
at his table and in his bed. Perhaps there, she told herself, they could find each other again.

All she could think of now was her need to return to
him, to seek Hugh out, to try to win him back. And each
time she traveled from one campfire to the next and was
told she had just missed ap Evan, her desire intensified.
Now she had found his camp and, if he said what she
needed to hear, she could return to Ainsleah by harvest,
certainly no later than All Hallow's Eve.

"By all the saints!" Meghan swore. "Will he not
come?"

She started to rise, then settled back with a wry grin.
There was no room to pace in the crude shelter.

Then the hide over the door lifted and, stooping, ap
Evan entered. He was not a large man, but his quiet

authority filled the cramped space. He smiled at Meghan, acknowledging her frustration. Quirking an eyebrow, he held up a mug and she filled it as he studied her, his dark features impassive, his eyes calm, his face lined by long years spent in the open. He seemed to weigh something within her then, satisfied, he spoke. "Do you need to leave today?"

He knew of her desire to return to Hugh. But she could not leave without his word.

His dark eyes laughed, then he frowned. "I must have time to settle my affairs, as few as they are, and to locate the men you want. Several days, four at most, then I can leave with you."

"You'll come then—to Cleitcroft?"

"Aye. Did you think I would not?"

Shame flushed Meghan's translucent skin. "I didn't know," she admitted. "So little is as it once was."

Ap Evan nodded, his mouth tight. "I'll come but I may not stay. I'm not one to place my neck in a foreign yoke. 'Twill depend on your lord. Will you wait and return with me? The mountains are not safe, not even for ab Owen's daughter."

Meghan's need gripped her again. "I cannot. I've been away too long. I must go to Cleitcroft, then home."

"Wales is not your home, lady?"

"My home is with my lord," she answered, knowing she could lose him by making such a statement.

"So it should be," ap Evan agreed, relieving her. "God's laws come before politics and he is your beloved lord, God blessed."

Meghan smiled her gratitude at him and ap Evan stood. "Selig waits, lady, with the horses."

"You knew I would not stay?"

"I did." Ap Evan smiled. "I loved, too, once."

Rising, Meghan frowned. "My lord," she said, "has gone to court."

"I know. There is little the Normans do that we do not know."

"But he is not one for court. I don't know why he is there. Mayhap to put me from him."

Ap Evan studied her, sensing the fear beneath her words. "Mayhap. Then I'll return here, and you with me."

He smiled and after a moment she returned it. He was right. She could only move with life, all her plans and hopes depending on fate's whim.

He ducked under the door and Meghan followed him out, blinking in the bright sunlight. Selig was waiting with the horses, her wolfhound with him. Mounting, Meghan looked down when ap Evan spoke. "Go carefully," he warned. "Rumor has it that Caradoc is about."

"But he is dead," Meghan whispered.

"Not so. Somehow he lived and he has not forgotten you. Ride forthwith to Cleitcroft. You'll still not wait and ride with me?"

Meghan swallowed a lump of fear and, smiling a confidence she did not feel, shook her head. Waving to ap Evan, she kneed her horse and was gone.

Gasping, Hugh struggled up from a dream of suffocation, of a noose about his neck, a pillow firm on his face, water over him, under him, with no surface to it. His eyes jerked open and he stared up at the curtains of an unfamiliar bed. He scowled, unable to remember anything of the night before, then he warily, painfully, turned to look at his companion. The movement created a pain that skewered his eyeballs to the back of his skull. He stared at the woman, thought to shake his head to clear it, and, remembering the pain, changed his mind. He blinked instead. She did not disappear.

Her mouth was agape, displaying her few remaining teeth, and a whistling snore issued from around them. There were pockmarks poorly concealed by blotched makeup and her hair was a bright, brittle orange, dried and frizzled. She lay on her back, a bolster beneath her, her head thrown back to expose the slackness under her chin which her whimple would normally have concealed. Loose flesh sagged from her large bones. As Hugh stared, she turned, her huge breasts flowing from her armpits and falling on the bed.

Frowning, Hugh lay back and closed his eyes. How had he come there, he wondered, and with what company? She was no lady of the court; he would have known her. And she was no whore. The fire and one guttering candle showed that the room held some tasteful objects. She was the widow or wife of a merchant or a well-to-do tradesman, he guessed.

He must have been drinking—and too much. He remembered boisterous companions and his own feigned joviality as he matched them drink for drink, the cost coming from his own purse. They had been celebrating something—the execution of Davyd ab Gruffydd!

Hugh's eyes flew open and he winced. There was no pleasure in the memory as the details slowly came back to him.

It had been a rare October day, the sky clear as midsummer, the warm air holding just a touch of crispness. The smell of unwashed bodies, of the generously spiced foods offered by grimy peddlers, of gutters overflowing with waste, had all been heavy on the slightest breeze. The crowd had been a shoving, laughing, jeering mass, but under its cheer there had been the smell of the mob, of a predator aroused and waiting.

Hugh had ridden with the court to the execution. Edward had kept him close by, aware they shared something more than the observing of a criminal's just punishment.

The king's face had been set. His irrational hurt and anger at Davyd had smothered much of the guilt and loss he might have felt. Davyd had rejected him, had refused the role of proselyte, and in so doing had spurned his lord in a way Edward could not forgive. Even had Edward been willing to forgive him, the nobles, the lawyers, and the clergy, would not have allowed it.

Aping their monarch's grief, the people of the court had arranged their features in sorrow, but their eyes had been avid with rapacious curiosity.

Davyd died with as much dignity as his manner of death had allowed. It had not been the smell, the malicious stares, or the execution that had driven Hugh on a blind drinking spree. He had seen both torture and death.

And it could not have been guilt over the man, Davyd ab
Gruffydd, Hugh insisted to himself. He, Hugh fitz Alan,
was innocent in that matter.

Suddenly, Hugh's stomach turned inside itself, its contents surging to his throat. Twisting off the bed, his feet
became entangled in the bedclothes. Silently cursing every
saint he could think of, his head a spinning ball, he desperately kicked his legs free and groped under the bed for
the chamber pot. He jerked it to him as the vomit spewed
forth while a voice in the back of his mind thanked each
saint he had blasphemed that the pot was empty.

The retching seemed to go on forever, threatening to
tear his stomach from its mooring. When at last it eased,
Hugh weakly wiped his mouth on the silken bed covering
and looked about the chamber with hollow eyes.

The woman's breathing remained undisturbed and he
was grateful that she had not awakened. An ewer of water
sat on a chest across the room and he tried to rise, but
found his legs too weak. Cradling his head in his arms,
he waited for the return of his strength.

It was not the drink that had sickened him, Hugh
admitted. It was self-disgust.

Hugh thought of why he had come to court. His anger
at Meghan's leaving had quickly faded and he had missed
her with an unbearable intensity. Her scent had haunted
their bedchamber and wrapped about him in his bed. The
castle's vaulted ceilings had echoed back her laugh and
Hugh had caught himself turning toward the whispered
sound of her footfall many times a day.

The knowledge that she was so close had preyed most
on his mind. His eyes had been ever drawn to the distant
dark mountains of Wales. Each day he had fought his
desire to find her, to bring her home. But to do so would
have meant possibly losing her forever. She had said she
would return and he had only to wait.

But the waiting had been hard. The ample and giving
body of the miller's daughter had not eased his need.
Though his religion was no more than a part of the pattern of his life, he had found himself attending to the
priest's sermons for comfort and praying fervently for his
wife's safety. Had she been there, Meghan would have

likened his anxiety to that of a woman waiting for the return of her lord from war.

His people had finally driven Hugh from Ainsleah. They had constantly reminded him of her by avoiding the mere mention of her name. He had seen sympathy in their carefully averted eyes. Yedda had gone so far as to remove Meghan's chair from the high table and Hugh had angrily ordered it put back, knowing its absence would be as much a reminder as its presence.

Gradually, his pride had rebelled. His loneliness and need had reverted once again to anger. Unconsciously, he had felt the need to prove to his people, to his wife and to himself that she was not necessary to him. Suddenly all his emotions had erupted in the appealing idea of a visit to court.

His present thirst driving the memories away, Hugh pulled his body up by the bedclothes and moved to the ewer, holding to the wall for support. He lifted the jug itself. Filling his mouth, he sloshed the water about, then spat it into the rushes before swallowing a little. Tentatively drawing a breath, he felt a wave of dizziness and leaned his hands against the table, his head low, waiting for it to pass.

For three months he had played the games of court. He had traveled with Edward and his family. He had hunted and hawked. He had shared quiet moments with his king, moments of rare understanding between two men, moments all too few and all too short. He had jousted with the king's knights and left them bewildered by the intensity and anger of his attack. He had been questioned often of his lady, the eyes of both men and women sly and smug. He had truthfully told them she was at home, as she was, and had enjoyed their disappointment at his words.

Slowly his disgust with court and with himself had grown. He had begun to avoid the men who saw him as a way to reach Edward Longshanks. He had tired of the women whom he took with an anger they mistook for passion. Soon he had sought his pleasure and oblivion with the people of London—the soldiers, merchants, whores, merry wives, and widows. That was how he must have met the woman on the bed.

Cautiously, Hugh stared at her then dropped his eyes, shuddering less from the sight than from disgust with himself. He knew that, were Meghan to become as scarred and worn from the birthing of his children, he would still find her as desirable as he did now. Smiling ruefully, he waited for the pain the thought of her always brought but found only a feeling of intense emptiness where his love had been.

Incredulous, he turned his gaze inward and probed the part of him that had needed Meghan. He found nothing but desire turned apathetic and love faded to indifference.

For several moments he refused to believe it, frantically trying to reason back the love that had driven and sustained him for so long. He felt hollow without the hurt and need, and desperately searched for them, sensing he was incomplete without them. Then he surrendered, the loss hitting him like a physical blow, knocking the breath from him. Leaning his head in his cradled arms, he gave in to dry sobs that racked his body. With each heave of his shoulders, he relinquished his desire and need.

Somehow his love had died with Davyd. He had watched the execution, his face impassive, but satisfaction had raged within him. It had seemed as though Davyd died, not for his crimes against England, but for his crimes against Hugh. Hugh had tasted revenge at the death of the man who may have intimately known his wife. Self-disgust swept over Hugh, that he should so gloat over the death of a noble man. Cold sweat chilled him. Tremors shook him. When they passed, they took with them his love for Meghan. Somehow, she was to blame for the joy and the exultation he had taken in another man's torture.

As Hugh's weeping eased, the hollow deep inside him became filled with purpose. Remembering the long years of waiting, suddenly and clearly, he saw their waste. The time he should have spent acquiring land and siring children, he had passed lusting after a wench whom no sane man would have ever thought to wife. He had been a fool. Edward himself had warned him. And Edward was

right, Hugh told himself. Because he had not believed his
king, he had wasted six years of his life.

Meghan was just another woman, more beautiful than
most—and there were those who would argue that—but
really no different. He had let himself be seduced by the
shape of an eye, the curve of a breast, but such things
put no coin in the coffer. Meghan's passion, her intelligence, and her spirit had drawn him, but they were things
a wise man sought only in a mistress.

Hugh felt his strength return as his resolution grew. He
stood, his knees no longer shaking, and glanced about for
his clothes, blood singing through his veins. His thoughts
flew as he dressed. Aye, he agreed with himself, I've
been a fool, but no more!

Hugh's mind filled with plans. He would return to Ainsleah. If his wife was not there, he would find her. If she
agreed to return home to stay, to be docile and biddable,
then he would take her back. If not, he would leave her
to her Wales and be done with the bitch! Once free, he
would find another wife, one with land and the proper
turn of mind, a small, plump thing like he should have
sought before.

Reaching for his cloak, Hugh heard the bells of London and, crossing himself, paused to listen. They rang for
Lauds and he had several hours yet before true dawn.
Time enough to find his men, to take leave of Edward,
and still make a full day's journey. The king would regret
his going, but he would be pleased that Hugh had finally
rid himself of his passion.

Lifting the latch, Hugh felt an overwhelming sense of
freedom. Laughing at the sheer joy of it, he closed the
door behind him.

Chapter 29

The sun was low as Selig and Meghan rode down the trail to Cleitcroft. The pastures they passed through were lush and green. In the distance, beyond a haze of hills, lay England. The defile behind the round, dark keep was streaked in misty gold and purple. A flock of birds wheeled through it, disappearing into the shadows then appearing again cast in purest white in the slanting rays of the sun.

Meghan, a perplexed frown between her eyes, was looking at the deserted village. No smoke rose from the houses. No women stood gossiping in their doorways. No children played in the wide road. The keep, too, appeared abandoned, the drawbridge down, the portcullis raised, no sentry walking the walls.

As they rode through the village, Meghan's gaze remained on the castle, apprehension expanding within her. A bowshot's distance from the walls, Selig grabbed her bridle, halting her. Meghan looked at him, but he only shrugged, his face as bewildered as hers. Releasing her horse, he pointed toward England, gesturing them away from Cleitcroft.

Meghan stared at him, her frustration rising. She envisioned the time she had spent away from Hugh as wasted, her labor worthless, her plans and hopes shattered. Sudden rage drowned all caution, and her heels slammed into her mount's sides. The horse leaped forward, almost unseating her. She heard Selig's guttural shout and the pound of his horse's hooves behind her. Her hands lifted to help her mount leap the space between the earth and the rising drawbridge before she realized that she was riding into a trap.

Desperately she jerked on the bridle, wheeling her horse about, his hooves slipping on the smooth wood. Clinging to him, Meghan battled to drive him back over the rising slope, but the animal's scrabbling efforts failed and he fell, twisting to cast her from him.

Meghan's breath escaped in a rush as she hit the hard-packed earth of the ward. Her head struck in a blow that brought stars. Selig's raging roar remained unheard through the thick walls and the pounding in her ears. She gasped, trying to suck air into her lungs. Gradually, her breathing eased and she started to roll over, fear driving her to motion. But a heavy foot pushed her back, pressing into her stomach. Blinking against the pain in her head, she opened her eyes, knowing before she saw him who held her pinned to the ground.

"Caradoc," she stated.

He was a bulky, menacing shadow silhouetted against the sky. His laugh was gloating. Bending, he snatched the knife from her belt and shoved it into his own. He jerked her longbow over her head, grinning as he snapped it in two and tossed aside the two broken halves. His foot pressed against her abdomen, all his weight behind it, then he released her and stood back to watch her rise.

Meghan crouched back on her heels and lifted her gaze to the sky above Caradoc, not wanting to accept his presence. He would not help her rise, she knew, nor did she want him to; his touch, however casual, would sully her. She waited until a remnant of strength returned, then stood, her knees shaking. At last, she looked at the weasel-faced man who stood at Caradoc's shoulder, remembering him as having been briefly with Davyd, then her gaze turned to Caradoc. "Where is Humphrey Thorley?"

Caradoc laughed, his voice too high for so large a man. "He feeds the carrion," he answered, nodding toward the defile. "But why do you ask after an Englishman when there are Welshmen to greet you? Do you not recognized my faithful Harlen?"

Meghan stared at Caradoc, numb with disbelief. Humphrey could not be dead! Not when she had just found him as a friend!

"You scorned my Harlen," Caradoc mocked, "when you were with Davyd. He did but want a taste of what you gave so freely to others. You did have him banished. 'Twas not a nice thing, sister mine, and he does resent it. But I told him you would make amends. When I am done with you, 'twill be his turn. And you will be more biddable then, won't you, sister?"

"Where are the people?" she heard herself ask.

Caradoc shrugged. "Those foolish enough to fight are dead. Those fast enough ran to the hills. Those wise enough to see they could not stand against me are here. But do not look to them. They know well what will happen should they try to aid you. I chose my time well," he boasted, his face as smug as a well-fed cat's. Most of your Norman lord's men were gone. You, too, and that dumb giant with you. 'Twas an opportunity I could not resist. And you trained him well in Welsh hospitality, that Humphrey Thorley. He did not turn a bard from his door or one he thought a bard. A simple matter of slitting one guard's throat and of lowering the drawbridge and the deed was done."

Meghan gazed at him, not seeming to understand. "And Glenna?" she asked.

Caradoc chuckled and spread his hands in a parody of regret. "She was an old hag. Such women become slow. She could not outrun a man on horseback—or his lance."

No more questions came to her stunned mind and she waited for grief to come. It didn't. It was as though all emotion was dead within her.

Caradoc returned her calm gaze, then grew uneasy. His eyes darted away and he shook himself to cast aside a sudden disquiet. "Ah, but come, sister mine," he shrilled, "I am remiss. I will show you to your chamber."

He reached for her elbow, but Meghan stepped back, eyes cool. Shrugging, he laughed and gestured her on before him. She went; there was little else she could do. There was no place to run, to hide, no place he would not know of. He had found her in all of them when they were children. All she could do was wait.

She led the way up the stairs and paused in the hall. Smiling, Caradoc motioned her on up the stairs to the bedchambers and, bowing, waved her into the room that had been hers. She hesitated, her fear of enclosed places rushing over her. But he grabbed her arm and swung her around. His fist descended against her face in a blow that knocked her onto a pallet, its force ringing her ears.

Swaggering over her, Caradoc grinned. "Do not fret, sister mine, you'll have company soon enough. Do you think I would deprive you of anything? Your Norman lord took what I wanted, but I'm not one to mind a bastard's leavings. And you seem not to mind a bantling, not that I expect the same welcome. But 'twill come, once I've taught you my ways."

His lips curved in anticipation, then he left the room, the door slamming behind him with the sound of a bar being dropped across it. Never had there been a bar before.

Meghan rose, driven by fear to rush to the door, to scream, to plead, to promise anything to be released. Then she fell back, her eyes tightly shut as she fought to control her terror.

She had no candles or torches; Caradoc would not have allowed her any. She tried to pull her thoughts into some order. Selig must have escaped, but how could he tell anyone of her plight? Godfrey, lame as he was, could not come to her rescue, even if he wanted to. And despite all his courtesy and kindness, Godfrey would do what he thought best for Hugh, even if she were to die for it.

And Hugh, he could well still be at court. Even if he was at Ainsleah and could understand Selig's pantomime, he might choose to do nothing, as well. She might not even be his wife now—he might have put her from him. And even if he did come, what could he do? He once had said it would be many months' work to take Cleitcroft.

Slow tears flowed over Meghan's cheeks. Just to have him come, she thought, would give her such comfort. Just to know he cared enough. Just to know he was there, outside the walls.

Meghan sensed Caradoc's approach up the winding stairs and pulled herself from a restless sleep. The light of a torch blazed into the room, blinding her. Caradoc's distorted shadow was cast across the room to her feet and Meghan jerked them back. But the light itself was sorely welcome.

Caradoc held up the torch, his face still hidden, and chuckled. "Ah, sister mine," he gloated, "you've been weeping! Have you so missed me?"

His words were slurred and his hand shook as he placed the torch in a wall bracket. He was drunk, Meghan realized, and perhaps more dangerous because of it. His enflamed gaze moved over her as she crouched against the wall. His large tongue moistened his red lips. His eyes gleamed with an obscene, forbidden purpose, his need to inflict pain flickering in their depths.

Meghan stared at him, mesmerized. Trapped, she watched as he removed his clothes. Then he kneeled in front of her, swaying slightly, his hairless nakedness leperous in its whiteness. His hand grazed over her face. She drew back, sealing herself to the wall. He tucked a stray strand of ebony hair behind her ear. "Will you not let down your hair for me, sister?" he asked, giggling at the absurdity of his request.

Her eyes were wide with horror and Caradoc laughed, his mirth rippling over her shrinking flesh. His eyes glowed as his mouth lowered to hers. His lips felt clammy. His tongue pushed into her mouth, its taste of ale and salted fish twisting Meghan's stomach. When he drew back, his face was smooth with confidence.

"I had hoped," he slurred, "that you would fight me, at least at first. But you've always wanted me, haven't you? I could tell in the way you walked. So rigid, as though you were afraid to tempt me with the sway of your hips. I could see it in the way your eyes avoided mine, as though you were afraid 'twould tell me of your lusts."

The stunned look fled from her eyes. Then she spat full in his face.

The unctuous handsomeness of Caradoc's features twisted as he wiped the spittle away. His fist struck her face, knocking her head against the wall, stupefying her. Through the roaring in her ears she heard him pour forth obscenities. She felt his hands ripping at her clothes, tearing her cloak from her, jerking her about as though she were weightless. Her belt was flung across the room. Her tunic was forced up over her head. The relentless pressure of his weight pushed her down. His hands explored her, twisting, pinching, seeming to delight in the way she flinched away from him. His mouth moved moistly over her, fouling her with its damp touch.

Then something snapped in Meghan. Her fear vanished and she began to fight. Her hands clutched his hair and pulled his head away from her breast. Her teeth sank into his shoulder. Her knees doubled up, seeking his soft belly. Her body turned beneath his, fighting his violation.

She heard his laugh as he blocked her knees. His hands grabbed hers, twisting until she released her grip, then his fist descended into her face again.

Meghan tasted blood as her head reeled. His lips claimed hers again, sucking. She felt his knee drive up, forcing her thighs apart. She kicked, aiming for his groin, and he caught her leg, pulling it up, twisting her to him. Her body went rigid as she felt his hardness press against her.

Caradoc twined his fingers in her hair and turned her face to his. His lips were moist, his eyes glinting as he watched, wanting to see her pain and disgust as he took her.

But Meghan smiled. "Caradoc," she said, "remember Glenna's puppy, the one you killed?"

His mouth grew slack with sudden apprehension.

"Remember, Caradoc, how you ran away to the hills to escape our father's wrath and when you returned, 'twas all forgot, or so you thought—but then you ailed. Your belly swelled and ached. Your bowels turned to water. You thought, in truth, that you would die. So did we hope. And you accused Glenna. But 'twas not Glenna who found you with the puppy, was it?"

Meghan paused, sensing his withdrawal. "Remember how I found it, its belly slit and its body pinned to the earth with your knife? I would have killed it in mercy, but you held me and forced me to watch it die, you laughing, me crying. 'Twas Kay who found us, who killed it. He would, methinks, have killed you, too, had you not run. Even he, though, had forgot by the time you returned. But not I!"

Caradoc stared at her, his face bewitched.

"You thought 'twas Glenna who cursed you," Meghan said. "But she dared not for fear of our father. But she had taught me well, had Glenna, though I dared not go too far. I did not want her blamed for my deed. Now ab Owen, too, is dead and I will not hold back a second time."

Caradoc's manhood grew flaccid against her. He started to back away, then paused, reason overcoming fear. "If you are a witch," he demanded, "why haven't you flown away?"

Meghan laughed while she frantically searched her memory for what witching lore she had heard. "For that I must have aconite, belladonna, and hemlock, aye, and the fat of an infant dead at birth. But to curse you, I need but a hair from your head, a fleck of your skin from under my fingernail."

Her nails dug into his shoulder and he jerked away, falling to the floor in his haste. Sitting up, she clasped her knees in her arms, her eyes catlike in the torchlight.

"A bit of dirt, too," she added as he yanked his clothes on and fought to get into his hose. "This place abounds in such. Some spittle and a straw, of course, or any sharp object to drive into the heart or belly or groin, depending on if I wish a long death or a short one."

He whirled to the door then stopped, her belt catching his eye. Picking it up, he turned back, need for dignity fighting his fear. "Methinks I'll take this," he told her. "By rights, 'tis mine. And you are mine, too! Don't think that I am done with you!"

Meghan only smiled and he groped for the latch, his eyes still on her. His fumbling fingers found it and he jerked the door open, then slammed it behind him, the bar thudding as he dropped it into place.

Meghan's smile fled and her body began to shake. Her breath came with hard gasps into lungs starved by fear.

He would come back. His twisted reasoning would find a way to turn her threat against her. He would convince himself she was lying. He would find a way to render her weaponless, to turn her weak again.

Shuddering, Meghan forced her arms from about her knees and stood, her legs shaking. The memory of his mouth on hers, of the suffocating weight of his body, twisted her stomach. Frantically, she searched for a chamber pot, knowing as she did that Caradoc would not allow her such dignity. Her stomach drove her to the far corner, where she retched until, exhausted, she cradled her head in her arms.

The thought of Caradoc touching her forced her at last to rise. She felt violated, her soul defiled. Moving unsteadily to a table, she lifted the jug of water to her mouth. Her lips welcomed the cool purity. She swallowed carefully, willing her stomach to remain calm. She wanted so much to spill the water over her, to wash away the slime of Caradoc's touch, but she set the ewer back on the table. She might have more urgent need of it later.

Head aching, face swollen, she drew on her tunic. It felt loose without the belt and anger at Caradoc filled her, giving her the will to creep back to her pallet. Lying down, she pulled Hugh's cloak over her and gazed at the torch. In his haste, Caradoc had at least left her that. But it would not burn long.

Her thoughts clung to Hugh, wanting him, needing him as she never had before. His touch would wipe away the filth she felt, could cleanse her soul. But she dared not hope for or trust in him. If he failed her, she would have no will left to fight or live. She would be more vulnerable than ever before. Her mind, she knew, would retreat into the limbo in which she had dwelt after her child's death, so deep she would never find her way back. She dared not even think of Hugh. She had to find another source of strength, one strong enough to sustain her.

Kent ap Evan might come but he, too, would be powerless. Selig might not have gone to Ainsleah. Perhaps he prowled about the walls looking for a means to rescue her. Hugh, Selig, Godfrey, ap Evan—none of them could help her. None could give her something to cling to. Then soft words came to her: "Had I not a wife and nine children, girl, I would have long since asked your father for you."

Suddenly Davyd seemed so close, giving her the strength that had sustained him for so long. She felt again the love that was great enough to relinquish her, to refuse the little she could offer. She turned to his image, saw again his accepting eyes, felt again his mouth light as a moth on hers, asking nothing where so many had demanded. He would have come to her, she knew. He would have given her strength. But he was a prisoner of the English, awaiting his fate as surely as she was awaiting hers.

Slow tears flowed as she thought of Davyd locked away from the earth he loved, from the sun, from the wind on his face. Her body shook as grief welled up, grief for Glenna and her lost wisdom; for Humphrey, gentle although he was a man of war, hiding his tenderness behind gruff, blunt ways.

With Glenna, she had lost the last support from her childhood, the woman she had turned to on her mother's death, the woman who had raised her. Glenna had given her so much, had given her wisdom, her strength, her courage. She had lived a life of peace in a land torn by war and she should have died peacefully in her bed, her hand in Meghan's. Somehow, Meghan thought, she should have been there, should have protected her.

And Humphrey! So plodding, so staid in his ways! But they had somehow become friends. He had understood her grief and had comforted her. She knew she could never replace the grumpy, grizzled warrior.

Both of their deaths seemed her fault. If she had not insisted on coming back to Wales, Caradoc would have had no use for Cleitcroft. He would never have come back and both Glenna and Humphrey would still be alive. If she had not been so stubborn, thinking that only she could save Cleitcroft, she would never have gone into the hills to seek out ap Evan. Then, perhaps, she could have stopped Caradoc, could have seen through his disguise. If she had not left Hugh after their marriage, perhaps Caradoc would have forgotten about her. And Humphrey was naturally suspicious and distrustful. If only she had not insisted he learn and abide by so many of the Welsh customs and courtesies, he would never have turned his back on anyone, bard or no. But he had been so proud when he pleased her! Now he was dead.

It seemed her grief would never ease, her sorrow never lessen. She cried for herself, trapped and without hope, with nothing to cling to but the memory of the gentle man Davyd who had loved her.

Chapter 30

Ten days after he left court, Hugh was but a league from Ainsleah. He and his men were weary. He had pulled them from their wenching, gambling, and drinking and given them only a few hours to become sober, to settle their debts, and to say farewell. They had set out early that same morning, still befuddled and resenting him.

Seldom stopping at monastaries or castles, they had camped instead beside the road. They had ridden through the late autumn rains. Their beds had been earth and rock, always cold, often wet.

They had not questioned Hugh. If they grumbled, it was among themselves and Hugh was thankful they did not press him. Perversely, he cursed the system that produced such blind obedience. Yet he half hoped that one of them would ask, giving him an excuse to vent the temper building in him.

The release and exultation he had felt ten days ago had ebbed as tension's quiet, unyielding grip had claimed him again. But he had not lost his purpose. In his mind Meghan was no more than a property to be kept or discarded depending on the circumstances. He could not care whether she stayed or went.

After driving his men for ten days, he suddenly felt reluctant to reach Ainsleah. It no longer offered comfort. When he thought of the questions to be asked him, the problems he would have to deal with, he felt only fatigue.

Ignoring his men's palpable eagerness, Hugh drew his horse to a slower pace and looked about the familiar landscape.

The road ran as straight as an arrow's flight across the heath, then turned to parallel the creek for a third of a league. Moonlight silhouetted each shrub and contour of land, marking each feature with a detail eerie in the cold glow of night. A silent wind blew shreds of silver-rimmed black clouds over the full moon and shifted the topmost branches of trees growing from the creek bottom, their boughs skeletal against the indigo sky.

Then the road dropped into darkness to follow the creek, becoming a jungle of brush and trees that emitted a dank odor of damp and rot. The air became oppressive, slowing the pace still further. The men crowded closer, their gape-mouthed breathing audible in the spirit-haunted night. Sensing their fear, Hugh reluctantly urged his weary horse to a faster pace.

They had to travel only a short distance more before the road dipped across a shallow ford and rose out of the creek and over cultivated land. The fields lay in naked, fallow ridges. From habit, Hugh glanced right and left, measuring by the stubble the harvest's success and the industry of each villein.

The village seemed to huddle into itself. In the square, a huge pile of wood and straw was heaped awaiting the bonfire of All Hallow's Eve, its flames intended to drive away the spirits of the dead that would walk again that night.

No light glimmered and no curious face peered out as they rode by, yet Hugh sensed the fear within the hovels. Awakened by the sound of horses, the people might wonder if the riders were humans or ghosts. From somewhere came the thin cry of an infant, quickly hushed.

At last they drew up before the gates of Ainsleah. Standing in his saddle, Ralph Ramsden cupped his hands around his mouth. Before he could shout, a torch appeared on the parapet. The gatekeeper usually slept deeply and it was often the work of half an hour to rouse him. Scowling, Hugh wondered why he was now awake in the dead of night.

Ralph answered the guard's challenge and the draw-bridge was lowered, the portcullis raised. Still puzzled, Hugh led his men into Ainsleah and found the people of the castle also awake. Men gathered in groups fell silent when they saw their lord pass by. The fire pit had been fed and its flames cast grotesque shadows on the walls.

Foreboding gripped Hugh as he dismissed his men and started up the keep stairs. All he wanted was a hot meal, a bath, and to sleep into the morning. Never had he wanted to avoid anything as much as what awaited him in Ainsleah's hall.

Above him, the portcullis of the keep was up, the huge, steel-studded door open, and Godfrey stood there. He spoke no welcome and the light of the torch he held etched his scowl. He swallowed hard, then forced the words from his lips. "Selig is here."

"And my lady?" Hugh asked hoarsely.

"He came in without her not an hour gone. He was staggering in his shoes, had ridden his horse to the ground. I've not tried to query him. He eats now."

Godfrey's words came like a blow to Hugh's breast-bone, paralyzing him. Selig would have fought to the death for Meghan. Unless, he thought, she ordered him from her. But he would not have gone. Unless she had somehow eluded his guard. 'Twould be something she would do. . . .

With the sudden knowledge of the grief he would suffer if he lost her, his emotional apathy dissolved. He needed her, wanted her, would challenge the very gates of hell for her. If she still lived.

His feet felt leaden as he entered the hall. The house-hold women stopped plying Selig with food, their eyes on Hugh. Several of his knights, waiting to question Selig, drew back, silent and apprehensive. Yedda moved first, rushing to Hugh with words of condolence, stammering how, after all, it was possibly for the best. God worked in ways unfathomable to His servants.

Hugh shoved her into her husband's arms. Rage blinded him when he thought how the man he had trusted had failed and he dared not move. At last, he walked to Selig.

Pulling out a chair, he swung his leg over its back and set down.

His voice emerged calm and controlled, surprising him. "Is my lady wife dead?"

Selig squinted, then shrugged, his eyebrows knotted. He shook his head.

"She may be, but you do not think so?"

Selig nodded vigorously.

"Where is she, then?"

Selig pointed to the walls and drew a cylindrical form with his hands. It hovered there as the other hand lifted to mold hills and mountains.

"Cleitcroft?" Hugh demanded, relaxing when Selig nodded. Then a thought struck him. "And Humphrey?"

In a gesture that left no doubt, Selig drew a finger across his throat.

"Then another man holds Cleitcroft—and my lady? Or does she stay of her own will?"

Selig shook his head vehemently.

"Who holds her?"

Consternation settled over Selig's features. Then he grinned. Striding to the fireplace, he selected a charred stick and returned to the table. With one movement he swept away the goblets, trenchers, and food, leaving only the white cloth. Swiftly he drew a stick figure, with a gigantic mustache on the round head. Next to it, on its right, he drew another, a triangle from its waist transforming it into a woman. Then he added six more with mustaches, all male. Beyond them, he drew another woman. Switching to the left, he marked down yet another woman and next to her, a man. Rapidly, he crossed out the woman to the left, then the one to the right. He emphatically marked out, too, all the male figures to the right, leaving only the single man far to the left, the woman to the far right, and the man in the middle. This last he crossed out before looking hopefully at Hugh. Seeing Hugh's frown, he pointed to the remaining woman and jammed his middle finger into the fist of his other hand in an ancient, obscene gesture.

"Meghan?" Hugh guessed.

Selig nodded and ran his hand over the figures, oblit-
erating all but Meghan and the male. Hugh scowled as
Selig stared at him, willing him to see. Then his features
brightened and he drew a shield on the male figure, adding, with a gesture of triumph, a bar sinister.

Hugh's frown only deepened, then Yedda gasped,
"Caradoc!"

"Caradoc?" Hugh whispered. "Her bastard brother,
the one she went to afore?"

"Aye," Yedda agreed, then honesty conquered her
disapproval. "But she did not go to him, but against
him!"

Hugh's gaze clung to her, wanting to believe but not
daring to. "How do you know?"

"I saw him once. She would not go to him. She hates
and fears him. And you, my lord," she stated. "You saw
him. At Flint. My lady said."

Hugh's frown deepened. Then a man's features leaped
to mind, features smooth and bland, then twisted with an
obscene suggestion as he looked at Meghan. Hugh shuddered. He remembered Meghan's fear as she stared at
Caradoc.

"No," he agreed, terror seeping into his soul. "She'd
not go to him."

He straightened away from the table. "We can leave
at once with the full moon," he stated. "All the men you
can spare, Godfrey. Ralph, tell them to prepare the
horses, to eat now as we'll not take time again tonight.
Yedda, get me food and pack more. Go, all of you!"

Selig half rose from the table, his eyes bright with
appeal and anticipation. Hugh saw him and his eyebrows
knitted into a refusal. Then he shrugged. "Aye, and you,
Selig, though I would know by all the saints how she was
taken!"

It was several days before Meghan realized Caradoc
was starving her. She had awakened late, her body
bruised and aching, her mind numb. The square of light
on the floor reflected from the high, small window had
told her it was midday. Uncaring, she had watched it
slowly move across the rushes, then up the stone wall,

becoming shorter as it climbed. Soon it was gone, plunging her back into darkness. But she still had water, she thought. It should last several days and food she could live without a while longer.

Meghan watched the light fade, her throat dry as dust, but she would wait to drink, she promised herself, until she could barely see. But not too long. It would be too easy to stumble in the dark and knock over the ewer.

Dreams of Caradoc, Hugh, and Davyd haunted her sleep that night and the night after. Her bastard brother came to her in nightmares, his pale eyes huge, gleaming with his lust and cruelty. Or he would be there in the dark, a threat she could only sense. She would try to escape, moving as though she walked through water, knowing that he could see where she could not, that he watched her efforts and laughed. She would wake in terror.

Hugh would come to her, his expression laughing or teasing or soft with love. She would run to him, but his features changed, becoming harsh. The miller's daughter would appear, moving into his arms and they would smile, mocking her.

Davyd brought her comfort. He would banish her heartfelt hurt. He would enfold her in his arms, demanding nothing. His words would be soft and caring and his eyes gentle before he was torn from her by a force much stronger than death, a force so great that she dared not challenge it. Yet he always left her stronger than before, left her in a sleep disturbed only by sorrow and grief. Until the dreams began again. . . .

On the third day Meghan woke late. The square of light had already touched the wall. Her mind was lucid, yet the chamber walls seemed far away and her body weightless. She made no movement toward the ewer, remembering how, half asleep, she had drained it of its last sweet drops.

Yet she felt only peace. It would pass. Soon thirst would drive her to panic, hunger to pleading. But now she savored her languorous serenity.

It took her a moment to identify the scrape of the bar being lifted and she scowled, resenting the intrusion. Her eyes rested apathetically on the laden tray being borne to her. She did not feel fear until she saw the serving girl, who she did not recognize for a moment through the bruises blackening her eyes. The girl's nose was puffed and she breathed shallowly through cut lips.

"Enid?" Meghan whispered, forcing herself to sit up.

She identified the ferret-faced man behind Enid, and met his gaze. Whatever he said or did, it did not matter. Only Caradoc held the power to defile her with his gaze, to reduce her to a frightened, stunned animal.

Under Meghan's steady stare, Harlen looked away, his mocking words dying. Instead, he jerked Enid around and kicked her when she stumbled, shoving her out the door. Meghan watched them go, too weak and powerless to intercede.

Slowly, she turned toward the tray. She stared at it, fighting hunger; to gorge herself would only make her ill. When she judged her resistance strong enough, she picked up the jug of water and drank carefully. Then she ate a very little before putting the tray from her. She would eat again in an hour's time, in the time it took the square of light to climb a quarter of the wall.

What game was Caradoc now playing? Perhaps he hoped she would gorge herself only to vomit and be left more hungry than before. Perhaps he hoped she would eat a little and save the rest. Then he would take it from her, leaving her to rue her abstention. Frightened, she hid half the food in the dry ewer.

Perhaps he thought to alternately starve and feed her into submission. Why didn't he just take her and slit her throat? But he wanted her defeated, a mindless, beaten thing. Her death would not give him that. Perhaps his design was to drive her into submission by no apparent design at all, to let her think she had found a thread in the pattern, then destroy the pattern itself.

Perhaps he had no plan at all, only his own mad whims. That was the most frightening thought of all.

Enid brought more food that evening and the next day and Meghan found she resented the intrusion. The walls no longer pressed in on her; the room had become a sanctuary. Although she welcomed the food, she dreaded seeing Enid. The girl brought concerns from outside that Meghan could not solve and she was thankful the girl was not allowed to speak. Harlen was no more than a meddlesome insect.

Only the square of light did Meghan greet with pleasure and mourn when it vanished. But with the night Meghan was able to summon Davyd. Sometimes it seemed as though he was really there with her.

It was midmorning of the fifth day when Caradoc came again. He swaggered and glanced about, his wrinkling nose, the two men with him watching. "It stinks of a jakes in here, sister mine. Can you not use a chamber pot?"

His comrades giggled and Caradoc met Meghan's impassive gaze. She allowed no fear or apprehension to show on her features. Nor did she mention that he had allowed her no chamber pot. He hoped to goad her into self-defense. To answer would be to acknowledge him.

"And you, sister mine," Caradoc continued, "look like a whore after a hard night—after several hard nights."

Meghan didn't reply and her hands stayed at her sides, ignoring the impulse to smooth her hair. She refused to hear the twitters of his men.

Shifting under her gaze, Caradoc realized he could not drive her to protest. But he knew what would rouse her. "You've guests, sister mine," he said. "Guests who will delight in seeing you, methinks."

A flicker of interest briefly touched her eyes. She walked proudly to the door, then paused, not wanting to leave her sanctuary. Without her eyes on him, Caradoc found courage. He seized her arm, twisting it behind her back and forcing her out the door and down the stairs. Halfway down, Meghan stumbled, thrown off balance by a jerk on her arm. Caradoc let go of her with a shove that sent her sprawling. She bounced from the rough wall, one bare shoulder scraped and bleeding, and fell face first into the hall.

Dazed, she pushed herself to her knees and stared at the blood welling from her nose. Caradoc twisted his fingers in her hair, yanking her head up. "Sister mine," he taunted, "I've never seen you clumsy."

The laughter of his men rang in her ears and she heard the hesitant, false mirth of her people join in.

"Ah, sister mine," Caradoc continued, "we cannot have you greet your guests appearing so. Methinks they'll believe we do not take proper care of you."

He smeared the blood over her face, shoved her through the passageway, down the steps of the keep, across the ward, and up the narrow steps of the outer wall. His fingers dug into her hair, forcing her head up. "Look, bitch," he whispered, "at who comes to honor us. I had not thought he would value you so."

Meghan blinked in the bright sunlight. Her heart pounded in her chest and she willed it to be calm, not daring to hope.

The village lay a long bow shot away and she had to stare before her vision adjusted. Then she saw the huddle of men and horses and recognized the colors and escutcheon of Hugh fitz Alan. A sob swelled her throat and she forced it back as she saw the sudden stir Caradoc's appearance roused in Hugh's men.

Her brother's roar rang in her ears. "Bastard! Norman bastard! Norman bastard, I would have word with you, a word in truce."

Meghan kept her eyes on the huddle of men, willing Hugh not to trust Caradoc, but he rode toward them, Selig beside him. Not wanting to face him, she lifted her eyes to the mountains. Shame coiled in her, and fear of what he would think when he saw her face battered and her body held so intimately by Caradoc.

Hugh and Selig were halfway up the path when they halted. Caradoc laughed. "No, brother bantling, 'tis not near enough. If you dare not trust me, mayhap the word of your lady wife will do. Or mayhap, you are not fool enough to place faith in such a guileful bitch!"

Caradoc released Meghan. Her gaze touched Hugh's. She swallowed then called that it was clear.

Hugh examined Caradoc, distaste so strong it nauseated him. He would deal with him in time, if he had to track him to the ends of the earth. His eyes moved to his wife. He studied her, seeing the blood and bruises mottling her features, her hair matted and dull. Yet she held her head proudly. A cold fury surged through him and he vowed that he would somehow reclaim her, that he would kill the man who had so mistreated her.

"You value this bitch, do you not?" Caradoc demanded.

"She is mine," Hugh answered, knowing he could find no better way to express his need and love. "As is Cleitcroft."

Caradoc chuckled. "Think you so? Ah, but they are in my possession, methinks! Would you like them back, bantling?"

"I will have them back," Hugh stated.

Meghan felt Caradoc's fingers dig into her wrist and knew he, too, heard Hugh's calm certainty. "How would you do such?" he challenged. "My father built well. If you think to starve us, I will slit her throat. Aye, and her people's with her. I will burn Cleitcroft to the ground! How will you take her, bantling? Mayhap she does not want to be returned. Mayhap she likes being in my arms and under me in my bed!" His hand covered Meghan's breast and squeezed. "She likes bastard pricks, does this one!"

"I will have her back," Hugh repeated, ignoring the taunts.

Caradoc's laugh broke, the eyes of the man across the defile chilling him. If there was a way, he realized, Hugh fitz Alan would find it. But there wasn't.

"Aye, mayhap you'll have her back. Mayhap I'll return her to you when I am done, when she bores me. And you'll find her more biddable, more docile than when she left you, I warrant. The bitch likes a strong hand. Aye, and mayhap with a bastard in her belly. How would that be, brother bantling? The wife of a bastard big with the bastard brat of her bastard brother. 'Twould take a score of priests a dozen years to trace all the sins of such. Would you like that, bantling?"

Hugh did not answer. His face was hard, as though molded from some harsh, unyielding metal and his eyes were cold with purpose.

Meghan returned his gaze, trying to find some softness, some hint of love, and saw only determination.

"I will have you back, lady," he told her, his voice harsh. "You belong to me, all said."

He held her gaze a moment longer, then turned and rode back to his men. She stared after him, wanting to believe but unable to hope. The rage in his eyes had chilled her, had seemed to say it was only because she was his that he wanted her, as he wanted Cleitcroft.

The certainty in his words was denied by his doubts as Hugh rode back to the village. He knew that the hope he had tried to give her was hollow. Perhaps she was better off dead than in the hands of the demented man who held her. Hugh was no closer than ever to forming a plan for taking Cleitcroft and, with his wife as hostage, his hands were all the more tightly tied.

She was so near, yet so far beyond his grasp. She had stood so proudly, had his Meghan, but her terror had reached across to him. In her eyes he had seen the ghost of the madness that had claimed her after the death of her unborn child. It would take little to drive her back into it, far beyond his reach.

Hugh forced himself to consider Caradoc's possible—probable—rape of Meghan. The thought of that obscene body taking hers drove bile to his throat. Yet his rage did not touch her as it had when he thought of Davyd; she would have gone to him in love, not by force. Hugh wanted to hold her, comfort her, to cleanse the stain of Caradoc from her body with his own, to remove all memory of this time with his love.

It was not until he dismounted among his men that Hugh noticed the Welshman and his three companions. He was not a large man, Hugh noted; his body was the slim, agile one of his people, yet there was a quiet strength in his dark eyes that seemed to match Hugh's own. Under his hand whined a wolfhound that Hugh recognized as Meghan's.

"He came while you were there," Ralph explained, pointing toward Cleitcroft. "He's Kent ap Evan, ab Owen's man, and he knows a way into the keep."

"Do you?" Hugh rapped.

"Aye, 'tis hard and has to be taken at dark, but it can be done."

"Does Caradoc know of it?"

Ap Evan frowned. "No," he stated. "Ab Owen was fox enough to build a bolt hole and, as much as he loved his bastard, as blind as he was to his faults, he did not trust him. He told only his sons—and me."

"And does my lady know?"

"Methinks not."

Hugh stared at him, allowing himself to believe, then he turned his face to his saddle, breathing in deep gulps, his shoulders shaking as though with sobs. When he turned back, his face was composed. "Show me," he ordered.

Ap Evan kneeled down and drew a diagram in the earth with his knife.

Chapter 31

They moved out in the deep dusk. Hugh took eight men, four of his own and the four Welshmen. He had hesitated until ap Evan had reminded him that they were Meghan's men in a way that no Englishman could understand. Nor was there anyone better able to pluck Caradoc's guards from the walls of Cleitcroft than a Welshman with a longbow. Hugh's mouth had quirked and the Welshmen had come.

With only a couple of hours before moonrise, they set a hard pace down the narrow goat path to the defile's bed. The last part of the trek would be the hardest and they must not be caught by the moon on the barren tower of Cleitcroft. The Welshmen moved silently, their soft leather boots finding footholds that the others missed, avoiding rocks that rolled under English feet and fell clattering to the valley below.

At last they reached the narrow bed of the defile. In the blinding dark, ap Evan led them with uncanny certainty. Hearing the whispered prayers behind him, Hugh grinned. He, too, was touched by a superstitious awe inspired by the Welshmen. He missed the weighted swing of his hauberk against his thighs, even though he knew it would encumber him, and the jangle of an army on the march.

At last they came to the base of Cleitcroft's tower. It extended up forever, a bulky pinnacle black against the sky. Not hesitating, ap Evan led them up, finding handholds and footholds in what appeared to be a sheer wall.

He located a path that circled around, doubled back, and twisted around to climb higher. Clinging to crevices with fingers and toes, they inched along above the straight drop to the valley below.

Chilled with sweat, Hugh both cursed and blessed the agility and strength of the Welsh. His legs shaking, his fingertips bleeding, his tendons aching, he damned Gavin ab Owen forever for the construction of a castle so impregnable and thanked him for having the foresight to hide a secret entry within it.

Then they were there. The rock leveled, allowing a man to stand upright and gaze down the way he had come if he dared. With only a glance at the moon's first glow, ap Evan led them around the base.

At a spot where the path widened, he stopped and waited for the men behind him. The other Welshmen joined them, longbows across their backs, knives in their belts. Hugh's men straggled into view. Selig emerged out of the night, a battle-ax in hand. Ralph appeared behind him, a grin on his boyish features despite the blood welling from a scrape that had stripped flesh from his forehead to jaw.

One more man came up and Hugh asked about the last. "Down there," he answered. "And he be fear-struck." Glancing down, he hastily jerked his eyes away and moved closer to the wall.

"God's truth," ap Evan chuckled, "I had not expected so many to make it. We're eight and that is enough to do the deed. My men will lead that one down there to safety come morning."

Kneeling, he worked his knife into the joining of two blocks of stone. At last one gave way, a slab scarcely as thick as a man's hand. Pulling another, thicker rock away, he revealed a black space large enough for a man. On his back, he wiggled into the hole, disappearing. Then his soft call came to them. Hugh checked the sword slung over his back before lying on his belly to follow.

The tunnel seemed endless as he wiggled through the twelve-foot wall. He thought of the tons of rock above him, held only by the stone he touched with every movement, and he forced himself to concentrate instead on the glow he could see in front of him. Then ap Evan was pulling him into the light of a torch.

Hugh glanced about the storeroom and up at the trap door ap Evan had told him was about ten feet above. One after another, the Welshmen emerged, their eyes glowing with the excitement approaching insanity with which they welcomed battle. Ralph came next, his jaunty grin still intact. They waited for Selig. His passage was marked by scrapings and grunts that seemed to echo in the cellar. When he appeared, his shoulders were scraped and bleeding but a grin lighted his scarred features. Finally Hugh's last man was through.

Standing with legs braced, Selig hoisted Hugh to the trap door. Wincing at its squealing hinges, Hugh lifted it. An ancient woman faced him, her eyes wide. She started to scream, then stopped at an abrupt shake of Hugh's head. Her stringy, age-spotted hands alternately crossed herself and formed the sign to ward off evil.

"Mother," he whispered, "we've come for your lady."

Her hand flew to her mouth as Hugh heaved himself through the door. Finding a ladder against the wall, he lowered it into the storeroom and the others emerged.

Hugh drew his sword, as did Ralph, and Selig unslung his battle-ax. The Welshmen strung their longbows, fitting arrows into them.

Hugh's glance touched his men once more, then he led the way to the hall. There was no need to tell them Caradoc was his; that they knew.

Meghan sat in the rushes, her hands bound to the leg of a massive table. She longed for nothing more than the sanctuary of her prison chamber, but she would not be allowed to return there, that she knew. Caradoc no longer needed her. He was already bored with her. He would use her, then give her to his men. Then he would kill her.

Caradoc had tied her to the table when they returned from the parapet. In the hours since, he had prodded and kicked her. He had wound greasy fingers in her hair, forcing her head back to smear his mouth on hers, to force food or ale down her throat until she choked, to force her to watch the rapes of Enid and two other women taken with Cleitcroft. And sometimes he ignored her, wondering how to proceed, wondering if he could best lead the Norman bastard with Meghan alive or dead.

Now Meghan no longer cared, only wanting it to end. The drunken yells and obscenities of the men no longer touched her. Caradoc pulled her hair again and her head lolled back to meet his drunken gaze with an apathetic stare. He grinned as he rubbed the sole of his boot down her ribs, his eyes gloating at her pain. Then he grew bored and released her with a yank.

She closed her eyes against the pain, then opened them. Her gaze drifted past the kitchen passageway then halted, not daring to return, afraid her mind had conjured the image from the spark of hope still in her. Then she looked back.

Hugh stood there, his broadsword clasped in white-knuckled hands, its point hovering an inch above the floor. His eyes held hers, implacable, then they shifted to Caradoc with a hate so hot it froze. To his right stood Selig, to his left, ap Evan.

The Welshman raised his bow and his arrow winged across the hall into the back of the man opposite Caradoc at the table. It appeared to sprout there, the man's body nourishing its growth. He slumped forward, his astonished gaze on Caradoc in mute appeal. Then his head crashed down.

Caradoc stared at him, nostrils widening. His eyes, meeting Hugh's, were stunned, then gleeful. Rising in a motion astonishingly fast for a man of his bulk, Caradoc leaped to the tabletop, his chair toppling. He laughed, strutting where he stood, his hands on wide hips. "Ah, bantling!" he mocked. "You've come to me in my own lair. Welcome to you!"

Caradoc hesitated under Hugh's cold gaze, then his sword jumped from its scabbard into his hand and he leaped to meet Hugh.

Meghan was aware of what took place on the edges of her vision—the Welshmen's arrows scarcely taking wing before others appeared in the long arcs of yew, Selig's battle-ax moving with a speed that turned it into a glitter of metal and wood. Ralph, too, leaped into the fray, a war cry on his lips, wielding his sword with ease and skill.

Meghan kept her gaze fixed on Hugh and Caradoc, not daring to hope; to do so might destroy the core of sanity remaining to her. The thought of Hugh dead held Meghan's heart in her throat, yet a part of her judged them dispassionately. Hugh was the taller, his reach longer, his movements swifter. But the breadth of chest, the width of shoulder, the unnatural thickness of his wrists, built by years of wielding his broadsword, gave him a false look of sturdiness. His bones were long and fine, his waist slim, his hips and legs narrow as Meghan knew so well from the hours of love they had shared.

Caradoc had the bulk and brute strength to carry a lighter man down before him. Beneath the sleek fat were muscles that swelled from years of trying to better his brothers.

Meghan had seen tournaments in England and the battlefields of Wales, but this was different. There was no roar of spectators, no battle cries, no wailing of wounded men. Only ap Evan, Selig, and Ralph remained, resting against the wall, all who would fight them dead. They, too, watched the battling men, Meghan forgotten. The others had left to clear the rest of Caradoc's men from the parapets.

Caradoc and Hugh fought on. The clang of their swords echoed and re-echoed from the walls until it seemed to ring inside Meghan's skull. The whisper of their feet in the rushes was harsh. Their grunts came from the gut and their breathing seemed to be torn from their lungs.

They circled each other, wielding their swords in both hands, the torches turning the blur of blades into shimmering arcs of light. Each fought to weaken the other, to corner him, seeking a point of vulnerability, a moment of carelessness, finding none. They were equals, the balance shifting between them so quickly that only a trained eye could see it.

The other men returned, their work on the battlements done, yet still Caradoc and Hugh struggled. Perspiration poured into their eyes, yet neither blinked. Caradoc's grin became a grimace of gruesome glee. To destroy this man, to deny him to Meghan, was the deepest hurt he could deal her. That his own death would follow was but a vulgar joke, the pain he inflicted well worth the cost.

Hugh's features were a stark mask. Only his eyes were alive, silver with hatred. His shoulders and arms ached from dealing blow after blow, from holding firm against each blow returned, from the shocks of pain that traveled up his raw nerves from the living metal of his blade. He saw Caradoc's sword swing down and brought his own up to meet it, knew as he did so that it was a feint. He saw the blade hover, saw it change course to strike his own; forcing it up, exposing him from shoulder to groin.

Meghan gasped just before Hugh spun away, Caradoc's blade cleaving the air where he had stood a fraction of a second before. As he turned, Hugh lifted his sword higher and brought it down with all his strength against the juncture of shoulder and neck laid open by Caradoc's feint.

Stumbling back, surprised by Hugh's recovery, Caradoc felt the point of Hugh's sword graze his tunic. His foot slipped in the rushes. His arms flailed as he fell, his bulk shaking the huge timbers. He lay on his back, stunned, his arms outflung. Then he grinned at Hugh standing over him, sword held in both hands above his head, poised to strike. Caradoc released his sword, tossing it from him, and he turned his hands palm up in an ancient gesture of supplication.

"Brother," he said, laughing, "I yield."

His eyes gleamed. Fitz Alan's honor, the code he had sworn to uphold, would not allow him to slay an unarmed man. That it was a code Caradoc scorned seemed a monstrous joke on Hugh.

Time halted. Hugh hesitated for only a second, but his nerves screamed for release. Each man waited, willing Hugh to do something, anything. Meghan stared disbelieving as she saw the point of Hugh's sword waver. Kill him! Oh, kill him! she thought so vehemently that she wondered no one heard.

Caradoc, too, saw the hesitation and his grin broadened, then in the next instant, he saw Hugh's pur-

pose. His eyes started from his head. His lips opened to
plead from a mouth gone dry just before Hugh's sword
descended with all his remaining strength. It struck Caradoc in the center of his breastbone and cleaved through
to strike the floor, the blade snapping with the power of
the blow.

Hugh straddled Caradoc, the sword's hilt still in his
hands, his eyes fixed on the death mask of his foe. Then
a tremor shook him and weariness swept over him. The
journey from court, the too brief pause at Ainsleah, the
relentless ride to Cleitcroft had all taken their toll.

But the night's work was not yet done; he had yet to
claim his wife.

Tossing the useless hilt away, he wiped the sweat from
his face with a shaking hand. His gaze lifted to his wife
where she sat, her face against her bound hands, her
shoulders shaking with dry, heaving sobs.

"My lady," he whispered, his voice hoarse.

For a long moment Meghan didn't respond, then she
turned her face to her lord. The perfection of her face was
marred by Caradoc's blows, by the food and drink he had
smeared into it, yet she somehow retained her beauty.
Beneath the grime and bruises Hugh saw strength and
unyielding pride. All the terror she had felt for him, all
the need and love, had been wiped from her features by
the fear that he did not want her.

Hugh searched her face for a sign of need or love and
found none. "Did he bed you, lady?" he asked. To know
she had been defiled and degraded would give him the
excuse he searched for to comfort her, ignoring the calm
arrogance in her eyes.

"No," she answered. "Nor his men."

Meghan saw nothing in his eyes but harsh possessive-
ness. Yet she had to know. "My lord," she said, "why
did you come?"

"Because you're mine." Hugh rubbed the base of his
skull, unable to find better words to express his love and
need. Fatigue blinded him. "And I do not relinquish anything that is mine."

Meghan closed her eyes, not seeing Selig go to her or
Hugh's wave ordering him back, ordering all the men to

their duties. All she could see were the long years ahead, years of bearing child after child conceived in a passion-less bed, of watching him go to a mistress each time his seed took root. All she could see was a life of cold ani-mosity growing into an all-consuming hatred or total indif-ference. That she did not think she could bear, not with the memory of the days of love they had shared ever between them. It would be better to be cast from his life forever.

She watched Hugh bend over her brother and jerk the gold link belt from under him. Freeing it, he walked to her and tossed it down, then kneeled to cut her bonds.

Staring at the dark hair curling on his neck, remem-bering how it had once twisted around her fingers, damp from lovemaking, Meghan felt the loss of him grip her. Her thoughts flew to her mountains and the freedom she would never know again. She saw her brothers and her father alive in their pride then dead, and it seemed as though her sorrow was for all of them. She heard again her own oath—she would never love a man of war, would never watch as he rode off to battle, would never wash his corpse when he returned thrown over the back of his horse.

Laughter at that proud and foolish girl caught in her throat. The knowledge that she did so love threatened to burst into pain. She would be willing to break all those oaths to have Hugh laugh at her once more, his eyes soft with affection. She would gladly bear the pain and sorrow such loving would bring to have him hold her once more. But she could not bear his disdain, his indifference.

"My lord," she whispered to his dark head, "let me go. Put me from you. Find a more biddable wife, one who will bear your children and bring no dishonor to your name."

His hands faltered on the last strands of rope. Raising stark eyes, he stared at her. "No!" he answered. "Never!"

"Please, my lord," she pleaded, her hands clutching his. "I'll stay in Wales. I'll make no claim on you or yours. I'll do nothing again to rob you of the respect due you. Your clergy will be sore pleased to rid you of me.

I'll stay at Cleitcroft. You'll be well rid of me. Let me go!''

Hugh's laugh was filled with pain. "You forget, lady. Cleitcroft is mine!''

Meghan rushed on, all discretion gone, filled with a need to escape the distaste in his eyes. "Then I'll go into the mountains. There are men there yet who would welcome the daughter of Gavin ab Owen. Or I can go to Davyd, be with him in prison.''

Pausing Meghan heard the echo of her last words and she grabbed at them. Davyd would need her. She could stay with him until Edward sent him to his death. He wouldn't refuse her a second time.

Not seeing Hugh's rage, she repeated, "I can go to Davyd! Edward would not deny me, not if you set me aside. And Davyd has need of me. Please, my lord!''

Meghan's fingers had clasped his. Her eyes clung to his face, searching for a softening. Only with the halt of her words did she notice his set features. She watched him stand, her eyes still holding a hope she refused to relinquish.

The conflicting emotions Hugh had felt from watching Davyd die flooded over him again in a wave of rage, remorse, and nausea. Pity and shame followed. Then he became numb. The memory of her face turned up to Davyd at court, of her grief on hearing of his capture, the rumor that he had been her lover—all no longer touched Hugh. His cold, uncaring mind analyzed his memories and he knew he had found the words with which to hurt her as she had hurt him.

"Davyd is dead,'' he stated.

Hugh saw disbelief leap in her eyes then die with the last of her hope. She closed her eyes against stinging tears and saw Davyd's gentle face again. How could he be dead when he had seemed so alive in her dreams?

"I would know how he died,'' she stated.

Hugh's features grew taut. "My lady,'' he told her, knowing she would ask anyway, "methinks mayhap 'tis not a thing you should know.''

Meghan shuddered, remembering that Davyd had told her he thought Edward would devise him a new death.

But, with all the cruelty in the world, how could there be such a thing? Lifting her head, she gazed about the hall, not seeing the grimly set faces of Selig and ap Evan, the pitying ones of Ralph and the others. It was as though she and Hugh were alone.

"How did he die, my lord?" she asked, staring at the hands clenched in her lap. "I must know."

Hugh released his breath. "He was hanged as punishment for the murders he did commit," he answered, "but they cut him down before he lost all life. For profaning the week of the Lord's Passion," he continued, noting the shaking of her shoulders, "they disemboweled him."

Meghan bent lower over Hugh's feet, her arms wrapped around herself as though to protect her own belly from the torture dealt Davyd. The sight of her beaten beneath his words turned a knife of self-disgust in Hugh. He welcomed the pain he inflicted on himself as he said, "Yet English justice is tempered with mercy."

Hearing her hysterical laugh, Hugh smiled in sardonic agreement. "Aye, but it is!" he told her. "They did not wait for his death but did behead him for plotting against the life of the king."

Meghan became aware of her tears falling on his booted feet. Her soundless sobs seemed to rip through her as she wept as much for Hugh's deliberate wounding as she did for Davyd. She felt soiled and used. Her tears on his feet reminded her of the woman of sin who had washed the feet of Jesus. Meghan wondered dully if that woman, too, had felt so used. But I am not adulterous, she protested to herself. I did but love Davyd in my thoughts and never over my lord.

"Where is he?" she asked at last. "Might I have his body brought to Wales?"

"No, my lady," Hugh said. He hesitated, but she would one day hear of it, whether he told her or not. "The head they sent to London to place on a spike next to Llewelyn's. The rest they quartered and sent to Northampton, York, Bristol, and Winchester. Winchester and York quarreled over his right shoulder and I know not which won."

Staring down at Meghan, Hugh felt a hollow victory. "My lady," he said softly, "I would have you rise."

Slowly, carefully, she rose. Her body felt old and bruised, but she refused his hand. Her features were swollen, her eyes almost closed from weeping. Her mouth looked wanton in its scarlet puffiness.

"Was he your lover?"

Meghan inclined her head as though to hear the echo of his question before she could comprehend it. Then her face lighted up. Suddenly she understood why he had degraded her. Her faint smile broadened. "No, my lord," she answered. "I swear by all that is holy, he was not. Nor was any man but you."

She lifted her chin. "But I cannot claim the virtue as mine, for I did offer myself to him. He did reject me."

Reading the rage and pain in Hugh's suddenly naked expression, Meghan laughed softly. Abruptly the mirth fled and her jaw clenched with a need to hurt him. "Methinks my belly, swelled with a bastard's get, repulsed him," she whispered through clenched teeth. "Or mayhap he would not go where a Norman by-blow's touch had sullied."

Hugh's hand lifted and she turned into it, accepting the blow, welcoming the pain. It spun her around and across the littered table. She lay there, stunned. Her arm was under her and beneath her fingertips was the knife Caradoc had discarded on sight of Hugh. Slowly she rubbed the blade, then her fingers closed around the hilt.

Meghan did not know if she intended to use it or not. Even as she pushed herself from the table, she knew he saw the knife. It was not until he advanced on her, gaze on the weapon, that the humiliations and hurts dealt her surged forward in a rush of rage. They blinded her until all she felt was the need to strike back. Rising in one motion, a sob announcing her intention, she mindlessly flung herself on him, the knife poised.

Grabbing her wrist, Hugh turned her other arm behind her, holding her tight against him as she fought. Shaking his head in a mute refusal of her purpose, he stared into her contorted face, stunned by the depth of her enmity.

"No!" he whispered. "No!"

Twisting her wrist around, he forced her hand up between them, the knife pressed upward toward his heart.

Meghan shuddered, still gasping for air. Her head drooped against his chest as she tried to accept what her rage had driven her to do. Never would he believe she had not wanted him dead, could *never* want him dead. So deep was her despair, she did not hear Hugh say her name until he repeated it.

Reluctantly, she met his gaze and when his hand tightened on hers she became aware of the knife she still held. In his eyes she read his purpose. "No, my lord. Oh, no!" she cried, shaking her head. "Holy Mother, no!"

She tried to release the knife, but Hugh's fingers closed harder on hers. His eyes commanded her as his hand forced hers relentlessly up another fraction of an inch. "You know how. You know where. Haven't you dealt such afore to dying men?"

Desperately, Meghan fought Hugh's grip. Her breath came in sobs. But his hand gripped harder, cutting her fingers into her wedding band. Feeling the slight relaxation as he readied himself to drive the blade home, she jerked back with all her strength. But his hand did not move. Sobbing, Meghan pleaded again, "No, my lord! Please, no!"

"Why not, lady? Who would know? Tongueless Selig could not tell and your Welshmen never would. And they would rid you of my men at your command. See? They already hold them with their bows. You could tell that I died at Caradoc's hand and there would be no one to prove the lie."

Reading no softening in his eyes, her desire to fight abandoned her. She relaxed against him, the delicate bones of her hand seeming to dissolve under his. He felt her tears on his neck, the feather softness of her breath as she whispered still again, "Ah, no, my lord, no!"

He released his grip, his fingers peeling hers from the knife hilt. It fell in the rushes and she shuddered against him. Her sobs turned to tears of gratitude and her lips moved in a silent prayer as her arms encircled him, clinging to him.

Holding her, his eyes closed against his grief, Hugh concluded that only Meghan's fear had held her hand. Briefly, he considered her plea to be let go.

All along he had believed that the few times he had felt her mouth melt under his, the few times her body had responded to his in passion, had signified more than a momentary lust. All along he had believed that under her fear and stubbornness there was love. But he had been wrong.

Yet he could not let her go. She was his wife, his responsibility, and he could not let her return to the mountains to live the life of a fugitive.

Other men had marriages of indifference and animosity, yet they sired children. Their wives served them in exchange for protection and the facade of respectability. Meghan would have to learn to do so. How such men found joy, if they found joy, was something he would wonder about later.

Hugh unwrapped Meghan's arms with gentle hands. Holding her from him, he studied her swollen features. "Take my lady to her chamber," he ordered Selig.

"No, my lord!" Meghan whispered. "I beg not there!"

Closing his eyes with weariness, he sighed. "Not there, then. Take her to Glenna's house. And, ap Evan, the crone in the kitchens—have her prepare my lady for me."

Ap Evan's eyes flicked from Meghan's stunned features to Hugh's drawn face. "You are weary, fitz Alan," he commented. "You verily shake with it. Should you get a child on her this night, 'twould be a weak, spindly thing!"

Hugh acknowledged ap Evan over his wife's bowed head and his mouth crooked into a mirthless smile. "Then 'twill die, will it not? And I will sire another."

Their eyes remained locked as Selig picked Meghan up in his huge arms. Ap Evan watched until she and Selig disappeared through the passageway to the ward. Swinging back, he faced Hugh once more. "Your lady," he informed him, "told me you were a doughty knight, that you have an unusual understanding of our people and our ways. But she did not tell me you are a fool—a fool in the ways of women!''

He stared at Hugh, reading the rage in his eyes, the pain and the need. Shrugging, he left in search of the old woman who cowered in the kitchens.

Chapter 32

Hugh did not go to Meghan until dawn.

She submitted to the old woman's ministrations. Her body was scrubbed until it was bright pink. Her hair was washed and dried and rubbed with rose petals until it gleamed ebony once more. Then, unable to summon fear or anger, she crawled into bed to wait and fell quickly into a dreamless sleep.

The dog's whines and the nuzzling of his wet nose awakened her. Yearning only to snuggle deeper into the nest of furs, she tried to ward him off but gave up. With a yawn, she pulled a robe over her head.

Shaking out the floor-length, milk-white folds, she remembered when she had last seen it—a lifetime ago. She had been hardly more than a child. Her father and brothers had been alive. She had not yet seen the demand in Hugh's eyes when she sat listening to Glenna's rambling wisdoms while the old woman painstakingly stitched the wide, convoluted green and gold Celtic band around the robe's hem. It was Glenna's bridal gift, the robe she was to wear on her wedding night.

Smiling wryly, Meghan wondered if Glenna, using the hemp seed, had ever foreseen the circumstances in which she would first wear it. But Glenna would not have finished it if she had seen such a vision. Biting her lip to force back sudden tears, Meghan smoothed the soft wool and shook her head, refusing to succumb to self-pity.

Her hound's whine reminded her of his need and Meghan let him out the door. Leaning against the frame, her arms wrapped about herself against the morning chill, she watched the gangling animal lope through the village from one familiar site to another, sniffing for alien scents, marking his own. She gazed about, wondering if this would be the last dawn she would see from her birthplace.

The sun had not yet risen, its promise just glazing the mists in a tinge of pink. Smoke rose from the huts occupied by Hugh's men and settled in a low veil in the heavy air. A lone bird chirped once.

Sighing, Meghan looked for her hound. He had stopped suddenly in his ambling, head lifted, ears alert, his eyes on the tall, slim man who was walking down from the castle. A growl stirred in his throat. He turned to look at his mistress and, receiving no command, faced the stranger again. Dropping to one knee, Hugh whistled the dog to him, snapping his fingers. The hound approached, stiff-legged with suspicion, and sniffed at the outstretched hand. His shaggy tail at last waved acceptance and, his head pressed against Hugh's thigh, he submitted to the fingers rubbing behind his ears.

Standing up, Hugh gazed at the waiting woman. His stride was steady as he approached her. His eyes held no desire, no promise.

Meghan bowed her head before turning back into the house. Blocking the dog's entrance with his knee, Hugh followed. He glanced about, noting the whitewashed walls, the strings of garlic and onions, the scarlet cloaks, and the bows and lances of men long since dead. A brightly painted chest stood in one corner. A pallet covered with furs lay against one wall. His eyes returned to his wife.

Meghan knelt before the hearth, her lips moving in a soft incantation as she fed embers that had been banked the night before. At last, satisfied, she knelt back on her heels.

Her hair gleamed ebony against the white of her robe. The room's dim light muted the bruises on her translucent skin and her eyes were green and clear. Her mouth was red, the lower lip full as she drew it between white teeth in an unconscious gesture of apprehension.

Hugh felt desire surge through him. He wanted her as he never had before, but he drove the need back. Such passion had no place in the life before them.

His weariness, only its edge taken from him by a few hours' sleep, assailed him again. He watched as she came to him on firmly placed feet. Her eyes were lowered as she took his cloak, unclasped his baldric, and hung them on a peg next to the scarlet cloaks. Her hands were steady as she drew his surcoat and his tunic over his head.

Noticing the scar gleaming red and sore on his shoulder, Meghan pushed away the desire to press her lips against it. "Queen Eleanor told me, lord," she said, "that you had been wounded."

"Aye, at Dolwyddelan. A lance."

Meghan didn't reply, unable to think of what to say. Kneeling, her hands on his shoes, she asked, "When do we leave Cleitcroft?"

"In two days, mayhap three."

Hugh stared down at her. She had to be told how things were to be, what he demanded of her. There must be no misunderstanding between them. It would be difficult enough as it was.

"There, at Ainsleagh, lady," he said, "you will assume responsibility of my house. You will warm my bed and birth my children. You will greet my guests with quiet courtesy. You will leave me no more."

Her hands motionless, she considered the life he described, overwhelming despair catching in her throat. At last, she asked, "And there is nothing else you require of me, my lord?"

For a brief second, Hugh's face became naked, then his features grew stern once more. "Nothing else, lady."

He stared into her proud, closed face and realized he could not use her as he had intended, could not take her with such cold, passionless purpose. His jaw clenched. He turned and removed his baldric and cloak from the peg.

"My lord?" Meghan whispered.

Hugh turned back to his still-kneeling wife.

"Where do you go?"

"To the keep. Ap Evan spoke true. I am sore weary for such work."

Had she really seen naked pain in his face? Meghan wondered. Was he, too, unable to admit his need, if he felt any. His face was set, yet there seemed to be torment in the depths of his eyes. She felt hurt and loss well up, suffocating her, and knew she could not relinquish her love so easily. "My lord," she stated arrogantly, "you dishonor me."

Hugh's head tilted as he tried to understand her anger. "Would you have me stay, lady?" he asked at last.

Not answering, unwilling to plead, Meghan stood there, tears flowing down her cheeks. She tasted her tears' salt and raised a hand to her face. "Why, Hugh," she wondered, "do you always make me weep?"

She turned from him, her hands clenched at her sides. At last she said, "You told me once that you wanted me for passion, for warmth, for joy, that you would give to me of life, not death. Do you now deny your words, my lord?"

Staring at her proud back, Hugh refused to believe he had heard her, unwilling to chance hurt again. Then his breath went from him in a sigh. The desire he had driven from him rushed back to choke him with its intensity. He touched her hair with trembling fingers, his breath warm on her neck, the fragrance of roses in his nostrils. He felt her stiffness as he undid her braids and ran his fingers through her hair, watching the blue-black waves gleam under his hands.

"My lady?" he whispered.

Slowly, carefully, Meghan turned, pulled by the desire and wonder in his voice. Seeing the need in his face, she knew her own expression betrayed her love. She rested her forehead on his naked chest. Waiting, not daring to breathe, she felt his hands touch her shoulders, holding her, then he gently pushed her from him. Gasping at his rejection, her eyes closed against the cruel satisfaction she knew would be on his face, she heard him speak her name. Pride once more claiming her features, she looked at him.

His gaze clung to her face, his eyes taking in each feature as though he could not look away. His hands moved to the brooch at her throat, his fingers steady as he unclasped it and slowly pushed the robe over her shoulders to fall to her feet. His eyes moved over her, touching her high, round breasts, her small waist and flat belly. He noted the faint lines at her slim hips, put there by the carrying of his child, then his gaze drank in the rest of her.

The touch of his eyes brought Meghan a hard ache of desire. She felt as though his hands and his mouth caressed each part of her. Need for him gripped her in a painful throb that Hugh recognized in the parting of her lips and the droop of her eyelids, yet she wanted to prolong the moment, to hold its welcome hurt a while longer. She smiled, her eyes gleaming. "Would you have me turn, my lord?"

His eyes laughed back and he drew a circle in the air. She turned to display her proud back and small bottom. She felt his hands touch her shoulders and she stepped from under them to face him again, feeling suddenly shy and inexplicably frightened.

"Little one," he whispered and her eyes flew to his, warmed by the promise in their depths.

Hugh drew a finger along her jaw and pushed a hand into the thick mass of her hair. His mouth lowered to hers and a moan rose in her throat. Her lips opened under his, her tongue meeting his, clinging with a sweetness he had not known before. Her hands touched his arms and moved to his shoulders, curling into the hair at his neck and drawing him closer. Pulling his mouth from hers, Hugh pressed it against the soft flesh of her neck, shaking his head in incredulous wonder.

"Please, my lord!" she sobbed. "Oh, please!"

Lifting her, he carried Meghan to the bed, dropping down with her. He felt her open to him, felt her urgent hands pressing him into her with a demanding need. Then he moved into her, claiming her.

Her body tilted and parted to him with an abandoned submission that brought a groan to his throat. Her soft croon of love became a sob and his own voice whispered her name in harsh, marveling joy. His body seemed to move of its own accord, plunging into her, loving her. He felt her unrestrained response as she gave to him, took from him, moved with him. He held her, wanting it never to end, feeling, even as he fought it, the demand for culmination. He took her to the heights of passion, the love and need in his voice lifting her above her fear into total surrender, carrying her with him into the spinning, throbbing oblivion of complete fulfillment.

He held her cradled against him, his hands moving over her curves. His mouth tasting the salt of her tears, he found himself in awe that, when he had at last let her go, she had suddenly become his.

And she was his, Meghan knew. He would ride away from her to heed Edward's call too many times. And she would wait for his return, would walk the walls in worry. One day, too, he might come home to her tossed over the back of his horse, his proud, hawklike face mottled with blood.

But first there would be love and joy, happiness and fulfillment. They had lost so much. So many people had died. Somehow the deaths and the mourning of them would bind her and Hugh closer, Meghan knew. Somehow, out of the despair and destruction of war, they would become stronger people, would build a better life, taking for themselves the best customs and traits of both the Welsh and the English.

And they had each other, their need and joy, their love! Always, she knew, his hands would arouse desire in her. His eyes would tell her of his passion whether alone or in a crowded room. And she would grow warm in response. Always his body would take her to the heights of passion, as hers would to him, responding, needing, wanting.

There would be children. Ah! but she wanted his children! She wanted to feel his child move within her, to feel its mouth at her breast, tugging at her, the tiny fists kneading. She wanted to see the wonder and joy on Hugh's face, to feel his hand on her belly as he felt the child move within her for the first time. She wanted to see his face gentle with love and joy as he watched his child take his first steps and ride his first pony. They would be Welsh-dark, these children of theirs, Meghan thought triumphantly.

Snuggling closer to Hugh, Meghan closed her eyes, almost asleep, and then she was lying in bed, the bed at Ainsleah, her body languorous with the fatigue of childbirth, the child small in the curve of her arm. Hugh was there, sitting on the bed, and in his hands was his birthing gift to her, a puppy, long-legged and gangling, the tongue swiping at his chin. Behind him stood the merchant who had brought the little female wolfhound from Ireland.

Meghan's throat contracted with the joy of it. Then she saw two hawk-faced men, brothers dressed in armor that she knew would not be seen for a hundred years. One wore the scarlet cloak of Wales. The other bore the escutcheon of fitz Alan. Their shouted words Meghan could not make out, but the thwack of a knife slammed in the wood of the table they leaned across, nose to nose, jerked her from sleep.

Hugh rose over her, his face a frown of concern. "Little one," he said, "did you dream?"

Meghan blinked at him, an inexplicable sense of intense sorrow at the edge of her mind, then it was gone. "I think I did," she whispered, "but I can't remember about what."

She reached up to draw him down for a kiss. "Know you, my lord," she said, "a man called Owen Glendower?" Hugh shook his head and she shrugged. "'Tis of no matter. 'Twas, methinks, but a name I heard shouted once in a dream."

Then she smiled, her finger tracing the line of his mouth. "Tell me, my lord," she whispered, "how 'twill be for me at Ainsleah."

Hugh brushed the hair from her face, his heart tightening with joy as she pressed her mouth into the palm of his hand.

"You will assume management of my house. You will warm my bed and birth my children. You will greet my guests. And you will leave me no more."

"And will there be anything else, my lord Hugh?"

"Aye," he answered, one eyebrow crooked, his gray eyes laughing. "There will be joy in the doing of it."

Meghan's eyes danced as her tongue teased between his fingers. "And why is that, my lord?"

"Because 'tis your woman's duty," he told her with smug male complacency. "And because you love me."

Her eyebrows puckered in thought and she sighed. "Aye, I warrant I do. And you, my lord?"

The corner of his mouth jerked in an attempt to control his grin. "I married you, didn't I? Skinny, dark, next to dowerless thing that you were. You are mine, all said. I only ask that you hold your female tongue that I may sleep. 'Tis hard labor, pleasuring a lusty wench like you, and I am weary!"

Breaking into laughter, he caught the fist she swung and flipped her to her back. Holding her, he grinned as she glared at him, his body covering hers until her indignant struggles ceased. "My lady," he said, "do you mean to tempt me?"

Still angry, Meghan ignored his teasing. "Think you, my lord, that the chase is done? That I will be ever the meek, biddable wife the world and Edward would have for you?"

The laughter faded from his eyes and they grew warm with love. "My lady, may all the saints and the Holy Mother help me for a fool were I to think—or want—such!"

Her fingers touched his lips and he pressed his face into her neck, breathing in her warm fragrance. "Ah, little one," he sighed, "I love you!"

At noon, Kent ap Evan knocked on the door as Hugh had asked him to do, bending down to comfort the whining hound. Hearing nothing but a faint rustle, he rapped louder, then inclined his head. He listened with admiration to Hugh's questioning curse as to the nature of the ancestors of whoever disturbed him and his wife, to his derogatory comments of any children that person might sire, and their children's children after them. He had begun his profane wishing of the pox, impotence, all matter of inconveniences and suffering forever on the intruder, his family, and his livestock, when his words were abruptly cut off. A moment later ap Evan heard a soft laugh ending in a sigh of pleasure. He grinned.

Snapping his fingers for the dog, he walked back up the road to the castle, his whistle clear on the crisp autumn air.

Kate O'Donnell

Kate O'Donnell was born in Spokane, Washington and raised on a ranch in western Montana, where she attended Missoula County High School and the University of Montana. In addition to being a writer, she is a certified hypnotherapist in the fields of creative and athletic enhancement, and she especially likes working with children. She enjoys painting, downhill skiing, walking beaches, and reading and has a weakness for Irish and British history. She now lives in Palo Alto, California with her two sons, Gregory and Gary.

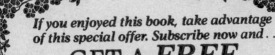